Heroes:

By Sydney Carr

Copyright

I dedicate this book to the stalwart folk of the Mining Community of Ashington who worked and played there from 1867 to 1988.

Author's Notes.

The terrace of the Sixth Row that this book is based on is fictional. Whilst the Sixth Row was very much a real place, numbers 50 to 60 depicted within these pages never existed. There were only ever two terraces of the Sixth Row, the fictional short Row in this book would have been located on a small area of allotments sandwiched between the end of the actual Sixth Row and the north end of Cross Row. All other locations in the book I have described as I remember them in 1958 Ashington.

All characters in the book except one are fictional.

Dialogue where appropriate is written in Geordie/Pitmatic dialect with the words spelt phonetically; these are not spelling mistakes or typing errors. For those readers not familiar with this dialect, I have listed the Geordie/Pitmatic words I have used along with their meanings at end of the book. I have not included words that should be easily understood. The pronunciation of Geordie/Pitmatic words I leave entirely to the reader.

Table of Contents

Chapter 1
Hang On

'Tom, Tommy!' Ian gasped as he clung desperately onto his younger brother; just managing to keep his head above the freezing water of the stinking marsh. 'Come on man Tom, help me,' he pleaded as he felt the strength slowly ebb from his thin thirteen year old body that shook uncontrollably from the icy water and mud that held them both in its sucking grip. The cold that had slowly crept through his muscles, burning his extremities and stealing his strength and energy, seemed now to be gnawing at his bones as the pain and feeling of desperation, slowly robbed him of the will to fight.

Tommy had stopped shaking and was no longer wailing in desperation, only an occasional moan from him let Ian know that he was still alive as he gripped him with frozen hands, wondering if anyone would find them and rescue them from this nightmare.

Was it a nightmare? It had only been a few short hours ago that they were both lying half asleep in their bed that was piled high with old blankets and overcoats to keep out the bitter cold of the particularly icy February of 1958. The 'Saddle-Back Tankie' that chuffed its way past their end of terrace colliery house toward Coneygarth Drift Mine to collect that nights coal-filled wagons meant it was seven o'clock, time for Ian to leave the warmth of their shared bed and get ready for his paper round.

Careful not to bump his head on the sloping ceiling of the bedroom they shared with their sixteen year old brother Mike, he pulled on his well-worn jeans and large woolly jumper that had been handed down to him last year. Tommy yawned from below the blankets and whispered, 'Are ye still teking me te the Regal te see 'Old Yella?'

'Yeh, if Aah get me deliveries finished in time,' Ian whispered back, frightened to speak loudly in case he woke their Dad who had staggered home drunk again the night before to find the family all in bed. None of them wanted to be about when he fell through the door drunk, angry at the world as always, and ready to lash out at any of them who might be foolish enough to be still out of bed.

Their Mother Jane had been in bed pretending to be asleep but cowering below his blankets; Ian had heard his Dad's raised voice as he bumped his way up the stairs and into his bedroom to berate his wife for not been downstairs when he arrived home. Then, judging from the awful sounds that came from their bedroom, his father began torturing his mother until eventually her ordeal ended and all was quiet, apart from her gentle sobbing that he listened to until he eventually fell asleep.

Ian walked into the kitchen and found his Mother and Mike already there, Mike taking the bleazer down from the front of the roaring fire he had just lit in the black leaded kitchen range.

Dark patches showed below her intensely beautiful but sad eyes as Jane poured tea into a cup and smiled gently at Ian before saying, 'Now sit down and have your jam and bread with your tea!' Then with a far off melancholy look in her eyes, she smoothed her loose fitting maroon dress and sat down at the small kitchen table to drink her own freshly poured tea, her hands trembling slightly as she remembered the horrors of last night.

Walking across the cold lino floor and onto the 'Clippy Mat' of the Spartan but immaculately clean kitchen, Ian grabbed the two jam sandwiches and stacked them one on top of the other before biting into them and spluttering through a mouthful of mushed food, 'Aah hevn't got time man Mam, Aah'll be late if Aah divin't hurry.'

'Whey ye should get oot of yer bed urlier, shudn't ye, Mike said as he grabbed his younger brother round the neck and roughed his hair none to gently. Mike was an apprentice electrician at the colliery and a keen and talented footballer who also knew he was good-looking, having inherited his father's looks but thankfully none of his morose, bad tempered ways.

'Sod off!' Ian said as he wriggled free and stepped into the tiny room that doubled as a pantry and washroom, containing a small Belfast sink and the only tap in the house. Scaring his face with a splash of water, he dried himself on the course, blue and yellow striped, colliery issue towel hanging behind the pantry door and combed his thick black hair into some semblance of order before walking back into the kitchen where Jane scolded, 'Get back in there and clean your teeth young man.'

Annoyed at the further delay, Ian stepped back into the pantry and quickly brushed his teeth rinsing his mouth out below the running cold-water tap.

'What time will you be back Pet, you are taking Thomas to the matinee aren't you?' Jane asked Ian, almost pleading, in her gentile accent that had acquired the odd Geordie word during the sixteen years she had lived in Ashington, the huge and thriving mining village fifteen miles north of Newcastle.

'I am if I finish me grocery deliveries before one o'clock,' he answered as he strode to the back door at the foot of the stairs where his battered, green imitation leather jacket hung on a peg along with coats from the rest of the family. Pulling it on he ran out through the yard and across the concrete surface of the back lane to their netty that stood at the end of a row of outside toilets, coal houses and air raid shelters running in parallel to the houses of the third and last terrace of the Sixth Row. The netty was not a place to linger on a cold and frosty February morning, especially when it entailed placing your bare arse onto an icy old porcelain throne that only had two narrow pieces of damp wood on the rim! Ian was in and out in very quick time!

In the meantime, having prepared some jam and bread for Maureen who had just turned sixteen, Jane wiped her hands on her apron that picked her out from all the other pinny wearing housewives in the Colliery Rows and said, 'Michael go upstairs and tell Maureen her breakfast is ready and be quiet, I don't want your father woken yet.'

It wud be better for all of us if he didn't wake up at all,' Mike hissed meaning every word, loathing as he did his father for the drunken, wife and child beater that he was. Jane was horrified at her son's scathing but understandable statement but made no effort to scold him as he dashed quietly up the stairs.

Ian was soon scuttling along the short terrace of houses whose roofs at the 'Back' sloped down to just above the pantry windows, unlike the 'Fronts' overlooking the gardens that were normal height above two bedroom windows. He ran down the second terrace of the Sixth Row that consisted of smaller two up and one down cottages and past the black creosoted wooden Scouts hut that guarded the red-leaded, steel-sided 'Rec Bridge.' The bride stepped across the six shunting lines of the colliery and led into the Miner's Recreational Sports Fields, Gymnasium and open countryside beyond.

Smoke from freshly lit fires hung above hundreds of chimneys in the still quiet streets on this frosty Saturday morning as he hurried on through the cuts between the terraces of the Fifth, Fourth and Third Rows, uniform in their drabness, brightened today by their frost covering their long rear gardens.

Ian's pal and fellow 'Paper Lad' Reg, was waiting for him at the end of the Third Row gardens, next to the little Methodist Chapel where he had attended Sunday School until he was eleven. Reg was blowing into his hands and jumping up and down, making a show of trying to keep warm but knowing that he had just left his house on the corner of the

Third Row a few moments before he arrived; Ian knew Reg's antics were all for show.

Taller and skinner than Ian with tousled blonde hair and an insane grin that rarely left his gaunt face, he yelled, 'Hoo blidy lang de Aah hev te wait on ye, before ye get oot yer stinking pit in the mornings?'

'Ye've just got yersell oot of yore blidy stinker, 'Ian shouted back, 'I can see ye hevn't even teking yore pyjamas off man! Aah didn't kna you wor posh enough te have blidy pyjamas like!'

Reg looked down and seeing that his pyjama top was sticking out from below his black serge jacket, he struggled briefly to tuck it into the waistband of his baggy navy blue trousers.

'Bugga off man,' Reg shouted back and they raced off to Willington's Newsagents in Highmarket, the street of shops that served this part of town. The tall figure of Mr Willington opened the locked door to his shop and turned over the 'Closed' sign to show the world that he was 'Open' just as the two panting lads stepped into his newly refurbished business that included in one corner, an enticing 'sweets' counter.

He did not say a word to them as they walked to the rear of the shop and sorted the piles of newspapers into order in accordance with the two handwritten notes he had placed on top of them. On the way out of the shop, with the strap of the heavy bag of newspapers cutting into his shoulder, Ian said to Reg, 'See you at one for the flicks.'

'Aye catch ye later.'

Turning his coat collar up to keep the cold wind out and to stop the strap of the paper bag from chaffing his neck, Ian began the boring chore of walking up and down the long, seemingly never ending Rows or as the locals referred to them, 'The Ra's', dodging angry dogs, icy patches and the odd miserable 'owld bugga' complaining that their paper was late! He was thinking of how the money he was saving would help him buy a second hand bike that would provide him with the mobility he needed to do a morning and evening paper round and

5

so make more money that could be used to help his Mother. Nick, his Dad was an underground labourer and as such, did not make a great deal of money, a high percentage of which he spent on beer!

A damaged knee prevented Nick from working on the coalface where miners earned the best wages, shrapnel from a German hand grenade had caused the injury during a rear guard action at Dunkirk in 1940; an action that saw him win the Military Medal that he displayed in the old glass fronted cabinet in the sitting room. It had left him with a limp, a grudge against the army that invalided him out and the Colliery for not giving a 'War Hero' a better paying job. On the other hand, it did help him win his beautiful wife Jane who had been a newly qualified nurse at the hospital he had recovered in after his escape from France. She had fallen for his good looks and at that time, his flashing smile and cheeky Geordie banter, subsequently falling pregnant to him with dire consequences! Nick and his pregnant new wife had moved in with his parents in the Sixth Row and there they stayed. Nick had taken over the house when his Father died after falling down the stairs in 1947 and his mother moved to Newbiggin to live with her sister.

At half past eight, Ian collected the five bob he had earned from Mr Willington for his week's work and headed up High Market, through the small plantation next to the Sandstone Church of The Holy Sepulchre standing opposite the Co-op shops at the 'Store Corner.' The Co-op marked the start of another stretch of shops that ran down to the Portland Hotel and on into town.

Wilson's was the largest grocery store in this part of the town and the only one that required a grocery delivery boy, a sought after and lucrative job that Ian had waited twelve months for Ray the lad before him, to leave to start work at the pit. Ian had lied that he was Fourteen and had had the job for four weeks. It was a job he was very keen to hold onto it as he made over a pound a week on wages and tips.

The heavy and unwieldy delivery bike with its small front wheel with the large basket above it was already propped up on its stand outside of Wilson's when Ian arrived. Walking through the busy shop to the rear, Margaret one of the young sales girls was cutting up a large block of Cheddar Cheese into smaller blocks before wrapping them in heavy blue paper.

'Here Bonny Lad,' she said, surreptitiously handing him a thin sliver of cheese that he covertly grabbed and pushed quickly into his mouth savouring the treat that he knew she would have for him.

'There's five boxes already made up and a few more to come so you better get a move on Ian lad,' she said, nodding toward the boxes of groceries stacked by the rear door. He quickly looked at the addresses on the boxes and saw that most of them were for regular customers down Wansbeck Road and Green Lane but that one was for Home Farm out on the outskirts that would take time to deliver. He realised that the last one might well prevent him from finishing in time for the cinema, especially as Margaret had said there was more to come!

By eleven o'clock he had delivered four boxes down Wansbeck Road and was delighted with the one-shilling and thrupence he had made in tips and was now struggling to pedal against a strong and bitterly cold west wind toward Home Farm, keen to get it delivered as there were three more boxes waiting back at the shop. With his head down and standing on the pedals to keep the bike moving into the wind, he struggled along Highmarket toward the Zebra Crossing totally oblivious as to what was going on around him. Consequently, he did not see the large brindle dog that had stopped at the crossing and sat down for a second before standing up to trot over the crossing; straight in front of him.

Seeing the dog at the last moment, Ian braked hard, his feet sliding from the pedals causing him to straddle the cross bar, crushing his testicles and skinning a shin on the back of a pedal. Letting out a low, slow moan he slowly fell to his left taking the heavy bike with him ending up lying on his side with the bike still between his legs. Painfully and slowly, he sat up holding his crutch and looked into the huge broad face of the big Brindle that was wagging its tail furiously having avoided the front wheel of the bike easily.

As Ian wriggled his left leg from beneath the bike, the dog turned and looked at the spilled contents of the basket, sniffed at the groceries and then gently grasped a tin of baked beans in its huge mouth and trotted off back across the crossing and down the cut between the houses!

By the time Ian had freed himself from under the delivery bike, the dog was gone and he did not feel much like chasing after it as the pain in his groin was still quite severe. The small, rotund Mr Stott came scuttling out of his Post Office and helping Ian reload his bike and remount, he said, 'That saved me having to give that beast another tin of Lassie but I'm sure he'll come and raid me again the morn.'

The statement went over Ian's head and he continued his journey to the collection of buildings at the side of the road out of Ashington that made up Home Farm, saying to the middle-aged woman who opened the door, 'Am sorry Missus, there's a tin of beans missing.'

Furrowing her brow, the woman said, 'What de ye mean missing, were they not checked at the shop before ye left?

'Ian nodded, 'Aye, tha wor, but a big dog knocked me off me bike and stole them!'

Shaking her head in disbelief the woman said, 'Do ye really expect me te believe that, are ye telling me that a bandit dog knocked ye off yer bike and pinched a tin of beans?'

'Aye Missus, whey he didn't really knock me off, Aah fell off when he ran in front of me but he did pinch a tin of beans!'

'Whey that's a bloody likely story, noo off ye can and get me another tin before Aah phone Wilson's and tell them ye've lost a tin of beans!'

Ian dejectedly pedalled the half mile back to Highmarket, bought a tin of beans from Pearson's store and peddled back to Home Farm where the frosty reception continued; no tip was forthcoming.

It was after one o'clock by the time he arrived back at Wilson's and then delivered the last three boxes. He knew he was going to be too late for the start of the matinee but if he hurried, he might be able to pick Tommy up from home and still get to the Regal before the main feature had begun.

As he hurried home along the cuts between the Third and Fourth Rows, he saw a lad from his class at school walking toward him with the big Brindle bandit dog, 'Hello Syd, is that your dog?' he asked.

Syd stopped and patted the bruiser of a dog that was wagging its tail madly, 'Aye it's Butch, my Dad got it a few days ago, he's great isn't he?' 'Am just teking him for a tin of Lassie.'

'He's blidy great alreet, he doesn't need a tin of Lassie; the big bugga pinched a tin of beans from me!'

Syd looked at Ian as though he was mad and said, 'Aye reet, who are ye kidding, Aah'll see ye later, haway Butch,' and he walked off toward the shops with the dog trotting alongside him with what Ian was sure was a smile!

A few minutes later he arrived home breathless and just a little weary and hurried inside where his Mother was peeling potatoes dug up last year from the side garden where Mike and he tried to grow as many vegetables as they could to help feed the family.

Knowing his dad would be at the 'Fell em Doon' Working Mans' Club until at least two o'clock, Ian relaxed and asked, 'Where's Tommy Mam?'

Jane did not answer, instead she stood up, grabbed his arm and led him to the kitchen table and gently forced him into a chair next to his pretty sister Maureen who was wearing her best red woollen jumper over a skirt that was struggling to contain umpteen starched petticoats.

With an unexpected firmness in her voice, Jane said, 'You are going to have some soup and bread before you do anything else,' and placed a bowl of thick, steaming lentil soup in front of Ian who was unable to resist it, devouring it so fast, it almost burned the skin from his mouth and throat

As his Mother walked into the sitting room, he greedily wiped the bowl clean with a crust and asked Maureen in a mocking voice, 'Me Mam seems a bit strange teday, are ye seeing yor sweetheart Terry the sefternoon then Maureen?'

She blushed scarlet and checking to see that her Mother had not heard the quip, whispered angrily, 'Be quiet Man, if me Mam and Dad finds out I'll be in big trouble, we're gannin te the Wallaw te see Elvis in Jail House Rock, noo shut up.'

Jane walked back in to the kitchen with a magazine and sat down in the fireside chair as Ian asked again, 'Where's wor Tommy then, if he's coming to the pictures we'll hev to gan noo or we'll be ower late?'

Tutting at her son's heavy Geordie accent, Jane said, 'He thought you weren't coming so he's gone across the Rec with Roger and Billy Grundy to watch Michael playing football'

'That's not good Mam, those two are alwas up te bother; God knows what tha deeing?'

Jane nodded and said, 'Well can you go across and see if you can find him and take him off to the Regal,' pleased and relieved that Ian and Maureen would both be out before Nick returned from the Fell em Doon.

Ian was at all happy pleased at his Mother's instruction as it meant he would probably be too late for the matinee but not trusting the other two lads, he said, 'Aye all right, I'll gan ower and look for him.' Tommy was only eight and not the biggest of lads, but what he lacked in size; he made up for in spirit and was adventurous and fearless.

Zipping his jacket up, Ian hurried along the street, past the grey net curtains hanging limply at the dirty kitchen windows of the Grundy's house and on down the second terrace. He crossed the Rec Bridge as a Tankie below shunted coal wagons, puffing white steam up through the openings between the wooden slats of the bridge. Reminiscent of a scene from a spy movie; Billy and Roger Grundy emerged laughing from the white steam clouds just as Ian ran forward to try and catch the last damp blast.

'Where's wor Tommy, me Mam said he was with ye two?' he demanded as the two bedraggled younger lads stopped in front of him.

The older and heavier built of the two, Billy, whose jeans were wet up to his thighs and whose heavy wool pullover was doing its best to swallow him, looked at Ian and said, 'He's still ower at New Moor, we've been looking for Moorhens eggs but couldn't find any and we got soaked so wa ganning hyem but he's still looking.'

'I thought you were going to watch the football? And looking for Moorhens eggs - are ye two daft or what, it's far too urly for them man, they divint start nesting till next month!' Ian said angrily, realising he was going to have to walk the length of the sports fields and around the back of New Moor small holding to find Tommy and there was always the chance that Tommy had already walked along the main road to the Sixth Row and he would miss him completely.

'Hev ye's just come from the marsh?' he demanded, wondering if Tommy was still looking for eggs.

Freckle faced and weasel like, Roger wiped a dew drop dangling from the end of his pointed nose with the back of the shiny sleeve of his ill-fitting jacket; pushed back his round, wire framed National Health specs that were fastened at the back with a piece of dirty elastic and

11

answered, 'Nur, we went to the Rec Hall te get dry and wor there for a bit before Joe chased us oot.'

'Tommy had better be alreet!' Ian warned the two lads, concerned that his younger brother was alone on the Marsh. He hoped he had either gone back to watch Mike playing football or gone home the other way but felt he still had to check to make sure and ran down the steps off the bridge and jogged into the Rec and across to the football field with its backdrop of pit heaps and collection of colliery buildings. He could see it was half time as the players and coaches of the two teams were huddled together at either end of the pitch and saw much to his annoyance, that Tommy was not one of the few spectators, realising he would have to go to New Moor to look for him.

He stopped by the goal posts where Mike's 'Ashington Colliery Apprentice's' Team were discussing tactics and waved at Mike who ran over and said, 'Are ye stopping for the second half, we're winning two nil?'

Ian explained what had happened and Mike cursed Roger and Billy before saying, 'Whey ye better gan and find him, are ye still ganna tek Tommy to the pictures then?'

'Nah, it's too late noo, I'll just kick his arse and take him hyem,' Ian replied dejectedly.

I'll see yer later then, a couple of the lads are coming back to wor hoose te listen te me new record, 'Singing the Blues,' Mike said and ran back to join his team.

As he jogged off toward New Moor just a few hundred yards away, Ian had a mental picture of Mike and his pals nodding their heads, tapping their feet and snapping their fingers to the beat of the music playing from the old radiogram in the sitting room, trying as they did to look cool, 'Daft buggers.' Ian thought.

Despite the bitter cold, he was sweating by the time he reached the back of the smallholding near the marsh as he slowed to a walk not, wanting to draw the attention of anyone and be chased off. Once past the out buildings, he walked across the frozen field that still had patches of frosted grass in the hollows and became boggier with every step as he neared the marsh that was only 50 yards from the Ashington to Ellington Road. He cursed loudly when he could not see Tommy and thought that he probably had walked home along the main road to look at the construction site of the new NCB Area Workshops.

The main part of the marsh had a fringe of ice around the belt of frosted reeds where the moorhens normally nested and Ian could see where the lads had churned up the mud and reeds in their fruitless search for eggs. Thinking he was too late, he turned to leave when he noticed something moving the stubby reeds and disturbing the water on the far side of the marsh! Curious as to what was the cause of the ripples he walked carefully around the marsh, trying in vain to keep his cheap leather shoes dry as he peered into the reed bed still unable to see what was there. Whatever it was, it was near the edge of the reeds, just before the deep water about fifteen yards into the marsh.

He could just make out a dark shape and was beginning to think some sort of animal had got itself into difficulties when realisation hit him like a thunderbolt! Without thinking, he charged headlong into the marsh toward the almost motionless figure and straight into trouble. He immediately lost both shoes in the sucking mud that lay just below the surface of the freezing water as he struggled to move forward in the ever-deepening quagmire.

Quickly thigh deep in water as the mud below gripped his knees bringing his mad rush almost to a stop as he struggled in vain to lift his legs free to reach his brother who he could now clearly see lying almost completely submerged and barely moving in the reeds ten foot in front of him. Hearing the commotion Ian was making, Tommy raised his head and looked at his brother and Ian saw that his face was as pale as marble; his lips blue and pulled back in a terrible grimace that bared his teeth as his body shook in uncontrollable spasms, the desperate look in Tommy's eyes drove Ian on.

Realising he was never going to reach him standing up, Ian threw himself forward into the marsh letting out an involuntary gasp as the icy water shocked his body that had been warmed by his exertions. Half swimming, half crawling, he ploughed toward his brother as the marsh did its best to prevent him from reaching him. Using clumps of reeds as leverage, the same clumps that Tommy had probably used to walk on before slipping into the mud, he slowly inched closer until he was almost able to grasp him just as he felt the mud suck his legs down, clamping him to the spot.

Wriggling and thrashing with all his strength, he reached forward, just managing to take hold of the back of Tommy's collar and pulled with all his might. Nothing happened, no movement at all, he was stuck fast and by the look of him, Tommy was unable to help himself as the back of his head kept dipping into the freezing water. With great difficulty Ian wriggled a little closer and managed to place his right arm under Tommy's head and grasping his shoulder as tight as he could, he tried to pull him free while keeping his head above the water. Tommy looked at Ian through staring eyes that looked as though they had shrunk inside his white face as he tried in vain to speak.

Shivering violently, Ian said, 'Hang on while Aah torn me sell roond and I'll drag ye oot but yer ganna hev te help me.' Staring back with empty eyes, Tommy did not answer; he was far too weak from his ordeal to respond. It seemed to Ian that it took him for ever to wriggle and heave through the mud until he was lying alongside Tommy, ready to try and pull him free but he eventually managed to slide both arms around him and started to heave. However, despite his efforts, it was impossible to move Tommy as there was nothing solid to lever against and the more he heaved the more he felt his legs slide deeper into the icy mud, quickly draining what energy he had left.

'Through quivering lips, he gasped, 'Haway Tom man, help me, we've gotta get oot of here,' but there was no response from his brother, he was almost motionless. With mounting alarm, Ian realised that he was not going to be able to get him out on his own and now he did not think he had the strength left to free himself.

Wiping mud from Tommy's ashen face, Ian said, 'Hang on, Mike'll get us oot, he's boond te come looking for us,' and pulled his brother's head onto his shoulder trying to keep it out of the water. He saw that Tommy had stopped shivering and moaning but did not know if that was a good sign or not and continued to talk to him as the cold slowly stole the warmth from his own body, slowing him down, confusing him, disorienting him until he thought he was lying back in their shared bed snug below a monstrous pile of blankets.

Having won the match 2 -1 and after showering in the Rec Hall, Mike was in a jubilant mood as he, Hank and Geordie walked along the Sixth Row discussing the goals and their part in them. They stopped outside number 57 where tall, blonde and the distinguished looking, thirty eight year old, ex-army Sergeant, Edward Thompson was polishing his blue, five year old Jowett Javelin.

'How did ye get on lads?' he asked as he wrung out his tattered chamois leather.

'Thrashed them two te one,' solidly built and broad-faced Hank replied for them.

'Hardly a thrashing!'

As they walked on, Mike shouted back, 'Aye it would hev been more but Hank kept missing the blidy goals, he needs new blidy specs!'

'Bugga off, at least I scored!' Hank retorted as they walked into Mike's; dropping their ex-army haversacks containing their muddy football kit at the back door before they walked through the kitchen and into the sparsely furnished but immaculately clean sitting room.

Jane, who had been sitting by the fire knitting a jumper for Tommy when they burst in, sprang up and whispered worriedly, 'Sshh, don't wake your father up, he went to bed an hour ago when he got back from the Fell em Doon!'

Looking sheepish, Mike said, 'Sorry Mam, we better not play me records then,' and ushering the other two lads back into the kitchen he asked his mother, 'Where's wor Tom and Ian then?'

'At the cinema, they've gone to see a film about an old dog I believe'

'Nur they haven't, I saw Ian and he said he was too late as Tommy was still ower at New Moor looking for bords eggs and that he was ganning te get him and come home!'

Frowning, Jane was immediately worried, asking, 'What time was that?'

'About an hour or so ago maybe a bit longer,' said Mike realising that the boys should have been home long ago. Jane's stomach began to churn, she knew Ian would have brought the reckless Tommy home and felt mounting panic as she thought of the marsh and its dangers.

Mike was already heading for the back door saying to his two pals, 'Come on ye two we'd better gan and look for them and I'll kick both their arses when I find them.'

Following the three of them to the yard gate, Jane shouted 'Hurry lads, God only knows what has happened to them,' then almost to herself she pleaded, 'Please God not now, not now!'

As they began jogging down the street, Edward Thompson stopped cleaning his car and asked, 'What's the matter?'

As Mike quickly explained what had happened, Jane ran down to them and was about to ask Edward if he would drive the lads to New Moor, just as he opened his car door and said, 'Jump in lads, we'll be there in five minutes in this,' and nodded reassuringly at Jane as he climbed into the driver's seat.

A few minutes later under a darkening sky, he parked the Jowett on the verge of the road next to a gate adjacent to the marsh and all four scrambled out climbing the gate to look across at the marsh hoping to see the two boys but there was no sign of them.

Mike said, 'I cannit see any sign of them maybe they' went home alang the owld path?

Straddling the gate and balancing himself on the middle rung, Edward cast left to right, then up and back and right to left, searching the marsh for any sign. On his third sweep, he saw a shape that was out of place deep in the north side of the marsh, '*There, over there!*' he shouted as he pointed, realising with horror it was the shape of a boy!

He immediately took charge of the situation and barked orders; 'Geordie, you and Hank run up te the hoose and ask them to phone for an ambulance and see if they have any planks or something we can crawl on; come on Mike let's get..,' but he didn't finish, Mike was already sprinting across the frozen field.

Ian was still talking to Tommy, at least he thought he was as he looked up and watched the sky darken; 'Was it that late already, we'll miss our tea if we don't get home soon,' he thought as he felt his head slip beneath the water for the first time! The water initially felt warm and comforting until its icy bite snapped him awake – he lifted his head and spat out filthy water but immediately felt himself beginning to slip back just as he heard voices that seemed to be coming from down a long tunnel. The voices seemed to give him energy; enough for him to shake Tommy and through numbed lips, whisper, 'Hang on Tom, Mike's here.'

Without thinking, Mike ran full tilt into the freezing marsh and almost reached his brothers before the mud sucked the speed and momentum from his run leaving him struggling just a few feet short of the boys.

'Throw your-self forward onte yer belly,' shouted Edward as he waded in. Mike fell forward reaching with both hands, just managing to grasp hold of a tuft of reeds next to Ian and pulled himself alongside his brothers as Geordie and Hank came running toward the marsh carrying a large sheet of corrugated iron.

Ian heard someone shout, 'Hang on for the wriggly tin to crawl back on or ye'll get yersell stuck as weel,' and then everything turned into a kaleidoscope of confused images of faces, grasping hands, grunts, shouts and Mike's voice saying gently but firmly, 'You can let go Ian lad, I've got him now.'

The kaleidoscope continued; hands grasping him pulling him across a tin sheet; Mr Thompson strong and silent lifting him and running across the field with him in his arms. Then a glimpse of Mike and one of his pals kneeling over Tommy on the bank of the marsh; the back of a car and a blanket being flung over him; his Mother's distraught face and finally, his Father's angry staring face and the smell of stale beer on his breath!

Chapter 2
Rescue

Mike had managed to hold onto his brothers until Edward reached him and the corrugated iron thrown onto the marsh but it was still a monumental struggle to pull the two lads free. They then passed them back onto the tin where Geordie lying on top, was able to grasp the boys and pass them back to Hank who was standing knee deep in the marsh. Edward and Mike then helped to free each other from the mud and back over the tin to firmer ground.

By the time they hauled themselves free, Hank was carrying out the Holger Nielsen method of artificial resuscitation on a lifeless Tommy as skinny Geordie wrapped himself around Ian in a vain attempt to pass on body heat.

Edward again took charge; feeling Tommy's neck he thought he felt a very faint pulse and nodded to Hank to keep working as a portly, middle aged woman came panting down from the small-holding with an armful of blankets and gasped, 'The ambulance is on its way.'

Edward thought that they probably had arrived too late for poor Tommy but that there was a slim chance that they might be able to be resuscitate him. Looking at Ian he knew what he needed now was rewarming to prevent him from worsening so he barked, 'Mike wrap Tommy in one of these blankets and Hank keep at it until the ambulance arrives, Geordie come with me and we'll take Ian home to his mother and let her know what's happened!'

Standing nervously at the gate to the small yard of her house, Jane was trying to keep calm, trying to convince herself that her precious boys would come running down the back lane, carefree and full of fun. That thought was quickly dispelled when she saw the Jowett swing into the lane and accelerate toward her, she felt her knees go week and her heart leap into her throat, 'Oh my God no please no,' she begged as Edward braked hard bringing the car to a shuddering stop next to her.

He leapt out of his car and grabbed her shoulders and said, 'You are going to have to be strong for your lads, lass!'

'My God, what's happened?' She pleaded.

'They've both been in the marsh, Ian needs warming up straight away but little Tommy, whey, he will be on his way to hospital; the ambulance was just arriving when we left.'

Jane had opened the rear door of the car as a mud spattered Geordie stepped carefully out cradling Ian whose face was just visible inside the heavy cream blanket he had been wrapped in. Pulling the blanket back a touch, she looked at her son's ashen face and said, 'Bring him up stairs and we'll get his wet clothes of him; Edward will you go next door and fetch Mrs Galloway.'

Upstairs Jane struggled to keep her emotions under control as she stripped the sodden clothes of Ian and rubbed him quickly down with a towel before placing him in Maureen's bed. She was piling blankets on top as stout, 5ft tall Aggie Galloway rushed breathlessly into the room; 'Eeee the poor bairns,' she said as she helped Jane straighten the blankets on top of Ian.

Jane took a deep breath; stood up and composed herself before saying, 'Aggie can you please find some hot water bottles, there's one in the bottom of the wardrobe there but will you please borrow some more and after you've filled them, place them around Ian but make sure they are not touching him and when he's ready give some very warm tea and there's a tin of tomato soup in the pantry, see if he'll have that in a while, I'm going to the hospital in Mr Thompson's car.'

Turning to a gaping and awkward Geordie she said, 'Geordie will you wake Mr Shepherd up and tell him what has happened and can you please light a fire in here?' She did not want to have to contend with

Nick and his foul temper now and she was sure that the sight of Edward would make it worse although she did not know the reason for the open hostility between the two men.

Geordie nodded, 'Yes,' but did not relish the task of waking Nick Shepherd; especially as he would have had a good few pints at lunch time!

Knowing she could rely on Aggie, Jane rushed down stairs to where Edward was anxiously waiting. 'Even in her distressed state she still looks beautiful,' Edward thought as he stepped forward and he asked, 'How is he Jane?'

'I think he's going to be alright but how is my little Thomas?'

'He didn't look too good Lass, but I felt a pulse and Mike was doing his best for him.'

Jane, gasped slightly as Edward spoke and with a faint quiver in her voice asked, 'I realise you will need to change your muddy clothes but will you please take me to the hospital Mr Thompson?'

Edward nodded, 'The mud will dry Lass, the priority noo is te get ye to hospital te see yer bairn, haway,' and after Jane took her navy blue woollen overcoat from behind the back door, he led her outside and opened the car door for her before rushing around to the other side to climb in behind the steering wheel. Swinging the Jowett into a three point turn to get out of the end of the street, he could see out of the corner of his eye that Jane was trembling and ached to take her in his arms and comfort her but instead said, 'Hang on, we'll be there in a few minutes.

Aggie Galloway was the epitome of what people meant when they called someone 'the Salt of the Earth,' always ready to lend a hand to anyone who needed it, she had genuine 'heart of gold.' Despite years of trying when she was younger, she had no children of her own, either herself, or more likely the dependable in all other matters, Mr Galloway were not firing on all four cylinders and neither of them ever felt like sharing their problem with any Doctor but they did enjoy trying to produce a baby! Now in her late 40s she was content with her lot and loved the children in the street and was always ready, should any of the kids be unfortunate enough to be close enough, to grab and hold one to her ample bosom while she wiped a dirty face with the corner of her pinny, after first spitting onto it of course!

Because of her size and the fact that she never walked slowly, always seeming to be in a galloping hurry, the kids affectionately called her the 'Gallowa' not just because of her name but because of her resemblance to a pit pony or Gallowa, the name given them by the miners. The Gallowa was in full gallop mode; after tucking Ian into bed, she grabbed the blue rubber hot water bottle from the tiny single door wardrobe in the corner of the bedroom and trotted down stairs, leaving Geordie standing forlornly trying to pick up the courage to go into the next bedroom and wake up Nick Shepherd.

After filling the kettle and nestling it into the glowing kitchen fire, Aggie galloped off next door and did the same with her kettle before puffing upstairs where she opened the bottom draw of her chest of draws and lifted out a brown stoneware hot water bottle. Trotting back down stairs with it, she left it by the hearth ready to be filled once the kettle boiled.

Needing more bottles, she began knocking on doors but by the time she reached the Grundys she had only managed to obtain one from Mrs Holloway at number 58. She paused for a second outside the Grundy's wondering if it was worth knocking on the door of her impoverished neighbour before she knocked.

Roger, accompanied by 'Monty' the Grundy's scruffy, forever foraging black mongrel, opened the door and before Aggie could speak he shouted, 'Mam the Gallowa's at the door,' and turned and walked back into the kitchen.

Aggie snapped, 'Get Doon,' and swatted Monty when he jumped up to greet her and sniff to see if by chance she had any food on her person, This was his normal procedure and he was used to being swatted and told to 'Get Doon,' and probably thought that was his name as folk were constantly shouting it at him!

A few seconds later, the once handsome but now homely and prematurely wrinkled, pinny wrapped figure of Flo Grundy shuffled to the door.

'Eeee hello Aggie pet, what canna dee for ye,' she asked wondering if one of her lads had been upsetting her neighbours yet again.

'Red faced and breathing heavily from her galloping, Aggie gasped, 'Hot water bottles, hot water bottles, we need as many as we can get, young Ian Shepherd is nigh on froze te death, he fell in the wetter ower at New Moor and we need te get the poor bairn warmed up.'

Flo grabbed Aggie by the arm and dragged her into the miserable, concrete floored kitchen that contained six battered chairs grouped around an old pine table, two of the chairs being occupied by Billy and Roger with a third Grundy, 13 year old Jake, sitting on a cracket stool by the fire reading a comic

Flo grabbed the soot blackened kettle from the hearth and as she filled it in the pantry, ordered, 'Billy nip upstairs and get the hot wetter bottle from the bottom of me bed,' and turning to Aggie, said, 'Go on pet, I'll fetch it alang as soon as I've filled it.'

Aggie raced out as a very sheepish looking Billy ran upstairs followed by a madly barking Monty who thought it was a game. Jake put his comic down, he was worried about his pal Ian, they went to school together and although Ian was in the 'A' class and he was in the 'B', they were good friends and had had some great escapades together. 'Aah hope he's alreet Mam, shall Aah tek the bottle alang?'

Happy to let her only sensible lad take the bottle, Flo said, 'Aye,' before turning to glare at Roger who was trying to tuck his dirty neck

23

down inside his grubby collar in a vain attempt to hide his head and disappear.

'Mind if Aah find oot ye two hev had out te dee with this yer deed!' she snarled, she might be scrawny but she ruled the roost in the Grundy household, the broom handle being her favourite method of dishing out punishment when it was needed, which was often.

Watching the kettle boil, Jake remembered that he had seen his dad put a stoneware hot water bottle behind the empty beer crate at the back of the tiny pantry and rushed in to reach under the shelf and behind the crate. He dragged out the heavy bottle and handed it over to his Mother saying, 'I thowt I'd seen me Dad put this in there.'

Flo took the bottle and shook it feeling the liquid inside splash to and fro, 'Aah wondered where this had got te, Aah hevn't seen the blidy thing for ages,' and stepped back into the pantry where she unscrewed the stoneware stopper and poured out the strongly smelling amber liquid from the bottle. The smell was too much for even an inquisitive Monty who tucked his tail between his legs and ran back to his place of sanctuary on a tattered blanket on the floor next to Jake's cracket.

'Bah that smells blidy aaful, Aah hope that dorty wee bugger of a father of yours hasn't been pissing in this bottle or I'll give him a right yarking when he gets hyem from Portland Park!'

Geordie had put off waking Nick Shepherd up and instead built a fire in the tiny cast iron fireplace and now that it was burning well, he decided that he had to wake him and he had also decided that he need not be there when Nick actually got out of his bed. Still afraid for his own safety, he picked up the small coal shovel with its sharp raised edges that he had used to fetch coal for the fire and holding it like a club; he took a deep breath and quietly pushed open the door to the second bedroom, peering into the curtain-darkened room. He could

24

just make out the double bed at the other side of a tiny unlit fireplace but there was enough light to enable him to walk quickly over and timidly shake Nick.

'Mista Shephaad, Mista Shephaad,' he whispered drawing no response from Nick in his beer induced sleep. After trying three more times with the same result, Geordie steeled himself and grabbing Nick by the shoulder shook him violently and almost shouted, *'Wake up man Mista Shephaad!'*

Sitting bolt upright, Nick swung a wild punch at the horrified Geordie who; just managing to dodge the blow, dropped the small shovel in fright and ran back to the door and turned around blurting, *'Ye need to get up, yore Ian's next door nearly deed from caad and Tommy's been teking to hospital and might be deed and yer Missus's has gone te see him we Mr Edwards.'* He did not wait to see if Nick Shepherd had heard or understood him, he thought 'Noo's the time te get oot while I still can,' and closing the door behind him, bolted down the stairs and out the back door just as Aggie came puffing back in with a hot water bottle wrapped in a tea towel.

Just after ten o'clock that morning, Nick Shepherd the War Hero, Disabled Veteran, Pit Labourer, part-time drunk, wife beater, child slapper and part time human being had staggered downstairs with a parched throat and raging headache wearing the vest he had slept in and his half fastened creased suit trousers that he had just pulled on. Standing at the kitchen door, he scratched the stubble on his chin, rubbed his lame knee, bent slightly, farted loudly and coughed his chest rattling smokers' cough before walking across to the fire and spitting disgusting green phlegm into the back of the flames.

Having ensured all their kids were out of the house, Jane stood by the pantry door warily watching her husband's morning routine with distaste and just a touch of hatred but also with pity for the shell of a

25

man that had once been the dashing soldier who had swept her off her feet. The man to whom she was locked too in a loveless and abusive marriage that she did not know how to escape from, not with four children to consider!

She felt that she had no one to turn to for help, nowhere to go to escape the man she depended upon, the man who had slowly robbed her of her self-esteem, the man who had through violence and intimidation, dominated her for the past seventeen years and robbed her of any say in their children's future.

However, the drunken violence he perpetrated against her last night had changed everything; after failing to fight him off she had had to endure his assault whilst stifling cries of pain and anguish, desperately not wanting to disturb the children. When Nick had finished and contemptuously pushed her aside she had lain sobbing waiting for him to fall asleep so that she could escape the bedroom. Later as she climbed out of bed, she looked down at him and knew she would take no more abuse from this wretched man.

Nick spat, 'Tea, where's me frigging tea?

'It's on the table; I poured it when I heard you coming down the stairs.'

'I'll hev a bacon sandwich we it,' he demanded as he lit his first cigarette of the day.

Knowing with dread what her husband's reaction was going to be Jane said in a quiet but firm voice, 'We haven't got any bacon, you left me short of money again this week and I couldn't afford to buy any.'

Banging his fist on the table, Nick exploded, 'Aah give you enough to put what I want on this blidy table,' and turning, he grabbed Jane by the throat and spat into her face, 'Yer nee fucking good in bed anymore and ye cannit even fucking feed me, ye bloody fucking useless women.' Pushing her back, he thrust her up against the pantry door as she fought to stay on her feet, he raised his right hand to strike Jane but she had foreseen this. Having spent the night in wretched misery, she was ready; she would tolerate no more abuse and swung the wooden hand brush she had concealed behind her, smacking it into the side of her husband's head!

Releasing his grip of her throat, he staggered back as Jane strode forward and continued to strike him again and again, propelling him back into the sitting room. The rage that she had held from the previous night when he had raped her in her own bed exploded from within her as she forced him backwards with more blows screaming, 'Never again Nick Shepherd, do you hear me you will never raise your hand to me or my children in this house again!'

Nick fell backwards over the step between the two rooms and held both arms up to protect himself from his wife's unexpected onslaught. Seeing him cowering on the floor, Jane flung the brush down and stepped back and whispered, 'Never again Nick,' turned and walked to the back door, took her coat from the hook and pulled it on. Fastening her coat, she walked back to Nick who had recovered enough to sit up.

Feeling utter contempt for the cowering disgrace that was her husband and just a tad euphoric at having finally stood up to him, she said quietly, 'I'm going to the Co-op to buy some bread to go with the soup I have made the boys for their lunch, if you want anything you can give me some money to buy it instead of wasting it on beer at the club!'

Still shocked, he spat, 'Yer frigging mental woman, I'll swing for ye one of these days and I'll spend my money on what I want,' but flinched when Jane bent down to pick up the brush.

Jane looked down at him and said, 'In that case the least we see of each other the better, I'll be sleeping with Maureen from now on,' and turned and marched out of the house.

Nick sat between the two doors for some time, trying to make sense of what had just happened; slowly realising that things were never

27

going to be the same again, he felt a black rage building up inside him – 'Why was his life so bloody shity?' He realised he had just lost his power over Jane, and remembered that Mike too had begun to defy him openly; he was losing control of his family! He also had to contend with Edward Thompson living just a few doors away. His long-time, supposed friend and ex-army pal, who had been with him at Dunkirk, was the only one who knew the truth of what happened back then. Despite Edward never mentioning the firefight they were both in, Nick felt as if Edward kept the truth of the firefight as a Sword of Damocles dangling above his head.

He picked himself up and angrily but stupidly punched the sitting room door, skinning his knuckles and wincing in pain, 'Shite,' he cursed before drinking the cup of luke warm tea Jane had poured earlier. 'Fuck this,' he thought to himself and decided to wash, shave, and bugger off to the Fell-em-Doon, he needed a drink and he had his little side-line to attend to.

A while later, having had a good few pints and having made a few quid running his under the table betting racket, he had limped into an empty house just after two o'clock. With no one to argue with he had flung his jacket on the sofa in the sitting room, kicked off his shoes and staggered back through the kitchen and upstairs pulling his tie off and unbuttoning his shirt before sitting on the edge of the bed. Muttering to himself, he had fallen back on the bed still wearing his trousers and shirt and quickly fell into a drunken sleep.

He was dreaming that he was half way down the pit shaft and someone was standing at the top shouting at him but he was too far away to hear when suddenly someone grabbed his shoulder and tried to drag him to the bottom!

Springing up in bed, he lashed out at whoever or whatever grabbed him and then jumped out of bed, his left foot standing on the sharp edge of the small coal shovel that Geordie had dropped! As he felt the shovel cut painfully into his foot he heard Geordie babbling at the door something about Ian being nearly deed and Tommy being deed but the pain from the cut made him jump and fall forward, his head colliding with the old varnished dressing table, clattering Jane's meagre supply of cosmetics from the top, across the floor.

Now in a blind rage from the cut to his foot, bang to his head and filthy hangover he staggered to his feet, kicking a hairbrush into the corner as he snatched open the door of the darkened bedroom and stepped squinting into the brightly lit small landing. 'What the fucks going on?' he demanded as he balanced on his weak right leg, squeezing his left foot with his hand to try to lessen the pain and stop the blood that was now flowing quite alarmingly.

Adding to his confusion, Aggie Galloway appeared in the doorway of the other bedroom and scolded, 'Be quiet ye noisy sod, yer bairns in here half deed and here ye are drunk as usual.' Aggie had no respect for him, nor did she have any fear of the dishevelled drunken figure in front of her and waited for him to compose himself.

Still balanced on his lame leg, Nick asked, 'What the fucking hell is ganning on?'

Aggie spat back, 'Divinit ye dare swear at Mr blidy Nick Shepherd, I'm not a feared of ye, noo shut up and listen!' She told him as much as she knew and was shocked when he again began swearing when she told him that his wife had gone to the hospital in Edward Thompson's car.

When she finished she said, 'I think you better go and see your lad noo, he keeps on opening his eyes but he is very poorly mind.'

Nick looked at her contemptuously and hobbled to the top of the stairs before saying, 'Aah will as soon as I've been doon stairs and wrapped sumat around me foot and had a cup of tea.'

She may have only been five foot tall but 'The Gallowa' was not having that; grabbing him by the arm she dragged him into the cosy bedroom that was lit by a glowing fire and pushed him toward the bed piled high with blankets where Ian's diminutive towel wrapped head, was just visible on the pillow. Nick felt himself forced forward and leant over the bed to stare into Ian's still ashen face just as he opened his eyes for a second or two.

'He looks alreet te me!'

'Ye wouldn't kna alreet if it smacked ye in the gob and ye need to sober up if yer ganning te the hospital to see poor Tommy.'

'He's ganning te hev te wait until I'm ready te gan, anyway he's mother and hur blidy fancy man are we him,' snarled Nick as he hobbled out the room and down the stairs where Jake Grundy was standing with two hot water bottles cradled in his arms.

The glowing stub of a cigarette hanging from his bottom lip identified the cold and tired Albert Grundy as he walked quickly along the street to reach the comfort of a roaring fire. He was looking forward to a wee nip of something special to warm him up after a freezing afternoon at 'Portland Park' watching the 'Colliers' beat neighbouring Blyth Spartans 3-2 in the local Derby. He had his well-worn, grey Mackintosh fastened tightly around his skinny five foot five inch frame and his cap pulled down snugly covering his bald head that anyone rarely saw as he rarely took his cap off.

Monty received a swat and a terse, 'Get bloody doon dog,' from Albert as he stepped out of the cold and into the hall where he took off his Mac and hung it on the peg on the back of the door. Adjusting his blue pin stripe suit that was shiny with wear and a lack of cleaning, he walked into the kitchen where all of his family were waiting for him, all that is less for 19-year-old Ronnie who was in the Far East completing his National Service.

Flo was standing by the huge, black kitchen range with a metal spatula in her hand looking at the egg she had just put in the frying pan nestling in the glowing coals of the open fire. She turned and smiled a sneering disconcerting smile at her husband and said sweetly, 'Sit yoursell doon Albert pet, ye must be frozen after standing watching the match all afternoon and Aah bet you've had nowt to keep ye warm other than a beer or two?'

Not sure where this was going, Albert sat down at the table where Billy and Roger were seated with elbows on table, faces in hands watching their father and mother expectantly.

Flo took a plate of food from the oven and deftly lifted the egg from the pan and slid it onto the plate saying, "Here ye are Pet, yer favourite, spam fritters, chips and beans with an egg wor Jake got oot of the Hindhaugh's hen cree at the back of the Fourth Row.'

Sitting on his cracket, Jake smiled, as he pictured himself at seven o'clock that morning sneaking into the Hindhaugh's garden to lift four eggs, as usual no one had heard or seen him and the Hindhaugh's must think by now that their hens were the worst layers in the Ra's!

'By that looks champion Lass,' said Albert as Flo placed the plate of food in front of him.'

'Aye noo just before ye tuck inte to it, can ye tell me hoo lang ye've been pissing in the hot wetter bottle?'

'What the bloody hell de ye mean woman – pissing in what bloody hot weter bottle, retorted Albert, annoyed at Flo's nonsensical question as she kept him from his food.

'The hot wetter bottle in the back of the pantry, the one ye've been pissing in?

A look of horror spread across Albert's face as he pushed back his chair and scrambled to his feet to shuffle quickly into the pantry, emerging a few seconds later, 'What have ye done we the hot wetter bottle that was in their?' he demanded.

'Oh ye brazen bugga, yer, yer admit ye've been pissing in the bottle de ye,' spat Flo as Monty who had been sitting staring at the food on the table, jumped up and began barking at what seemed to him to be very much like a new game.'

'Aah hevn't been pissing inte owt woman, noo where's me hot wetter bottle?'

'Oh, I see, noo ye divint piss at aall and it's wor blidy hot wetter bottle not yor's and I've lent it te the Shepherds for poor Ian cos he fell in the marsh!'

'Lent it! Lent it! For God's sake what did ye dee we the whisky that was in it?'

The penny dropped for Flo; now she knew what the foul smelling liquid was that she had poured down the sink and that made her angry, very angry.

''Whisky!' she snarled, 'whisky, since when could we – you afford whisky when we cannit afford to put clathes on the poor bairns' backs and hiding it in a hot weter bottle?' She picked up the spatula and began beating Albert on the back, spitting, 'Ye blidy sneaky, little thieving bugga, who blidy dare ye?'

Cowering under her blows, Albert retreated toward the back door as Monty, wanting to join in the fun grabbed his trouser leg and hung on as Flo chased Albert around the kitchen and back into the pantry along with Monty who was still hanging on.

Flo turned and picked up Albert's dinner that was minus a couple of handful of chips that had found their way into the Billy and Roger's mouths. She handed the plate of food to Jake and said, 'Here Bonny

Lad, get that doon ye, that miserable owld bugga is getting nowt te night.'

Jake took the plate and perched it on his knees as he pushed three chips and half a spam fritter into his mouth.

Dragging Monty along, Albert marched out of the pantry determined to retrieve his dinner but was stopped by his spatula wielding wife who spat, 'Nur ye divint, yer getting nowt stay away from the lad!'

Realising his bounty was in danger of being snatched back by his father or Monty who had let go of Albert's trouser leg and was now standing with his nose inches from the food, waiting for an opening, Jake wrapped his left arm protectively around the plate and in between swatting his Father's hand and Monty's nose, stuffed the food into his mouth as quickly as he could.

As Flo continued to smack their father with the spatula, Billy and Roger joined Monty, crowding Jake, desperate for a spare morsel of food that their brother was protecting. Picking up the last piece of spam, Jake pushed it into his mouth and handed the plate to his two younger brothers who took it greedily, snatching at the chip but it was Monty who tilted his head and expertly flicked the egg with his tongue, straight into his mouth where it disappeared without trace. Licking the grease from its lips, Monty then pushed back in for a chip and some beans.

Later, sitting forlornly by the kitchen fire, as he painfully eased his spatula battered shoulders, Albert ate three slices of toast as he mourned the loss of his precious whisky.

Nick gave Jake a withering look before hopping with some difficulty into the kitchen as he clutched his foot in an effort to stop the bleeding. Reaching the pantry he snatched the neatly folded towel from the rail behind the door and ripping a strip off, hobbled back to the table and sat down on one of the chairs to wrap the strip tightly around his foot. Feeling sorry for himself and very angry at events earlier in the day he contemplated what to do next when Maureen walked in and up to the fire to warm herself.

He grabbed her arm and demanded, 'Where the blidy hell have ye been, I've telt ye before that I want ye in this hoose before it gets blidy dark?

Shrugging off her father's grip, Maureen lied, 'I went to the pictures with Mary Holland and I've been in her hoose next door watching television,' she did not want him to know that she had been to the cinema with Terry and had been canoodling with him in his sitting room for the past hour!

'Whey there's been a right carry on here, Ian's in yor bed half droond and Tommy is away te hospital nearly deed, or so that blidy nosey bugga next door says.'

Not fully understanding what he was prattling on about and noticing he had several red marks on the side of his face, Maureen was worried that he had done something to her brothers and rushed up stairs and into her bedroom, straight into Jake Grundy's back. Brushing past him, she saw Mrs Galloway tucking blankets back in after having placed the hot water bottles that Jake had brought, next to Ian.

'What on earth has happened?'

Aggie stood up and put her arm around Maureen who was taller than her and pushing her gently toward the old chair by the bed, said 'Come and sit doon lass and I'll tell ye what's happened cos Aah doot ye'll get any sense from yor Dad.'

Nick hobbled into the sitting room, pulled on his jacket and shoes, the right one with some difficulty due to the strip of towel wrapped around it. Still not certain in his own mind what he was going to do he gingerly walked to the back door and taking his grey overcoat down from its hook, he yelled up the stairs, Am ganning to the Medical Centre

34

then on te the hospital te see hoo Tom is.' Fastening his coat and pulling on his trilby, he limped off in the dark, heading for the Colliery Medical Centre, next to the Pit Head Baths and just behind the Eleventh Row, half a mile away.

On hearing Nick shout upstairs, Aggie whispered to Maureen, 'I think he thinks that they'll hev taken Tommy to Ashington Hospital but I doot that, they'll hev teken him to the Fleming at Newcastle!'

After her fight with Nick, Jane had walked to the Co-op deep in thought at having at last found the courage to stand up to him. She now had to work out what was going to happen next, divorce was something only Film Stars did; here in Ashington, if you had problems in your marriage you were expected to work them out behind closed doors – 'marriage was for life' was the way it was and the local way of life. She had no money of her own and nowhere for her and the children to go, her father, her only living relative would be delighted to hear of her predicament and she knew he would revel in being able to tell her, 'You married the spiv, you will have to live with the consequences.

Robert Trevelyan had been prosperous enough before the war, his small factory churning out aircraft parts but in 1936, with the 'Clouds of War' gathering and fuelled by the countries need for warplanes and lots of them, business had boomed. By the time War was declared in 1939 and with the aid of Government money, his factory had doubled in size and he was making more money than he could have dreamt of when he took over his late father's business in 1918. His father had built his factory up from a small garage to a factory making engine parts for the newly formed Royal Flying Corps but had to hand over the running of the factory to Robert in 1917 when he was diagnosed with cancer, dying just six months later.

35

Robert had always been an inveterate snob but he became even more so when in 1920 he married the beautiful socialite Rosalind Richmond (nicknamed Rolls Royce by her friends because of her initials and expensive tastes) and bought Huntly Court, the beautiful old manor house on the outskirts of Coventry, just a mile from his factory. They had enjoyed the thriving social scene of the 20s and 30s, the only rain on his parade was that Rosalind, having given birth to Jane, was then unable to bear any more children and he desperately wanted a son.

Sent to an independent girls' school just outside Brighton where she did reasonably well, Jane left on her 17th birthday in 1937 to spend six months on the Mediterranean with her mother. It was during this break before she went up to Cambridge that she saw that war with Germany was inevitable and resolved to do contribute. In 1938, despite her father's angry protests, 18-year-old Jane joined The Queen Alexandra's Imperial Military Nursing Corps and left to begin training at 'The Royal Victoria Infirmary at Netley, near Southampton. It was here in August of 1940 whilst undergoing her final training that involved treating injured soldiers returning from Dunkirk, that she fell pregnant to Nick Shepherd, the wounded War Hero!

Writing to explain to her father what had happened, she had expected her father to be angry but was horrified when she received his short reply – '*I no longer consider you to be my daughter, you are not welcome here and we do not wish to hear from you again!*' Jane did manage to speak to her mother once in the following years and although her mother regretted what had happened, she was unwilling to go against her domineering husband's wishes.

Discharged from the Nursing Services in disgrace, Jane married Nick who had rushed her into the marriage thinking he was marrying into money but instead found himself with a pregnant wife, discharged from the army and with nowhere to live. He took her to live with his parents in the very basic and cramped confines of Number 60 the Sixth Row where Jane found everything from the dialect, the food and the living conditions completely alien after her privileged upbringing. She did grow to love Nick's parents but Nick and her struggled to live of his War Pension and meagre colliery labourer's wages.

Nick continued to be charming to Jane, hoping that her father would forgive her but as time passed and it became clear that it was not going to happen, his attitude began to change and the viscous, self-obsessed, self-pitying Nick emerged. After the sudden death of his father in 1947 at only forty-nine, his mother quickly moved in with her sister in her flat in North Seaton Road, a terrace of houses on the edge of the road into the Victorian fishing and mining village of Newbiggin by the Sea. This left Nick free range to bully and eventually strike Jane and worse.

The only contact she had with her parents was in 1951 when she found out from her Father's Solicitor that her mother had died of a stroke and had been buried in the church near the family home. When she received no answer from the letter she had written to her father, she used her paltry savings to travel by train to Coventry and visit her mother's grave to say goodbye and returned the same day without attempting to see him.

Walking back from the Co-op Jane had resolved to explore divorce or at least separation from Nick, one thing she was sure of was that she would no longer allow herself or her children to be bullied or struck by him!

Sitting in the front of Edward's car on the way to Newcastle, her problem with Nick no longer mattered, she was desperate to find out how her little Tommy was and that was all that mattered now. Edward had driven Jane straight to Ashington Hospital where the staff informed them that Tommy was being taken to the Fleming Children's Hospital just of the Great North Road as it enters Newcastle and they had set off along the A1068 through Bedlington and on to the A1 pulling up outside the stately red bricked hospital just after six o'clock.

Dashing through the heavy oak door Jane stopped in the panelled hall, desperately searching for someone to show her where her boy was. Seeing a young woman sitting at a desk beyond the hall she rushed up to her and asked, *'Tommy Shepherd – my son, he's been brought here by ambulance, how is he, can I see him, which ward is he in, please where is he?'*

'Please calm down Mrs Shepherd, your son only arrived a few minutes ago,'

Jane cut her off, 'I am calm; I just need to know if my son is alive?'

He is Mam!' Mike said as he walked up to his mother brushing dried mud from his clothes, 'He's alive but he's oot of it and the Doctor says he is very poorly, they were discussing putting him in a bath to warm him up, that's when they chased me oot but wor Tom's a fighter, he'll pull through.'

Jane grabbed Mike to her and clung onto him as her pent up emotions got the better of her and she cried deep sobs of relief at the news that Tommy was still alive. Edward joined them and stood silently to one side as Mother and son comforted each other until Jane released Mike from her arms and began hurling questions at him, asking how Tommy was, what had they done and where he was, most of which Mike was able to answer.

Edward spoke quietly to the receptionist before joining them, saying gently, 'Someone will come out to talk to you as soon as they have stabilised Tom, so I think we should wait here.'

They almost had to restrain Jane to stop her from charging through the wards looking for her son, eventually calming her but she could not sit, instead she paced to and fro waiting for news; it was almost an hour before a dour faced young Doctor approached them.

'Mr and Mrs Shepherd, I can take you in to see Tommy in an hour or so but I have to warn you that he is very ill, his chances of pulling through are quite good and we are doing everything we can to rewarm him slowly and bring him back.'

Jane had to cling onto Mike for support as the Doctor continued, 'His pulse is stronger now but we have to be very careful that we don't try to warm him too quickly as that could be very dangerous but we are very hopeful.'

'Very hopeful!' what does he mean by that Jane thought before begging, 'Can I see him please?'

'Not while he is in the bath I'm afraid but if you and Mr Shepherd take a seat we should be able to get you into see him in an hour or so – just so long as there are no complications.'

'I'm not Mr Shepherd,' said Edward, 'but thanks Doctor we'll be here.' and led Mike and Jane back to the seats.

With her head bowed and deep in thought, Jane rocked slowly back and forwards with Mikes hand grasped firmly in hers until she suddenly announced, 'He's going to be alright, my Thomas is going to be alright – I suppose his Father should be here but I don't even know if he is aware of what has happened?'

'We're better off withoot him here Mam,' Mike whispered.

Placing his hand gently on Jane's shoulder Edward said, 'It looks as if it will be a while yet before they let you see Tom, Aah can drive back home and bring Nick back, I think he should be here as well.' Jane nodded and Edward quickly headed back to his car for the thirty-minute drive back to Ashington.

Chapter 3
Recovery

Despite the pain in his head, the sound of voices forced Ian to reluctantly open his eyes and find out where he was. He had been dreaming he was swimming in an ice-cold sea looking for Tommy who he had been holding a few minutes before but now he wondered why Jake Grundy was swimming toward him talking about soup! As his eyes slowly focused he could see a pendant light with a floral shade hanging above his head, 'Strange,' he thought,' whys is the light in Maureen's bedroom hanging in mine and why can I smell tomato soup?'

Despite feeling heat all around him, his bones felt cold, very cold and he tried to speak but before he could, Maureen's worried face appeared above him, 'He's awake look, he's awake,' she said and he felt her hand stroke his face.'

'Aah knew he was ganna be alreet man, he's as hard as owt,' he heard Jake Grundy say from the end of the bed.

Then even stranger, he heard 'The Gallowa' say, 'Let's see if we can prop him up and I'll give him some of the soup.' Hands gently lifted him into a slightly raised position as pillows were adjusted behind him and blankets tucked in around him and as Mrs Galloway stepped back he could see from the glow of the fire burning in the small fireplace that he was in Maureen's neat room but why, and why were Mrs Galloway and Jake there?

As Aggie advance on him with the bowl of soup in one hand and a spoon in the other, he remembered!

'Where's Tom, where's wor Tommy?' he croaked.

'Hush noo bonny lad, Tommy's alreet, yer mam's we him at hospital, I'm sure he's ganna be champion,' Aggie said, not at all sure if that was the truth but she knew she could not have Ian worrying about his brother, not at the moment anyway.

Aggie's words sunk in but Ian was not convinced; picturing Tommy's lifeless body lying by the marsh he whispered through tear filled eyes, 'Are ye sure, he's ganna be alright?'

'Aye, he's going te be fine,' answered Aggie as she guided the soup laden spoon carefully toward him; the tomato soup tasted creamy and really very good as he felt it slide down his throat, warming him inside as he took gentle sips.

Jake leaned over the end of the bed and asked, 'Are ye alreet Ian marra?'

Does he look alright, Maureen scolded from her chair.

'Whey man am just asking like,' Jake answered feeling uncomfortable and foolish in front of the very pretty Maureen, he always felt as if he was a clumsy stupid idiot when he was near her, or any other pretty lass for that matter and could feel himself blushing as Maureen looked at him sternly. 'Aah best be off then,' he heard himself say, keen to hide his embarrassment.

Ian croaked, 'Hang on Jake,' as he struggled to swallow the last spoonful of soup Mrs Galloway had poured into his mouth.

Jake turned back and waited while Ian composed himself.

'Will ye dee my paper roond the morn Jake?'

Before Jake could answer, Mrs Galloway butted in, 'Of course he will Pet, noo divint ye worry aboot that, ye need te get yer strength back.'

Grinning madly and happy that he could help, Jake asked, 'Aye I'll dee it nee bother, what time dee Aah hev te be there like?

'Eight o'clock.'

'*EIGHT O'CLOCK!*' Jake spluttered, 'It's Sunda the morn man, what aboot me lie in?'

Ian croaked a warning to Jake, 'Watch oot for the Alsatian in the Forth Ra!'

'What Alsatian?'

'The big black one in the Fourth Ra!'

'Oh that thing, whey am not frightened of that man,' lied Jake.

Mrs Galloway put down the soup bowl on the tiny dressing table in front of the window and shushed Jake out of the room saying, 'That's enough noo, just mek sure you are there on time and look after the poor lad's job for him, noo go on get yerself hyem.

Jake nodded and said, 'Aye aall reet, am ganning te Howard's to watch the Tele,' and skipped down the stairs thinking 'Deliver papers at eight in the morning, blidy hell!'

After the buxom and matronly nurse in the Medical Centre cleaned Nick's foot, closed the cut with four neat stitches and gave him a tetanus jab, he limped down to the bus stop near the Store Corner and caught the bus to Woolworths and hobbled round to the Hospital. His foul mood was not helped as he passed groups of early evening revellers heading out to enjoy Saturday night in one of the many Social Clubs or perhaps the Arcade Dance Hall. In addition, a few of his cronies were expecting to collect their winnings from him at the Fell-em-Doon and West End Club and would be none too happy if he did not show up!

His foot hurt like hell and he felt even more anger when he was told that Tommy had been taking to Newcastle, exploding, *Frigging hell*, that's Aah'll Aah need to kna, I've frigging come aall the way here for blidy nowt, frigging champion,' then stormed out, and limped to the bus station to catch a bus back to High Market.

Edward was also well on his way back to Ashington, not relishing having to deal with Nick whom he had known all his life. They had grown up in the Sixth Row, played wild games together and gone to Wansbeck and Bothal Schools together. They started work at the

43

Colliery at the same time, Edward as an apprentice electrician while Nick went to work underground. They began dating girls together but this had led to their first falling out, Edward being unhappy at the way Nick treated girls and he in turn was resentful of Edward's apprenticeship.

When war was declared, they both rushed to join the Royal Northumberland Fusiliers but for very different reasons. Edward had listened to events in Europe on the radio and horrified by the Nazi Monster that looked as though it would devour any country that did not submit to its will and joined to do what he thought was necessary to help stop them. Nick had no such notions but when an angry father and three of his sons vowed to 'sort him out' after another one of Nick's conquest's fell pregnant and was forced into a back-street abortion before being sent South to go into service; Nick escaped retribution by leaving with Edward to join the Fusiliers.

The following year, after spending the period known as the 'Phony War' in Belgium, the two Sixth Row lads found themselves in the same infantry section fighting desperate 'Rear-Guard' actions as the British Expeditionary Force and a huge chunk of the French Army retreated to Dunkirk.

Driving through the dark Edward remembered the day in late May of 1940 when their battered platoon were ordered to occupy a farm dominating a vital crossroads. Having suffered several casualties, the platoon was down to just 18 unwounded and needed a rest. Their section led by the huge Corporal Turnbull from Morpeth, was the strongest of the three, still having the Bren light machine gun team of a Lance Corporal and two, plus four riflemen, which included Edward and Nick.

It was raining heavily, the first rain they had had for ages and they were all wet, exhausted, hungry and increasingly worried that they were going to be left behind but none more so than Nick who complained constantly and bitterly and had hinted to Edward that they should leave the platoon and make their way to the Dunkirk on their own. Edward had been horrified at the suggestion and warned Nick to 'keep it together' or he would sort him out. There was no longer any friendship between the two, Nick having demonstrated on more than one occasion that his main priority was to stay alive and sod everyone else.

With their khaki uniforms sodden and heavy from the persistent rain, the platoon took cover in the ditch by the cross roads a hundred yards from the farm, waiting as their young but worn out Platoon Commander, Lieutenant William Cartwright, carefully scanned the buildings and surrounding trees with his binoculars, looking for any sign of life. Satisfied that the farm was empty he called over Corporal Turnbull and ordered, 'The farm is deserted, get your Section up the farm track as fast as possible and occupy the buildings while the rest of us keep the crossroads covered. Once you are in, position the Bren to cover us and the crossroads and we will join you, we need to get the four wounded under cover as soon as possible.

Corporal Turnbull listened intently before returning to his Section in a crouching run and gathering them together, he briefed them. 'Right listen in, we are going up to the farm to set up the Bren to cover the others, Bren Team up the left side of the track, Rifle Team on the right,' he paused while his men nodded. Then speaking directly to his Lance Corporal, he said, 'When we get there Jim you set the Bren up in that gable window at the front so that you can cover the rest of the platoon and the crossroads.'

Turning to the Rifle Team he said, 'Ed and Nick search the buildings for any food and drink before the rest of the Platoon get there,' and to the other two men he said, 'You other two secure the rear of the farm, got that?' They all nodded; keen to get into shelter and to see if there was any food or drink in the farm.

Corporal Turnbull held up his thumb to the Lieutenant and on receiving the signal to go he stood up and said, 'Right lets go, come on quickly now!' The Bren Team doubled over to the left of the track and began moving along the hedgerow toward the farm as Edward led the four riflemen to the right side, Nick making sure he positioned himself to the rear, hugging the hedge as close as he could. Not expecting any trouble, Corporal Turnbull walked straight down the centre of the track urging his men on, keen to get into the farm and out of the rain.

Unfortunately for the Section, the farm had been occupied by a fast moving German Reconnaissance Section who had hidden their four motorcycle and sidecar combinations in one of the barns.

Behind the gable window of the farm; devoted Nazi, battle hardened Feldwebel Henrik Richter watched the section of Tommie's approach the two dilapidated stone gate posts that marked the entrance to the farmyard. Confident that he and his men would deal quickly with the advance section, he tapped the coal-scuttle helmet of the Machine Gunner who had the butt of the MG34 pulled tight into his shoulder; his sights on the advancing Bren Team. A few feet inside the room and hidden by a net curtain at the window, the German machine gunner pressed his trigger as did the rest of the German Section which had been hiding in the downstairs rooms!

Edward dived instinctively behind the right hand gatepost when he heard the first burst of the MG34 spitting bullets at eight hundred and fifty rounds per minute smashing into the Bren Team, killing all three in two seconds. The second burst shattered both of Corporal Turnbull's legs and ripped open his stomach, bowling him backwards where he lay with his head and shoulders propped up by his small pack. The two men behind Edward were also dead, killed by rifle fire from the downstairs windows.

Nick had also reacted quickly, throwing himself down behind his two dead comrades and wriggling desperately trying to burrow himself

46

below the dead men. The Platoon's other two Bren guns opened fire on the top window from the road as the remainder of the men in the other two Sections also began pouring fire from their Lee Enfield rifles into the farm as fast as they could operate their bolts.

Edward wriggled to the left of the post and began firing round it into the window nearest him, seeing a shape fall as he fired. The situation was desperate; the MG 34 was now engaging the rest of the platoon pinning them down with short accurate bursts as Richter ran down stairs to gather his remaining men together. Of the five he had left there, one was dead and another was in his final death throes.

Richter checked that the safety catch on his MP38 sub machine gun was off and moved toward the side door of the farm ready to outflank the 'Tommie's' just as a mortally wounded Corporal Turnbull, ignoring the excruciating pain he was in, pulled the pin from a smoke grenade and lobbed it fifteen foot into the farmyard. The German Machine Gunner saw the movement and switched his aim putting another short burst into Turnbull, before switching fire back to the Platoon as his assistant fed another long belt of ammunition into the machine gun.

As the smoke quickly built, Edward knew he had to act immediately; rising into a crouch, he took a hand grenade from his ammunition pouch, pulled the pin to let the clip fly. Still crouching, he ran into the smoke stopping fifteen yards from the farm and threw the grenade up into the gable window where it exploded as it landed, killing both men of the machine gun team instantly.

Turning he sprinted back through the gate, throwing himself to ground next to where the dead Bren Team lay, dropping his rifle to grab the Bren. He struggled briefly to free the light machine gun from the tangle of bodies before placing it on its bi-pod and wriggled behind it, just as Richter and the three remaining Germans barrelled out of the farm, through the smoke toward left-hand side of the gate, unaware that Edward was there.

He fired three six rounds bursts knocking the Germans into an untidy heap. He then waited for what seemed an eternity for the fire from his own Platoon to stop but it could only have been a few seconds after which, slowly rising with the Bren he began to cautiously walk forward when to his surprise, Nick appeared from the other side of the track!

Nick ran up behind Edward and grabbed his arm saying 'Are they all dead?' Edward tried to pull away to check that the Germans were neutralised but that couple of seconds cost them both dearly. Terribly wounded, with blood pouring from a stomach wound and more dribbling from his mouth, Richter hurled a 'Potato Masher' hand grenade at Edward and Nick before falling back onto his lifeless comrades.

The grenade landed short but still had a devastating effect, Edward was blown off his feet from the blast, a piece of shrapnel smashing into his steel helmet, knocking him unconscious and tearing a 3 inch slash across his scalp. Also blown of his feet, Nick felt shrapnel rip into right knee smashing the kneecap and bone behind it.

Screaming with pain, he sat up grasping his knee and saw the big German NCO pull himself into a sitting position, raising his right hand in surrender as he tried to hold his intestines back in with his left hand. Nick reached for the Bren that Edward had dropped and pointing it at the German a few yards away, squeezed the trigger, emptying the magazine into Richter, just as the remainder of the Platoon, led by the Lieutenant, swarmed past him.

The smoke had hidden most of the action from the Platoon and the Lieutenant had been unable to make out who had thrown the grenade that had taken out the MG34 but seeing Nick lying wounded with the Bren in his hand, assumed that he had and that he had killed the German NCO and three men with him.

After ensuring the farm house was safe, Lieutenant Cartwright walked back to where the medic was strapping up Nick's leg and kneeling beside him said, 'Outstanding work Shepherd, I never knew you had it in you, bloody well done.' Nick did not reply, he was in too much pain from his wound, beside he was not about to tell anyone that he had been cowering below two dead comrades during the firefight and, as far as he knew, no-one else was left alive to say otherwise.

Twenty minutes later, while another platoon occupied the farm, a truck arrived from Battalion to collect Nick and the other wounded, whisking them to the rear and relative safety just as the Lieutenant bent over Edward to take his identity tag. Unfastening the neck of Edward's shirt, the young Officer noticed him twitch slightly and feeling for and finding a pulse, yelled, 'GET THE MEDIC HERE, NOW!'

Due to the confusion of the fighting around Dunkirk and the chaotic rescue by the Navy and small boats; Nick was unaware that Edward had survived and had been evacuated on another ship the day after him. Nor was he aware that it was 14 months before Edward remembered in detail what had happened at the farm and by that time, Nick had been presented with the Military Medal, married and had been invalided out of the army, nor did he know that Edward, was in the Western Desert fighting with the 8th Army.

Edward decided that nothing would be gained from telling anyone what had really happened and soldiered on until the end of the war leaving the army in 1946 with three stripes and a chest full of campaign medals.

Edward arrived back at the Sixth Row just after 8 o'clock, knocked on the door of Number 60 and walked into the kitchen where Maureen was standing by the fire waiting for the kettle to boil to make a pot of tea.

She looked at Edward and asked, 'How's wor Tommy?'

'Holding his own Pet, but he is very poorly.'

'Thank God, I was worried sick he might have died.'

'Whey he's not oot of danger yet but it looks as if he is going to be OK,' said Edward, not wanting to worry her more than necessary. 'Hoo is young Ian?'

Maureen smiled and said, 'Tucked up in my bed with Mrs Gallowa fussing ower him and he's talking which is a good sign.'

'Whey I'm pleased to hear that, is it alright if Aah gan up and tell him aboot Tommy?'

Maureen nodded and Edward turned and climbed the stairs, quietly opening the door to the bedroom made cosy by the glowing fire. Sitting nodding in the chair by the bed, Aggie Galloway looked up as a floorboard creaked when Edward stepped in.

'Is he awake?'

Aggie looked at Ian, touched his cheek and smiled saying, Aye, he's a fighter this one.'

'Edward stepped over to the bed and said, 'So's his brother.'

On hearing voices, Ian opened his eyes and saw Mr Thompson smiling down at him, fearing the worst and with tears welling up in his eyes, he croaked, 'Wor Tom, wor Tommy, hoo is he Mr Thompson?'

Edward put his hand gently on Ian's shoulder and said, 'He's okay Ian lad, thanks to you he is going to be alright.'

Relief swept over Ian, easing some of the tension that had gripped his weakened body, releasing tears that streamed down his cheeks and onto his pillow. Having been certain that Tommy had perished and that Mrs Galloway had been hiding the truth from him, he sobbed uncontrollably at the news that he had not lost his younger brother.

Feeling his own eyes cloud with tears, Edward patted Ian and left the room, nodding to Aggie who picked up a towel and began gently wiping Ian's cheeks while talking to him quietly.

Maureen poured Edward a cup of tea which he took gratefully, enjoying the sweet taste, realising he was very thirsty. Holding the empty cup out for a refill, he was just about to ask where her Dad was when the back door swung open and a furious Nick stormed in.

Nick was tired, his foot hurt, his leg ached, he was hungry, thirsty and had a raging headache and here was Edward Thompson, the only man that knew he was a coward, the man who had whisked his wife off in his flash car, the man who was always calm, always right, the man he hated with a vengeance, and he was drinking tea in *his* house!

Nick hobbled up to Edward and spat, 'What the hell are ye deeing here and where's me blidy wife Thompson?'

Edward stepped back from Nick, not wanting to have a confrontation with him, not just now anyway, 'She's at the hospital with Mike, I think Tommy is ganning te be Ok, I've come te tek ye ower te see him.'

'Hev ye noo, whey isn't that just blidy hunky blidy dory - Edward Thompson looking after every bugga whether they want him to or not, whey sod ye, I'll get a bus ower mesell,' hissed Nick.

Trying to remain calm, Edward offered, 'Divint be silly man, come on I'll hev ye there in half an hour and Aah'll wait and bring the three of ye back later.'

Listening to the exchange, Maureen said, 'Go with Mr Thompson man Dad, me Mam needs you there and ye'll get there a lot quicker.'

Nick gave Maureen an angry look and snarled, 'Divint ye tell me what te de; that bitch doesn't need me, she made that clear teday and Aah divint need hur either and anyway she's got her blidy fancy man here to look after hur!'

Controlling his mounting anger, Edward said quietly, 'Look man, ye need te see yor bairn in case out happens, so for God's sake get in the car and I'll have ye there in half an hour!'

Nick stood fuming quietly for a few seconds, desperately wanting to smash something into Edwards face but afraid to do so as he knew Edward was far stronger than him.

Gathering his thoughts, he spat, 'Maureen give me a cup of tea noo,' and turning to Edward growled, 'I'll gan we ye te the hospital and ye can drop me off at the door and bugga off, me and *my wife*, will get home wor sells.'

Edward was about to argue but thought better of it, the main thing was to get Nick to hospital to see his son as soon as possible, so he nodded and walked out to his car, climbed in and turned it around to wait for Nick.

As Nick finished his tea, Maureen ventured, 'What happened to your face, you've got some red marks and bruising on the side?

Nick felt the bruising on side of his face, remembering Jane's retaliation that morning and lied, 'Aah bumped me heed when I fell ower when I cut me foot on the blidy shovel some idiot left in the bedroom.'

Maureen thought it was a pity no one had the pleasure of giving her father what he was always so keen to dish out but said nothing as he finished his tea and limped out to climb into Edward's car.

The atmosphere in the car on the drive to the hospital was colder than a Siberian winter; not a word, look or glance was exchanged during the short journey and when Edward pulled up outside the hospital, Nick climbed out, slamming the car door as hard as he could and hobbled off inside to find Jane. Parking up, Edward decided that despite Nick's angry outburst, he was going to wait and see if Jane wanted a lift home.

Sitting alone in his car Edward remembered the first time he had seen Jane; home on a weekend pass a few weeks before D Day, he had arrived late on Friday night and the following morning he was leaning on the fence, cup of tea in hand enjoying the spring sunshine. Looking up the street he saw a raven-haired woman step out of the yard of the end house, she had the hand of a small boy in her left hand and an even smaller girl's hand in her right; they were all smiling and laughing as they walked toward him

The sun shining brightly behind them silhouetted her slim shape but hid her face in shadow until she was just a few yards away and he was able to see how beautiful she was. She was wearing what looked like an expensive but well-worn yellow dress with a matching cardigan draped over her shoulders, fastened by the top button at her neck. Her black hair brushed back from her face, it glistened in the sun, accentuating the brightness of her dress. The faces of the two children shone with the radiance of an early morning scrub as they giggled with their mother.

Edward stood up and attempted to fasten the top buttons of his khaki shirt and smoothed back his unkempt blonde hair before clearing his throat and offering, 'Good morning, you'll be Nick's wife and these his bairns then?'

Jane stopped and smiled a widely, answering, 'Yes I'm Jane and this is Michael and this little angel is Maureen,' Maureen had moved behind her Mother's leg and was smiling shyly at Edward who quickly bent forward to say hello but before he could, Nick limped up behind. He snatched Maureen up in his left arm and taking Jane's arm with his right hand moved them quickly on giving Edward the slightest of nods. It was the first time the two men had seen each other since the skirmish outside Dunkirk and Nick made it clear that he was not prepared to talk to Edward, not that Edward was at all concerned, he was thinking how beautiful Jane was and how on earth had she ended up with a no-hoper like Nick Shepherd.

Edward's own love live had been less than successful. When he rushed into the army, Mary his childhood sweetheart promised to wait for him and write every day, which she did for a whole six weeks until she wrote, 'I do not think I can waste my best young years waiting for someone who might not come back!' Devastated, Edward was even more upset when he received a letter from his mother telling him, that Mary had married one of his friends and that she had heard that a baby had been borne just a few months after the ceremony!

The war had prevented him from finding another girl and now the girl of his dreams had just walked past him with the man he despised!

Here he was twelve years later, still in love with the woman that was married to the waster that had been his friend and they were living just three doors away! Having returned to work at the colliery as an electrician, he had moved back in with his parents but was about to leave. Having slowly saved a modest sum of money he had left work at the colliery a couple of years earlier to run his own electrical business and had just been appointed as a sub-contractor for the electrical installations of the large new council house estate. With business beginning to grow, he was planning at last to move out of his parent's home and into a house of his own in Wansbeck Terrace that he was in the process of buying.

Nick received a frosty reception from Mike and a very worried Jane who said quietly, 'The Doctor has just been out to say that they have managed to stabilize Thomas's pulse and his temperature is climbing slowly so they believe he is through the worst of it - but have warned that there may be complications or side effects but that it is too early to tell yet.'

'Waat bloody complications and side effects?'

'They didn't say but it could be respiratory or even brain damage!' Jane answered, just managing to hold back her tears.

The three of them were allowed into see Tommy for five minutes before the Ward Sister suggested that they went home and got some sleep and to come back in the morning as, for the time being, there was nothing more that could be done.

It was well after Ten o'clock when they walked out of the Hospital into the freezing night air; Jane and Mike heading for Edward's car.

Where ye ganning?' demanded Nick.

'To get into Mr Thompson's car and go home.'

He snarled, 'We're not ganning hyem we him, we'll get the bus,' and grabbed her arm to pull her away.

Mike continued toward the car as Jane stopped and pulling her arm free, looked at Nick and said firmly, 'You can go home any way you wish Nick Shepherd but I am going in that car, have you forgotten what I said this morning, I am not dancing to your tune anymore!' and turned and walked across to the car.

Edward had watched them walk toward him and witnessed the exchange of words; unsure of what was happening he stepped out opening the back door and said, 'Come on and get in out of the cold, you will have missed the last bus so I thought I'd better wait and give ye a lift hyem. Jane climbed into the back seat behind Edward while Nick climbed into the other side and Mike into the front. On the drive back to Ashington, Mike filled Edward in on Tommy's condition while Jane and Nick sat in the back in frosty silence.

When Edward pulled up outside number 60, Jane thanked him for the lift home as Nick jumped out without saying a word, slammed the car door behind him and hobbled angrily into the house, sitting down at the kitchen table where he took out a cigarette and lit it.

Jane and Mike rushed straight upstairs, eager to see how Ian was and found Mrs Galloway asleep on the chair by the bed with Ian lying motionless below the heaped blankets. Jane held her breath and reached forward to touch her son's face, wanting to confirm that he was alright just as Maureen came in behind them, she had been sleeping on Ian and Tommy's bed in the attic bedroom, 'He's alright Mam, he just asleep again.'

Jane touched Ian's face gently before turning, 'And Tommy is going to be alright as well thanks to Ian and you Mike, we better have something to eat and get to bed as I'll be going back to the hospital tomorrow morning. She woke Mrs Galloway and thanked her for help, grateful that she had a next-door neighbour that she knew she could rely upon.

Downstairs, Maureen took a pan of mash and sausages from the oven that she had cooked earlier and dished it out on the plates she had arranged on the table. Nick looked at the food, stubbed his cigarette out in the mash on his plate, picked up a sausage, stuffing into his mouth, he hobbled upstairs to bed, leaving Jane Maureen and Mike seething at his behaviour.

Maureen and I will sleep in your bedroom tonight Michael, you will have to sleep in the sitting room until Ian is better and back in his own bed, then I'll be moving in with Maureen.' Her two oldest children looked at each but neither said a word both happy that their Mother was finally moving out of their abusive father's bed!

Chapter 4
Deliveries

'Just five mair minutes and I'll get up,' Jake Grundy thought to himself as he lay huddled in his bed below a pile of thread bare blankets, topped off with a couple of old over coats. Monty, who had borrowed into the bedding by his foot and was now trying to get himself comfortable at Jake's expense, had woken him a few minutes earlier.

Jake looked at the flimsy curtains on the window of the bedroom he shared with Ronnie when he was home on leave and noticed that judging from the sun shining in, it was a bright morning outside; a good morning to deliver newspapers. He thought, 'No hurry, it can only be about eight o'clock and being a few minutes late wouldn't matter that much, would it?'

He heard his Mother shout from the foot of the stairs, 'Jake, Jake, JAKE YE LITTLE BLIDY SOD YE, ANSWER ME!'

Pulling the blanket from his mouth he shouted back, 'Waat man?'

'Waat time did ye say ye were delivering papers teday cos it's nearly half past eight?'

'Jake leapt out of bed like a scalded cat and nearly leapt straight back in again when his bare feet hit the ice cold lino! 'Blidy hell it's frigging freezing,' he muttered as he pulled on the jeans and jumpers he had thrown on the floor the night before.

Ten minutes later, he ran into the shop straight passed Mr Willington who was serving a customer and to the back of the shop where Reg was still sorting out Newspapers. 'Am Aah late, Aah thowt, Ian said Aah had te be here at nine o'clock.'

Reg looked at the scruffy, dishevelled Jake who had a large dewdrop dangling from his nose and noticed that he had fastened his jacket buttons in the wrong holes further creasing and wrinkling his already creased and wrinkled black jacket.

'Nur we start at eight cos we have te sort the papers oot forst. Aah only fund oot aboot Ian this morning from wor Terry, he went around te see Maureen last night and she telt him what had happened. Aah thowt Aah would hev te de a double paper roond this morning but this is champion if ye ganna de Ian's roond.'

Tall, thin and bespectacled Mr Willington joined them and looking down at the unkempt grinning Jake asked, 'What are you doing here lad?'

'Ian Shepherd asked me te de his paper roond until he's better.'

Shaking his head, Mr Willington thought for a few seconds before saying, 'Aye whey that's good of ye lad but only until he comes back, Reg will tell ye what te do and mek sure you get all the papers delivered by ten.'

'Nee bother,' Jake answered, wondering if being a paper lad meant you could help yourself to free sweets but thought he wouldn't ask too early!

A few minutes later, he was struggling down First Row stuffing papers into letterboxes in accordance with Reg's pencilled scribbles. Being a Sunday the bag was particularly heavy as most folk got two or three papers each; The Sunday Sun, News of the World and Sunday Post seemed to be the favourites.

Many of the houses did not have letterboxes, so Jake just rolled up the papers and stuffed them into whatever crevice he could find. He thrust papers behind the door snecks, behind fence posts of the small yard fences or, in some cases just left them on doors step until he became bored with having to look for somewhere to put them. He began pushing them into the nearest available letterbox to the house number – 'They'll mek sure they right folk get them,' he convinced himself as he pushed on into the Third Row.

His method of delivery seemed to be going OK until the door of a house he was stuffing newspapers into opened, 'What ye deeing lad?' asked the man who opened the door. Wearing slippers, he was in shirt and trousers with his braces dangling and a newspaper under his arm, he was obviously on his way over to the outside toilet across the lane and in a bit of a hurry.

Stifling a snigger, Jake answered, 'Whey am delivering yer papers, this is number fowerteen isn't it?'

'Nur ye sacklass little bugga, this is number sixteen noo sod off and put them in the right hoose.'

Jake nodded and walked on throwing the papers into the yard of the next house as he couldn't be bothered to walk back two houses and the bag was still very heavy!

By the time he reached the middle of the Third Row, his method of delivery had become even more haphazard, stuffing papers anywhere that he happened to be when he pulled out the next bunch for delivery. He was tired, cold and just a bit pissed off at having his lazy Sunday morning routine upset so did not really care if one or two ended up at the wrong address, he was sure they would sort it out themselves.

He called into his Aunt Martha's at the end of the Third Row and scrounged a cup of tea and slice of toast that he took his time eating and only left after she asked, 'Ye best be ganning if yer ganning te get them papers delivered Bonny Lad.'

Lifting the still heavy bag onto his shoulder, he said 'Ta da,' and left, walking wearily around to the Fourth Row where the big black Alsatian stood waiting on the pavement fifty yards in front of him. 'Bugga!' he thought his brave statement to Ian the night before forgotten as he stopped and stared at the dog that was staring malevolently back!

'I'll just cross ower the road and walk roond the blidy thing,' he thought and started to walk to the other side but stopped in the middle when he saw the dog mirroring his movement. Apart from him and the

59

dog, the street was empty and just a little ominous! Jake was suddenly aware of the silence and side stepped an old newspaper that the cold wind tumbled past as he and the Alsatian continued to stare at each other!

Feeling more than a little afraid to approach the black dog, he gulped and adjusted his paper bag into a position that would enable him to dump quickly should he have to run for it. Continuing to stare into the eyes of the dog that appeared ready to pounce if he moved forward, Jake thought the scene reminded him of Gary Cooper facing the baddies in 'High Noon,' only this baddie might eat him. He tried moving back to the path but the dog again copied his movement and did so again when Jake moved back to the middle of the narrow back lane.

Still unsure what to do, his mind was suddenly made up for him when the Alsatian lowered its head menacingly and advanced a few steps toward him, 'Bugga this,' said Jake and turned and ran back a few yards into the entrance of one of the brick built air raid shelters dotted between the outside toilets and coal houses. Emptying the papers on to the floor he stepped out, glanced to make sure the dog was still further up the street and then made a dash for the end of the Row, nipping round the corner where he stopped and peaked back to check that the dog had not followed him.

It was still standing sentinel in the middle of the street, daring Jake to come back but he had no such intentions and walked down the road in between the ends of the First to Sixth Row on one side and the ends of the Seventh to Eleventh imaginatively named Rows on the other. At the end of the First Row he turned into High Market and walked toward Willington's to dump the empty paper bag and to see if any free sweets might be in the offing after all his hard work!

Opening the door to the newsagents, he unsuspectingly walked nonchalantly into a maelstrom of anger from people wanting to know where their papers were or why someone had delivered them to the wrong address! Realising immediately that he was in trouble, Jake thought, 'Bugga,' turned quickly around and tried to leave but Mr Willington grabbed him by the shoulder and dragged him to the rear of the shop.

'Wait here,' he ordered Jake before turning to placate his angry customers that was no easy matter but he promised to ensure everyone would have their papers within the hour. As the shop emptied, he turned back to Jake who was impossibly, trying to look innocent.

'Right, ye little waster, what have ye been up too?

'Just delivering yer papers Mr Willington, that's aall, why like is sumat the matter?

'Sumat the matter!' the enraged shop owner growled, 'There'll be sumat the matter if you can't produce the newspapers yer were supposed to deliver!'

A few minutes later Jake led Mr Willington into the air-raid shelter and pointed to the heap of abandoned newspapers, 'Aah left them here cos the big black dog wudn't let me past, Aah was ganning te come back later and deliver them, honest,' he lied.

Glaring down at Jake, Mr Willington found himself having to stop himself from smiling and putting on an angry scowl, snarled, 'Ye'll deliver them now and I'm coming with ye te mek sure you do it properly and the first thing I'll show ye is hoo te deal with that dog.'

Waiting for some fun, the dog had not moved as Jake slung the reloaded paper bag over his shoulder and stepped back into the street. Pushing Jake gently in the back, Mr Willington said, 'Go on just march down the street and ignore the dog, I'll be behind you.'

Jake gulped, hitched up his jeans, adjusted the bag and marched across the lane, onto the pavement and toward the dog, whose eyes had remained firmly fixed on him. He was so frightened of the dog, that he forgot why he was there until Mr Willington said loudly, 'Number 22 Jake, their papers lad ye've just walked past it.'

Flinching at the order, Jake stopped and without taking his eyes off the dog, walked backwards five paces, his eyes remaining fixed on the beast even as he pulled out the newspapers and stuffed them into the letterbox. Another nudge in the back and he marched forward again as the dog surrendered the path and moved to the middle of the lane.

'That's it just ignore it and it won't bother you!'

Jake thought, 'That's alreet for ye te say, yer reet taall and that blidy dog is nearly as big as me,' but once past it he felt relief and as his cheeky confidence came rushing back, said, 'That's alreet noo Mr Willington Aah can manage noo.'

Not prepared to risk upsetting any more customers, Mr Willington accompanied Jake for the rest of the deliveries, taking the sack from him at the end of the Sixth Row and saying, 'Right seven o'clock tomorrow morning don't be late and let me or Ian down, ye can nip home now.'

'Ur Aah was ganna come back te yer shop we ye, te maybes get one or two sweets for me hard work this morning?' said Jake cheekily.

'Ye'll get me foot up yer backside if I have any more of your cheek, now go before I find someone else te deliver them.

The following few days were hectic and tiring for Jane, she and Maureen had rushed to the hospital on the first bus on the Sunday morning to find that Tommy was continuing to improve but that the doctors were still concerned that there may be complications! They were only allowed to see him for five minutes but spent a couple of hours sitting in the waiting room, hoping that they may have been allowed in again before they left for home. She travelled back to the hospital on Monday and Tuesday to spend the thirty minutes allowed with Tommy on each day.

Maureen stayed at home to look after Ian, she had gone into Pearson's grocery shop in Highmarket to explain what had happened and that she needed a few days off to help her Mother.

More concerned with looking after his illegal gambling than looking after his sick sons, Nick did not bother taking off time to visit Tommy. He and Mike had gone back to work on Monday, neither saying a word to the other, the resentment between them palpable.

Tommy appeared to be recovering rapidly from his ordeal; when Jane walked into the ward on Thursday he was sitting up in bed reading the Beano but threw it to one side when he saw his mother walk in and stifling a cough, asked enthusiastically, 'Hiya Mam, can Aah come home teday?'

Jane smiled as she looked at her little boy whose skin looked so pale, accentuated by the dark circles under his deep blue eyes and stroking his face gently, said, 'Not today Pet, hopefully you will be home at the weekend, the doctors just want to do a few checks before they let me take you home.'

Bored with his confinement, Ian had felt well enough to get out of bed on Wednesday, he was keen to see his friends and get back to his jobs to ensure he could continue to save. Despite his mother's protests and much to Jake's relief, he was ready to begin delivering papers by Friday.

After having devoured a huge bowl of porridge sweetened with jam, Ian escaped his Mother's hugs and pleas to 'Take it easy,' and 'be very careful,' and was zipping up his washed and dried imitation leather coat as he walked quickly down the lane into the frosty clear morning.

He was startled when Jake sprung out of his back yard and yelled, 'Shit the bed hev ye?'

Ian looked at Jake who had obviously not had a wash, his curly hair was uncombed, there was sleep in the corner of his eyes, jam on the corner of his mouth and his battered baseball bootlaces were untied.

'Waat are ye deeing?' Ian asked as Jake first fastened the buttons of his black serge jacket then bent down to fasten his laces.

'Mr Willington asked me te gee ye a hand teday te mek sure yer alreet and he promised te give me an extra bob, so I had te come we ye, didn't Aah?'

A few minutes later, having met up with Reg the three of them walked into the newsagents and headed to the back to sort out the papers but Mr Willington stepped in front and put his hand on Ian's shoulder, 'How are ye lad, are ye sure you are okay to do your round?'

Ian was perplexed and embarrassed at this show of concern and answered quickly, 'I'm okay.'

However, Mr Willington wasn't finished, 'How's your Thomas, I hear he is still in hospital?'

'Aye he is but he's alright as weel, I think he's coming home temorra.'

'Well if he is alright it is all down to you, you should get a medal for what you did.'

Even more embarrassed, Ian slid his shoulder from Mr Willington's hand and walked to the back of the shop to join the other two. He had not even thought he had been brave, he was just helping his brother so couldn't understand why Mr Willington had said so, in fact he thought it was his fault that Tom had got into trouble and had expected to be in bother for having done so!

Sorting newspapers, Reg said, 'Ye might get the Victoria Cross medal for bravery.'

Jake elbowed Reg in the ribs and said mockingly, 'Divint be daft man, the ownly give that to sowldgers for killing thoosands of Gurmans and Japs and he hasn't killed any bugga, has he!'

Ian's paper round took longer than normal, not because Jake was more of a hindrance than a help but because quite a lot of folk stopped him to pat his back, tell him 'Well done,' or enquire about his health. The worst however was when the gargantuan Mrs Armstrong waddled out of her door in the Third Row and wrapped her huge mutton like arms around Ian hugging him to her enormous breast and belly saying, 'Eeee, Bonny Lad, iviry body is taalking aboot ye and who ye saved your little brother, yer a little champion, pet.'

Buried under massive breasts and with Mrs Armstrong's smelly pinny suffocating him, Ian just wanted to escape and breathe again but had to wait until she released him from her bear hug and patted him on the head. Shoving her paper into her hands, Ian muttered, 'Thanks Mrs Armstrong,' and quickly walked away blushing madly.

Jake was laughing almost hysterically and had to stop to get his breathe back before saying, 'Aah thowt that was the last I was ganning te see ye, I thowt she had pulled ye inside hur, aall Aah cud see was yer legs hanging unda hur arms!'

Jake's nemesis, the black Alsatian was waiting as he and Ian continued into the Fourth Row!

'That blidy dog hates me!'

Ian gave Jake a derogatory look and said, 'It hates iviry body man, ye canna let it see yer scared.' Despite Ian's confidence, Jake was scared and ran across the lane, climbed over the wall between a couple of coal houses and air-raid shelter and ran along the track at the bottom of the Fifth Row gardens coming out in the cut a few doors past the dog and leant nonchalantly on the wall waiting for Ian. Ian continued up, posting the newspapers while ignoring the dog that looked at him menacingly but gave ground when he reached it.

Thirty minutes later the two of them walked past Gibson's garage toward the Victorian red-bricked Bothal County Secondary School standing between the end of Third Row and beginning of Long Row, facing the main road with the miners' retirement cottages at the other side. Jake was shoving Halfpenny chews into his mouth so fast that Ian thought he was going to choke, 'Aah didn't see you buy them, did Mr Willington give you them?'

Jake grinned through a mouthful of half-chewed chews, and answered with spittle running down his chin, 'Nur not really.'

After walking through the wooden gates into the playground, past the entrance to the hall and across to the school kitchens, they were quickly surrounded. It was Ian's first day back at school and the lads in his class and others were all keen to hear the story of the Marsh rescue. Ian was answering as quickly as could until Geordie Robertson pushed his way through. Universally disliked, he was in the year above Ian, he was taller, heavier with broad features and curly fair hair above piercing pale blue eyes and was handy with his fists, lashing out any of the younger or smaller lads who strayed into his space.

Having pushed his way through none to gently he looked down at Ian and spat, 'Whey looka here, it's the big frigging hero; Shepherd the hero, he looks like a little piece of shite te me!'

Ian glared back at the bully as Jake stepped forward and said, 'Why divint ye just piss off and leave us alen,' and was rewarded with a backhander that split his lip and sent him staggering backwards. Jake was even smaller and thinner than Ian and no match for Geordie but he still scrambled to his feet to fight back but was beaten to it by Ian who launched himself Kamikaze style at the big lad.

Swinging madly, Ian determined not to let the bully over power him, landing a few wild punches as he waded in but the lad was too big and strong and threw Ian to the ground kicking him twice as he fell. Ian knew he had to get up and scrambled to his feet as Geordie landed another two swinging kicks, the last one to Ian's back, bowling him over again as lads scattered before the charge.

A voice roared, 'STANDSTILL!'

Ian's Class Teacher, the tall and powerfully built Mr Haig waded in, pushing boys out of the way, grabbing Robertson by the scruff of the neck, 'You're in trouble now lad,' he warned.

Geordie struggled in vain to free himself from Mr Haig's firm grasp and snarled, 'They started it Sir,' but was drowned out by a chorus of, 'No they didn't it was you,' by the other boys.

With Geordie held firmly in his right hand, Mr Haig looked at Jake's split lip and announced, 'You'll live Grundy,' and turning to Ian asked, 'are you all right Shepherd?'

Ian rubbed his back and said, 'Yes Sir, I'm alreet.'

He marched Robertson off to the Head master where he received three stinging blows of the strap to his outstretched hand, bringing tears to his eyes as he silently vowed vengeance on Ian and Jake!

Walking into the kitchen after school, Ian was met by his mother who said, 'Ian there's a man here from the Ashington Post and he wants to talk to you about rescuing Tommy.'

Looking into the sitting room, Ian saw a young man in an ill-fitting grey suit sitting on the settee sipping a cup of tea. 'Aah didn't rescue Tommy Mam, wor Mike rescued us both.'

Standing up, the Reporter said, 'I have already talked to Michael at work but he said you were the real hero, so if ye don't mind, can I talk to you about it?'

Jane gently nudged Ian into the room where the Reporter coaxed the story out of him with a series of questions before saying, 'Well done lad, ye are a wee hero, your story will be in next week's 'Post', be sure to tell all your friends to buy a copy noo.'

Mike and Jane rose early on Saturday morning and after preparing breakfast for Ian, they both left to catch the bus to Newcastle, Jane carrying a brown paper carrier bag containing warm clothes for Tommy to wear for his journey home. As she walked to the bus stop, her arm linked through her handsome son's arm she reflected on the events of the past week and considered their options for an uncertain future.

She had barley spoken to Nick all week and he on his part, had spent much of his time either at work or at the Fell em Doon. When Ian had moved back into his own bed, she had moved into Maureen's bedroom, rearranging the furniture to make room for the single bed she had borrowed from Aggie, who never asked why Jane needed another bed.

Visiting the hospital had reminded Jane of how Nick had prevented her from returning to nursing after Tommy had begun school but now she saw trying to become a nurse again as a necessity if she was ever going to make a life for her and the children without him. She knew she would have to retrain but believed that with her and Maureen working, and Mike on his apprenticeship, they should be able to manage financially without Nick - dependant on where they lived.

Concerned that Ian was still not fit enough to deliver groceries on Saturday morning, Jake persuaded him that he needed his help. He was also concerned that he felt so concerned over Ian's condition and was surprised when he realised he cared so much about his pal, 'Aah suppose that's waat friends are aall aboot?' he thought as he pulled his battered baseball boots over his stockings that were in danger of having more holes than material!

Hitching up his jeans, he pulled on his jacket and ran outside and down the lane to catch up with Ian who had given up waiting for him after Mrs Grundy sent him upstairs to wake her Jake up.

Lying curled up on the bed; Monty had wagged his tail as Ian had dug below a pile of blankets and overcoats to find Jake. He had to shake him several times, ignoring his pleas to 'Bugga off man,' before Jake reluctantly made a move to get up. When he did get up, the vision of him standing shivering in just a grubby vest, rubbing sleep from his eyes was too much for Ian, he retreated downstairs where Mrs Grundy smiled at him through a haze of woodbine smoke and offered him a cup of tea.

'No thanks Mrs Grundy, Aah've just had one thanks,' he said. Having drunk tea there before he knew that the tealeaves would have been used several times already with more heaped upon them and that it would taste vile. In fact the strong and bitter stewed tea he'd had there before had left a foul taste in his mouth for ages.

After delivering the Saturday morning papers, with Jake shuffling along behind him, Ian walked into Wilson's just after nine o'clock where once again, he was treated like a hero. There was much patting of his back and Eeeing and Oooing from the girls, all of which left Ian burning with embarrassment and Jake unnoticed as he grinned inanely. By the time the ruckus had died down, Jake had eaten breakfast; a slice of cheese and two slices of boiled ham that he had quickly slid off the greaseproof paper where they were waiting to be wrapped by Patsy, one of the younger shop assistants.

As Ian looked at the addresses on the already packed boxes of groceries, Patsy looked at the small piles of cheese and ham and turned to look at Jake who had not quite managed to swallow the last slice of ham. Feigning anger, she glared at Jake who, trying to look innocent looked up at the ceiling and swallowed hard, gagging as he did so.

Patting him on the back none to gently Patsy bent down and whispered in his ear, 'Careful lad, we divint want ye choking before we tek you down to the Polis Station, now do we!' Seeing the look of horror on Jake's face, she grinned at him and pushed him toward Ian who was carrying the first box out.

Ian said, 'Grab the next box and fetch it oot tha both for Green Lane.'

With the two boxes loaded into the hamper of the delivery bike, Ian lifted the back wheel off its stand, clipping it into position as Jake tried to rest the handle bars from his grasp saying, 'Haway man, I'll dee the pedalling, ye aren't up te that yit!'

Ian pushed Jake back, 'So that's why ye've come ye just want te hev a ride on the blidy bike, whey yer not ganning te ride it with groceries in cos knaing ye, ye'll crash and spill the groceries, ye can ride it back though.'

That was how they spent the rest of the morning, Ian riding the full bike to deliver the groceries with Jake riding it back; the last two trips with Ian balanced precariously in the basket. By eleven o'clock, they had just one large box left to deliver to Home Farm! Ian did not feel up to it but was not sure that he could trust Jake to deliver it on his own. After loading the heavy box of groceries he said, 'Look Jake, I'll let ye deliver this last one te Home Farm as am too knackered but divint mess aboot cos Aah divint want te lose me job and, mek sure ye bring the bike straight back here.

'Aye nee bother man, but mind, am keeping the tip on this one!' said Jake as he mounted the bike and pushed off, wobbling toward the Store Corner.

Ian watched his friend pedal off with just a little trepidation before collecting his pay from the Manager; he had decided to give Jake his share of the one-pound and tips after the safe delivery of the last load.

Despite the heavy and awkward load Jake was enjoying himself, it was a cold but sunny morning and he was warm from his exertions and expected a big tip for the long ride out to Home Farm. The only downside was that he was hungry and thirsty and he was finding it increasingly difficult to take his eyes off the goodies in the basket, especially the bottle of Lucozade wrapped in orange cellophane.

The temptation was too much; he stopped opposite Bothal School and heaving the bike up onto its stand, eagerly searched through the groceries. 'A drink forst,' he thought and taking the bottle of Lucozade out, he carefully untwisted the cellophane and unscrewed the hard stopper. He should have unscrewed the stopper as carefully as he had unwrapped the cellophane; shaken by the journey in the basket the contents fizzed out through the neck soaking Jakes sleeves and face as he tried to swallow the fizzy liquid!

'Bugga,' he spluttered as he wiped his face with his sodden sleeve before replacing the stopper. Carefully, he re-wrapped the cellophane but was dismayed at how much Lucozade had been spilled and drunk and hoped that it would not be noticed. He also hoped that no one would notice that the carefully rewrapped boiled ham was one slice less now than when he loaded it!

When the door opened at Home Farm with his mischievous grin spread across his cheeky face, he said, 'Hello Missus, here's yer groceries.' Placing the heavy box at her feet, he held out his hand for a tip and rewarded with a thru penny bit that he thrust into his pocket before turning quickly away. He pushed the bike onto the road pedalling away as fast as he could but not back to Wilson's he was a lot closer to home and decided he could return the bike after he had something more to eat!

At home, Ian had made himself a cup of tea and sat at the kitchen table to drink it while eating the pease pudding sandwich his mother had left for him. Nick was at the pantry sink having a wash and shave in readiness for his morning at the Fell-em-Doon. He had not seen much of his family that week and had started to eat at the pit canteen before coming home from work. 'The foods better and there's more than Aah get served here,' he thought, 'plus Aah can afford it noo that Am making a few more quid we me little betting racket.'

'Pour is a cup of that tea lad,' he demanded as he dried his face.

Not wanting anything to do with his father, Ian took a last slurp of tea and said, 'Aah've got te gan oot,' and hurried out the back door grabbing his jacket as he went. He had intended to walk toward Wilson's, hoping to meet Jake on his way back from dropping the delivery bike off but stopped when he saw the bike propped against the fence of the Grundy's backyard!

Annoyed at Jake's misuse of the bike and worried that he could be blamed for not returning it, he was about to confront his friend but thought, 'I'll tek the bike withoot telling him and see what happens!' Bending below the height of the fence he grabbed the handlebars and pushed the bike clear of the Grundy's, quickly mounted and cycled off to the shop.

As he was putting the bike away in the rear yard the Manager came out with a bottle of Lucozade and said, 'Ian lad, I've just had a call from Home Farm complaining that the bottle of Lucozade ye delivered isn't full so ye'll hev to take another one oot te them, divint bother bringing the other one back.'

Ian took the bottle and replied, 'Righto, I'll just walk there then and then I'll gan straight hyem,' and set off for the farm. It took him 20 minutes to reach the farm where he swapped the bottles, the Farmer's wife saying, 'Aah divint kna who that's happened becos the wrapping's still on it?'

Ian unwrapped the cellophane from the bottle as he walked home and saw that the paper seal had been broken and carefully stuck back down – 'The bloody sod!' he thought, 'I wonder what else the bugga did?

On the journey to Newcastle Jane discussed the future with Mike, telling him that once Thomas had fully recovered, she wanted to seek a divorce from Nick but that she was worried that they would end up homeless as the colliery house was obviously in Nick's name and if they divorced, the NCB would evict them. Mike said that he was sure they would be able to manage without his Dad but Jane still had grave doubts.

When they left the bus at the Town Moor, a bitter North East wind hurried them along to the hospital where they were keen to get out of the wind and keener still to take Tommy home. Walking quickly through the reception hall, they hurried along imposing corridors up to the Sister's office of the ward where Tommy was a patient. Jane noticed that his bed was empty and thought that he must already be up, waiting to go.

The Sister was sitting writing at her desk as Jane knocked and said, 'Good morning Sister, we've come to take Thomas home.'

Placing her pen on the desk, the Sister looked up, the smile on her face disappearing when she recognized Jane, 'Aah Mrs Shepherd, I'm afraid Thomas won't be going home today, he became very poorly last night and has been moved to another ward, the Doctor believes he has pneumonia.'

Jane grabbed Mike's arm, squeezing it so hard as she listened to the Sister that Mike winced, she also felt as if the room had disappeared and all she could see was the Sister's mouth as she continued. 'He is obviously in the best place for him and it is lucky we found out before he went home, he is stable but as I said he is very poorly'

Jane interrupted, 'Can I see him please?'

'It's not visiting hours until this afternoon but under the circumstances I think you should speak to the Ward Sister who can tell you more than me.' She directed Jane and Mike to the Isolation Ward where the Sister allowed them to look through the glazed door to see Tommy lying with a drip attached to his arm and an oxygen mask covering his face.

The Sister put her hand on Jane's arm and said, 'The Doctor examined him again an hour ago and said that although his

73

temperature is high, he is stable and we will obviously be taking good care of him.'

'Thanks,' Jane said, 'will I be able to go in and see him?'

'I'm afraid not, not today, he is to be kept very quiet, he needs rest and lots of it but you should be able to get in to see him tomorrow but it's best you ring first.'

Jane knew better than to push to see Tommy and knew that he was in safe hands, 'How long do you think his recovery will take?' she asked.

'That depends on how strong Thomas is but I would think at least two weeks – if there are no complications.'

'There's that phrase again,' Jane thought, 'no complications', poor Tommy has had enough complications, and our lives are complicated enough.'

Mike turned from staring at his young brother and placing his hand on his mother's arm, said hopefully, 'Wor Tommy's a fighter Mam, he's ganning te be alreet!'

Jake was running up the short slope from the Sixth Row to the Fifth, desperately searching for the missing delivery bike when he saw Ian coming along the Fifth Row from the direction of Long Row. He stopped and waited, trying to concoct an excuse for the missing bike as Ian walked approached him with his jacket collar turned up against the bitter wind blowing down the Row behind him.

Sliding the bottle of Lucozade behind his back, Ian stifled a smile as he walked up to a clearly nervous Jake, 'Alreet Marra?' he asked.

Jake rubbed his hands nervously and answered, 'Aye champion, there's just one little problem like!'

'Waat's that then?'

'Yer bike - whey not your bike - the delivery bike.'

'What aboot the delivery bike?'

Jake rubbed his hands even harder and looking down at his feet, almost whispered, 'It's lost.'

'Lost, hoo can a bike get lost, wad de ye mean like, lost?'

Jake said loudly, 'Aah mean it's lost, gone; disappeared; yer kna – lost!'

Finding it difficult not to laugh Ian said, 'Nur, Aah divint kna, hoo can it be lost, lost from where?'

'From ootside wor hoose,' Jake muttered, lowering his head again.

'Ootside yor hoose, what the heck was it deeing ootside yor hoose?'

'Aah was hungry so I went hyem te get sumat to eat before Aah took the bike back to Wilson's and some bugga has nicked it man.

'Ur, so noo it's not lost, it's been nicked, has it?'

'Aye it hes man, sum buggas nicked it from ootside wor hoose, noo what are we ganna dee aboot it?'

'Waat de ye mean, we? Ye've lost it, ye are ganning te hev te buy a new one.'

Jake went scarlet and spluttered, 'Buy a new one! Buy a new one! Are ye blidy mad man, where the blidy hell am Aah ganna get the money te buy a frigging bike?'

'Jail for ye then Jake,' said Ian, bringing the bottle of Lucozade from behind his back and slowly taking the top of before taking a long swallow.

Jake looked at the bottle and demanded, 'Where did ye get that?'

'This? From Home Farm, tha blidy angry like, the reckon someone drunk haf of it before they delivered it and the Manager made me deliver a new one and wants money for the new one Jake.'

Jake was having difficulty containing his anxiety and was now swaying sideways as he rubbed his hands, 'Blidy hell, blidy hell, waat am a ganna dee noo?'

'Hev a drink of Lucozade and we'll gan hyem.'

Jake grabbed the bottle and took a swig before saying, 'But waat aboot the bike man?'

Laughing Ian said, 'Aah took it back te teach ye a lesson,' and ran off.

Jake grasped what had happened and set off after him shouting, 'Yer rotten swine yer.'

Chapter 5
Shocking News

On Monday morning, having had restless night worrying about Tommy, a very tired Jane was sitting reading 'Get Well Soon' cards that his friends at Wansbeck School had lovingly drawn and signed. The morning before, she had walked round to the public phone box next to Bothal School and phoned the hospital to find out how Tommy was – 'Holding his own' she had been told and also not to bother going to see him as he was sedated. The Doctor had also told the Ward Sister that there was to be no visitors until Monday afternoon at the earliest!

Deep in thought, a loud knock at the door startled her and standing quickly, she smoothed her hair and straightened her apron as she walked quickly to the door, opening it to the Postman.

'Morning Missus, are ye Missus N Shepherd?'

Jane nodded and the Postman said, 'Aah've a registered letter her for ye te sign for Hinny.'

Taking the large A4 envelope, Jane signed the small brown book the Postman held out to her before walking back to the kitchen table placing the envelope in the centre and stepping back to stare at it, wondering whom it was from, and what it contained.

Taking a deep breath, she sat down at the table and picked it up to look at the postmark - 'Coventry!' Jane's mind was in turmoil as she thought of her Father and wondered if the letter was from him and why would he be contacting her after so many years of silence? Taking a knife from the draw under the table, she carefully slit open the envelope and withdrew several sheets of neatly typed paper; looking at the sender's address, she recognised the name; Messrs Roddick and Penrose, Solicitors!

With some trepidation, she began reading the letter, written in a pithy formal style;

Dear Mrs Shepherd,

It is with regret that I have to inform you that on the 11th of January this year, your father, Mr Robert Thomas Trevelyan took his own life. After a post-mortem held in the first week of February your father was buried in his family plot on the 11th of February.

Following a request made by him in a letter to me before his suicide (copy enclosed for your information), I have delayed informing you of these matters as he stipulated he did not wish to have you attend his funeral.

A tear rolled down Jane's cheek as she placed the letter on the table, unable to continue as she thought of this final snub from her father and, wondered why he committed suicide. Composing herself, she began reading again;

I have to make you aware that your father died in bankruptcy after a downturn of his Company's fortunes and several years of financial mismanagement of which I am not at liberty to discuss. Suffice to say that creditors have laid legitimate claim to all of his remaining assets.

Jane was shocked and saddened by the contents of the letter, especially as it appeared that her father had still been unable to forgive her even at the end. The news of the collapse of his business was a surprise, it had been so prosperous at the outbreak of World War 2, not that she had ever harboured any thoughts of an inheritance, but the biggest shock came in the second half of the letter.

I now have to inform you that you have a half-brother, Master Ralph Rorke Trevelyan who was borne on the 12th day of June 1944. He is currently a pupil of Rugley School but will have to leave at the end of this half-term on Friday the 21nd of March due non-payment of school fees. You may wish to take over the payment of these fees, thus allowing him to complete his education at Rugley.

'A brother, I have a brother!' Jane said aloud, stunned by the revelation, her brain trying to fathom out how she had a half-brother who was borne when her mother was still alive! She continued reading, keen to find out more.

In return for rescinding all parental rights and any contact with her son, your late father paid, Master Trevelyan's mother, Miss E Rorke a substantial sum of money. As we do not know her whereabouts, Miss Rorke, we have been unable to inform her of the death of Mr Trevelyan.

You are the only known living relative of your stepbrother and as such may wish to accept responsibility for his future. Your late father did set up a small trust fund for his son of which I am the executor. Should you accept him into your family, I am prepared to provide an allowance from this of £5 per week for his upkeep. In anticipation of your willingness, I have also taken the liberty of purchasing train tickets for his journey from Coventry to Ashington at the end of the current school half term on the 21st of March.

Jane read the last paragraph that contained details of how she was to conduct further contact with the solicitors and then looked at a sealed envelope with written upon it, 'Mr R.T. Trevelyan's letter to his daughter Mrs Jane Shepherd.' Jane could not bring herself to open it, afraid that it would contain more recriminations or spiteful remarks, as it was clear from the fact that her father did not want her to know of his demise or funeral until it was over that his attitude toward her had not changed. Placing the letter along with the Solicitor's letter back into the envelope, she placed it in the back of one of the drawers in the sideboard in the sitting room. Standing quietly by the sideboard, she thought, 'I cannot begin to consider what to do while my Thomas is lying desperately ill in hospital; it will have to wait until I have the time and the mental strength to deal with it,'

Preparing herself for her trip to see Tommy, she realised it was only eighteen days until her brother would be joining them, unless she took action to prevent him coming! She was angry that in the midst of her terrifying fears over Tommy that her father had caused her even more misery and worries; how would Nick act when she told him her younger half-brother was coming to live with them? How would the children re-act to having her brother come to live with them? How would he fit in? What was he like? Would he want to come? How and why did her father have had a child with another woman while her mother was alive and had she been aware of this? All of these questions filled her head as well as the constant nagging worry over Tommy as she sat deep in thought on the bus to Newcastle.

Allowed at last in to see her sickly son, she was delighted when managed a little smile for her, as with laboured breath, he attempted to raise himself in his sick bed. Jane gently pushed him back down and touched the side of his face feeling the heat from the fever still raging inside his frail body.

The nurse had told her that he was doing well and they were hopeful he would make a complete recovery in due course, as long as there was 'No complications!' Jane had to stop herself from screaming when she heard that dreaded phrase again.

On the way home she resolved not to tell Nick about Ralph until she had discussed the options with her two oldest children, their opinions were far more important to her than his were, he would have to accept their decision when she told him and she was prepared to defy him if he should go against their wishes.

With many questions nagging away at her, Jane walked to the public phone box on Tuesday and rang the Solicitor, hoping for answers. He told her;

Ralph used the old pronunciation of his name, Rafe.'

Rafe believed that Jane's mother, Rosalind was his mother.

Jane's mother knew about the boy and had agreed to the surrogacy as she could no longer bear children and her husband who was the last of the Trevelyan's, was desperate for a son and was determined to father a boy no matter how many times he had to try if the babies were girls. She was however, obviously very upset and very angry and understandably, refused to play the part of the boy's mother although she was always kind to him.

Her father's business had been in steady decline after the war and he had made matters worse when he fired some of his workforce to save money – a bitter and prolonged strike further damaged the business when his main customer left for another company. In a desperate attempt to keep the company viable, her father had invested heavily in a new building and equipment but when he failed to attract new customers he was left with crippling debt.

Jane pushed her last few coppers into the coin box and asked, 'Is Rafe aware that he might be coming to live me?'

Mr Penrose, the Solicitor cleared his throat before answering, 'Yes Mrs Shepherd but have you considered allowing him to continue his education at Rugley, you will be aware that it is one of our most prestigious public schools?'

Jane thought that the Solicitor must have no grip on reality if he thought even for one moment that she could afford to pay public school fees for her half-brother.

Besides, what about her own children and said, 'No Mr Penrose I have not, if he comes to live with me, he will be treat exactly the same as my children and he will attend the local school.'

There was a slight pause before Penrose replied very tersely, 'That is entirely up to you Mrs Shepherd.'

The Solicitor explained that he would forward a cheque weekly for £5, commencing on Saturday 22nd of March and that unless he heard from her again, Master Rafe would arrive at Ashington at 4pm on Friday the 21st. Jane thanked him for his help and walked home wondering what she was going to do. 'Would a boy from a privileged back ground survive here let alone fit in with her family?' She then thought about her own upbringing and how difficult it had been for her to settle into life in a tiny shared miner's house but she had and now she felt as if it was the only life she had ever known! The brisk walk home helped her rationalise her thoughts and by the time she stepped through her back door, she had made her mind up and was resolved on a course of action.

At breakfast on Saturday of the following week, Jane waited until Mike and Maureen were at the kitchen table, Nick was still in bed and Ian on his paper round, before saying, 'I want you to be here at seven o'clock tonight after your father has gone to the Fell-em Doon, I have something very important to discuss with you.'

Maureen was first to answer, 'But Mam, I'm going to the pictures tonight!'

Mike added, 'And I'm ganning te the 'Tute with Hank and Geordie, then we're ganning te the flicks!'

Jane tapped the table with her hand and said, 'Now listen, you will be here, no arguments and I do wish you wouldn't speak so crudely, I take it the 'Flicks' Michael, is the cinema?'

'Aye OK Mam, Aah mean Mummy Dear,' Michael replied, smiling at his mother who smiled wryly back at her son.

Maureen said, 'I bet this something to do with ye not sleeping with my Dad anymore, and we are all happy yer not mind?'

Jane rubbed her daughter's shoulder affectionately and said, 'It has very little to do with your father and that's all I'm going to say at the moment so please no more questions.

She spent most of the day worrying how Mike and Maureen would take the news and wondered what she would do if they rejected the idea of having another addition to their family. She had expected Nick to accompany her to visit Tommy and was annoyed but at the same time relieved when he said, 'Aah've got business te take care of the sefternoon,' and pushing a half crown across the kitchen table continued, 'Here buy him some grapes and chocolate or sumat.'

She did not argue with him, glad that she would not have to tolerate his company on the bus journey to and from Newcastle and left the money lying on the table until he had left for the Fell-em-Doon before picking it up.

Finding Tommy's slow but steady recovery was continuing and having sat holding his hand for half an hour whilst she talked quietly to him lifted her spirits, bolstering her for her talk with Mike and Maureen later in the day.

Nick left the house just after seven o'clock as Jane sat nervously sipping a cup of tea at the kitchen table. Mike and Maureen were in the sitting room listening to Sonny James singing 'Young Love' on Mike's newly acquired record. Ian was watching television at Howard's, two doors down.

Hearing the back door close, Mike stepped into the kitchen and said, 'Howay then Mam tell us what this is all aboot then.'

Jane picked up her tea, walked into the sitting room and sat down in the armchair in front of the glowing fire. Mike sat down next to Maureen on the sofa and waited while his mother stared into the fire for a few seconds before turning to look at them.

'I have a brother!'

'What?' Maureen exclaimed.

'Blidy hell,' Mike said grinning madly, 'that's a torn up for the books like!'

Jane smiled nervously and continued, 'It was as much a shock to me as it is to you.'

'Eee, I have an uncle,' Maureen said, imagining a middle aged, well-dressed man smoking a pipe!

'Yes you have an uncle and what's more you will get to meet him very soon.'

'Why; is he coming to visit us?' Mike asked.

'No,' Jane paused before adding, 'he is coming to live with us.'

Mike exploded, 'Waat, live with us, there's nee room for another bloke here Mam.'

Jane smiled and said quietly, He's not a bloke; he's a boy, the same age as Ian actually.'

'Blidy hell,' exclaimed Mike.

Maureen gasped, 'Goodness me.'

The two of them listened intently while their mother explained how she had received the letter, its contents and her talk with Mr Penrose whilst now and again holding her hand up to stop questions from both Mike and Maureen, and did not tell them that he was a half-brother!

'So there you have it, I would like Ralph or should I say Rafe to come and live with us, it will cost us nothing but a bit of love and understanding as the small allowance will be sufficient to clothe and feed him, what do you think?'

'Where is he ganning te sleep?' Mike asked.

'There is just enough space in your room for another single bed and that will have to suffice for the time being unless you want to sleep in here on the sofa bed?'

'Nur that's fine but we'll have te get another bed and everything.'

Jane nodded and said, 'Yes we will, does that mean you are happy for him to come to live with us?'

Mike smiled and answered, 'Aye of course man, we are all the family the lads got, so he'll hev to come here.'

Maureen was at the stage where she did not much care for her three brothers let alone a fourth but was intrigued by the whole thing and said, 'Yes, he will have to come here,' then lied as she asked, 'Now can I go, my friends are waiting to go to the pictures with me?' Blonde-haired, blue-eyed Terry was waiting at the end of the street to take her to the pictures, not her friends and she looked forward to snuggling up to him in the two-seater sofa seats in the Buffalo Cinema.

Jane felt a huge surge of relief at their acceptance of the situation and said, 'Yes of course but I want you in by ten o'clock and please, the pair of you do not tell Ian about Rafe, I will tell him but not just yet.'

'That was easy enough' Jane thought 'but how would Ian react to the news that he was going to have an Uncle living with them who was his own age and how would Nick take the news?'

Trench coat collar pulled up and trilby pulled down against a steady drizzle as he tried to emulate George Raft; Nick limped past Bothal School heading for the Fell-em-Doon but stopped outside the brightly lit, huge double windows of Gibson's Garage Showroom. Of the three cars on display he stared covetously at the gleaming smooth lines of a red, five-year old Riley One Point Five and imagined himself cruising along, window open with his beautiful wife sitting next to him smiling. 'Nee blidy chance of hur smiling for me!' he thought as he took out a Capstan, turned his back to the wind and lit it with his stainless steel lighter. 'I will have that car though, just another good week like the last one and I'll have the deposit for the £185 they are asking for it,' he thought as he limped across the road to the Fell-em-Doon.

In addition to taking bets in the Fell-em-Doon, Nick had gone to the popular bar of the Grand Hotel in the centre of town last week and begun taking bets there. Ashington had over twenty Working Men's' Clubs but only three pubs; it was these three pubs along with the Fell-em-Doon that he focused his racket. It was just a bit too risky to try it in other clubs where he was not a full time member

Walking into the tobacco smoke filled Bar Room of the 'Doon', he took off his hat, shook off the rain drops, walked up to the bar and smiling at the slim, blonde barmaid said, 'Me usual Ginny Pet.'

Ginny smoothed her tight black skirt, aimed her breasts at him, smiled a red-lipped smile back, and said, 'Anything for you Nick.'

Pouring a bottle of Double Maxim, she placed it front of him and held her hand open. He placed a half crown into her palm and held onto her hand mouthing silently, 'Later?' She smiled and nodded as Nick turned to join a couple of men sitting in the corner of the bar.

Ten years younger than Nick, Ginny was besotted by his flash dress and cocky manners and had been taking him back to her seedy flat a few doors along High Market for a quickie several times a week for the past few months. It was a relationship she was keen to build on but for Nick, she was a convenience, a little distraction from life and she was by no means the only girl he had or was dallying with.

Maureen was madly in love, the way only a young girl in love for the very first time could be, her every waking minute was spent thinking about Terry's twinkling eyes and his passionate embrace and kisses. She had thought that by 'going all the way,' with him may have changed their relationship for the worse and that he might have felt differently about her and she worried that he might leave her for another more virtuous girl. However, she had been wrong, ever since they had made love in his sister's house early on New Year's Eve whilst they baby-sat his niece; Terry had been even more loving and attentive. They had managed to find the opportunity to make love a few times more since then but she worried needlessly that her mother could tell that she was no longer a virgin and was rightly terrified of the consequences should her father ever find out.

Ian spent the evening at his tall and heavily built friend, Howard's neat and well-furnished house, Number 58. Sitting on their huge, plush floral sofa with Howard and his chubby but pretty, 15 year old sister Mary; they were glued to the small wooden boxed 12 inch television. They were watching the Rock and Roll TV programme, 'The Six Five Special,' and unhindered by grown-ups, they snapped their fingers and tapped their feet to the beat of Don Lang and Tommy Steele. Howard's parents had left to watch the first showing of 'The Abominable Snowman, at the Regal and would not be home until nine o'clock as they would call in at the 'White House Club for quick a drink after the film.

Mary grabbed a very reluctant Ian's hand and dragged him off the sofa when Don Lang backed by his band sang Buddy Hollies 'Brown Eyed Handsome Man' 'Haway, Ian and I'll teach you hoo te jive,'

'Nur man, Aah divin't want te blidy jive!'

'Whey yer ganning te so hang on!' and grasping Ian's hand, Mary spun, twirled, side-stepped and jived her way around the bemused lad, sending her loose fitting skirt and petticoats flying high revealing her shapely legs as she yelled instructions at him. He was a fast learner and quickly began to enjoy the dance until the pair of them collapsed giggling onto the sofa when the music finished.

Cheered on by Howard, they had a couple more jives as the programme continued, Mary giving an embarrassed Ian a very tight hug after the last one saying excitedly, 'Ye'll hev to come to the Tanner Hop next week and we'll show everybody how te really jive.'

'Not me Mary, I'm not ganning te any dances, that's for cissy's man.'

Howard nudged Ian in the ribs and sniggered, 'Whey the way ye were dancing there, does that mek ye a big cissy like?'

'Sod off man,' Ian said, 'noo that that's finished are we ganning te play Monopoly?'

The three of them played the board game until just before nine o'clock when the back door swung open and Howard's parents, George and Mary rushed in out of the cold damp March night. Shaking coats and hats in the passageway, they scurried across to the kitchen fire where Mrs Holland placed a large paper bundle on the open oven door before they jostled each other good naturedly to warm themselves in front of the well banked fire.

'Eeee, it's aaful oot there again tonight,' Mrs Holland said, turning her portly figure around so that her back was to the fire before hitching up her skirt to warm her ample bum.

George Holland, six foot two and eighteen stone gave way to his wife and said 'By yer mek a blidy good bleazer Mary Hinny but ye divint leave much heat for the rest of us!'

Ian enjoyed being in the Holland's house, it was a happy comfortable home, full of love and life. He also loved the way the huge Mr Holland was with his family; he obviously loved them all and constantly showed it through words and gestures. 'If only my Dad was like him!' He could not remember the last time he had heard his father say a kind word to any of them but remembered the stinging slap across the face he had giving him three weeks ago when he refused to hand over his paper round money. He also remembered all the other slaps, punches and kicks his father had dished out over the years. He had also noticed that lately, when Mike was about his father was much less violent and no longer hit out at him, obviously afraid of retaliation, as Mike grew older and stronger.

'Whey Aah better be ganning hyem,' Ian said as he helped Howard pack up the game.

'Had yer horses Bonny Lad, I've got ye a patty and chips for ye, we called in at Cutherbertson's on the way hyem from the Regal and bought wi's aall supper.'

He said politely, 'No thanks, you didn't have to get me any,' but Mr Holland was not having that, 'Yer sitting doon we us lad, noo come on join us up at the tyeble.'

Ian enjoyed the patty, chips, bread and butter and strong tea that Mrs Holland made but most of all, he enjoyed the cheerful banter around the table before he left to run through the now pouring rain the twenty yards home. Curled up in the armchair in front of the fire in the sitting room, Jane was reading a magazine that she laid down when he Ian walked in smelling of rain.

Rising from the chair, she and put her hand round his shoulders, guided him to the sofa and sat down with him preparing to tell him all about Rafe. However, when Ian told her of dancing to the music on the television, Monopoly and patty and chips, she decided she did not want to spoil his happy mood; she would tell him tomorrow and tomorrow when she was also going to have to tell Nick!

It had been a busy night for Nick, a couple of beers at the Doon before catching the bus up to the bus station and walking across the road and along to the 'Grand' the imposing sandstone Hotel and pub that dominated the main cross roads in the centre of the town. He spent two hours there touting for business, managing to interest half a dozen or so of the regulars into placing a few bets on the mid-week races at Doncaster.

Two of those interested were the McArdle twins, 30 years old tough and vicious hard men from Blyth; they had been steadily making their presence felt in Ashington and quizzed Nick on the extent of his little racket. Nick saw nothing suspicious in their questions and was happy enough to outline his below the table betting and his plans for expansion to the two swarthy but smiling thugs.

He finished his night off back at the Doon, followed by forty minutes with the very accommodating Ginny before limping home through deserted streets and rows as the rain endeavoured to drench him to the skin. Standing in a silent house, warming his hands in front of the kitchen fire, he cursed his loss of control over Jane and plotted revenge!

The following morning, with Mike sitting next to her, Jane sat at the kitchen table peeling potatoes for Sunday dinner. She had asked him to be there when Nick rose and had told him of her intention to tell him about Rafe including him coming to live with them in five days.

Nick did not come down stairs until after eleven o'clock, 'What's this, a deputation?' he snarled when he saw Jane and Mike sitting at the kitchen table staring at him.

'I have something to tell you and I would like you to listen without flying off the handle,' Jane said quietly.

'Divint ye tell me waat te de and waat not ye dee womin, if ye've sumat te say te me spit it oot noo, Aah canna be deeing we ye.'

Mike placed his hand reassuringly on his mother's as she said, 'My father is dead.'

'Ha! Whey divint expect me to be upset aboot that,' Nick spat as his mind went into overdrive. 'Hing on noo, does that mean he's left ye the business or money or sumat?' he asked trying hard to hide his greedy expectations – 'at last the owld bastard's gone and I might reap the reward of putting up with his frosty stuck up daughter for all these years,' he thought as he waited expectantly.

'There is no business or money, nothing, he committed suicide and was penniless!'

'Blidy fucking champion, the owld get still gets the last laugh on me, the fucking twat, aall these years Aah've hung on hoping he was ganning te leave me, Aah mean, ye some money, the blidy useless waster,' Nick snarled, kicking the coal scuttle, scattering coal across the kitchen floor.

He was about to walk to the back door to go to the nettie when Jane said with some trepidation, 'I have found out that I have a thirteen year old brother and he's coming to live with us on Friday!'

'Nee buggas coming te live in this hoose with oot my say so, what the fuck de ye think this is woman, a blidy doss hoose and hoo the hell are we supposed to feed another bildy mooth?'

Jane stood up and placing her hands on the table she looked at her husband with some contempt and said in a voice that quivered with anger, 'I have endured you hitting me and the children for far too long, I have also had to put up with your lack of concern on how they are doing as well as your boozing and womanising and your total lack of feeling for us, well, all that has changed Nick.'

He stepped toward and warned, 'Be careful lass cos Aah'll blidy swing for ye if yer not careful,' but hesitated when Mike sprang from his chair and stood silently next to his mother.

Jane touched Mikes arm, 'Nick you no longer have the right to tell anybody what to do in this house, my brother is coming to stay with us and that is that and you don't have to worry about paying for him, he has a small allowance for his upkeep.'

Pulling his dangling braces over his shirt Nick hesitated then said quietly, 'That's alreet then, hoo de I get this allowance te feed him?'

Jane shook her head, 'You don't, it will be paid to me by cheque and I will feed and clothe him, you don't have to be involved at all.'

'Hoo are ye ganning te cash a cheque we haven't got a blidy bank account hev we?'

Sitting down, Jane said quietly, 'You might not have one but I have, I put my Co-op dividend money into and anything else I manage to scrimp, how do you think I manage to put clothes on your children's back's?'

Furious at his inability to intimidate or best Jane, Nick stormed out across the lane into the netty where behind the closed door he beat the wall hammer like with his fist in silent anger and frustration.

Down the lane, Howard struggled to keep his bike in a straight line but it was very difficult with Ian straddling the luggage shelf and Jake perched on the crossbar. 'Stop trying te steer man,' he yelled at Jake who was clutching the handle bars.

Ian yelled from the back, 'Gan canny man ye'll crash inte the blidy coal hooses if ye not careful.'

Howard managed to gain some forward speed and this helped balance the load but just as he approached the end of the Row and just when he thought he had his bike under control, Edward turned the corner in his Jowett. Howard panicked and wobbled into a battered metal dustbin, knocking it over and scattering the contents as the three lads spilled out across the road. Edward braked and sat smiling at the chaos in front of him and beyond where the dustbin lid was rolling sedately down the lane, eventually running out of momentum and falling over on the kerb half way down the street.

Climbing out of his car, he helped the lads to their feet and checked that they were all okay before asking Ian, 'Hoo's your Tommy?'

Ian hitched up his jeans and pulled his pullover down before answering, 'Me Mam says he's a lot better Mr Thompson, Aah haven't been allowed te gan and see him but Aah think he will be home next weekend.'

Turning to climb back into his car Edward said, 'Whey that's good news as Aah hurd he had developed pneumonia, tell your mam and dad that....'

He did not finish his sentence, Nick had come out of the toilet and seeing Ian talking to Edward, yelled, 'How, Ian, get yersell doon here noo.'

Ian looked angrily back at his father and shouted, 'I'm playing with Howard and Jake.'

'Get doon here noo, I winit tell ye again,' shouted Nick.

Edward said quietly to Ian, 'Ye best gan hyem lad, nee need te mek matters worse.'

As Ian walked reluctantly home, Jake asked Edward, 'Hev ye come back te live here again then Mr Edwards?'

'Nur lad, Aah've just come for me Sunday Dinner, ye canna beat yer mam's Sunday dinners noo can ye?

'Any bugga can beat my Mam's, nee meat, hard tetties, cabbage that Aah hate, turnip that's harder than the tetties and claggy lumpy gravy, and mind she winit let us leave owt; it's aaful man!'

'Aah hurd that, Aah'll tell yer mam what ye said,' Albert Grundy said as he stepped out of the air-raid shelter he had converted into a shed cum workshop by knocking a door and window into the substantial brick walls. Wearing a pair of greasy and dirty NCB navy blue overalls, equally greasy boots and an even greasier peaked cap set jauntily on the side of his head; a half smoked woodbine that was stuck to his bottom lip waggled precariously as he spoke. 'There's nowt wrang we yer mam's dinner, ye should be grateful for whaat ye get, there's thoosands of kids roond the warld that would love a dinner like yer mam's.'

'Where they can hev mine, I divint mind,' Jake said as he climbed onto the back of Howards precious bike for another ride.

'Hoo's your motorbike then Albert?' Edward asked?'

Rubbing his hands on a filthy rag, Albert replied, 'Aye whey ye kna it's coming alang champion, Aah should have it running like a sewing machine any time noo.' He had been saying the same thing for the past two months but despite Albert's best efforts, Edward had not heard the engine of the 1953 red James Cadet burst into life, but Albert was not going to give up on it

He spent any spare time he had in his air-raid shelter repairing other blokes' motorbikes and mopeds for a few shillings, or a chicken or whatever they had to offer for a few hours of his time and effort. He generally managed to carry out the repairs but he was struggling with the James. He had bought it for £10 from a woman in Green Lane who had said it had been her son's motorbike but he had not looked after it, resulting in a seized engine. When the son had left to carry out his National Service, he had abandoned the motorbike at the back of their garage. 'Sum folk hev got mair money than blidy sense,' Albert had told Flo, 'Aah shud be able te mek a few pund when Aah sell it.'

Flo's response had been, 'Aye and pigs might be blidy fly!'

He also made cracket stools for anyone foolish enough to admire his handiwork. Sophisticated joinery they were not, owing more to large nails and screws for their rigidity than elegant tongue and groove joints. However, he enjoyed making them and it kept him from under the 'Missus's' feet, which was very important to both of them.

'De ye need a cracket for yer new hoose Eddie?' he shouted.

Laughing, Edward shouted back, 'No thanks Albert, Aah already hev two that ye made me!' and climbed into his car and drove it to the end of the street to turn around and drive back and park outside his parents' house. He looked forward to Sunday dinner especially as his new contract was keeping him so busy he had to live off fish and chips, having no time to cook for himself in his new home in Wansbeck Road. He also hoped that he may find the opportunity to see or talk to Jane but those opportunities were very rare.

Having prepared Sunday Dinner, Jane gave Maureen final instructions on when to place various pots and pans on the fire or in the oven before cleaning herself up and applying makeup ready for her trip to Newcastle to visit Tommy. She had watched Nick leave for the Fell-em-Doon just after twelve; they had not spoken since the earlier argument and not wanting to have another, she did not ask him if he was going with her. Mike was playing football in the Sunday league so would not be accompanying her to visit Tommy.

She pulled on her dark blue, slim fitting coat and, tying her favourite floral scarf loosely around her shoulders, she hurried out the back door and down the back lane to catch the bus from Highmarket. Edward, who had been talking Albert Grundy outside the air-raid shelter, saw her coming and quickly crossed the lane to speak to her.

'She looks as beautiful as ever,' he thought as he smiled as she approached, 'Off te see young Tom?'

She smiled back and said, 'Yes, he's a lot better; I have to hurry to catch the bus.'

'Aa'd be happy te run ye over, save you hurrying for buses?' Edward said hoping she would accept.

'Thanks Mr Thompson, that is very kind of you but I think it's best if I catch the bus but thanks anyway,' and she hurried on down the Row.

Chapter 6

Rafe

On the following Friday as they sat down on the bus that would take them the mile from Highmarket to just over the Station Bridge in the centre of town, Ian asked, 'Hoo come you have just fund oot that ye have a brother then Mam?'

Pausing to gather her thoughts, Jane replied carefully, 'Well, your grandfather has not spoken to me for a very long time and as no-one else had told me; the first I knew was when the letter from your grandfather's solicitor arrived.'

'Why do I hev to come to meet him though?' Ian asked, curious as to why his mother had stopped him from going to school just to meet a new uncle.

'I thought you would be good company for him and help him settle in, it's all going to be a bit strange for him.'

'No stranger than having an uncle coming to share your bedroom!' Ian thought to himself. It had been a tight squeeze putting a third, newly bought on HP bed into their attic bedroom but there was just sufficient space to stand between the new bed and Mikes leaving three foot between the bottom of them to Ian and Tommy's bed that was at right angle to the other two.

'It's ganning te be crowded the morn night when Tommy comes home and there's four of us in there.'

'It will be cosy!' Jane said patting Ian on the knee.

Staring out of the grimy window of the steam train as it chugged across the iconic Tyne Bridge, the tall and slim, thirteen year old Ralph Rorke Trevelyan was an excited but worried young man! He eased his striped school tie and adjusted his maroon and very expensive Rugley School blazer as he prepared to leave this train at Newcastle Central Station to find the train for Ashington. His whole world had collapsed around him; although never really close to his father, his suicide had left him feeling lost but worse, he had lost the security and sense of purpose he had felt at Rugley School.

The solicitor, Mr Penrose had been kind enough on his first visit to Rafe, explaining the death of his father, the collapse of his business and the uncertainty of Rafe's future. He had said there was a possibility that he may be allowed to continue at Rugley but that decision was not his to make.

His House Master had accompanied him to his father's funeral which had been a dismal and harrowing affair made worse by the news from Mr Penrose that everything in his home had gone, all that he, Rafe, owned was what he had at school, a school that had not received fees for two terms.

It was another two weeks before Mr Penrose came to visit again, informing him that he had made contact with his sister who was prepared to 'take him in' but was not prepared to meet the cost of his school fees. The Headmaster had expressed his regret that the School was losing a promising sportsman and popular boy and wished Rafe well in all his future endeavours and told him he was to leave at the end of term.

In the huge curving Newcastle Railway Station, it took Rafe thirty minutes to organise himself and his luggage and find the train for Ashington sitting patiently waiting for its passengers in a quiet corner where the line from the Northumberland mining villages terminated.

His ebullient personality and almost haphazard way of breezing through life had helped him through the difficulties of the past month but now he worried if his newfound sister would accept him. He was still unaware that Jane was a half-sister but knew that his father had disowned her for some scandalous act during the war. This piece of information had worried him – was she a truly awful woman who would be horrible to him?

Mr Penrose had also told him that her circumstances were less than plush and was therefore just a tad concerned that his new home would not be as comfortable as his last but he was looking forward to meeting his nephews and nieces and hoped they would like him

Ashington Railway Station consisted of a small entrance hall flanked by a ticket office on one side and a waiting room on the other, with toilets, stores and a Station House spread along the canopied platform. The platform on either side of the tracks served passengers travelling to and from Newbiggin upon Sea where the line terminated and in the other direction to the various towns and villages that straddled the line to Newcastle.

Standing on the platform opposite the Station buildings enjoying the late afternoon sunshine, Jane and Ian watched the steam train chuff into Station, the engine slowing to a hissing halt under the bridge with carriages stopped neatly along the platform. Ian scanned the men amongst the twenty or so passengers who stepped down from the train, expecting one of them to come over to introduce him-self but all of them hurried by and up the steps to Station Road.

Turning to look up at his mother, he asked, 'Has he missed the train then?'

'No, there he is,' she said pointing to the tall blonde haired boy in school uniform who was wearing a perplexed expression on his striking face. Seeing Rafe wander off toward the rear of the train, Jane and Ian hurried to catch up with him.

'Rafe, Rafe,' Jane said loudly as they caught up with him.

Rafe turned and looked at the beautiful woman who reminded him of the woman he thought was his mother and the dark haired boy wearing a well-worn but very clean and well cared for navy blue serge jacket over equally well-worn grey flannel trousers and highly polished black shoes.

'Ah, hello you must be my sister Jane?' Rafe said politely.

Ian looked incredulously at Rafe and said, 'Ye cannit be me uncle, yer ower young te be me uncle man!'

'Sorry, I didn't quite catch that?' Rafe answered wondering what language the boy was speaking.

"Ye, hoo can ye be me uncle when yer nee owlder than me man?'

Looking even more puzzled, Rafe was about to speak but Jane interrupted, 'I'm sorry Ian pet, I thought I had told you that Rafe was the same age as you, anyway, Rafe I'm very pleased to meet you,' and shaking his hand that he had thrust at her, she bent slightly and kissed him on the cheek.

'This is your nephew Ian who wanted to come to meet you this afternoon.'

Ian looked at his mother and said, 'Yer made me come, am supposed te be at school.'

Rafe thrust his hand at Ian and grinning from ear to ear, said, 'Hello Ian, yes I am your Uncle Rafe, crazy isn't it?'

Ian was won over by Rafe's broad and engaging grin and knew instantly that he liked his uncle, 'Aye Hullo, am very pleased te meet ye,' he said shaking Rafe's hand vigorously.

'Where's your luggage Rafe,' Jane asked as the guard waved his flag and blew the whistle signalling that the train was leaving.

'There it is,' he answered pointing to a porter carrying a large leather suitcase and a large canvas and leather sports hold all.

'We should be able to manage them between us,' Jane said stopping the porter.

'Waat aboot the trunk Missus?' the porter asked.

'What trunk?'

Rafe stepped forward and pointing to a huge trunk that had been left where the Guards van had been said, 'That one, it has all my clothes and books inside.'

'Ye've got a lot of clathes for one purson!' Ian said incredulously.

Jane thought for a moment and said to the Porter, 'Can you please take it across to the Dairy and I'll meet you there.' Then turning to the boys said,' come on bring the cases and follow me.

With Rafe, Ian and the Porter following, Jane crossed the lines at the bottom of the platform, through the ticket hall and into the milk dairy next to the station and up to the glass fronted office by the entrance, 'Wait here.' She ordered as she tapped and walked in to talk to the white coated man inside. She emerged a few minutes later with the man who spoke to the Porter before the two of them wheeled the trunk to the side of the office.

Giving the Porter sixpence, Jane said, 'That's that organised, the milkman will deliver the trunk tomorrow, come on we've a bus to catch.'

'Oh haven't you a car? Rafe asked.

'A car, Aah wish we had!' Ian replied, 'we've got te catch the bus ower the bridge by the post office, howay, let's carry yer bags ower.'

Struggling over the railway bridge with Rafe's baggage, Ian was excited at having another brother and felt compelled to point things out to him while Rafe enjoyed listening too and getting to grip with Ian's Geordie twang!

'That's the coouncil offices and that's the Mine's Rescue Station below.'

Rafe stopped on the middle of the bridge and looked northwards over the other side, 'What strange looking hills, they look almost man-made?'

101

Ian followed his gaze and laughed, 'Tha not hills man, tha pit heaps and tha great for sliding doon, howay, noo look doon there, that's the TA Hall and the other way, doon past the Post Office is the cricket club and library.'

Waiting for the bus and listening to the two boys chatting none stop, Jane was thrilled that they were getting on so well and hoped that her other children would accept Rafe as readily as Ian had done.

On the bus to Bothal School, Ian kept up his commentary, 'That's Crisps, the toy shop and newspaper shop, am after a night time job there.'

Rafe managed to interject, 'My goodness, are you really starting work at night, but you are only thirteen?'

'Just a newspaper roond man, not a proper job like, that's the polis station and courts, that's St Aidans, the Catholic Church and tha school's behind and here's the Regal, the best picture hoose in Ashington.'

Rafe was taking it all in but had also noticed the long row of houses on the opposite side of the street. 'There's an awful lot of those houses and they all look the same,' he said.

Jane interjected, 'That's the Seventh Row, there are eleven rows here all together; we live in the Sixth Row.'

Rafe was shocked, 'You mean you live in one of those tiny houses?'

Ian quickly answered, 'Aye but not exactly the same, wor's has three bedrooms and they've just two and, we live next to the railway line and country and tha trees and bushes behind wor lavvies that are great for playing in.'

Ian pointed out the road down to the Institute and Swimming Pool, then Wilsons from where he delivered groceries, the Church at the Store Corner, the plantation, Willington's the Newsagents, Pearson's where Maureen worked and finally Bothal School when the bus pulled to a halt opposite it.

As they crossed the road, Ian said, 'That's where Aah gan te school, will Rafe be ganning there with me Mam?'

'Yes for the time being he will.'

Rafe looked at the mainly one story red-bricked Victorian school and said, 'It is very small isn't it, where are the playing fields?'

'We use the sports fields' ower the Rec' Bridge near where we live,' Ian said as he struggled with the heavy sports holdall.

The three of them struggled on through the cut between the school and Long Row, past the garden at the end of the Fourth Row, through the cut between two terraces of the Fifth Row and down the slope of the concrete road to the gap between the two terraces of the Sixth. Despite the cold they were hot from carrying the heavy suitcase and holdall and stopped to change grips.

Rafe looked down the Row and saw what he thought was a mini riot! 'What on earth is happening?' he asked.

Ian looked at the gaggle of kids further down the street and said, 'Football, it's just me friends playing football.

It was like no game of football Rafe had ever seen, a gang of six or seven lads were hacking, kicking and elbowing each other as they attempted to kick a battered leather ball in whatever direction they happened to be running. In addition, a scruffy black dog was adding to the confusion by running amongst them barking madly while having a quick nip at whatever ankle was closest. There appeared to be no structure to the game, no passing, no teams, every boy appeared to be playing for himself – it was pandemonium but did look exciting.

Picking up the luggage, the three of them struggled toward the footballers who had been too intent on kicking the ball too notice them until Jake spotted them and quickly scooping up the ball, ran over followed by the remainder of the lads and the still barking Monty.

The lads grouped themselves around Jake leaning against each other, sweating and panting from their game, the two smallest wiping dewdrops from their noses with the back of their tattered jumpers.

Rafe looked at the lads, noting Jake's infectious grin and battered clothing; Howard as tall as himself but heavier built looked clean, tidy and very well fed. Reg, tall gangly, narrow jawed and hook-nosed. Behind him, Geordie Turnbull the eldest of seven from the other end of the Row, and who always had a permanently bewildered frown. At the back, two smaller very scruffy younger kids, Roger and Billy Grundy sniffing dribbling snot back up their noses, Roger sporting a very red and sore looking Sty on his right eyelid.

It was Jake who spoke first, 'Aah thowt ye were ganning te fetch yer uncle, who's this posh bugga?

Smiling, Ian said, '*This is my uncle*, this is my Uncle Rafe; he's ganna live with us.'

'Another one for the gang then,' Reg said as Rafe stepped forward.

'Hi everyone, yes I'm Rafe and I'm very pleased to meet you all.'

Jake laughed and mimicked, 'Hi everyone, I'm Jake – he taalks just like ye Mrs Shepherd, right posh like.'

Jane replied, 'Well he is my brother Jake, now we must get him home, he has had a long day and I'm sure you will all get to know each other tomorrow,' and turning, she continued down the street followed by Rafe, Ian, the lads and a still excited Monty who let his feelings be known by barking loudly.

They had one more obstacle to overcome before they reached home – Aggie Galloway appeared at her gate smiling, 'Eeee, hello Jane Pet, isn't it lovely to see Ian up and aboot and who's this bonny young man ye've got there, I was telt ye had a brother coming te stay?'

Jane smiled, 'You heard correct Aggie this is my brother - my younger brother Rafe, Rafe say hello to Mrs Galloway.'

Dropping his suitcase, Rafe smiled charmingly and stepped forward, 'Hello Mrs Galloway, How do you do?'

Aggie ignored his outstretched hand, wrapping her arms around the much taller Rafe and snuggling into his chest, replied, 'I am very well young man and I am delighted te meet ye.' Then releasing the very embarrassed lad she said to Jane, 'By lass you've got some bonny laddies in yor hoose, ye can let me hev one of them if they get ower much for you!'

Smiling, Ian said awkwardly, 'Thanks for looking after me when Aah was poorly Mrs Galloway.'

'My pleasure bonny lad,' she replied before placing a plump hand on either side of his face and planting a big wet kiss on his shocked face.

Jane led the escape, followed by the two boys who were keen to leave before Mrs Galloway offered any more hugs or kisses.

When Rafe put his suitcase down in the kitchen, he was shocked at how small the house was and how poor the furnishings were but hid his shock and disappointment by looking at the kitchen range with its inviting and warming fire, saying, 'This is very cosy!'

Jane smiled at him, 'I know it's not what you are used to Rafe but I'm afraid it's all we have, it took me a while to adapt but I'm sure you will settle in.'

Rafe now felt like a clod, his sister who was less than well off financially, had agreed to take him in and look after him, 'I'm so sorry, I didn't mean to appear ungrateful and I'm sure I will love it here, it's just that it is all a bit strange at the moment.

Ian said, 'Wait till ye taste me Mam's cooking it's the best and we've got corned beef, tetties and dumplings tonight, ye'll love it.'

'I'm sure I will,' said Rafe, 'the food at Rugley was blooming awful.'

Laughing, Ian mimicked Rafe, 'Blooooming awful,'

Jane filled the kettle, plugged it into the socket next to the pantry door, and said, 'A cup of tea first then I need to talk to you about Mr Shepherd, Rafe.'

Ian grimaced at the mention of his father as Rafe looked around him and asked Ian quietly, 'Excuse me Ian but where *is* the loo?'

'Waat's the loo?'

Rafe hesitated, 'The lavatory, the loo, you know the toilet.'

'Ur ye mean the lavvy, the netty, the bog! It's ower the lane.'

'No seriously I really need to go, where is it?'

'Aah've telt ye, it's ower the lane.'

'Over the lane, do you mean it's outside on the other side of the street?'

'Aye, that's right, that's where all the lavvies are, come on and I'll show you which one's wor's.'

Rafe followed Ian out of the house and across the street to where the green doors of two coalhouses stood. 'Is it one of these?' asked Rafe.

'Nur look here, the forst door,' Ian said pointing to two doors that were down a tiny cut, facing the side of the coalhouses.

Rafe stepped inside as Ian looked in and said, I normally pinch a bog roll from school or Mike nicks one from the pit baths but it's that shinny skid stuff, that's why there's newspaper hanging there as weel.'

'Thanks but I just want a pee, but where does one wash one's hands?'

'One washes them back ower the road in the pantry, that's the ownly sink we hev.'

Emptying his bladder with some relief, Rafe asked, 'You mean you don't have a bathroom, where do you have a bath?'

Ian smiled and answered, 'Did ye see that lang zinc thing hanging on tha wall in the yard, whey that's the bath, we fill it we hot weter and hev a bath in front of the kitchen fire.'

106

Rafe was horrified, 'Are you saying that I have to bathe in front of everyone in the kitchen - that there's no privacy.'

'Only if you want te, We're too owld for that noo but Tommy still has one there, ye'll hev te gan te the Pit Baths like me or ower the Rec te the Rec Hall.'

The smell of food greeted them from the kitchen when they walked back in as Jane opened the oven door and slid six dumplings into the large stew tin that was simmering away. Pouring cups of tea for the three of them, she said, 'Sit down Rafe and let's talk.'

She explained how difficult it was living with Nick and that he did not eat with them, taking his main meal at the Pit Canteen. She warned him that Nick had a foul temper and that it was best that he kept out of his way whenever he could; this upset and annoyed Rafe, 'How could anyone be so mean?' he thought.

As he listened intently to her every word, Jane told him about the accident in the marsh and that Tommy was coming home the following day and then said, 'Maureen and Mike will be home from work shortly and they are so looking forward to meeting you.'

It was difficult to get a word in edge ways at dinner, Mike, Maureen and Ian bombarded Rafe with questions which he did his best to answer until Jane said 'That's enough now, give him a chance to eat his dinner, you have all the time in the world to ask questions.'

After dinner, Ian helped Rafe take his suitcase upstairs and showed him the cramped space he would be sleeping in. I would keep most of yer clathes in yer suitcase, out ye have te hang up will hev to gan in the wardrobe in Maureen's room but there's not much space in there,' he said, looking in wonder at all the smart clothes inside the suitcase when Rafe opened it.

Rafe took off his jacket and hung it in the wardrobe before pulling on a Rugley School purple jumper, 'There's just my sports kit to sort out now,' he said as he followed Ian back down stairs and into the kitchen where they had left the large Holdall.

Jane stopped clearing the table and nodding toward the sitting room, said quietly, 'Rafe, go and say hello to your Uncle Nick.'

Feeling very uneasy, he walked into the sitting room where Nick was sitting in the armchair in front of the fire smoking, 'Hello Uncle Nick, I'm Rafe.'

Nick turned and stood up before slowly looking Rafe up and down saying, 'Are you now?' He noted that Rafe was as tall as he was, a good three was or four inches taller than Ian and that, he was blonde-haired with striking blue eyes and clean good looks.

Rafe held his hand out but Nick ignored it and turning his back on Rafe, sat back down in the chair and took another long drag from his cigarette leaving Rafe to stand in awkward embarrassed silence.

Ian nudged Rafe in the back and said, 'Haway the let's see what ye've got in yer sports bag.' They spent a few minutes examining the contents; rugby ball and boots, cricket gear, a set of boxing gloves and boots, running shoes, two tennis rackets and three balls, everything except a football!

'Didn't ye play football at your school then?'

'Yes they did but I chose to play rugger instead, it's a much better game.'

Brushing his teeth in the pantry, Mike came out and stated, 'Niver, football is the best game by a mile man.'

Jane made them close up the bag and store it in the lean-to shed on the gable end of the house but not before, they had taken out a cricket bat and tennis ball for a game in the back lane using a dustbin for stumps. Within minutes, most of the lads in the Row had joined them, all of them trying their best, fast or spin bowls, googlies and full throws to hit the dustbin that Rafe protected, hitting every ball with nonchalant ease until Ian caught a careless tap that was greeted with loud and triumphant shouts of 'HOWZAT!'

The cheering dragged Jane from the pantry where she was washing dishes, to the back door where she was joined by Mike who was leaving to meet his pals for a night at the 'Tanner Hop' at the other side of town. 'Isn't it lovely that Rafe and Ian have hit it off,' she said smiling.

'Aye they're like mismatched twins,' Mike replied as he left for the dance.

Keen to take some bets for tomorrows races, Nick limped to the 'Doon' just after eight o'clock, 'At least it's not frigging raining tonight,' he thought to himself as he fiddled with the flick knife he had bought at 'Peter's Surplus Stores' that afternoon. He had decided that he needed a little extra protection now that he was regularly carrying a wad of cash and, more stories of the McArdle twins ruthlessness had come to light – 'Just for self-defence,' he told himself.

Chapter 7
Comings and Goings!

Despite the strange surroundings and the occasional sound of a steam engine shunting coal trucks, Rafe was surprised how well he had slept, he was of course used to sleeping in a dormitory with a dozen other boys but they had considerably more space between the beds than there was in the attic bedroom of his sister's house. He had been awake for some time listening to the sounds of steam engines shunting coal wagons a few hundred yards away but was reluctant to get out of the warmth of his bed until Ian shook his shoulder and said, 'Haway then, it's time ye were up if yer ganna de the paper roond we me.'

As Nick had not mentioned whether or not he was going to accompany Jane and Mike to the hospital to collect Tommy, Jane had thought it a good idea for Rafe to spend the morning with Ian. With Maureen at work, she did not think it sensible for him to be in the house alone with.

Standing in the corner of the kitchen where the Milkman had placed it, Rafe's trunk stood like a silent monolith as the two boys sat down at the table. 'Porridge, this is just like Rugley,' Rafe said as he took the bowl of steaming cereal from Jane.

'There's Jam, honey or sugar if you want it sweetened,' Jane said as she filled another bowl for Ian.

Ian asked, 'Mam, wor Tommy's ganning te be alright, isn't he?'

'Yes he is Pet, but he will be spending some time on the sofa in the sitting room until he is fully recovered but I thought you knew that?'

'Aye Aah did, Aah was just wondering when he would be able te play ootside like?'

'Not straight away but it won't be long, why?'

'Aah thowt I'd get him a present like, ye kna te welcome him hyem.'

Rubbing his hair affectionately, Jane said, 'Ah, that is sweet of you but I thought you were saving your money for a bike, I hope you're not going to spend a lot?'

'Aah kna that he's alwas wanted a pair of roller skates so am ganning te buy him a pair, Aah'll soon save me money up again.'

Unable to answer, Jane nodded and walked into the pantry to catch the tears that were filling up her eyes and silently thanked God that Ian had inherited his father's good looks but none of his nasty traits.

Maureen came down the stairs, walked into the kitchen but turned suddenly and ran out across the road to the toilet. 'Ye've scared wor Maureen that much she's runaway Rafe,' Ian joked.

As Rafe smiled and answered smoothly, 'I have that effect on all the girls!' Jane walked to the kitchen window to look across at the toilet, a worried look clouding her face.

'Jake gave me a hand with the papers and grocery deliveries for the forst couple of weeks after Aah was bad but I divint think he'll be oot his bed teday, he likes his weekend lie in,' Ian said to Rafe as they walked briskly to Willington's meeting up with Reg at the Third Row.

'Mr Willington this is my Uncle Rafe and he's ganning te come with me te see what delivering papers is like in case ye tek on another lad,' Ian said as the three of them walked into the Newsagents.

Rafe stepped forward and thrust out his hand, 'How do you do Sir?'

Taken aback by the immaculately dressed Rafe's manners and speech, Mr Willington grabbed his hand and muttered, 'Champion son, I'm champion and you are Ian's uncle?'

'Yes Sir I am but there is only a month's difference in our ages and I do hope that you will be able to provide me with employment.'

'Aye well the crafty bugga knows that I'll be wanting a lad te take on Wansbeck Road, Green Lane and Park Villas next week as I'm teking on more customers.'

Delivering the papers that morning took longer than normal, the few folk that they bumped into were keen to find out more about the well dressed, polite boy who thrust his hand at them and introduced himself as, 'Rafe, Ian's uncle.'

Back at number 60, in slippers, crumpled shirt, trousers with dangling braces, unshaven, unkempt, smelling of stale beer and cheap perfume, Nick stood at the foot of the stairs and snarled at Jane in the kitchen, 'What time are ye ganning te pick Tom up?'

Surprised that he had even remembered, Jane replied, 'Mike and I are catching the eleven o'clock bus.'

'That's not waat Aah asked ye woman, waat time are ye due te pick him up at the hospital?'

'Twelve.'

'Aye, whey Aah might tek ye in me car.' he said before hurrying out and across the street to the toilet, leaving Jane and Mike looking at each other wondering if they had heard him correctly – 'car?'

Nick new they would be curious as hell and took his time over the road before lighting a cigarette and limping back into the kitchen to sit down at the kitchen table waiting for the inevitable questions.

'Okay Nick, what car, how can you afford a car when we can barely afford to live?' Jane demanded.

'Whey since ye left my bed it's none of your blidy business waat money Aah hev or waat Aah de with it, anyway ye are getting another five pund a week for that blonde haired simpleton of a brother of yours. If ye must know, I'm getting a car this morning and I'll tek ye te pick they bairn up in it.'

Jane was perplexed, how could he possibly afford the money to buy a car? 'How can you buy a car when we barely have enough money to survive Nick?'

Placing the teacup he had been slurping tea from, back on the table, Nick took a long slow drag from his cigarette and snarled, 'Aah've got ways of making money and if ye want some of it then ye'll hev te be a proper wife te me again.'

Jane looked at him with disgust and whispered, 'That will never happen Nick Shepherd.'

Anger building up inside him, He spat back, 'In that case divint expect any more money from me and divint ask any more questions cos yer not entitled te blidy kna.'

Mike who had stood in the doorway to the sitting room, spoke up, 'Aah know where ye getting yer money from, yer running a book at the Fell-em-Doon and if ye get caught ye'll get locked up.'

Nick rose from the chair and advanced menacingly toward Mike, 'Ye'd better keep yer gob shut if ye kna what's good for ye lad,' but when Mike stood his ground, he turned away and went upstairs to dress.

Having promised to fit a light in his parents outside loo, Edward Thompson parked his car outside his mother's house, climbed out and opened the boot to take out his toolbox just as Nick limped down the street. 'Aye Nick, I hear Thomas is coming home teday?'

Nick scowled at Edward and limped on without replying, he was off to complete the deal on the Riley at Gibson's and he couldn't wait to drive the car back and show Thompson that he had his own car and a very smart one at that. He had told Jane and Mike that he would be back by eleven to drive them to the hospital and there was to be no arguments, he was taking them to collect *his* son.

Ian and Rafe had eventually finished the paper round and were half way through the grocery deliveries at Wilson's where Rafe proved to be a huge hit with the young female shop assistants who all wanted to hear him talk in his posh voice which he was more than happy to do.

114

Much to Ian's embarrassment, Margaret grabbed him around the neck, gave him a peck on the cheek and said, 'He might have a posh voice and be a charmer but ye are still the best looking laddie roond here!'

As Ian set off with a delivery for Green lane, Rafe stayed in the shop helping Margaret prepare more deliveries, including weighing and packaging sugar and rice.

While the boys were enjoying their morning, Maureen was anything but! She had had another wretched morning feeling nauseas and had rushed to the toilets at the rear of Pearson's shop to throw up twice that morning as waves of panic driven fear engulfed her. What was she going to do? She had missed another period, she must be pregnant; her life was finished! What would Terry do if she told him; he was only 16, the same age as Mike! She couldn't let her father know as she was sure he would throw her out, her mother was the only one she thought might help her but she could not bring herself to tell her?

Completing the paper work for the finance on the car had taken longer than Nick had thought; it was after eleven before he finally drove the Riley out of Gibson's, turned left and parked opposite the chip shop a 100 yards past the Fell-em-Doon. Tooting the horn of the Riley, he looked up at the grimy window above the chip shop and saw Ginny pull back the curtain and wave before she hurried down stairs and out across the road to climb in the passenger seat next to him.

Wearing a tight fitting pink jumper, she thrust her breasts at Nick and pouting her bright red lips and whispered as sexily as she could, 'This is beautiful Nick, ye 've got te take me for a quick ride before I start work.'

Nick couldn't resist, she looked red hot and sitting behind the wheel of his new car, he certainly felt randy, 'You look blidy gud enough te eat,' and slipping the clutch he drove off, heading for a quiet spot at Sheepwash down on the banks of the River Wansbeck a mile away.

Jane was furious, it was after eleven, Nick had not turned up and the Newcastle bus had left, the next one would not be for another 40 minutes making them an hour late to collect Tommy! Standing at the gate watching for signs of his father, Mike was not surprised when he had not turned up and seeing Edward wiring the light fitting in his parent's outside toilet, he walked down to talk to him. Mike explained what had happened and asked if Edward could take them to the Hospital as otherwise they would be very late.

A few minutes later Edward drove out of the Sixth Row with a relieved Jane and Mike aboard and headed for Newcastle as Nick and Ginny made violent love in the front seat of the Riley!

Nick sat back in the driver's seat and lit a cigarette as Ginny pulled her panties back on and slid her black skirt down from around her waist, smoothing the wrinkles before twisting the car's interior mirror to check her make up. As she applied a fresh layer of lipstick, Nick said, 'It's quarter te twelve, Aah'd best drop ye of at the Club and get roond te wor hoose and pick me missus up, Aah've got te tek her to Hospital te pick the bairn up and am late but that's just frigging tough.'

Ginny leant over, rubbed the inside of Nick's thigh and asked, 'Why divint ye move in with me Nick, ye'd be far better off than living with her and all them bairns?'

He opened the car window and flicked the stub of his cigarette out, 'Ye niver kna Pet, Aah might just de that one of these days soon,' and started the engine before driving slowly out from under the trees where he had parked, heading back to Highmarket.

After finishing delivering the groceries, Ian and Rafe had stopped at Badiallie's Café for a Pepsi and a Kit Kat each before walking along to

Crisp's toy shop and newsagents where Ian was set on buying roller skates for Tommy.

Inside the shop, examining a pair of skates with metal wheels, Ian was interrupted by Rafe who had picked up a set with rubber wheels, 'These look as though they are much better than those ones Ian.'

'Aye they are, they are the new sort but tha five bob more than these and Aah want te buy wor Mike a pair of shin guards for his borthday on Tuesda.'

Rafe looked at the two sets of skates and said, 'My Father said that you should always buy the best quality you can afford as it will save you money in the long run.'

Ian thought for a moment and said, 'Aye, Aah think he is right like, Tom will love the rubber ones and he'll use them all the time and tha much betta made, that's it then, Aah'll buy them.'

Having dropped Ginny off at the Fell-em-Doon, Nick drove slowly into the Sixth Row, hoping there would be many folk about to admire his Riley, he wasn't disappointed. Three of the Turnbull brood were playing cannon at the corner but stopped when they saw the sleek red car and ran after it shouting and cheering, gathering around it when Nick stopped next to Albert Grundy who had come out of his little workshop to see who was making all the commotion.

'Whey am beggared Nick lad, that's a belter ye've got there.' Albert said as he used his greasy rag to swat George, the eldest Turnbull off the running board of Nick's car.

A self-satisfied smile spreading across his face, Nick replied, 'Yep it's a 1951 one and a half litre RMA, goes like the clappers.'

Albert walked slowly round the car, swatting kids here and there until back at the driver's side, he looked down at Nick's smug face, 'Aah alwas thowt this model was underpowered, noo the two and a half litre, there's an engine, a bet one of those can gan like the clappers?'

117

Stung by Albert's remark, Nick spat, 'What the fuck div ye kna?' and drove off to the end of the Row where with some crunching of the gears, he carried out a three point turn before parking up outside his house.

As he climbed out Aggie Galloway came trotting over and asked, 'Hev ye won the pools lad, who on Earth can ye afford that?'

Nick brushed past her snarling, 'Mind yer an blidy business woman,' and stormed into the house. Expecting to have a confrontation with Jane, he was angry when he found the house empty and thinking they must have caught the bus he limped back out to his car where, Arthur Galloway had joined his wife to examine the sleek red Riley.

'Are ye looking for your lass?' Aggie asked as she and her husband stepped back onto the pavement.

'Aah've already telt ye te mind yer an business,' he spat as he limped around to the driver's side of the car.

Five foot ten inches tall, fifty year old Arthur Galloway had been toughened by years of work underground, he was not about to let Aggie be insulted by his loathsome next door neighbour; stepping forward he said firmly, 'How, divint ye speak te the Missus like that ye nasty blidy waster ye.'

Nick was at boiling point, 'now he was being threatened by a grey haired old git,' he let go of the car door and walked toward Arthur but stopped when he saw the Massive George Holland walk from his gate to join Albert.

Staring angrily at the pair, he snarled, 'Aah cannit be bothered we ye two, Aah've business to attend te,' and turned to limp back to his car.

Follow Nick back to his car, George waited until Nick climbed into the driving seat, then leaning forward warned, 'Aah wud tread very carefully and quietly if Aah was ye or ye might just get waat ye deserve, yer blidy lucky Aah was here cos Arthur wud have giving ye a reet gud fettling if ye had pushed him.'

Nick tried to pull the door closed but George held it open until Nick stopped pulling then gently pushed the door shut and wagged his finger at him as though he was a naughty child.

Maureen walked into an empty house just after one o'clock and after filling the kettle and plugging it; she spooned tealeaves into the teapot but had to stop when her fears and emotions got the better of her. Crying uncontrollably, she collapsed into the fireside chair where she rocked herself back and forth, tears streaming down her pretty face.

As Maureen sat crying, Ian and Rafe walked into the Sixth Row, both hungry and looking forward to eating whatever Maureen was preparing for them. The street appeared deserted apart from Howard who was cleaning his bike but stopped and stood up as they approached, 'Aah like yer faather's new car,' he said.

Ian looked at him incredulously and asked, 'Waat new car?'

'Yer faather's driving a big red Riley, it looks right good.'

'Whey I didn't know he was getting one,' Ian said as Mr Holland walked out of his house and joined them.

'So this'll be yer Uncle Rafe then?'

'Aye it is Mr Holland, Rafe, this is Howard's Dad.'

Rafe said, Hello Mr Holland,' and put out his hand a little timidly wondering if the huge man in front of him would crush it.

George Holland shook Rafe's hand and seeing the box in Ian's hand asked, 'What hev ye been spending yer hard urned money on then nipper?'

Ian opened the box to show him the roller skates and answered, 'Some skates for wor Tommy to help him cheer up when he comes home and Aah bought wor Mike some shin guards for his birthday and to say thanks, ye kna for saving me life.'

'That's a smashing thing te de lad but wor Howard telt me ye were saving yer money te buy a bike?'

'Aye, I was - I am it'll just tek me langer that's aall.'

Raising a huge hand, George Holland scratched his head as he studied the two boys before asking Rafe, 'So will ye be staying for lang then lad?'

'I hope so Mr Holland, it is the only home I have.'

Grinning at them, George said, 'Well in that case come we me the pair of ye, I have something that ye might be interested in,' and turned and walked into the house.

Ian looked at Howard who shrugged his shoulders and said, 'Aah divint kna what he's on aboot, ye better follow him,' and all three boys hurried after Mr Holland who walked straight through the house and out into the front garden. The gardens of the sixth were not quite as long as the gardens in the other 'Rows' but still over twenty foot long. In keeping with the majority of the others, the Holland's used theirs to provide vegetables but there was also a large patch dedicated for the almost religious local passion of leek growing. Many of the gardens had sheds or chicken huts and a couple had rabbit hutches where the occupants bred animals destined for their kitchens.

Sitting at the end of the garden, a wooden garage opened onto the rough alley way sandwiched between the gardens and the backs of the toilets, coalhouses and air-raid shelters of the Fifth Row. Opening the doors to the garage, Mr Holland said over his shoulder, 'Hang on noo,' and disappeared inside.

The penny dropped for Howard and he said excitedly, 'Yer ganna love this!'

Ian and Rafe listened in puzzled silence to the sound of the big man moving things about in the cluttered garage until he popped his head round the door and said, 'Ready?'

The two boys nodded their heads and watched as he slowly emerged with a bicycle that developed into a tandem as he pushed it into the alley. 'There ye are lads, just the thing for ye, it was bought ages ago for me and wor lass but we ownly used it the once. I'm far ower big for the blidy silly little thing and cudn't get the seat up high enough and wor lass is just ower big for riding bikes noo if ye kna what I mean.'

Ian and Rafe looked on in stunned silence as Mr Hollande wiped the bike over with a rag he had brought out of the garage, 'Whey waat de ye think, aall it needs is a gud clean, the tyres pumping up and some 'Three in One' oil and a bit of tightening and adjusting here and there?'

The boys did not answer, they just stared at the tandem until Mr Holland, thinking they were not interested, asked, 'Whey if ye divint want it, it's aboot time Aah sold it te somebody Aah suppose.'

Ian looked at Rafe and as they stared at each other, huge grins spread over their faces, Ian almost shouted, 'Aah think it's brilliant Mr Holland but I haven't got much money left to pay for it.'

'Pay for it! No lad, Aah divint want paying for it, it's yor's if ye want it, it's just teking up space deeing nowt, go on lads tek it, I'm sure ye'll hev some fun we it.'

Ian took the handlebars from Mr Holland as Rafe said, 'Thank you so much this is very generous of you.' The two lads wheeled the bike into their own garden and up to the lean-to shed where they turned the bike upside down, opened the shed, grabbed a bag full of tools and began tinkering with their newly acquired transport system. Close inspection and a bit of cleaning revealed that it was a 'Twickenham Eagle' with drop touring handlebars and 'Sturmey Archer' combined brakes and three speed hubs; 'This is a brilliant tandem,' said Ian.

121

'And very classy!' said Rafe.

Tommy found it impossible to sit still; every time he saw a nurse and despite being able to read the time on the clock at the end of the ward, he asked 'What time is it please?' Time appeared to be going backwards as he waited for his mother to arrive to take him home. 'Am going home teday,' he told anyone and everyone within hearing range. His excitement mounting as the clock struggled uphill to twelve and then she was there.

She bent over and gave him a kiss on the cheek that he self-consciously wiped off, shows of emotion were not something that he went in for but his emotions were boiling over as his mother picked up the paper carrier bag with the few bits and pieces he had accumulated during his three weeks in hospital. After he said his goodbyes and Jane her thanks, he took hold of his mother's outstretched hand and walked out of the ward and through the hospital to the waiting area where Mike waited with Mr Edwards. Again there was no great demonstration of affection, Mike ruffled Tommy's hair and said, 'Haway kidder, let's get ye hyem,' but those few words implied more than any gushing words could ever mean.

Edward's car pulled up outside Jane's house just after one thirty and as she stepped out the car with Tommy, she turned and said to Edward, 'You will come in for a cup of tea won't you?'

Inside, Maureen had pulled herself together and had poured boiling water into the teapot before placing the plate of cakes and pies that she had brought home from Pearson's, on the kitchen table. When her mother walked in with the Tommy, Maureen ran forward and much to his pretend disgust, gave him a hug which he shrugged off, saying 'Am starving hev you got owt to eat?'

Jane said, 'First into the sitting room, it's bed on the sofa for you young man and we'll bring you something through. Tommy did not argue, the fire in the sitting room looked cosy and the bedding on the sofa very inviting, he was soon tucked up devouring a slice of corned beef pie as if he hadn't eaten for days.

'Where's Ian and Rafe,' Jane asked Maureen.

'I haven't seen them Mam,' Maureen replied as Aggie Galloway walked in.

'Hello pet, hoo's the bairn then?' she asked Jane.

'He's fine and I think very happy to be home, he's in there, you can go in and see him.'

As Aggie walked into the sitting room, Ian and Rafe walked in through the back door, Ian with the box containing the roller skates asked, 'Is he home?'

Smiling, Jane replied, 'Yes he's on the sofa, go on in, he's dying to see the pair of you.'

The two boys stepped into the sitting room just as Aggie planted one of her 'Specials' on Tommy who was unable to dodge her show of affection and had to wait until she released him before he wiped his face with the back of his hand. On seeing Ian and Rafe, Aggie moved to one side and said, 'Here's yer bonny brother that saved ye and yer bonny new uncle.'

Tommy smiled at Ian as he approached the sofa; it was the first time since the accident that they were able to speak to each other, 'Alright Tom?' Ian asked self-consciously.

Tommy grinned and touching Ian's arm replied, 'Aye, I am noo.' That was it; those few words expressed the brother's love for one another, a love that was unbreakable.

Rafe had held back while his two cousins greeted each other but now stepped forward smiling, 'Hi Thomas, I'm Rafe, I am so happy to meet you at last, Ian has told me all about you, apparently you are a tad accident prone?'

Tommy looked up at the tall good-looking lad in front of him and said, 'Ye talk just like me Mam.'

'Well I am her brother so I suppose that's to be expected.'

Aggie chuckled and spoke up, 'Niver mind Rafe, we'll soon hev ye taalking proper like us, eh Tommy?'

Turning to Aggie, Rafe said, 'Whey aye man,' which made her chuckle even more.

Ian handed the box to Tommy and said, 'Here I got ye these, Aah kna ye've wanted a pair for a long time like.' Tommy lifted the lid and seeing the roller skates, was unable to speak as his emotions got the better of him and a tear rolled down his cheek. Unsure whether his brother was pleased or not, Ian asked, 'Aah can change them for something else if ye divint like them?' Still unable to speak, Tommy shook his head and hugged the skates in a demonstration of how much he was pleased with Ian's gift.

Leaving the boys in the sitting room, Aggie stepped into the kitchen where Jane asked, 'Will you have a cup of tea with us Aggie and a piece of cake or pie?' Not being one to refuse food, she pulled out the chair next to Edward and sat down reaching for a rock bun as Jane poured her a cup of tea.

Aggie took a sip of tea and looking at the calendar hanging on the wall by the pantry door, asked, 'Is that Scotland Jane?'

Jane smiled, 'Yes Aggie, that's Balmoral Castle.'

Aggie sighed, 'Eee, me and wor Arthur wud love te gan there on a holiday, mebe one of these fine days eh?' and took a large bite out of her bun as she stared wistfully at the calendar.

Nick had been busy taking bets and telling his regulars that he would be opening a book on Wednesday for the 'Grand National'. He was hoping to make a good few quid next Saturday, as just about everyone in the pubs and clubs liked a little flutter on the big race. After visiting the Portland and Grand, he popped back into the Fell em Doon for a whisky and to tell Ginny that he would be back to see her later.

Climbing back into his car, he drove around to the Sixth Row, wondering if Jane and Mike had arrived back from collecting Tommy and mentally prepared himself for some angry words from them for failing to drive them to Newcastle. 'Sod them,' he thought to himself, 'Aah've got me an life to live and I needed te be here to tek me bets anyway.'

Swinging into the Sixth Row his mood darkened considerably when he saw Edwards Jowett parked at the end of the Row, wondering why it was there he accelerated up the lane, screeched to a halt behind Edwards car and stormed into the house. In the kitchen the sight of Jane, Mike, Maureen, Aggie and Edward sitting at *his* table eating and drinking sent him into a rage, 'Whey just look at this, isn't this just fucking cosy noo. Iviry bugga enjoying themselves playing happy frigging families in my hoose, waat are ye deeing here noo Thompson?'

Edward rose to his feet and glared at the irate Nick as Jane said, 'I invited him in for lunch, he drove Mike and me to Newcastle seeing as how you didn't turn up when you said you would and we'd missed the bus.'

Consumed with rage, Nick spat, 'Aah did turn up ye stupid cow, Aah was just a bit late but could ye wait, nur not ye, ye jumped into that bugga's car – any chance te be we him ye fucking whore ye!'

Edward stepped from behind the table and said, 'Calm down Nick, it was Mike who asked for the lift not Jane,'

Mike joined in, 'Aye it was me that asked him seeing that ye couldn't even torn up on time te gan and pick yer son up!'

Nick glared maniacally at Mike and shouted, '*Ye can shut ye frigging gob an all, it's this cliver bastard here that Aah want oot my hoose noo and his fucking car moved from outside before Aah swing for the lot of ye.*'

Jane tried to calm Nick down, 'He's just leaving; now I think you should calm down and go in and see your son who ye haven't seen for three weeks.'

Nick was not about to calm down, 'Aah've telt ye woman, ye canna tell me what te de, ye nee frigging wife te me, this fucka here is trying te tek ye from me, just hang on noo,' he stormed into the living room ignoring the three lads who had been listening to him raging.

Scared at the sight of his angry father, Tommy jumped from the sofa and stepped behind Ian as Nick opened the display cabinet, grabbed his medal and stormed back into the kitchen and threw it at Edward, 'Here, ye've stolen me fucking wife ye might as well tek this as ye think yer entitled to it,' and turning to Jane snarled, 'Ye've made yer fucking bed, ye can sleep in it cos am off,' and limped quickly out leaving everyone staring at the door in bewildered embarrassment.

Aggie was first to speak, 'Eeee, that wasn't very nice was it, yer best shot of him pet,' and stood up putting her arm around Jane who had tears rolling down her cheeks.

Edward followed Nick outside and watched as he swung the Riley back and forwards to turn it around, knocking over a dust bin in his haste before roaring off down the Row. Mike joined him at the gate in time to see the car disappear round the corner at the bottom of the Row, 'We're better off withoot him, he's blidy mental.'

Edward said quietly, 'I better be ganning Mike, I think it's best if Aah stay away from ye all, I divint want te mek matters worse, tell yer mam will ye?'

'Aye, Aah will but what was me Father on about the medal for Mr Thompson?'

126

'Nowt lad, it's up te him te tell ye not me,' Edward said and climbing into his car, drove back to his parent's house.

Back inside Maureen, her own problem forgotten for the moment was consoling Jane as Aggie made another pot of tea – 'To calm every one down.' Tommy had climbed back onto the sofa as a stunned Rafe asked Ian, 'Does that happen very often?'

'Aye when he's drunk, then ye hev te be careful that ye not aboot or he'll daad ye as well!'

'Do you mean he hit you?'

'Aye, he used te hit us for nowt but noo that Mike's as big as him it's not as bad as it was.'

Tommy said, 'I hope the pig doesn't come back, Aah hate him!'

Rafe shook his head and said, 'Well we cannot allow him to bully any of us can we, especially your mother.'

Walking into the room, Jane heard Rafe's remark, 'There is no possibility of that happening again Rafe, his days of bullying this family are over, so all of you please try not to worry about him, I will deal with him from now on.'

Later, Ian and Rafe wheeled the resurrected Tandem from the garden into the lane and brought Jane and Mike out to see their new acquisition.

Delighted that here was at last something to lighten the mood and take the boy's minds off the events of lunchtime, Jane said, 'That's wonderful boys; I hope you thanked Mr Holland for his generosity?'

Mike looked at the bike and said, 'Whey it's a belter but who's ganning on the front and who's ganning on the back?'

Rafe leant on Ian's' shoulder and answered, 'Well, as Ian knows Ashington and I don't, I suppose he will have to steer and anyway as I'm taller than him. I'll be able to see over his head!'

'Sounds good te me, said Ian, 'howay then lowp on and let's gan.'

As they pedalled off, Jane shouted, 'Make sure your back in time for dinner.'

Parking the Riley in Highmarket, Nick walked around the back of the Fell-em-Doon and along to the rear of the Fish and Chip shop where he had taken the outside staircase to the landing on the first floor that led to Ginny's and another a door to stairs that dropped down to the side of the shop. Ginny had been about to go down town when Nick banged loudly on her door. 'Eee, Aah wasn't expecting ye this afternoon Pet but it's lovely te see ye, are ye after more....'

Nick stopped her in mid-sentence and brushing past her walked into the small flat, 'We need te talk, Aah want te spend the night here and we need te discuss waat we are ganning te de in the lang run.' He had certainly not intended to make any commitment to her, nor had he any long-term plans for the two of them; he just needed somewhere to stay while he decided what to do next but knew if he were to string her along that, he would have to tell her a few lies.

Ginny threw her arms around his neck and whispered in his ear, 'That's lovely Nick, I knew you wud come te me eventually, have ye brought yer things with ye?'

Taking her arms from around his neck, he answered curtly, 'Not yet, Aah'll get them the morn morning before iviry buggas aboot, noo de ye need te gan anywhere before ye gan back te work cos my chariot awaits ye?'

Ian and Rafe cycled around to the Store Corner, past Wilson's and into town and along Station Road as Ian took Rafe on a grand tour of Ashington pointing out cinemas, cafes and the wide-ranging mix of shops. They had had a few problems mastering the tandem but were enjoying the freedom of going where they pleased, eventually ending up at the Pit Baths and Canteen. Ian said, 'This is where I come for a shower and ye can get a meal in the canteen for a Bob, which reminds me, we need te get home, it's nearly dinner time.'

Jane served Toad in the hole, mash, peas and gravy to Maureen and the hungry boys and watched in awe as all the plates, apart from Maureen's, were soon cleared! Rafe and Ian talked excitedly about the tandem and their ride around Ashington while Tommy, who was wearing his skates, sat listening intently. Eventually Jane said, 'Ok everyone I'm just going to put Tommy back in his bed then the rest of us need to talk.'

Managing to convince Tommy that he would be far more comfortable without his skates, Jane sat back down at the kitchen table and said, 'We need to discuss money and how we are going to manage if your father does not return or if he leaves us.'

Mike said quietly and passionately, 'The sooner he buggas of the betta!'

'Yes Mam, we are all carrying scars from his attacks, both physically and mentally,' added Maureen.

Ian did not say anything; he had spent most of his young life terrified that he would upset his father over some trivia and receive another vicious battering, he had no love or respect for him and would be very happy if he did not see the miserable bully again.

Jane said, 'Okay this is how things stand at the moment, Mike and Maureen are both working but their wages are very small, I have spent some time looking at becoming a nurse again and will start retraining at Ashington Hospital later in the year. However I am starting work, serving in the baker's in Highmarket next week when hopefully Tommy will be back at school.' Her children and Rafe listened intently as she continued, 'I receive £5 a week for Rafe which will be very helpful but we are obviously going to have to be very careful on what we spend our money on.'

Ian spoke up, 'Aah'll start handing over me paper and grocery delivery money Mam, there's nee need te save for a bike noo that Rafe and me have got the tandem.'

Jane smiled at Ian and said, 'That will come in handy until we know how we are doing pet, thanks for that.'

Mike ruffled Ian's hair and said, 'Well done Young'un.'

Feeling he needed to add something to the pot that he had actually earned, Rafe said, 'Mr Willington said that I might be able to begin delivering newspapers next week so that will add a little more.'

'Aye and Rafe and me can gan doon te Crisps and put wor names doon for evening deliveries as weel,' chirped Ian, glad that he would be able to relax at home without fear of his Father.

Putting both hands flat on the table, Jane said, 'Well it looks as though we *might* be able to manage but we will have to do without luxuries for a while and we certainly will not be able to afford new clothes just now, you will all have to take care of what you have.'

Having listened to her mother spell out how every penny was needed, Maureen was overcome with worry, she would have to give up her job in a few months and how would she be able to cope with a baby when it looked as though they were going to be almost destitute. Unable to contain her worries and fears, she burst out crying and ran upstairs to her bedroom.

Thinking that his mother's statement on not buying clothes was responsible for Maureen's sudden departure, Mike said, 'Whey that surprises me, Aah didn't think that would upset her that much.'

Jane looked sadly at Mike and said, 'I don't think she is upset about clothes or not being able to buy new ones.' Quickly changing the subject, she looked at the huge trunk standing on end in the corner of the room, 'Rafe what have you got in your trunk, we are going to have to move it out of here tonight?'

Rafe had a 'eureka' moment – 'Good God Jane, I forgot, all my clothes, the one's that fit me are upstairs in my suitcase, half of the trunk is filled with all my old clothes that I have had since I started school three years ago, they are all too small for me' then looking at Ian said, 'but I know who they will fit!'

Gathering round the trunk, they all watched as Rafe unfastened the leather straps and then sprung the clasp open before swinging the two halves of the trunk apart, cascading clothes and books onto the kitchen floor. 'Sorry,' he laughed, 'I'm not a very good at packing!'

They sorted the books first; 'The Complete Works of Dickens, fought with the novels of Tennyson, Sir Walter Scott, Robert Louis Stevenson, Edgar Rice Burroughs, the Brontes and Sir Arthur Conan Doyle for space on the floor, overwhelming a scattering of text books. 'Father always made sure I had the best to read, not that I have read them all by any means,' said Rafe.

Jane nodded and picked up a leather bound copy of 'Jane Eyre', stroked the worn cover and said pensively, 'He did Rafe; this was one of mine!'

They organised the books by Authors and carried into the sitting room, where they stacked next to the sideboard against the rear wall – 'Until we get a bookcase,' said Jane.

Rafe began sorting through the clothes, excitedly handing them to a surprised and delighted Ian, 'Here my first school blazer and my walking out blazer,' he said as he handed over two expensive jackets that were followed by several pairs of trousers, shirts, pullovers, three pairs of leather shoes and a pair of tennis shoes. 'These were all just kept in my overflow locker instead of being sold off, what luck ay.'

Jane picked up the deep purple school blazer and looking at the Rugley badge on the breast pocket, said, 'I'll take the badge of this one and yours Rafe, you'll be the two smartest boys at school!'

Mike had watched with some delight as Rafe handed trousers and shirts over to Ian who stepped into the sitting room to pull on a pair of trousers before walking back into the kitchen beaming, 'Look, they're a purfect fit.'

Looking at the old clock ticking steadily away on the mantel-piece, Mike said, 'Ye two are ganna hev all the lasses chasing ye's when ye get dolled up in them fancy clathes.'

Jane added, 'None of you will need fancy clothes to have the girls chasing after you, you are all beautiful boys.

'Aye be that as may,' Mike said, 'Aah've got te get my suit on as it's time to take my new girlfriend to the pictures and then the Arcade.'

Jane gave a mock frown and asked 'And what new girlfriend is that?'

'A lass Ah met last week, she lives at Morpeth and is coming to see me here so she must be keen, she's a right bonny sixteen year owld lass and is still at Morpeth Grammar School.'

Smiling, Jane warned, 'Well make sure you behave like a gentleman and, make sure she catches her bus home.'

'She's not catching the bus home, her dad is picking her up in his car at half past ten at the Arcade before any bother starts with any drunks.'

Just after seven o'clock, Mike had butterflies as he met the dark haired, demure and very pretty Jennifer at Ashington bus station and was thrilled when she placed a leather-gloved hand in his as they walked the few yards to the Wallaw picture house. It was the start of an enjoyable night, sitting upstairs holding hands with her head on his shoulder, he did not feel the time was right to put his arm around her and kiss her even though he ached to do so.

The Arcadians were already in full swing at nine o'clock when they climbed the beautiful marble staircase of the imposing Co-op building to the Arcade ballroom on the top floor where only three couples were brave enough to be the first few on the floor for the first dance of the evening, a foxtrot. Jennifer did not hesitate, after handing in their coats; she immediately headed for the dance floor pulling a reluctant Mike after her.

She turned and asked Mike, 'You can dance can't you?'

Smiling he said, 'Sort of,' and then whisked her away skipping across the floor with her as though they had danced together many times. Later he told her that his mother had taught him and Maureen to dance when they began secondary school and had continued to teach them after they left school. The rest of the evening was a blur as they danced and chatted and danced some more.

Jennifer's father pulled up outside the Arcade in his Rover at exactly ten thirty and climbed out to meet Mike who was standing nervously at the kerb with Jennifer. Over six foot with chiselled looks and thick dark hair that had grey streaks just above his ears, Jennifer's father, Doctor Jonathon Metcalf looked Mike slowly up and down before saying, 'Well, at least you are on time,' and opened the front door of the car for his daughter.

Jennifer carefully pushed the door closed and said, 'Daddy this is Mike, I thought you could drop him off at High Market as we drive through!'

Grasping Mikes outstretched hand, the Doctor shook it firmly, noting Mike's strong grip and steady eye contact, 'Did you now, well I don't see why not,' and smiled as his daughter opened the back door of the car and climbed in followed by a nervous Mike. She held his hand for the five-minute drive to High Market and kissed him on the cheek when he said good night having already arranged to meet her the following weekend.

A crisp sunny March Sunday morning, spoilt only by the coal fires from hundreds of chimneys that sought to pollute the fresh air blowing

133

into Ashington on a gentle North Easterly saw Rafe up early, polishing the chrome wheels of the tandem in the back yard while Ian delivered the Sunday papers.

Hearing the sound of a car driving slowly up the street, he stood up, looked over the wooden yard fence and saw the red Riley with Nick behind the wheel drive up and halt next to the gate. Ignoring Rafe, Nick climbed out of his car and walked into the house and straight up the stairs to his bedroom, where he grabbed an old suitcase from the top of the wardrobe and began stuffing his clothes into it.

Rafe walked into the kitchen where Jane was sitting at the table preparing vegetables for Sunday dinner, chatting to Mike who was sitting opposite her drinking a cup of tea while in the background 'Two Way Family Favourites' played music and requests on the radio; neither of them had heard Nick enter and go upstairs.

Rafe said quietly to Jane, 'Nick's here, he's gone upstairs!'

Mike jumped up and headed for the stairs but Jane stopped him, 'Wait; let's see what he is up to. Rafe it's probably best if you go outside while he's here.'

Rafe nodded and walked back outside just as Nick stormed down the stairs and into the kitchen, ignoring both Jane and Mike who had both nervously stood up. Limping into the pantry, he grabbed his shaving gear and toothbrush and limped back out of the house without saying a word, leaving Jane and Mike staring at each other!

Mike spoke first, 'Does that mean he's gone for good Mam?'

Jane sat down and replied, 'As your Granny Shepherd would say, "I'm Buggared if Aah kna Bonny lad!"'

After Sunday Dinner, Ian and Rafe were discussing different ways to make money, Rafe not really contributing very much, just nodding his head in agreement as Ian went through money making schemes; 'There's wor paper roonds, ye'll be starting next week and we can check at Crisp's te see when they hev any vacancies for night deliveries. There's my grocery delivery job on Friday night and Saturday morning and this week, starting the morn night, we'll be able to hoy in some coals for at least a bob a load.'

Rafe interrupted his flow, 'Hoy in coals, what on earth is that?'

'Hoying in coals man, you kna, shovelling in loads of coals!'

'Rafe grinned, 'No I don't know, shovelling what coal where?'

Looking at him as though he was dim, Ian replied, 'Iviry body who works doon the pit gets a free load of coal once a month. It's dropped ootside the coalhooses and we gan around and ask if we can hoy - you know shovel the coal into the coalhouse for a shilling a load but ye've got te be careful cos there's a couple of men who do it for a living and they'll chase ye if the catch ye trying te hoy in their loads.'

'Who are these men that chase you and what will they do if they catch you?' Rafe asked with some concern.

'It's alreet man, they cannit hoy all the coal in, it's just a matter of knaing where they are working and then ganning to different streets. There's Robson, he's got a gammy leg and is not ower bright, that's why he is hoying in coals for a living but he just shouts and swears at ye but then there's Hooky; noo he is different, he's a right big bugger and as mad as out, he'll daad ye with his shovel if he gets the chance.'

'Charming!' said Rafe.

Ian continued, 'Anyway, we can make a few Bob hoying coal in, then there's tettie picking during Blackberry Week,'

'Tettie picking, blackberry week, you are going to have to explain that as well,' said a frustrated Rafe.

'Blackberry week is the Autumn school holiday and we'll both be fourteen so we can gan picking potatoes at one of the farms, it's ten bob a day and a pail of tetties each day plus there'll be lots of lasses there.'

'Rafe smiled sardonically, 'Sounds terrific fun!'

135

'What else, oh aye, selling firewood!'

'Explain please,' Rafe demanded.

'Whey ye can see that iviry body has coal fires, whey they need firewood to light them, so I saw pit props and chop them up into firewood and sell them but not around the colliery hooses as most of the men bring their own firewood home, I sell them te the private hooses down Wansbeck Road, Dene View and the council hooses around Park Villas, mind I dee have a few regulars in the Ras as weel. But it teks a lot of time walking roond we a few bundles of firewood.'

Rafe listened carefully before asking, 'Where do you get your pit props from?'

'That's the only snag, I sneak alang to Coneygarth Drift and tek one from the timber yard but I can only carry a couple at a time.'

'Isn't that stealing?'

Ian laughed, 'Only if ye get caught, besides they've got that much they'd never know any had gone.'

Rafe thought for a moment, 'So what we need is some means of carrying more than a couple of pit props at a time and then more than a few bundles of firewood at a time?'

'Aye that's right like.'

Rafe said, 'I have an idea,' and walked around the side of the house to the black, creosote painted garden shed, returning with the homemade barrow he had seen there yesterday. It consisted of a large and very strong black painted wooden box mounted on a large pair of sturdy pram wheels and strong wooden spars screwed to each side of the box, joined at the other end by a wooden spar to use as a handle.

"If we can fasten this to the back of the tandem we can use it to collect pit props and to carry the bundles of firewood once we have chopped them!'

Ian looked at the barrow and said, 'That's a brilliant idea, haway, I'll get the tandem oot and we'll see hoo we can fasten it on the back.'

The two spars were long enough to ensure the box of the barrow did not foul the rear wheel but tying the handle to the stem of the rear seat was not very successful; having lashed it with a piece of old clothes line they set of on a trial run but soon realised it was not very stable, as the handle slid under the rope.

As they were trying different knots, they heard a motorbike burst into life followed by noisy revving. Looking down the back street, they saw Albert Grundy straddling his James motor bike, twisting the throttle in triumph as he listened to the engine roar steadily.

'Bloody hell,' Ian said, 'look he's finally managed to get his motorbike started.'

Ian and Rafe abandoned their project and walked down the street to congratulate Albert whose noisy revving was beginning to attract attention. Monty was first to respond and came scampering out of the Grundy's house and began barking madly at the motorbike while taking the odd nip at both the bike and Albert. He was followed by Flo who, wearing her pinny and turbaned scarf, scuttled across the street and began swatting Albert with a tatty tea towel yelling at him to 'SWITCH IT OFF,' but Albert was not about to switch it off, it had taken him long enough to fix the engine, he was enjoying the steady roar.

Jake, followed by Billy and Roger came out next to see what the commotion was and as soon as they saw their father revving the motorbike, they began dancing round, cheering wildly. Albert smiled stupidly at Flo and let the clutch out, sliding his feet along the street to steady himself as he moved slowly off before quickly picking up speed. The Grundy boys ran alongside cheering but quickly gave up, unlike Monty who continued to chase Albert, while barking wildly as continued to try to bite the motorbike.

At the end of the terrace, Max, the Turnbull's Border Collie came scampering out the yard and joined the chase, barking at Monty and the motorbike while trying to bite both!

Ian, Rafe, Flo, Jake and the boys watched in dumfounded silence as Albert followed by the two dogs, turned the bike up the bank toward the Fifth Row and disappeared from sight.

'Flo shook her head and spat, 'Sacklass bloody bugger,' and walked back into the kitchen followed by her two youngest boys.

Turning to Ian and Rafe, Jake asked, 'What are ye up te?'

Ian answered, 'Trying to fasten wor barrow to the back of the tandem so we can use it like a trailer.'

The three of them walked back up to where the tandem was propped against the pavement with the barrow lashed to the back. Jake examined the outfit with a critical eye before declaring, 'Whey that's shite man, it'll slide aall ower the blidy place.'

Glaring at Jake, Ian said, 'We know man so unless ye've a better idea, shut up.'

As the three of them tried a different way of lashing the barrow handle to the bike, Mike who was leaving for a football kick about over the Rec, stopped and asked, 'What the blidy hell are you lot trying te de?'

Ian stood up and answered, 'Fasten the barrow te the bike but we cannit get it te swivel properly and stay in the centre.'

Mike looked at the rig and announced, 'What ye need is some sort of metal sheath attached to the handle that will slip over the stem of the back seat and I know where te get one!'

The three lads piped up together, 'Where?'

'From the band that fastens roond the tubs at work, they have a metal socket at the front for attaching the pony limbers too. Aah'll get one the morn and cut it up in the workshops to fit and then drill some holes in the band to fasten it te the handle, that should work champion.' He turned and began walking off for his game just as the sounds of a motorbike and the barking of a pack of dogs could be heard approaching the street!

Jake, Ian and Rafe ran past Mike, Jake shouting, 'It's me Dad coming back!'

Albert Grundy swerved into the street, he was having difficulty riding in a straight line as he tried desperately to avoid running over any of the large pack of dogs that were chasing him, his motorbike and each other, barking and snapping as they did so. He had collected more and more dogs as he had ridden the motorbike around the Fifth, Fourth and Third Rows before heading for home with his ever-expanding entourage of excited dogs. The pack consisted of dogs of all shapes sizes and pedigrees, all having a wonderful time as they chased their pray whose greasy overall trouser leg was in tatters as the dogs fought to bite him and his noisy contraption.

Albert eased the bike to a halt outside his house and switched the engine off hoping that would stop the dogs. Monty still hung onto his left trouser leg and was snarling and shaking it, determined to save his master form the noisy machine, meanwhile the other dogs turned on each other and a massive dogfight ensued! It was pandemonium; dogs barking and fighting, Albert swearing at Monty and the lads shouting at the dogs until Flo came running out of the yard swinging a bass broom!

She waded into the dogs with the broom, scattering them before her like grass under a scythe and soon restored a semblance of order as dogs scarpered back to wherever they came from, all less Monty who was still worrying Albert's trousers despite him having climbed off the bike to stand sheepishly in front of Flo, who ordered, 'Inside – Noo!'

Albert limped toward his house dragging Monty along until Flo smacked the dog on its arse with the broom; it let go and beat Albert in through the front door, just.

As Ian and Rafe walked back to the tandem, Rafe asked, 'Ian, what about Grammar School, did you sit an eleven plus exam?'

139

'Aye I did but I failed it as I knew my Mam couldn't afford to send me to Grammar and if she had it wouldn't hev been fair on Mike and Maureen, having extra money spent on me, but listen I was also supposed to sit a thirteen plus exam but I towld them I didn't want to sit it and I never towld me Mam so divint ye tell her.'

Rafe looked at Ian and said, 'That was thoughtful of you, I wonder if I would have done the same had I been in your shoes?'

'Aye, whey ye just aboot are noo!'

Chapter 8
The Hacky Dortys

The following morning walked down the back lane with Rafe, Ian felt very self-conscious, sure he was going to be embarrassed and suffer a lot of ribbing when they walked into the school yard, he was correct!

Jake had stepped into the lane as they approached and gave a long wolf whistle as they walked up to him, 'Blidy hell, Am not walking next to ye two toffs, ye look like blidy Little Lord Flontreloy or what iver ye call him!'

'Sod off Jake and shut up if yer coming with us,' Ian retorted.

He and Rafe were wearing the dark purple, Rugley School Blazers, white shirts with ties, grey trousers and highly polished black shoes, Jane had even managed to have Ian comb his thick black hair into some semblance of order.

Ian looked very smart but Rafe, despite having a few qualms about his first day at a new school, looked elegant, relaxed and confident. 'Is that all of it? It would fit into the quadrangle at Rugley' he asked, laughing as they approached the school.

'Yep, that's the lot; there are two playgrunds, one for the lads and one for the lasses.'

Rafe smiled and said, 'Brilliant - girls ay, there were none at Rugley!'

Twisting the arm of a skinny youth that he had just stolen two cigarettes from, Geordie Robertson looked up when he heard a commotion outside the entrance to the school hall next to the gate. Pushing the lad contemptuously to one side and followed by the snivelling Ray Smith, he walked across the yard from the toilets to investigate.

Ian and Rafe had been surrounded by lads keen to know who Rafe was and why were they dressed like Grammar School kids. 'He's my uncle,' Ian kept saying to disbelieving pals, until Geordie pushed his way through.

'Look at the state of these two ponces, waat a couple of frigging soft shites we hev here,' he sneered as he circled menacingly before stopping in front of Rafe who was the same height as him but much slimmer.

'Who the fuck are ye?' he demanded.

Rafe stepped back and with some disdain, looked Geordie up and down before answering in measured, cultured tones, 'I am Rafe Rorke Trevelyan, uncle to Ian Shepherd and friend to him and the rest of the Sixth Row chaps, who - or what are you?'

Taken aback by Rafe's confident reply, Geordie hissed, 'Piss off ye Soothern soft shite ora'll daad ye.'

Rafe gave Geordie a disconcerting smile and asked, ''Daad ye', is that some sort of threat you horrendous oaf?'

It took Geordie a couple of seconds to digest Rafe's rebuke, then he exploded, 'Right ye frigging ponce, Aah'll sort ye oot!' and swung a vicious right hook that met with fresh air, Rafe having stepped nimbly backwards as the surrounding boys quickly formed a circle.

Ian moved forward and warned, 'Watch oot Rafe, he's a right nasty bugga, let me fight him?'

Without taking his eyes of the puce faced bully, Rafe said, 'I can handle this cretin Ian old chap, never fear!' and snapped two very hard lefts straight into Geordie's bulbous nose that immediately trickled blood.

Wiping his nose with the back of his hand, Geordie surged forward swinging one fist after the other but Rafe side-stepped him, kicking his feet from under him as he lunged forward. Geordie crashed head first into the solid wooden door of the school hall and knelt there for a moment to regain control before standing and turning straight into a swinging right that rocked his head back and as he brought it forward, it met with a swinging left that knocked him back against the wall.

With the crowd cheering madly, Rafe stood like a professional boxer, secure behind his guard, and warned, 'I suggest you walk away now before I hurt you,' but Geordie was not listening to suggestions and pushed off from the wall and again lunged at Rafe finding only fresh air. Rafe then brought a crashing right onto the side of Geordies head that knocked him to the floor semi-conscious.

'Kick im!' shouted some of the lads as Rafe straddled the fallen bully and said in a matter of fact voice, 'I did warn you.'

Geordie looked up at Rafe and spat, 'Aah'll get ye for this ye fucking bastard,' and grabbed for Rafe's crotch but Rafe grabbed Geordie's hand and twisted it firmly bending it back against the wrist causing his opponent to wince in pain.

Rafe released his grip and stepping back said, 'I think we should leave it there don't you old chap?'

Ray Smith rushed to help Geordie up and snarled, 'We'll get ye for this ye bastard ye!'

Ian stepped forward and pushing his face close to Ray's, warned, 'If I was ye I'd keep me gob shut in case Aah find a fist in it!'

Ray got the message and he and his battered and scowling hero skulked off to the toilets for a fag as the younger boys crowded around Rafe all keen to touch the lad who had just humiliated the school bully.

After assembly Rafe was taken to the meet the Headmaster in his office where, after a ten minute interview, the tall distinguished Headmaster leant back in his chair and said, 'Once we have had an opportunity to review your results from Rugley you may well be transferred to either Bedlington or Morpeth Grammar School.'

Rafe thought of what Ian had told him the evening before and said, 'Thank you Sir but I do not wish to transfer to a Grammar School, I prefer to attend school here if that is acceptable?'

The Headmaster did not try to reason with Rafe and instead, said, 'We shall see, now off you go and join Mr Haig's Class, Three A.'

Rafe was disappointed with the rundown school and its amenities but did not say as such to Ian, beside which he was enjoying meeting the other lads in his class and more so the lasses who were all taken by his good looks, impeccable manners, charming smile and 'Posh' voice!

'Eeee, didn't he taalk lovely?'

'Aye just like the News Readers on the tele!'

'Aah love his blue eyes mind.'

'Who de ye thinks the best looking him or Ian?'

'Tha both smashing but Aah love Ian's cheeky smile.'

'Ye hev Ian and Aah'll hev Rafe eh?'

The whispers and giggles continued for the rest of the day with several of the girls following the two boys for a chat when school finished for the day. Rafe was enjoying the attention and was disappointed when Ian said, 'Haway then, we've got some coals to hoy in they've been delivering in the Ra's.'

At home they hurriedly changed out of their school clothes, Ian pulling on an old pair of flannel trousers and a threadbare jumper as Rafe asked, 'What should I wear?'

'Sumat owld that doesn't show the muck noo hurry up!'

'Right O,' Rafe replied then asked, 'Are there often fights at Bothal School?'

Ian thought for a second or two, 'Nah not really and if there are that swine Robertson is normally involved, why?'

'Some advice my father once gave me, I have just remembered it.'

144

'What advice was that?'

'Well, he said in his very serious way; "Never start a brawl - you will be branded a thug, always try to walk away from confrontation but never run - you will be branded a coward and become the target of bullies and,' Rafe deepened the tone of his voice, trying to imitate his father, "if as a last resort you have to fight back, then fight to win," I think it was good advice and advice I took seriously, after some initial bullying at Rugley I joined the boxing club and learnt how to defend myself.'

Ian smiled, 'Well ye did more than defend yersell teday, noo hurry up and get changed.'

While Tommy fought a fierce battle with toy soldiers on the rug in front of the sitting room fire, Ian stood by the fire in the kitchen and ate a jam sandwich as he waited for Rafe to change as Jane prepared another sandwich for her young brother. 'Try not to get too dirty Ian and try and keep out of trouble and make sure your back for dinner at six.'

Ian was about to answer but instead burst out laughing when Rafe walked in; he was wearing a rugby shirt that was two sizes too small accentuating his thinness but it was the baggy white cricket trousers that made Ian laugh. They were also old and no longer long enough for Rafe's legs leaving a four inch gap between the bottoms and his gym shoes.

'Heck man Rafe, Aah said something owld that doesn't show the dort, ye look like a cloon in them troosers man!'

Jane stifled a laugh and said, 'At least he will not spoil anything that still fits him, now go on get going, I want you back for dinner.'

Hurrying out of the house, the two lads picked up two large shovels from the coalhouse before heading down the street where Jake was waiting. For once Jake was speechless, he looked at Rafe then raising his eyebrows, looked quizzically at Ian who just shrugged his shoulders.

Jake looked at Rafe again and was about to speak but Rafe warned, 'Do not say a word!' Jake didn't, he just burst out laughing and was joined by Ian and then Rafe as they headed for the Seventh and Eighth Rows where there was 'loads' of coal to be 'hoyed' in.

They reached the Eighth Row first where they saw that Hooky was hard at work throwing coals into a coalhouse fifty yards down the Row.

'Howay we'll gan to the Seventh Ra before he gets there,' Ian said and they walked along to the next long row of terraced houses that stretched toward the town centre. Neat loads of coal had been dropped outside most of the coalhouses, some had already been shovelled in by husbands on nightshift or by wives who did not want to pay to have their coals 'hoyed in' but here was still plenty there to get stuck into.

Jake rushed off to the door of the house opposite the first load and knocked loudly on the door that was opened by a pinny wearing middle-aged woman whose flour covered hands showed she was in the middle of baking. Before Jake could speak she said, 'A shilling noo gan on, I'm in the middle of making me man's dinner!'

Jake rushed over to the coal and dragged the door to the coalhouse open and began throwing the coals in with easy practiced movements as Ian said to Rafe, 'Come with me for the first load then you can do the rest on yer an!'

With Rafe standing behind him, Ian knocked on the door of the next house with a load of coal outside and asked the bespectacled and attractive thirty year old woman who opened the door, 'Can Aah hoy yer coals in Missus?'

The woman did not answer immediately, she looked at Rafe in his ill-fitting rugby shirt and half-mast white trousers and began giggling! Composing herself, she took a deep breath before saying, 'Ahem, me man normally throws the coal in but I would just love te see that lang streak throw a load of coals in so gan on I'll give yer a tanner each!'

After dragging the coalhouse door open Ian turned to Rafe and said, 'Aah'll start up here hoying this lot straight in the back, ye shovel the lot by you forward te me and we'll have this done in ten minutes,' and began scooping up coal on his large shovel and with an easy swinging motion, 'hoyed' them into the back of the coalhouse.

With the woman leaning on her door, Rafe self-conscientiously dug his shovel into the pile of coal and with some difficulty lifted a half-full shovel of coal and threw it forward, most of it hitting Ian on the legs who shouted, 'Blidy hell man watch where yer hoying the coal!' The woman began giggling again as Rafe tried again unsuccessfully to scoop up a full shovel of coal and again threw it at Ian!

Exasperated, Ian walked around to Rafe and speaking as though he were teaching a toddler he said slowly, 'Look, push the shull inte the coal alang the ground, not straight inte the pile, that way it slides in easily and scoops up a full shull-full and when ye pick it up, swing it back first and when you hoy it forward let the shull slide through yer left hand a bit, the power coming from yer right, noo try that,' as he demonstrated the action.

'Oh I see,' said Rafe as he followed Ian's instructions and scooped up a full shovel of coal and 'hoyed' it deftly to the coalhouse door as the woman clapped her hands and said, 'Ah bet that's the forst time them hands have held a shovel?'

Rafe turned and smiled his charming smile and answered, 'Absolutely!' before returning to the task in hand.

Within a few minutes Ian and Rafe were either side of the coalhouse door 'hoying' coals in as fast as they could, racing to see who could hoy in the most. Finished they closed the door and stood smiling at each other as Jake joined them saying, 'Howay then, there's a lot more te de.'

Rafe looked at his hands and then his now not so perfectly white trousers and said, 'My God look at me I'm filthy!'

147

Grinning, Ian said, 'Aye yer hacky dorty!'

'Hacky dorty! What on earth is that?

Jake pushed his coal blackened hands at Rafe and said, 'Look man we're aall hacky dorty, ye kna filthy like!'

Grinning like a Cheshire cat, Rafe said, 'So I am now hacky dorty?'

'Yes man,' said Ian, 'we are all hacky dorty,' then after a second or two he said, 'That's us, we are 'The Hacky Dortys,' noo come on let's get even more hacky dorty and mek a few more bob.'

As they hurried along to the next loads of coal, Rafe shouted 'Up the Hack Dortys!'

Jake shouted, 'Hacky Dortys forever!' and the three lads continued on down the street hoying coals in where they could.

They had competition however and as they approached the end of the first terrace of the Row they could see a couple of other lads at work further down. Ian said, 'This is their Ra so we better try the next one,' and they headed up the road between the terraces that led to the other Rows and onto the colliery.

As they approached the Eighth Row, big, bald and bad tempered Hooky began to cross the road to reach the next terrace but stopped when he saw the three lads approaching him with shovels! 'Ye fugging little buggas betta not be hoying me coals in cos if ye are Aah'll fugging batta ye's' he shouted and raised his shovel menacingly.

Jake said, 'Come on, let's bugga off before he catches us, we can duck doon the Seventh and gan the lang way roond te the Ninth.'

Ian nodded and said, 'Aye, we divint want te upset him and anyway, it's the only way he can mek a living so haway,' but as he spoke Rafe walked straight toward Hooky! Hooky had not expected this, normally the lads always ran away when he threatened them but this queer looking lad was walking straight up to him.

Stopping in front of the puzzled Hooky, Rafe said firmly, 'Look here old chap, you cannot go around offering violence to strangers, it's

148

against the law you know, besides it is so easy to be pleasant and enjoy other people's company, now I'm sure you won't mind if my chums and I go along to the next street and 'hoy' in some coals?'

With a slack jawed dumfounded look, Hooky stared at Rafe as though he were a Martian as Rafe turned and smiled at a shocked Ian and Jake and waved them forward with a shout of, 'Come on he is perfectly harmless.'

Ian shouted, 'DUCK!' and without thinking, Rafe did so as Hooky's shovel swung through the air missing Rafe's head by inches, the momentum of the swing throwing Hooky off balance.

'*Run yer daft Bugga*,' screamed Jake as Hooky gathered himself for another swing at the 'cheeky daft bugga' in front of him. Rafe did not need Jake's advice; he was already sprinting toward them as Hooky gave chase for a few yards before stopping to shout obscenities at the three fleeing lads.

They made it to the Eighth Row without further incident and found several more housewives who were willing to pay a shilling for having their coals thrown in. By the time it was nearly six o'clock they had made six or seven bob each and were tired and happy enough to head to home for dinner, except Jake was not looking forward to whatever his mother had made.

'Am ganning te the pit canteen te spend a shilling on some proper food, Aah'll see ye later,' he said and headed up to the colliery as a heavy drizzle began to fall, hurrying Ian and Rafe home.

Rafe looked at the dirt covering his blistered hands and asked, 'What about all this dirt, how do the Hacky Dortys bathe?'

Ian smiled at him, 'Us hacky Dortys gan te the pit baths but not yet as the shifts are changing ower, we'll hev a quick wash, hev dinner then gan for a shower.'

As they walked up the Sixth Row they could see the Tandem parked outside their house and to their surprise saw that the large wooden

149

barrow was attached to it! Mike had been true to his promise and adapted a metal sheath from a tub and attached it to the front handle of the barrow. He had also taken off the rear seat and pushed the stem through the sheath and back into the tandem frame allowing the barrow handle to swivel easily.

He was waiting for Rafe and Ian as they walked into the kitchen that smelled of corned beef pie and gravy, laughing, he said, 'Mam telt me what ye were wearing Rafe but I thought she was kidding, what a bloody clip ye look!'

Rafe smiled, 'Thanks Mike, very kind of you to say so.'

Turning from the oven where she was taking out a large plate pie; Jane urged, 'Hurry up and have a wash boys, dinner is ready, Mike go upstairs and tell Maureen to come down for her's please.'

Tommy walked through from the sitting room and looking at Rafe asked, 'Are ye a clown Rafe?'

'Yes that's me Thomas, clown, buffoon and downright idiot, good fun ay?'

Tommy laughed and sat down ready to eat as Mike returned, 'She says she's not hungry Mam.'

With a worried frown clouding her face, Jane cut the pie and dished out slices to the four boys and then hurried upstairs to speak to Maureen who was lying curled up on her bed, still wearing her white shop coat and sobbing into her pillow.

Jane quietly sat down next to her daughter and stroked her raven black hair gently before saying, 'I think it's about time you told me what the problem is Maureen, don't you?'

Without lifting her head, Maureen sobbed, 'I can't Mam, everything is ruined; I wish I was dead,'

'Grabbing Maureen's shoulders, Jane carefully but forcibly turned her and lifted her so she could take her in her arms to comfort her. 'It can't be that bad and I'm sure we can sort it out but you will have to tell me what it is that's the matter but I think I know!'

Clinging to her mother, Maureen opened the floodgates, releasing a torrent of tears and emotions, blurted between sobs, 'Am pregnant! Everything's ruined, Terry won't want me with a baby, I'll lose him and me job, everything and everybody will find out and call me names, what am I ganning to do Mam, Am sorry, I'm so sorry Mam, will I have to go away? Aah've heard that lasses like me have to get rid of their babies and go away but I divint want to get rid of a baby, how could anyone do that, I've ruined everything!'

Jane slowly rocked Maureen until the crying subsided to sobbing and said in a calm voice, 'I'm a bit disappointed that it has happened, especially after having discussed this last year and I thought you would have had more sense but never mind, you are not the first girl that has got herself into trouble and you won't be the last, it is not the end of the world, just a problem we have to overcome together and there is no question you getting rid of your baby; that is if you are having one and no question of you having to go away, now how many periods have you missed Pet?'

Between sobs, she answered, 'Two Mam.'

'And Terry is the father?'

'Mam! Of course he is there's never been anyone else.'

'Does he know, have you told him yet?'

'No.'

'Why not, are you frightened to tell him?'

'I'm frightened he will be mad and leave me or hate me for getting pregnant man Mam.'

'It takes two to get pregnant Maureen so how can he hate you for something he has done, you are going to have to tell him we just need to think when is the best time and place.'

'I can't Mam.'

'Oh yes you can young lady, the sooner you get over this first hurdle the sooner we can sort things out, now when are you seeing him next?'

Jane's gentle and reassuring voice was beginning to calm Maureen, 'Wednesday night; we are supposed to be going to the Regal.'

'Okay, well instead bring him here and I'll make sure you have the house to yourselves for an hour, and then I will want to talk to the pair of you, how does that sound?'

'Alright Mam but I'm scared about how he will be.'

'Look Maureen, Terry is a lovely lad and from what I know of his family, they are decent people, I'm sure he will do the right thing by you, we have just got to decide what the right thing is.'

Downstairs, having finished their dinner, as the boys began stacking plates on the tiny drainer in the kitchen, Mike said, 'Aah'll let ye two do the washing up 'am off te the 'Tute' for a game of snooker with Hank, see ya's,' and walked to the back door, snatched his jacket off the coat hook and set off into the darkening evening.

Ian said to Rafe, 'We can't do the dishes until Mam and Maureen have had their dinners so we might as well go to the pit baths now, come on we'll gan on the tandem.'

As Rafe nodded, Tommy asked, 'Can Aah come?'

Ian shook his head and said, 'Nur man, ye kna Mam doesn't want ye ganning oot yet and she certainly doesn't want ye ganning te the pit baths, beside we're ganning on the tandem.'

Tommy jumped up from his chair and said excitedly, 'I can sit in the buggy, it'll be great man!'

'He could!' added Rafe.

'Howay then, grab towels and let's gan, we can peddle doon Wansbeck Road and Green Lane and then around Park Villas so you know where they are before ye start yer paper roond on Saturday, then we'll gan te the pit baths, it'll be nice and quiet by then.'

152

Clutching towels grabbed from the under stairs cupboard they hurried outside where Tommy quickly climbed into the barrow attached to the back of the bike and shouted, 'Come on hurry up.'

Rafe climbed onto the rear of the tandem and Ian the front and pushed off and headed down the Row just as Jake, fresh from his feast at the pit canteen walked into the Row. His hands thrust deep in his pockets and whistling Colonel Bogey as he imagined himself marching along with the British POWS to build the Bridge over the River Kwai!

Seeing the lads on the tandem pedalling toward him, he stopped and shouted, 'Haway the Hacky Dortys!'

Cycling past him, Ian and Rafe shouted back, 'Haway the Hacky Dortys,' and continued on and into the Fifth Row shouting their new 'Battle Cry'. Tommy joined in shouting and laughing madly, not sure why they were yelling 'UpThe Hacky Dortys.'

In the flat above the chip shop in Highmarket, Nick smoothed back his brylcreamed hair and pulled on his trilby at a slight angle and turned his head from side to side, admiring his dark good looks in the tarnished mirror that hung above the chipped washbasin in the corner of the room. Not for him the regulation flat cap worn by most of the men in Ashington, he was far too smooth to wear something so ordinary. Straightening his tie he picked up the keys to the Riley and left the flat and limped downstairs and out through the chip shop to his parked car.

He was feeling very satisfied with himself, Ginny was very accommodating, possibly just a little bit too much as her constant fawning could be boring, 'She probably thinks she has got her man,' he thought to himself as climbed into his car and drove the mile to the Grand Hotel. 'She's not a bad cook either, not in the same class as Jane but good enough, in fact she's not in the same class as Jane, apart from sex, Ginny couldn't get enough of it whereas Jane did not want any!'

The other bonus for Nick was that Ginny worked full time at the Fell em Doon giving him free range to prowl the other Working Men's Clubs and the three Ashington pubs touting for bets, in fact it was all quite satisfactory apart from the cramped conditions in the dingy flat.

Parking outside the Grand, he limped into the smoke filled bar, crowded with men in dark suits and flat caps, some in animated conversation, some sitting quietly sipping their beer. In the corner, half a dozen more were playing dominos very noisily.

After buying a pint, Nick joined three men standing at the end of the bar, 'Alreet fellas?' he asked as they turned and grunted back in response.

The tallest of the three, a gaunt but powerfully built six foot, middle aged man, pushed his cap back with a gnarled forefinger and said, 'Aye Nick lad, who's it ganning kidda, are ye teking bet's for the 'National?'

This was music to Nick's ears, 'Aye of course Stan, de ye want te put a couple of bob on the favourite or some other owld gallowa?'

'Whey Aah was fancying Goosander, it's gotta be his year, he was favourite last year and just got beat?'

The smaller, dapper man next to Stan added scornfully, 'Aye and he'll get beat again this year man, tell ye whaat Nick Aah'll hev a couple of Bob on the favourite, Wyndburgh.'

'Champion,' said Nick as he took the small hard backed, black book from his inside pocket and scribbled the bet inside then held his hand out for the money.

'Aye gan on then,' said Stan, 'Aah'll hev a couple of bob on Goosander.'

Nick took the bet and turning to the third man who had been watching silently with a disapproving look, asked, 'Whaat aboot ye then Harry, de ye fancy a wee flutter?'

Glaring at Nick, he answered, 'Not me Shepherd, Aah divint believe in hoying away me hard urned money on gambling and wasters like ye.'

Gritting his teeth, Nick snarled back, 'Aye ye alwas wor a miserable git Harry!'

Stan stepped between them and said jokingly, 'Aye that's right, Harry doesn't waste his money on gambling, he just wastes it on booze, isn't that right Harry?'

Harry relaxed saying, 'Aye as like as not Stan lad,' and turned his back on Nick who nodded to the other two before moving on to the domino players to tout for business. Within a few minutes he had taken a couple of quid and decided to try a couple of Clubs and come back later when hopefully the Grand would be busier. Placing his empty glass on the bar he said to Stan, 'See you later Stan, am off te the Central and 'Varsal for an hour or so, try and cheer that miserable fucker up will ye.'

Before Stan could reply, Harry growled, 'Aye fuck off Shepherd and rob some other stupid buggas.'

Laughing, Nick left the Grand, leaving the Riley parked outside, he hurried the couple of hundred yards to the Central Club behind Woolworths where after buying himself a pint, he started taking bets from the men in the busy bar.

Meanwhile Jane continued to comfort her distraught daughter, gently but firmly, slowly persuading Maureen that it was not the end of the world and that the family would help her through the difficult times ahead. She was in no rush to go back down stairs which was probably just as well as if she had discovered the recovering Tommy missing, she would have had a fit!

It was just after seven thirty when the three boys cycled back home and found Jane and Maureen's dinners still uneaten on the table! Tommy wandered off into the sitting room and climbed back onto the sofa as Ian went upstairs and knocked on his sister's door, 'Mam yor dinners are cowld, should Aah put them in the oven?'

155

Jane looked at her watch and rising from the bed walked over to the door and opening it said to the puzzled Ian, 'Yes Pet, we'll be down in a few minutes.' It was more like half an hour before they came downstairs and Jane took the food from the oven but neither of them had an appetite, eating very little and when Jane cleared the table, Maureen disappeared back upstairs.

Ian who had been making an 'Airfix' Spitfire with Rafe asked, 'What's up with wor Maureen Mam?'

'Nothing that need concern you; now you and Rafe can wash the dishes while I see to Tommy.'

Turning to her youngest boy who was lying on the sofa reading the glossy 'Eagle' comic, she said 'Right young man, you've been out of hospital a few days now so I think it's time you had a bath, I'll put the bath in front of the sitting room fire so that you are nice and warm, we don't want you becoming ill again do we?'

Tommy was about to protest and tell his Mam he had just had a shower but Ian, gesturing frantically from the kitchen for him to keep quiet, stopped him and he prepared himself for his unnecessary bath.

Having done well in the Central and Universal Clubs, Nick was back in the Grand at half past nine sitting in the corner supping another pint, letting the punters come to him to place their bets. He was just thinking of driving down to the Portland when the brooding, brutish McArdle twins slid into the chairs on either side of him, placing their beers on the table next to Nick's.

Joe McArdle asked, 'Nick lad, who the divil are ye?'

'Am champion Joe, how are ye two tonight?'

Pat answered, 'All the better for seeing you Nick lad, now then ye'll be taking bets for the big race on Saturday will ye?'

'Aye Pat I am; de ye want to put a couple of bob on?'

Joe leant forward and said quietly, 'We do Nick, we do just that.'

'Twenty quid each on that lovely little Irish hos, Mr What is what we want te bet,' said Pat sneering into Nick's face before adding, 'ye can handle that now can't ye Nick lad?'

Nick gulped visibly and stammered, 'Nnnur, am sorry lads me maximum bet is just two bob, that's all Aah can handle.'

Smiling hideously, Pat said, 'Now Nick lad, ye mustn't hev hurd Joe properly, it's twenty quid each on Mr What, got that?'

Fighting his mounting fear and panic caused by the two intimidating men, Nick's mouth turned dry and his collar suddenly felt far too tight as he replied desperately, 'Am sorry lads, Aah cannit handle that size of bet, Aah couldn't cover it, not forty quid on a eighteen to one bet.'

Placing his hand menacingly on Nick's arm, Pat said almost flippantly, 'No bother Nick, we'll just put ten pound each on it,' and slid four £5 notes across the table. Nick started to protest but the McArdles rose and both of them placed their heavy hands on the table and leaning toward him, Joe said, 'See ye on Saturday night for our winnings - should we be lucky Nick.'

Nick couldn't speak as he watched the two men pick up their beers and walk back to the bar. 'Mr What is an outsider, 'Wyndburgh or Goosander is boon te win and Aah'll hev twenty of their quid in me back pocket, fuck them,' he thought as he nervously played with the flick knife in his jacket pocket!

The rest of the week flew by for the family, Tuesday was Mike's seventeenth birthday that they celebrated with a few home-made cakes and a few seconds of embarrassment when Ian self-consciously handed over the shin-pads he had bought before Mike rushed off to catch the bus to Morpeth to see Jennifer.

On Wednesday, Ian and Rafe cycled along the railway line to Coneygarth where Ian showed his uncle where the timber yard was, 'Should we get some props now?' asked Rafe.

Ian shook his head, 'No it's too busy during the week; we'll come back on Saturday evening when it's quiet, besides I have a good few bundles of firewood at home and we need te sell them forst.'

Rafe settled into school and enjoyed being the centre of attention while it lasted, Patsy and Anne, two girls from the boy's class took to walking to the end of the Sixth Row with Ian, Rafe and Jake, even though it was out of their way. On Friday afternoon instead of leaving at the corner, the girls walked up the Row with the boys, stopping outside the Grundy's to chat and flirt. Jake did not linger as he knew his tea would be on the table and he did not want his younger brothers helping themselves to his meagre rations.

The other four had been chatting for half an hour when the very pretty blonde-haired Peggy Reagan from Number 56 walked up the Row in her Bedlington Grammar School uniform! Peggy had had a crush on Ian since they were at Wansbeck School together and she knew Ian liked her, so she was not best pleased to see two girls laughing and giggling with her 'boyfriend' and his posh uncle!

Storming up too Ian, she demanded, 'Who are these Ian Shepherd?'

Bushing, he stammered, 'Just two lasses from school like.'

'Are they now, well just you come with me, I have something to say to you in private!' and grabbing his arm, she dragged him along to her house two doors away as Patsy and Anne made 'Ooooing' sounds and Rafe looked on, bemused!

Dragging Ian into her backyard, Peggy said, 'Ian Shepherd, I thought you were my boyfriend, why are you with these two lasses, is one of them your new girlfriend?'

'Girlfriend,' Ian gasped, 'No man, they are after Rafe not me, Aah hevn't got a girlfriend.'

Peggy grabbed Ian by the shoulders and planted a quick kiss square on his lips and said, 'Yes you have and don't you forget it!' and stormed indoors leaving Ian shocked and puzzled but mainly thrilled at the kiss; he had always liked Peggy and always thought she was the bonniest lass around but he had never thought of her as his girlfriend! The more he thought about it the more he liked the idea and as he slowly walked back to the others he had difficulty in concealing the self-satisfied smile that was spreading across his face.

'Right Rafe am off hyem, are ye coming?'

Patsy asked, 'Is she yor girlfriend then?'

Ian hesitated for a second then said happily, 'Aye she is,' and turned to walk home as Rafe ran up alongside him and put his arm around his shoulder.

Smiling Rafe said, 'OK young man, as your uncle I feel it falls on me to warn you of the dangers of consorting with girls!'

"Sod of ye daft bugga,' said Ian.

Chapter 9
Nick has a bad day

Saturday the 30 March began promisingly with the sun shining brightly through Jane's bedroom curtains at number 60 the Sixth Row. She had moved back into her own bedroom but unsure if Nick was going to return she kept the bed the Galloway's had loaned her made up in Maureen's bedroom. With the sun lifting her mood, she was determined that she and the kids would have a happy and stress free day and rose early to prepare breakfast.

By the time Ian and Rafe had their now routine jostle at the tiny sink for their morning ablutions, Jane had a pile of toast on the kitchen table and was soft boiling the half dozen eggs she had been given yesterday by Mrs Williamson at number 53. Mike was already seated drinking a cup of tea as Maureen joined him in her white shop-coat.

Scooping the eggs from the saucepan into chipped egg cups, Jane said to Ian and Rafe, 'Come on you two, you need to get a move on if you are going to be at Willington's before half past seven.'

The two boys sat down at the table and decapitated the eggs before plunging soldiers of toast into the hot soft yokes as Jane pulled back a chair to join them. 'I want us all to have a good day today, I know things are a little tight with your father not being here but we can manage especially with me starting work at the bakery on Monday.' Looking across at Maureen sitting quietly drinking a cup of tea, she continued, 'We still have a problem or two to overcome but nothing we cannot handle as a family, now what is everyone up to today?'

Mike answered first, 'Aah've got te get the seed tetties planted this morning and if I hev time, some carrots as weel then the savvynoon Aah've a match on doon at the welfare and tonight I'm at the Arcade.'

Swallowing his last piece of boiled egg, Ian said, 'We've got wor newspaper roonds this morning, Rafe's first go so that should be fun, then I've me grocery deliveries and this afternoon me and Rafe are selling firewood.'

Rafe smiled and added, 'As Ian just said so eloquently, we will be busy!'

Jane stood up, 'Good, Tommy will be spending the afternoon down at the Turnbull's and I would like you all out between three and five as Terry and his parents are coming round for tea, we will have our dinner together at six o'clock okay.'

Ian and Rafe nodded as Mike looked at Maureen who was blushing deeply while studying the table cloth intently, he was about to speak but was stopped by a stern look from his mother.

Having had a good week - betting wise, Nick kicked off his morning with three slugs of whisky. 'The National' was the biggest race of the year and everyone liked a flutter and he had taken over fifty quid's worth of bets including the McArdles that had caused him some concern but he was also worried that the favourite Wyndburgh, might win as that would mean him just breaking even, still with a bit of luck he would make a killing!

As Ian hurried around the Ra's delivering newspapers, Rafe was getting used to lugging his heavy bag of papers as he studied the sketch of the streets that Ian had drawn for him the night before. He had found Wansbeck Road without problem and delivered a few papers in the terraces there before dealing with the large houses at the end of the Road. Green Lane led off from the bottom of Wansbeck Road and had also been straight forward; especially as there were only three papers to be delivered there; the problem came when he tried to find Park Villas!

Ian had said, 'Just walk straight up the road from the new Council Estate and you'll come to the Park, the Villas on the other side.' He had walked straight up the road, crossed over a railway line and found himself on a wide tree lined road where he found a sign that read 'North Seaton Road.' Knowing he had come in the wrong direction, he turned around and headed back the way he had come and stopped an old man to ask directions.

'Excuse me Sir, can you please tell me where I can find Park Villas?'

The old man stopped and looked Rafe up and down slowly; took out the pipe he was smoking and spat on the pavement before saying, 'Aye I can tell ye Bonny Lad, gan back ower the way Aah've just come and when ye get te the crossroads, torn reet and gan streit up ower ontil ye reach the Park on yer left, ye'll see the Villas just ower the other side.' Rafe thanked the man and pointed the correct way, he silently cursed Ian for not being clearer as he realised he had walked an unnecessary mile.

Ian was already delivering groceries as Rafe walked past the Park passing a group of lads playing football. One of them shouted, 'How ye big ponce ye, what hev ye got in yer handbag?'

Recognising Geordie Robertson as the lad who had shouted, Rafe ignored the remark and hurried on but to no avail, Geordie and three of the other lads ran after him, stopping him by standing in front of him at the edge of the Park.

Emboldened by his companions, Geordie pushed Rafe on the shoulder, 'Noo then fancy pants; let's see who hard ye really are?'

Rafe wanted to lift off the strap of the still heavy paper bag but knew that it would leave him wide open to an attack by the lads and instead stepped back to give himself some space but as he did so, two of the other lads stepped quickly behind him, closing him down. 'This is going to be painful,' he thought to himself as he watched Geordie ready himself for an attack!

Just as the lads were about to make their move, a blue Jowett Javelin pulled up alongside them and the voice that rang out from the open car window stopped the lads in their tracks, 'How lads, there's nee bother here noo is there?'

The four lads backed off as Edward Thompson climbed out of his car and walked around to the group on the pavement and while glaring down at Geordie, he said to Rafe, 'Hello lad, everything all reet here?'

'It is now thanks,' replied a relieved Rafe.

Towering over the four lads, Edward slowly looked at each one of them before saying, 'Aah kna who ye all are and Aah kna some of yer fathers, noo I'm telling ye this, if owt happens to this lad, Aah'll come doon on top of ye's like a ton of bricks, got that?'

Two of the lads muttered, 'Yes Mr Thompson' and beat a hasty retreat to the Park but Geordie and the fourth lad stood their ground, 'Ye cannit threaten us like that,' growled Geordie.

'Aah not only can threaten ye but Aah'll daad yer bloody lugs as weel if ye divint bugga off right noo ye cheeky little waster ye.' Geordie found himself alone as the last of his three pals ran off and with him, Geordie's boldness evaporated. Lowering his head he too turned and slunk back to the Park muttering under his breath.

Edward turned to Rafe and said, 'There you go lad, hopefully there'll be no more bother from them teday but ye need te get away from here now.'

Rafe held his hand out and said, 'Thank you sir, it was very kind of you to come to my assistance as I fear I could not have coped with all four at once.'

Edward gave Rafe a wry smile and said, 'Aye probably not but Aah reckon you could handle them one at a time eh? That's a bonny accent ye've got there, where're ye from son?'

'Rugley but I live in the Sixth Row now.'

'Well Aah niver, then you must be Jane Shepherd's brother I've been hearing aboot, hoo is iviry body?'

'I *am* Jane's brother and everyone is fine thanks.'

'Aah kna I shouldn't ask but hoo are ye getting on with Nick?'

'I don't think he cares very much for me but we see little of him since he moved out.'

Edward's brow furrowed, 'Moved out, where too?'

'Somewhere in Highmarket as far as I know.'

Edward stepped back, 'Look I'm sorry lad, I'm being far too nosey, just tell Jane that I'm asking after her and if there is owt Aah can dee for ye all, tell her te just ask, alright son?'

Rafe hitched the paper bag up and said, 'I will do Mr Edwards and thanks for coming to my rescue,' and turned to head for Park Villas as Edward nodded and climbed back into his car. He sat for a few minutes, to make sure Rafe was not followed by the other lads and to think over what Rafe had just told him – if Nick has moved out, how are they coping? He decided he would call on Jane tomorrow as he was going to his parents tonight for dinner and staying on for Sunday lunch. Deep in thought he drove slowly off and headed for Minorie's Garage to have the Jowettr serviced.

The pile of buttered bread disappeared rapidly from the plate in the centre of the kitchen table as Mike, Ian, Rafe and Tommy plucked off slices to dip into the broth that Jane had dished up from the huge saucepan simmering on the edge of the fire. Rafe, in his matter of fact way had told Mike and Ian of his little adventure and light-heartedly blamed Ian's scribbled map for him walking in the wrong direction.

Ian responded, 'Divint blame me if ye've got no sense of direction man, Aah showed ye where Park Villas was on Monday noo didn't Aah?'

'Yes you did but that was a few days ago, anyway I got there in the end thanks to Mr Edwards.'

165

Blushing slightly as she lifted a strand of hair from her face, Jane said, 'He is a good man and was very good to us after Tommy's accident.'

Mike nodded, 'He's a great bloke, he'll de owt for anyone and he's as hard as nails, he winit tek any cheek from sods like Geordie Robertson, just as weel he came alang when he did Rafe lad or Aah might hev had te find Robertson and kick his arse!'

Jane was horrified, 'Mike you will not, and please don't swear at the table!'

'Aye okay Mam, that broth was smashing but I have to be away noo te catch the bus te the welfare, I'll see you at six.'

Ian stood up, 'Aye me and Rafe hev firewood te sell so we'll see ye later Mam,' and he too headed for the back door as Rafe followed.

'Thanks Sis, see you later,' Rafe said as he left, bumping into Maureen arriving home from her Saturday morning shift.

After attaching the barrow to the tandem, Ian and Rafe loaded a dozen bundles of firewood into it and cycled off to sell them leaving Jane and Maureen to prepare for Terry and his parents, the Proudlocks.

Wednesday had been difficult for Maureen, telling Terry she was pregnant had been traumatic and she had done so through a flood of tears, certain that he would be at best, angry or at worst, storm out but she could not have been more wrong. He wrapped his arms around her and held her for ages before saying, 'Whey it's just as well that I love you if we are ganging te get married!'

They then talked for an hour or more, Maureen saying she had ruined both their lives; Terry responding by saying it was his fault and that they would have to do what was right for the baby and that he had decided a long time ago that Maureen was the only lass for him just that marriage would be a bit sooner than he had thought!

Jane had patiently and anxiously sat in the kitchen waiting for them to come through and when they finally appeared self-consciously holding hands, she released a huge sigh of relief before hugging them both saying, 'Well that's the first hurdle over; now young man you have your parents to tell.'

Terry looked worried as he said, 'My Mam will be upset and my Dad will be angry but even if I didn't want to, which I do, they would make me do the right thing or if Aah didn't they would throw me out I'm sure, but I'm dreading telling them.'

He had judged his parents reaction correctly, upset, anger and finally resignation when his Father said, 'Aye, whey you've made your bed lad, noo ye've got to lie in it, we'll need te discuss the matter with the lasses mam and dad te see what happens next!'

Nick was already well on the way to being drunk by the time Ginny left her flat for her lunch time shift at the Fell em Doon; despite Ginny's pleas not too, he had finished the quarter bottle of whisky he had bought the night before as he dressed for a last blitz on betting before the big race at three fifteen. Earlier he had carefully counted his takings of mainly shilling and two shilling pieces and placed them all in the old leather school satchel he hid under Ginny's bed.

Now, after admiring himself in the mirror he thought, 'The Grand first, then the Portland and then back here to the 'Doon' for the last few bets,' then checking that his black book was in his inside jacket pocket he picked up his car keys and left the flat.

A steady drizzle was falling and although he knew he should not be driving he was not prepared to wait for a bus, so drove carefully out of Highmarket and round into Station Road and along to the Grand where he parked clumsily with his front wheel on the kerb of the tiny car park. Inside he was soon successfully touting business as he supped a pint with a whisky chaser, too busy to notice the McArdles walk up behind him!

167

'Nick lad, collecting more money for our winnings I see,' Pat McArdle said as he placed his arm menacingly around Nick's shoulder.

Flinching and with a bravado he wasn't feeling, Nick replied, 'Look lads I hev been trying te find you te tell ye that I cannit cover ten pund bets, as Aah've telt ye's, me maximum bet is two bob so I'll give ye yer money back noo.'

Joe McArdle scowled at him and Pat squeezed his shoulder saying quietly, 'There'll be no handing any money back Nick lad, ye've teken our bet and that stands, now ye better have enough money to pay us if we win or we'll be taken that pretty red car of yours and an ounce of flesh in lieu if ye know what I mean!'

Nick made to protest but Joe silenced him by shoving a stubby finger to Nick's lips, 'We might be seeing you later Nick, yer living with the bonny Ginny now aren't yer lad so we know where te come should we be lucky, be seeing yer,' and the two of them walked off leaving him shaken and just a wee bit terrified that they might win.

Pushing his way to the bar, he demanded a double whisky to calm his nerves and gulped it down in one before limping outside to the Riley and roaring off back down town to the Portland where he hobbled quickly to the busy bar and ordered another pint with a whisky chaser. Downing the whisky, he picked up his pint and sauntered over to a group of lads sitting by the huge window at the front of the bar.

'Alreet lads,' he slurred, 'noo hoo fancies a bob or two on the big race?'

A tall, skinny lad who looked as hard as nails said, 'Aye go on Nick Aah'll hev two bob on ESB, I fancy his chances nee bother.'

'Good lad Tom, he's at twenty eight te one,' said Nick taking the money the lad handed over before scribbling the bet in the book.

The lad to the left of Tom shoved his hand in his pocket and pulled out a shilling and slid it across the varnished table, 'A bob on 'Hart Royal' Nick'.

Nick took the money as yet another lad banged a florin on the table and said loudly, 'Two bob on Mr What.'

Nick glared at the lad and snarled, 'Keep yer voice doon man,' then paused before saying, 'Fucking Mr What! Who gave ye that bloody tip, it's the forst time he's been in the race man!'

The lad said quietly, 'Nee bugga gave me the tip but Arthur Freeman's riding him and he knows his way roond Aintree, Aah fancy the little Irish horse!'

'That's all I need to fucking kna!' said Nick as he rose and limped to a group of men by the bar.

He spent another 30 minutes touting and drinking before driving the half mile to the Fell em Doon, where looking drunk and dishevelled, he limped inside. Ignoring the doorman's 'Aye Nick Lad,' he barged his way to the bar where Ginny gave him a withering look before turning to serve a group at the other end.

Nick knew he was drunk but he didn't care, there was till suckers willing to lose a bob or two on the Race and he was determined to take their hard earned cash. Loosening his tie he caught the attention of the barman and demanded, 'A whisky Bob.'

Bob looked at him, leaned forward and said quietly, 'Ye've had enough teday Nick, hevn't ye?'

'Give is a frigging whisky noo man.'

Bob reluctantly poured Nick a single whisky and took the money Nick pushed across the bar as Nick turned and steadied himself in an effort to stop the bar spinning before lurching over to two men he recognised sitting quietly at a table by the door. 'Haway fellas, de you want te put a couple of Bob on the big race?'

One of the two men was on the Club's Committee and after a quick glance at the other man, they stood up and took Nick by the arms and pushed him through the door and into the entrance hall, the Committee Member warning him, 'Yer drunk Nick and ye kna ye cannit tek bets in here and yer not in a fit state to be still drinking, noo bugger off hyem and sober up!'

Nick turned to argue but he was jostled out the door and left snarling and spitting on the pavement. Trying to focus his watery eyes as his head nodded drunkenly, he turned and felt his way along the buildings to the chip shop and staggered through the door, ignoring the woman cleaning the fryers as he groped his way up the back stairs to Ginny's flat where, weighed down by pockets full of silver coins, he flopped drunkenly into the one, old red armchair and immediately fell asleep.

He was dreaming that a great weight was pressing down on his head, crushing it slowly as his tongue swelled inside his parched mouth until he heard someone calling his name – 'Nick, Nick, NICK!, come on wake up, the race starts in a few minutes.' It was Ginny; she had finished work at quarter past two and hurried along to her flat to find him slumped in a drunken sleep in her armchair. She had taken his shoes off and undone his tie before making herself a cup of Nescafe and then spent some time tuning the radio to the Light Service to listen to the build-up to the Grand National.

Nick woke and sat forward rubbing his head with both of his hands, 'Me fucking heed is splitting, mek is a cup of tea,' then hearing the radio he spat, 'Fuck, what's the time?'

'It's ten past three they're getting ready to line up, what a state you are in Nick, you haven't sorted out the money and bets you've taking today and the winners will want paying tonight.'

Nick stood up and walked across to the sink between baby belling cooker and shelves stacked neatly with pots, pans and crockery and grabbed a cup filling it with water, gulping it down before staggering back to the chair. He needed to clear his head and think but he couldn't get past the thought of the consequences of Mr What winning!

170

The voice in the old wooden radio shouted, *'And they're off.'*

He sat up and said unnecessarily, 'Shut up and listen.'

'Goosander followed by Athenian and Never Say When lead the field to the first jump; they are all clear, not a single faller.

'Go on Athenian,' Muttered Nick.

'A faller at the third but it is Never Say When still leading followed by Goosander and Athenian with the favourite Wyndburgh and Hart Royal just behind, 'Over the Fifth and Never Say When still holding first place , a couple more fallers there...'

Nick shouted, 'Aah hope Mr Fucking What has faallen!'

'And now Beecher's Brook, the leaders all over safely but two more have fallen!'

'Who has fallen, where the fuck is Mr What?'

'Now, Canal Turn with its sharp left turn but there are no casualties....Valentines all clear and now Goosander takes the lead followed by Athenian with Never Say When dropping back to third...'

'Haway Goosander, but what aboot frigging Mr What, has he fallen?'

'Over ten and the order stays the same, Goosander and Athenian are neck and neck...'

Nick shouted, 'Thank God, nee sign of Mr What!'

'At the twelfth, Goosander holding on followed by Never Say When as Tiberetta and Green Drill move up.....'

'Nick was beginning to relax, there had been no mention of Mr What, hopefully he had fallen or he was well behind!'

'Near the end of the first round and over number fourteen as Green Drill beats Never Say When to third place, there are still twenty horses running as they come to the water jump with Goosander and Athenian still in the lead but Mr What is moving up to fourth as Richardstown falls...'

Back on his feet, Nick yelled, 'Where the fuck did he come from, come on Goosander divint let that fucking Irish nag catch ye!'

'Here they come into the country for the second time, Goosander still slightly ahead of Athenian but Mr What is gaining on them steadily as they approach jump seventeen...'

Nick growled, 'Fall for fuck's sake,'

'There over the seventeenth and now it's Mr What neck and neck with Goosander as Athenian drops behind with Never Say When and Wyndburgh moving past him...'

'One of ye's, any fucking one, just ride the fucka doon!'

'At the eighteenth, jockey Arthur Freeman is battling hard to take little Mr What clear of Goosander...'

Nick was jumping up and down, 'Come on Goosander, divint let the fucker past!'

'There's still a large field behind them at this stage of the race, more so than usual so anything can happen – over nineteen together, hardly a yard in it and behind them Athenian has come to grief...'

'Beechers for the second time, Mr What takes it bravely and is now edging ahead of Goosander as two more fall behind...'

Nick was beginning to panic, 'Come on Goosander for fuck's sake tek the fucker.'

'At the Canal Turn Mr What is well ahead of Goosander, Green Drill, Wyndburgh and ESB ...over Valentines and Mr What is increasing his lead as Goosander tires and Green Drill moves into second place...'

Nick screamed at the radio, 'Come on Green Drill, any of you fuckers; catch the bastard for fuck's sake!'

'No sign of tiredness from Mr What as the gap increases, he's now leading by three lengths - after jump twenty seven we have Mr What leading Green Drill, Tiberetta, ESB and Goosander but Mr What is now many lengths ahead as he comes to the last jump of all..'

Nick shouted, 'FUCK!'

'*Mr What takes the jump – he's Fallen-.*'

'YES,' shouted Nick.

'*No, he's alright, a brilliant recovery by Arthur Freeman as Mr What thunders on toward the post after what must have been his biggest fright of the race and finishes in great style over thirty lengths ahead of Tiberetta and a good fifty in front of Green Drill.*'

Flinging the empty cup he had been grasping throughout the race at the radio where it missed and smashed into pieces on the red floral wallpaper of the wall behind, Nick moaned, 'Shit, fucking shit, shit, what the fuck am Aah ganning te de, the McArdles will be after their fucking winnings, nearly fower hundred fucking quid, Aah hevn't got that man, am really fucked noo!'

Ginny ventured, 'Whey how much have ye got, surely ye can pay most of it off?'

Nick looked at her as though she was stupid and snarled, 'Aah've just ower a hundred quid and there's other winners te pay oot as well, the McArdles'll tek me money me car and me fucking face, am reet in the fucking shit noo man,' he said as panic engulfed him and he limped to the kitchen sink grabbing the small bottle of White Horse whisky he had hidden there. Shaking visibly, he unscrewed the top and took a long slug of the whisky almost choking as the kick of the strong alcohol hit his throat.

Ginny looked at the trembling, panic stricken figure, shocked that the 'War Hero' should collapse this way, 'Maybe you can reason with them Nick?'

'Hoo the fuck can ye reason we the likes of them?' he squawked as he took another long slug of whisky, 'I need te think before they get here.' Staggering back to the armchair, he sat down to pull his shoes on.

Ginny asked, 'Where are ye ganning?'

'Am ganning hyem, Aah've got a hundred quid float hidden in the cupboard under the stair's, Aah'll get that and give them another hundred and me car, at least that way, they might not fucking kill me!'

'Ye've got a Hundred pounds at Jane's? Asked Ginny'

'Aye, ye divin't think I'd bring it here de ye?' he said as he stood and took another long drink, leaving just a small amount of whisky in the bottle.

'Don't drive there Nick, you're too drunk, please walk, it's not far.'

He spat back, 'Aah'll fucking dee what Aah want woman,' but knew she was right and leaving the car keys next to the radio he fastened his coat that was still weighed down with pockets bulging with coins and stormed out the flat and headed for the Sixth Row a couple of hundred yards away.

Earlier, with freshly applied make up and wearing her best red coat, Sarah Proudlock, smoothed her blonde hair back from her temple before linking her man Jim and accompanied by a very solemn Terry, they walked from their house in the Third Row to the Shepherd's house in the Sixth A good looking upright couple in their thirties, they had been and continued to be mightily upset at the news Terry had given them on Wednesday night but 'what had to be done, had to be done,' they made that clear to Terry who had told them that he loved Maureen and wanted to marry her.

Jim Proudlock had expressed his feelings in the firm monosyllabic way typical of the tough miners who rarely betrayed their emotions in front of family. He would never let Terry know that he and his mother had to get married, albeit they were a couple of years older than Terry at the time but it was something he had hoped would not happen to his children as he remembered how tough their first few years of marriage had been. They would never have managed without their parents and

174

he was determined to give his lad his support no matter how stupid he had been.

Gathered in the Shepherd's sitting room, the meeting with Jane and Maureen had started off very formally but once everyone had expressed their desire that Maureen should keep the baby and that there should be a wedding as soon as possible, the atmosphere relaxed. The only tense moment came when Jim said, 'I've known Nick since Bothal School when he was in his last year and I was just starting, he was always in trouble and has never changed as far as I can tell and I divin't really want anything te de with him, so am glad to hear that he's gone!'

Sarah dug her elbow into her husband's side and glaring at him said, 'Be that as it may, these two obviously care for each other and your Maureen has always struck me as being a nice lass and Terry has always said that she was the one for him so we will just have to make the best of it.'

Sitting on the arm of the chair that Maureen was in, Terry blushed but put his hand gently on Maureen's shoulder. She had sat with her head lowered for most of the conversation but lifted it now and gave Terry a little smile as she fought back tears.

Placing a fresh pot of tea on the coffee table in front of the sofa, Jane said, 'So we are agreed, a wedding in the Methodist Chapel at the end of the Second Row as soon as I can book it and we'll have a quiet reception next door in the Toc H Hall?'

Sarah nodded and said, 'We'll help with the catering.'

Jim blundered again, 'Am glad there's been nee talk of visiting Fat Flora's or owt like that!'

Sarah was aghast! 'Jim, shut up will you!'

Maureen and Terry both looked puzzled not sure what Terry's Father was talking about but it was Jane who ended that conversation and their puzzlement. 'There was never a question about Maureen keeping the baby Jim, only what you and your Terry wanted to do.'

It was agreed that Maureen would move in with the Proudlocks after the marriage and they would have Terry's room until they could arrange something better which would be sometime, at least until Terry finished his apprenticeship. They talked for a while longer until just before four o'clock when Sarah said, 'Well we best be making a move Jim, Aah've yor's and the lads' dinner to check in the oven,' and standing she said to Jane, 'It's been lovely meeting ye even under the current circumstances, Terry said yer a lovely woman and he's not wrong, am obviously just worried aboot them.'

Jane grabbed Sarah and gave her a hug and without saying anything led the way into the kitchen; just as Nick burst in!

He looked wretched, his hair was uncombed, his jacket creased and baggy, his tie hung round his neck, he reeked of alcohol and he had a wild stare to his watery eyes, he was clearly drunk out of his mind!

Standing swaying by the back door he looked at the group of people standing in the cramped kitchen and tried to focus on who was who, 'What the fucking hell's ganning on here; a fucking party?' he slurred!

Jane was horrified, 'Nick I think you had better leave.'

'Shut up woman, what's ganning on here, why are the fucking Proodlock clan gathering here?'

Maureen pushed forward and grabbing her drunken father by the arm, she begged, 'Dad, yor drunk and you're going to ruin everything; just leave please.'

Trying to shrug off her grip, Nick snarled, 'Not till Aah kna what's ganning on here!'

Without thinking, Maureen blurted, 'Am going to have a baby and me and Terry are getting married now please leave,' and tried to push him back through the door.

'A fucking baby, yer bloody fucking slut, yer ownly sixteen and yer fucking aboot,' growled Nick as he pulled her hand from his arm and smacked her viscously with the back of his right hand, splitting her lip and sending her reeling backwards onto the floor in front of Jane and the Proudlocks. Terry jumped at Nick, wrapping his arm around his neck in a stranglehold, forcing him to bend forward into a crouch where he struggled in vain to break Terry's hold.

Stuck behind the women and the kitchen table, Jim Proudlock shouted, 'Hang on te him Terry and Aah'll give you hand to sort the waster oot,' but before he could get past, desperate to escape the vice like grip around his neck, Nick plunged his hand into his jacket pocket and pulled out the flick knife, clicking it open as he brought it clear.

Terry thought Nick had punched him in the side and stomach and couldn't understand why his strength had suddenly left him as he released Nick and crumpled to the floor.

There was a moment's silence before Sarah screamed, 'He's stabbed wor Terry!' and bent over her son blocking Jim again.

Nick looked down at Terry who had both hands to his stomach, blood oozing between his fingers and onto the floor and then looking at the blood-stained knife in his hand, he backed toward the door as Maureen screamed and Jane knelt down next to Terry.

Jim finally got past the women but Jane stopped him saying in a calm but firm voice, 'Let him go Jim, run over to the shop in Ellington Road and phone for an ambulance for Terry, quickly now.'

Jim did as ordered and ran out the door and saw Nick stumbling down the Row before he turned the other way and sprinted the fifty yards to the shop, bursting in, demanding to use their telephone.

As Jim phoned for an ambulance and the police, Jane was doing her best to stop the bleeding from the knife wound to Terry's side and stomach and ordered Sarah to press a towel to one of the wounds.

Maureen was distraught and was standing crying hysterically at the sight of the two women trying to save her boyfriend's life.

Looking up at his mother, Terry said through gritted teeth, 'By that bugga hurts a bit Mam.'

'Ye'll be alright lad, won't he Jane?' she said desperately.

Barely managing to control her own emotions, Jane looked at Terry and said with a confidence she wasn't feeling, 'Yes of course he will, it's only a cut to his side and not very deep and the other wound doesn't look too bad, he'll be fine as soon as we get him to hospital and stitched up. Now Maureen, pull yourself together and clean your lip up, you might need a stitch in it, I'll have a look in a minute.'

Standing peering through the net curtain of the big sash window in her flat watching for Nick returning, Ginny was shocked when she saw him running in his lame way past Pearson's on the other side of the street before bolting across the road causing a car to slam its brakes on. Seconds later he burst into the flat wild eyed and panic stricken and ignoring Ginny, grabbed the money satchel from under the bed and his car keys before rushing back to the door but was stopped by Ginny grabbing his arm.

'Whatever's happened Nick, where are you going?'

He turned and looking through her, he held his blood stained hand up and shouted, 'Aah've killed young Terry, Aah've got te get oot of here noo!'

Ginny held onto him, 'What are ye saying Nick, my God what hev ye done?'

'Are ye fucking deaf, Aah've stabbed Terry Proodlock noo let me gan, Aah've got te get the fuck away.'

Ginny hung on to him and said, 'What about me Nick, shall I come with you?'

'Fuck you an aall,' he snarled viscously and swung the heavy satchel at her head knocking to the ground as he bolted toward the door.

Lying on the floor Ginny yelled hopelessly, 'Nick I'm pregnant, don't leave me!'

He did not hear her cry as he ran down the stairs in panic stricken flight and burst onto the street, straight into Joe and Pat McArdle!

As Joe pushed Nick back against the wall of the house next to the Fish and Chip Shop, Nick screamed, 'Not now, not fucking now man, let me go!'

Pat McArdle joined his brother and held Nick against the wall as Joe snarled, 'Is that our money ye were bringing to us Nick lad, I hope ye've got three hundred and eighty quid in there for us?'

With tears running down his eyes, Nick spluttered, 'You don't understand, Aah hev te get away from here now, please let me go, Aah'll get yer money for ye Aah promise, just let me go!'

Pushing his face into Nick's, Pat growled, 'It looks to us as if you were trying to do a runner without paying us our winnings Nick lad, now cough up or face the consequences,' then punched him hard in the stomach causing him to vomit a stream of stinking beer, whisky and fear! The McArdles stepped back to avoid the torrent as Nick stood up and pulled the flick knife from his pocket and with vomit dribbling down his chin warned, 'Stay back or Aah'll fucking knife ye, ye bastards!'

They held back, watching the long bladed knife in Nick's right hand and the heavy bag in his left as he edged along the wall toward his car parked ten yards further down. Joe moved to his right and Pat to his left, both of them looking for a chance to jump the drunk but before they could make their move, a black car with bells ringing frantically, screeched into the top end of Highmarket with and raced toward them.

PC John Tate was at the wheel of the black Wolsley 6-90 police car responding to the message that there had been a stabbing in the Sixth

Row and the man responsible - Nick Shepherd was heading toward the Fell em Doon.

The sound of the police bells stopped the McArdles in their tracks leaving Nick to bolt for his car and running around to the driver's side, he climbed quickly in just as the police car raced past.

Sitting next to John Tate, portly PC Richard Williams said loudly 'Stop, stop, that's the bugger there.'

Tate; lean, fit and father of three, expertly brought the Wolsley to a screeching halt twenty yards past Nick as the McArdles ran off in the opposite direction. Both policemen jumped out of their car and ran back toward the Riley as Nick started up and accelerated toward them forcing them to jump clear as he raced off toward the end of Highmarket on the road to Morpeth.

Within seconds the two policemen were back in their car and speeding after Nick, John Tate racing up through the gears while PC Williams radioed events to the control room at Morpeth. Nick had a few hundred yards lead that was diminishing steadily as he recklessly threw the Riley around the left hander past Home Farm towards the junction at 'Coopers Corner' where he again swung the wheel hard over to the right causing the car to swing it's rear end out as he careened from the Newcastle road, onto the road for Bothal and Morpeth that was greasy from drizzling rain. With the police bells ringing, John Tate dropped two gears and swung the Wolsley round the corner before accelerating hard after the fleeing Riley.

'They're sending two cars out from Morpeth, hopefully we'll trap the bugga at Pegswood, shouted Williams as they sped toward Bothal and its notorious bank!

Adrenalin and whisky were fuelling Nick's headlong flight but did nothing to improve his driving ability as he sped past Bothal Barns cursing loudly as he fumbled to switch his headlights on in the darkening evening sky. He took his eyes of the road for a couple of seconds to find the switch and when he looked up he saw that the first sharp left hander of Bothal Bank was coming up fast, stamping on his brakes he swung the steering wheel hard-over and the car slid sideways into the corner; where he released the foot brake to try and straighten up but instead he fish-tailed around, the rear wheels bouncing off the right hand curb before the car swung the other way and bounced off the left hand one. In total panic, Nick stamped on both the brakes and clutch causing the Riley to slide down the steep greasy road toward the right-hand hairpin where it bounced over the curb and crashed on top of the low fence before sliding another 5 yards down the steep embankment to come to a crashing halt against one of the many trees that guarded the bank.

He managed to throw his arms up to protect his face but smashed his chest against the steering wheel, knocking the air out of his lungs leaving him gasping and dazed. The front doors of the Riley opened toward the rear and kicking open his, he held it open with his foot as he scrambled for the money satchel that had flown off the passengers' seat into the foot well, grabbing it as he reached into his pocket and pulled out the flick knife, determined not to be arrested.

John Tate brought the Wolsley to a sliding halt 10 yards from the fence that Nick had smashed through and both policemen jumped out and ran forward to either side of Nick's car. PC Williams was having difficulty negotiating the steep bank on the passenger side that was overgrown with brambles but John Tate had no such problem and wrenched open and pushed back the driver's door against its own weight with his left hand as he grabbed Nick with his right just as Nick turned and lunged with his right hand, driving the flick knife up and through the serge police jacket and into John Tate's madly beating heart, stopping it instantly!

PC Tate collapsed to breathe his last few breaths as Nick scrambled out and up the bank while PC Williams made his way around the front of the car and up to where his partner looked up at him with eyes whose spark had just departed.

Still unsure what had happened he knelt to help his comrade up but seeing that he was lifeless, he stood up and gave chase closing up on Nick at the top of the bank but as he did so Nick stopped, turned and swung the heavy money satchel straight into the policeman's face knocking him to the ground and relieving him of several teeth.

The satchel split with the force of the impact sending the silver coins cascading out across the road, many of them racing down the hill as Nick threw the empty satchel at the floored PC before running up the bank. It took PC Williams several precious seconds to regain his senses and by then Nick had crossed the fence at the top of the hill and was running north across open fields to the west of Coneygarth Farm. The PC stood up and yelled into the night air, 'Shepherd you bastard, you'll swing for this!' and turned to go to his fallen comrade as the bells of the police cars from Morpeth could be heard racing toward Bothal.

Ian and Rafe had had a good afternoon, they had sold all the firewood and had treated themselves to a Pepsi and crisps at Pieroni's Café before going into Crisps the newsagent and toyshop where they put their names down for the next available evening newspaper rounds. They climbed back onto the tandem and singing Guy Mitchell's 'Singing the Blues, they cycled through the drizzle to Highmarket, onto the Ellington road and to the rail crossing that was 50 yards from their home, totally unaware of what had just occurred.

They turned left onto the bramble sided path that ran alongside the railway line heading toward Coneygarth Drift Mine and the timber yard, Ian saying, 'It won't be fully dark when we get there but there's niver anybody aboot this time on a Saturday and we need te be back for dinner at six.'

182

'I'm ravenous,' said a very hungry Rafe as Ian slowed as they approached the lights of the Drift that shone brightly in a rapidly darkening sky. The drift consisted of one main structure of a brick filled, red-leaded steel framed building that spanned a spur from the railway where the coal wagons were filled. From this building a similar structure descended at 30 degrees to ground level concealing the huge convey belt that raced up from below ground carrying the hard won coal into the rail-wagons throughout the week apart from Saturday evening and Sunday. Behind this was another building which contained a lamp cabin, Overman's Office and around the back at a lower level, a boiler room that was used as a place of rest by the young lads who loaded tubs and trams with timber before going down the drift.

They stopped and climbing off the tandem twenty or so yards from the drift mine, pushed the bike silently past the buildings until they were adjacent to the timber yard beyond and turned the bike, hiding it behind the scrub next to the railway line where it was out of sight of anyone at Coneygarth.

Ian smiled at Rafe, 'Noo the commando stuff, we sneak in, tek a couple of props each, bring them back and de it again, follow me, keep quiet and de as Aah tell ye, right!'

Grinning madly Rafe nodded as he suppressed the urge to giggle and then slunk after Ian thoroughly enjoying their illegal escapade. Ian knew that if the watchmen found them, all they had to do was to tell him they were taking a couple of props for firewood and he would turn a blind eye but he chose not to tell Rafe that.

Hobbling panic stricken across the field, Nick could hear the bells of the police cars echoing through Bothal Valley and when they stopped he knew they had reached the scene of his crash – the murder scene! Looking up to the darkening skies, he felt the drizzle on his face and cried, 'Ye fucking idiot, ye've fucking done it noo,' and limped on toward the lights of Coneygarth Drift that shone like beacons on the other side of the muddy quagmire that was the path of the new road being constructed between Ashington and Pegswood to by-pass Bothal and the Bank.

Having worked at Coneygarth several times over the years he knew he could rest up in the boiler room while he decided what to do and headed for the timber yard in order to approach the boiler room in shadow. Climbing the small embankment to the yard, he turned back to look toward Bothal and could see torches flashing in the distance, about three quarters of a mile off! 'So much for lying up here,' he thought, 'I'll see if there are any bait bags with grub in the boiler room and then push on toward Ellington and swing roond toward Newbiggin and me Mam's.'

Ian crept silently through the huge stacks of pit props, heading for the easily manageable three footers, pointing them out to Rafe. He nodded and followed Ian to the stack and held his arms out as Ian pulled off two props and handed them to Rafe before turning for two more. As he did so he heard a scuffle behind him and turned to see to his horror that his Father, who looked like a demented, mud spattered ghoul, had his left arm around Rafe's neck and a wicked looking knife in his right hand!

'What the fuck are ye two deeing here?' Nick snarled.

Shocked at seeing his father in this terrible state, Ian blustered, 'We're just getting some pit props for fire wood Dad, let Rafe go man!'

Nick tightened his grip and said, 'Everything has gone te rat shit since this blidy frigging twat came, he's caused all the fucking bother I'm in, the fucking little shit.'

Rafe struggled to break free but Nick was too strong for him and forced the lad onto the ground pinning Rafe's arms back with his knees, he leant over the lad and sneered, 'What ye ganning te de noo ye

184

fucking little bastard?' and leaning back he spat into Rafe's face and ran the edge of the knife menacingly across Rafe's cheek.

Ian stepped forward and grabbed his father's arms, trying to pull him off but was rewarded with a back hander that sent him reeling.

Looking up at the crazed man, Rafe watched horrified, unable to move his arms, feeling the sharp point of the blade against his neck slicing flesh as Nick readied himself to plunge it in.

Nick's eyes suddenly glaze over and he pitched forward collapsing on top of Rafe like a dead weight. He quickly wriggled free to find Ian standing with a two foot long, stout timber strut clenched in his hands, 'Aah had te do it, Aah had to hit him; he was going to kill you!'

Rafe knelt to look at the back of Nick's head and saw that it was bleeding heavily, 'I think you've killed him?'

Tears welled up in Ian's eyes and he gasped, 'My God what am Aah ganning to do?'

Rafe was finding it difficult to think as he clutched the small cut on his neck to stop the trickle of blood, 'I don't know, do you think we should run away or what?'

Ian thought for a moment, 'Nur come on we'll find some body and tell them I've hit me father and he might be dead or something,' and walked forlornly off to the main building of the Drift. It took them several minutes to find a man in his sixties sitting in the lamp room reading a Western.

Ian blurted, 'We need help, I've just bashed me Dad on the back of the heed and Aah think he might be deed, we need an ambulance!'

The Lampman dropped his paperback and demanded, 'What the blidy hell are ye talking aboot lad and what's happened to his neck?'

'Me Faather stabbed him so I had to bash me faather on the back of the heed and I might hev killed him cos he's lying and not moving in the timber yard and there's blood all ower the back of his heed man!'

185

'Ye buggas better not be having me on, come on show me where he is,' and he limped after them as Ian and Rafe led him to where they had left Nick lying. As they approached the spot they could see torches in the field next to the Timber yard and just below them a policeman wearing an open, mud spattered overcoat, climbed the fence at bottom of the embankment and struggled up toward them.

'Hev ye seen a man with a limp running this way?' asked the panting PC John Stone.

The Lampman answered, 'Aah've seen nee bugga, just these two lads and this one reckons they've killed their faather!'

PC Stone looked at him as though he was mad and said, 'What the hell are ye talking aboot, a dangerous man was seen running this way, he's just murdered a Police Officer and bloody soon every policeman in Northumberland will be here looking for bloody Nick Shepherd!'

Ian couldn't believe what he was hearing and almost shouted, 'That's my Dad, I've just killed him, he's ower there,' and pointed to the stack of three foot props.

PC Stone looked at Ian and said, 'Your father! and you've killed him, what the hell are ye saying lad, how and why have you killed your father?'

'Cos he was ganning te kill Rafe with a knife, so I hit him on the back of the heed with a prop.'

PC Stone grabbed the two boys and pushed them toward where they had left Nick - he wasn't there! 'Are ye sods telling bloody lies?' he asked as Rafe bent down to look closely at where Nick had lain.

'Look,' he said, 'here's his blood, he must have just been knocked out and woken up and run off!'

Reflecting the overhead lights in its wicked blade from where it lay next to the props, the flick knife caught Ian's eye, 'There,' he shouted, 'there's his knife,' and stepping forward to pick it up he felt the policeman grab his shoulder.'

'Don't touch that son, it's evidence and blidy well spotted, noo the buggas not so dangerous!'

Two more mud spattered constables joined them to find out what was going on and as the bemused PC Stone tried to explain what appeared to have happened, the Lampman asked Ian, 'What were ye deeing here in the forst place?'

'Getting some props for firewood mister!'

As one of the newcomers blew his whistle to attract the other police officers still in the fields, PC Stone turned back to the boys and asked, 'And you say Nick Shepherd is your father and you bashed him on the head with a lump of wood and knocked him out?'

Ian answered, 'He's my father, this is my Uncle, and aye Aah bashed him on the heed when he was ganning to shove his knife in Rafe's neck.'

Rafe took his hand from his neck releasing a fresh dribble of blood, 'He was pushing the knife into my neck, see?'

Stone looked at Rafe's cut and said, 'Ye've been lucky lad a wee bit further back and that might have been your jugular,' then turning to the Lampman he asked, 'have you got a First-Aid kit you can stick a plaster or sumat on this lads neck?'

The Lampman nodded and led Rafe back to the Lamp Room but PC Stone held on to Ian as more police arrived from the direction of Bothal, 'A few questions lad, why were you meeting your father here?'

Ian was shocked, 'I wasn't, me and Rafe came here to get some props for firewood, we didn't kna me Dad was here, Aah hevn't seen him since he left home last weekend!'

'So he doesn't live with you anymore then?'

'No, he lives in Highmarket man, we didn't kna he was ganning te be here.'

'Right son, have you any idea where you father may be running too?'

'Whey we only live half a mile doon the railway line so he must be ganning hyem!'

Stone shook his head, took off his helmet and wiped the inside with a handkerchief he had pulled out of his trouser pocket, 'I doubt that lad, the police are already there, he stabbed a young lad there an hour or so ago, I would think that's the last place he would go.'

Ian couldn't believe what he was hearing, 'What young lad, has he stabbed one of my brothers?'

PC Stone turned and shouted to one of the other policemen that were now searching the timber yard, 'Alec, what was the name of the young lad that Shepherd stabbed?'

Alec turned and shouted back, 'Terence Proudlock, he's been teking to hospital.'

'That's my sister's boyfriend, gasped Ian, 'Why would he stab him? My Dad must hev gone mad!'

'Whey he's certainly cannit get in te any more bother than he is now son, now is there anywhere else he might run too, any relatives?'

'Me Granny at Newbiggin is the only one we have, she lives in North Seaton Road.'

With their bells ringing madly, two police cars raced into car park just below where they were standing, 'That'll be the Superintendent, come on lad, we need to tell him what's happened here and that we've got the knife thanks to you two,' said Stone as he put his hand on Ian's shoulder and led him toward the figures climbing out of the cars.

Nick was four hundred yards away hobbling along the railway line to Ashington, he was in a desperate condition, soaked, mud caked with blood oozing from his head, he had a raging thirst and the pains in his head from the effects of the whisky and the blow from Ian made it difficult for him to think. He dare not stop as he felt the coppers were right behind him but where to go? His lame knee was aching unbearably making any plans of running to Newbiggin impossible; anyway he needed money if he was going to get away.

'Money!' he thought, 'I still have a hundred quid hidden at home, Aah'll hev te get that but forst Aah need te hide and hev a rest.' He hobbled along the cinder track, past the large Granary stopping in the shadows 50 feet from the level crossing of the Ellington Road. On the other side of the road, he could see beyond the trees and bushes, the gable end of his house in the Sixth Row, so close but the place would probably be full of Police by now!

The road was quiet and almost free of traffic as he inched forward waiting for an opportunity to race over to the other side and the seclusion of the trees and scrub that separated the railway line from the back of the coalhouses and outside toilets of his street. He didn't wait long, and dashed safely over, scrambling over the wooden picket fence and crawling into the dark sanctuary of the dense scrub just behind his coal house.

He could hear voices but did not dare look over the wall for fear of being seen so instead, wriggled under thick bushes and lay down to rest and wait.

The ambulance that had arrived within ten minutes of Jim Proudlock making the 999 call was in the street barely ten minutes before it had turned and was racing to Ashington Hospital with Terry being attended to by one of the ambulance men while his distraught Mother and Maureen sat watching from the bench seat. Jim said he would go home to tell young Reg what had happened and take him on the bus to the hospital to see how Terry was doing.

As the ambulance pulled away, a black Ford Prefect pulled up in the space the ambulance had just left and a handsome, if untidy, tall blonde man whose hair looked as though it had not seen a comb for some time, climbed out, straightening his tartan tie and fastening his crumpled tweed jacket as he looked at the neighbours who had gathered to see what was happening.

Looking at Arthur Galloway, he asked in a Scottish lilt, 'Is this the Shepherd's house?'

'Arthur looked at the dishevelled man and answered, 'Aye, it is but noo's not the best time te call as there's been some bother!'

The stranger smiled at Arthur, 'That's why I'm here,' and walked into the back yard and knocked on the door.

Aggie Galloway opened the door and looking up at the tousled haired man, said, 'Noo's not a good time whatever it is, we are expecting the Polis!'

'That would be me, Detective Sergeant Norman, Mrs Shepherd.'

Aggie gave him a withering look and said, 'Am not Mrs Shepherd, she's inside, ye divin't look much of a polis te me but ye better come in.' DS Norman followed Aggie into the into the small kitchen to see Jane kneeling with her back to him, mopping blood up from the lino of the kitchen floor.

'Who is it Aggie?' she asked without turning.

It's the Polis Jane.'

Jane stood and turned, wiping a strand of hair from her furrowed brow and looked up into the startling green eyes of the Detective and said with a hint of annoyance, 'It has taken you long enough to get here!'

Looking into the worried face of the beautiful woman in front of him, Jamie Norman found himself momentarily lost for words, then stammered, 'Aye, I'm sorry Mrs Shepherd, it's a bit chaotic at the moment, the priority was to get all available Officers out looking for your husband and I had just finished for the day, someone had to come and fetch me, now if we can sit down somewhere perhaps you can tell me what happened here!'

Jane wearily dropped the blood stained cloth she was holding into the bucket by her feet and walked to the pantry to rinse her hands before saying, 'We can sit in here,' and led DS Norman into the sitting room.

Aggie, said, I'll put the kettle on Jane, I'm sure you could use a cup of tea.'

Jane was half way through describing what had occurred, when there was a heavy knock at the door; tutting; Aggie waddled to the door and opened it to look up at a tall uniformed Constable! 'One of yours is already here,' said Aggie.

'Yes, that's who I hev come te see, can ye ask him te come te the door please Mrs Shepherd.'

'Am not Mrs Shepherd, just hang on a minute,' and Aggie scuttled back to the sitting room and said, 'Sorry to interrupt but there's one of your lot at the door asking te see ye.'

DS Norman apologised for the interruption and walked to the door where the Constable took him into the yard to talk to him for a couple of minutes before he walked back into the sitting room looking very worried.

'Mrs Shepherd I have just been told that your husband has killed a police officer so this is now a murder investigation!'

Jane stood up, holding her hand to her mouth and almost whispered, 'Oh no, my God what has he done?'

DS Norman continued, 'They are drafting in policemen from all over Northumberland to search for your husband, apparently he ran off from Bothal with some of the local Bobbies hard after him, they will also appoint a DCI from Morpeth to take over the case but I have to stay here until he arrives and there will be a constable outside just in case your husband comes back this way but I should imagine that is very unlikely.'

Jane was about to speak but stopped when she saw a very worried Mike walk in.

'What's ganning on Mam; there's three cars outside, two of them are police, there's a policeman at the door and haf the neighbours standing in the street shaking the heeds and nebody will tell me what's ganning on!'

Putting on a brave face, Jane hugged Mike saying, 'You better come in here and I'll tell you what's happened, have you seen Ian or Rafe?

Mike stepped into the sitting room and nodded to the tall figure standing by the window, 'Aye, hallo, who are you?' he asked.

I'm Detective Sergeant Norman; I'll wait in the kitchen while you mother tells you what has happened.'

Jane told an incredulous and increasingly shocked Mike of what she knew then joined the DS and Aggie who were drinking tea in the kitchen, Aggie pouring two cups for them as Mike began to ask a question but was stopped by Jane, 'I'm worried about Ian and Rafe, they should have been home by now!'

Taking the cup of tea Maggie handed him, Mike said, 'They're probably still doon at Coneygarth getting some pit props to chop for firewood Mam.

DS Norman put his cup on the kitchen table and asked, 'Coneygarth, do you mean the drift mine?'

'Aye, Ian normally gans there on a Saturday afternoon and the fella their gives him a couple of pit props to chop up for firewood, why?'

Knowing that was the direction the chase had gone, DS Norman looked concerned, but said, 'Nothing, I just want to check something on one of the car radio,' and hurried outside.

'Where's Tommy Mam,' asked Mike.

'Down at the Turnbull's, Aggie has been down to see Mrs Turnbull and they're going to keep Tommy there until I go for him, he's having his dinner with them.'

A few minutes later, DS Norman tapped on the door and walked back in trying unsuccessfully to smooth his unkempt hair, 'Mrs Shepherd your sons are on the way here with the Superintendent, apparently they had a brush with your husband at Coneygarth but are both OK, so the search for your husband is being concentrated across the fields toward the Ellington Road with the possibility he might be heading for his mother's at Newbiggin.'

Jane was horrified, 'Brush with Nick, what do you mean, he hasn't hurt them has he?'

'Not as far as I'm aware but they'll be here anytime now.'

Rushing to the door, Jane was just in time to see another black Wolseley pull up behind the other two, hurrying down she saw Ian and Rafe climb out looking a little confused as they stopped to take in the scene. There was now more cars in the Sixth Row than anyone had ever seen at one time and at least five policemen were by their house as well as most of the neighbours, amongst them Jake and big Howard.

'Yer Dad's done it noo Ian,' said Jake as his mother pulled him back into the small crowd, clamping her hand over his mouth to silence him.

Wrapping an arm each around Ian and Rafe, Jane steered them quickly back to the house, ignoring the distinguished looking policeman who climbed out the car after the boys. Under the bright light of the kitchen ceiling light she turned to examine the boys and asked, 'Are you both alright, he didn't hurt you did he?'

Ian started to speak but Rafe beat him to it, 'We are fine Jane, Nick was going to stab me in the neck,' he said touching the large Elastoplast on his neck, 'but Ian floored him with a pit prop!'

'Aah thought I'd killed him Mam but I hadn't he's run off somewhere.'

'Oh my God,' Jane gasped, 'Are you alright Rafe, how bad is your neck?'

'Just a little cut, thanks to Ian but I fear it would have been worse if he had not bashed him on the back of the head!'

The house became more and more chaotic, first the Superintendent from Ashington arrived and then Chief Superintendent Garrity followed by DCI Fairbanks from Morpeth whilst outside several members of the press started to gather but were kept at bay by the police. Police cars and vans could be heard racing up and down Ellington Road, thumping across the level crossing as more and more police joined the hunt for Nick who laid shaking and shivering fifteen yards from his back door and a dozen or more policemen!

At nine o'clock, Chief Superintendent Garrity set up a Command and Control Headquarters in a mobile unit parked in the Granary yard a couple of hundred yards from the Sixth Row as he concentrated the search for Nick in the area between Coneygarth and Ellington. A dozen policemen were scouring the building site for the new NCB Area Workshops that contained a myriad of hiding places on the other side of the railway to the Rows

Four times Nick had to control his nausea and shaking as policemen scoured the scrub between the outhouses and railway, one of them almost prodding him with a stick but their search was not as thorough as it might have been as the general consensus was that Nick was heading for Newbiggin, nonetheless Garrity positioned a constable outside number 60 just in case Nick was stupid enough to return home!

Spending the night at his Mother's, Edward Thompson had been called in to help again, driving to Ashington Hospital just after ten to collect the Proudlocks and Maureen. Maureen looked tired and pale when she walked into the kitchen with Edward, stopping by the door to see who was still about. Apart from Tommy who was tucked up in bed, the rest of the family were sitting around the kitchen table drinking tea and eating toast. Rushing around to Maureen, Jane hugged her, asking, 'How is he?'

Maureen gave a relieved smile, 'He's out of danger, the Doctor said he was very lucky that the stab wound did not puncture anything vital and the other cut needed twelve stitches,' her emotions got the better of her and she clung to Jane saying, 'Oh Mam, I thought I'd lost him, I thought he was going to die but he will be home in a few days - what about me Dad, have they caught him yet?'

'Not as far as we know now come on and sit down and have a cup of tea, you look all in,' then looking at Edward, Jane asked, 'will you join us for a cup of tea Edward?'

Edward smiled at Jane but said, 'No thanks Jane, I better leave you all to get some sleep if that's possible but divin't forget, if there is owt ye need or want deeing just ask.'

Outside, Edward spoke briefly to the constable standing in the drizzle under the street lamp and then climbed into his car and drove down to his Mother's. By twelve o'clock everyone in number 60 was in bed but only the youngest was sleeping soundly; thoughts of the day's events thwarting any chance the remainder had to sleep.

After the last of the police cars left the Sixth Row, Nick waited for half an hour before peering cautiously over the wall between the toilets and coalhouses. Seeing the constable under the lamp he ducked back down, cursing silently to himself as he shivered; feeling hungry, thirsty and scared, very scared.

He heard Edward drive up and go into his house then a few minutes later heard him talking to the constable before driving down to his mother's. An hour later he listened as another constable arrived and talked to the first one for ten minutes before he took over the watch.

He drifted off a couple of times, waking with a start just after one o'clock; although he could here cars in the distant, the Sixth Row was very quiet and he again wriggled up and peered over the wall. PC John Doherty was smoking a cigarette as he stood quietly under the lamp post on what he considered to be a pointless task, 'The mad buggas niver ganna come back here,' he thought as he stubbed the cigarette end out with the toe of his boot.

Hidden in the dark, Nick stared at the constable wishing him to disappear but realising that was highly unlikely he began to consider his options including trying to make it to his mother's but as he watched, PC Doherty crossed the street and disappeared into the Galloway's toilet!

Nick was over the wall in a second and hobbled silently to his back door, key already in hand, he unlocked the door and stepped quickly in closing it quietly behind him. Standing with his back to the door with the stairs directly in front of him, he stood motionless, listening for any sound that might indicate he had woken someone. After a few tense seconds and hearing no noise, he quietly opened the kitchen door to his left and again stood quietly but this time he was savouring the familiar smells of his home! A wave of self-pity swamped him as he realised what he had thrown away; a beautiful wife and four great kids who, because of his evil ways, all despised him.

Feeling no remorse for what he had done, he wallowed in self-pity that everything and everyone had conspired against him. 'Well fuck them all,' he thought as he stepped into the kitchen and felt his way along the wall to his right until his hand fell with the familiarity of use on the small sneb that held closed the under stairs cupboard. Lifting the sneb clear, he gently opened the door and dropped to his knees to feel along the floor, being careful not to knock over Jane's collection of household cleaning paraphernalia. Moving a brush and pan delicately to one side he scrabbled to lift the lino in the corner for a few seconds before it moved allowing him to scoop up the five pound notes that were hidden there.

Easing himself painfully back to his feet he counted the notes – 'Twenty, at least they hadn't found my stash,' he thought as he pondered on how to make his escape from the house. He was far from thinking rationally, thirst, hunger and a blinding headache preventing him from being logical. 'A drink of water and food,' he thought as with cash in hand, he silently made his way to the pantry where he groped around in the dark before taking a glass from the top shelf and quietly filling it, swallowing first one then two more glasses of cold water savouring each glass as if it were nectar.

Walking back to the kitchen table he lifted the lid from the bread bin on the corner, took out half an uncut loaf and placing it on the table and picking up the nine inch bladed carving knife or gully, he began to cut through the bread when the door in the sitting room was thrown open and the light inside switched on, blinding him as he turned with the huge gully in his hand to see who was there.

'Dad, what the hell are ye deeing?' demanded Mike from the sitting room door.

Panicking, Nick snarled, 'Be quiet.'

Mike looked at the pathetic, wild eyed wreck of a man that stood before him; the man who had beat him more times than he could remember; the drunken bully who had abused his mother and battered his brothers and sisters and who was now a murderer. Switching on the kitchen light that further blinded Nick, he said, 'Give yourself up, there's no way ye can get away man!'

'Nick pointed the gully at Mike and growled, 'Put that fucking light oot and divint ye tell me what te de ye fucking little waster ye or Aah'll cut yer fucking heed off!'

Mike switched the kitchen light off and stood watching his father looking for an opportunity to jump him while outside, PC Doherty

197

standing outside the toilet fasten the buttons of his trousers, saw the light in the kitchen window go on then off.

Thinking it strange and worried that someone may have got into the house while he was relieving himself, he walked quickly across the street, sliding his truncheon from his pocket as he did so. 'Probably a false alarm or maybe one of them nosey bloody reporters has slid in behind my back?' he thought as he crossed the tiny yard and tried the back door handle – it opened and PC Doherty stepped in to look into the kitchen where he saw Nick Shepherd standing with a huge knife in his hand, his son to the right standing in the door to the sitting room silhouetted by the light shining from within.

Standing a good foot taller than Nick, Doherty was not easily rattled and he felt the urge to smash his fist into the killer's face, 'Put the knife down Shepherd, you're not going anywhere now ye murdering swine.'

Nick turned, pointing the knife at the big policeman, 'Get oot me way or Aah'll rip yer fucking guts oot,' he warned as he moved toward the door but John Doherty was not going to get out of the way, he had his truncheon resting on his right shoulder ready to bring it down on Nick's head if he got the chance.

Mike provided him the opportunity he needed, jumping forward he pushed his father hard, propelling him into the wall as PC Doherty, moving incredibly quickly for a big man, brought his truncheon down hard an Nick's hand knocking the knife free and then swinging it again, he smashed it into the side of Nick's face knocking him to the floor semi-conscious and bleeding from a cut on his cheek bone.

The Policeman was on him in a flash turning him over onto his face and wrestling his hands behind him. Kneeling on the middle of the killers back, he opened his overcoat to get at his handcuffs, 'Nip over to the Granary lad and tell them I have your father under arrest,' he said to Mike who was only too keen to oblige and hurried out the door as PC Doherty lifted the handcuffed Nick to his feet. 'That's it all over for you

Shepherd, ye'll be hanging from a rope in a few weeks' time, and it doesn't take us lang to hang a Police Murderer lad.'

The thought of the drop and noose breaking his neck was too much for Nick, his bladder released what liquid it had and urine dribbled down his leg staining his trousers as Jane, Ian and Rafe appeared at the bottom of the stairs to stare in disbelief at the wretched figure that had made their life so miserable.

PC Doherty reached down and picked up the money that Nick had dropped in the scuffle, 'Here Mrs Shepherd, you best take this, he's not ganning te need it where he's going and if I take it, it'll be tied up in red-tape for ever.' Reluctantly taking the money, Jane realised it was what Nick must have come back for and that it had proved to be his downfall.

The PC sat the wretched Nick on a chair as Jane ushered Ian and Rafe back upstairs saying, 'It's probably best if you stay upstairs out of the way, Mike and I will look after things down here and Ian, I don't want you seeing your Father anymore.'

Climbing back into bed, Ian said to Rafe, 'Aah bet ye wish ye'd niver come here?'

Rafe lay back in his bed, his hands behind his head and stared up at the dark sky through the tiny attic window, 'Are you kidding, I have never had so much fun and excitement in all my life, it's great here, especially being part of this crazy family.'

Chapter 10
Aftermath

The following day the last day of March dawned cold and grey; the drizzle had stopped during the night leaving the air heavy, damp and smoke filled, as fires were stoked or relit as the folk of Ashington began their day of rest. There had been little sleep for anyone at number 60, the family were all very tired and all but Tommy in a state of bewildered shock after the events of the past 24 hours.

Pandemonium had ensued after the capture of Nick; at least four police cars screeched into the Row disgorging a dozen or more policemen as more ran to join them from the other side of the railway line; all trying to get inside number 60. Chief Superintendent Garrity brought calm to the situation, ordering PC Doherty as the Arresting Officer and DCI Fairbanks to take Nick to Ashington Police Station for processing and questioning. He then ordered a continued police presence outside the house and the wind down of operations. Shortly after he talked to Jane for some time and before leaving, informed her that DS Norman would return in the morning to take statements but now the family should try and get some sleep.

By nine o'clock several reporters were being kept at bay by the policeman at the door as Aggie Galloway was admitted to once again lend morale and physical support to the emotionally drained Jane and her children.

Hugging a physically and mentally shattered Jane, she whispered, 'You're well shot of him Jane lass, noo sit yarsell doon and Aah'll make sum breakfast for the kids.'

Jane did not refuse Aggie's help nor did she refuse the huge metal casserole pan filled with mince and dumplings brought along by Mary Holland at lunch time who confided, 'Everybody in the Ra is wanting te help ye Jane, even that miserable Maggie Rutherford doon at 52 says she'll take yer washing in the morn for ye, she's ownly saying that cos she's got a new washing machine and she want's everybody te kna!'

Ignoring the throng of reporters who threw a barrage of questions at him, DS Jamie Norman arrived just after ten and, adjusted the collar of a clean and freshly ironed shirt, straightened his tie, smoothed down his hair that had been tamed somewhat by a smear of Brylcream and fastened the jacket of his best navy blue suit before knocking on the door.

Leading him into the sitting room, Jane did not notice that the tall, handsome Scots Detective had smartened himself up and after offering him a cup of tea, which he declined; she sat answering his questions politely. He took statements from Jane, Mike, Ian and Rafe, leaving at one o'clock to push his way through the reporters to reach his car as he noted the small crowd of nosey folk at the end of the Row. Driving past them, he noticed the McArdle brothers and wondered why they were there, 'That needs following up,' he thought as he sped away.

Just after three o'clock, Flo Grundy, accompanied by Jake who was carrying a large blackened, heavy metal pan, tapped on the door and sidled into the kitchen of Number 60, 'Hello Pet,' she said to Jane who was sitting drinking a cup of tea by the fire as she talked to Mike, 'Aah've browt ye sum of me special beef 'n' bacon broth that ye and the kids will love, it's wor lads favourite isn't it Jake?

Jake, who had just slid the heavy pot onto the kitchen table, pulled a face of disgust and shook his head while he lied, 'Aye Mam we love it, we cannit get enough of it.'

Jane was about to tell Flo that they had already eaten thanks to Mary Holland but thinking that would be unkind, said, 'That's very kind of you Flo, it smells delicious,' and lied again when she continued, 'we'll have it for our suppers, that will be a real treat for us all'

'Aah thowt it wud Pet, mind the bacon bits are a bit fatty but them beef bones are full of goodness, noo can ye make sure one of your lads brings the pot back by seven o'clock cos Aah alwas boil wor Albert's pit socks in it for an hoor or so on a Sunday night before Aah put them in the oven to dry so as tha nice and warm for him in the morning.'

Jane hid her shock and answered, 'Yes of Couse Flo.'

After Flo and Jake left, Mike lifted the lid of the pot, releasing an almost rancid stink that rose from the fat scum floating on the top of the stew made up of potatoes, onions, beef bones and small pieces of fatty bacon, 'Blimey Mam, look at these bones, they're what the butcher gives te folk for their dogs and that bacon looks rotten!'

'Mike, it can't be that bad surely?' Jane said as she too looked into the pot. 'Oh my God, we can't eat that,' she said, 'what are we going to do with it?'

'Whey we cannit feed it to Mr Stoddart's pigs cos it would kill them off, Aah'll throw it the bin when it gets dark and there's nebody aboot.'

Rafe, who had been reading in the sitting room, walked into the kitchen and asked, 'What on Earth is that smell?'

'Your supper, 'Mike said seriously, that's if ye can eat it withoot being sick!'

Rafe looked into the pot, then took a spoon from the draw of the kitchen table and used it to move some of the semi-congealed fat from the surface of the stew before scooping up a spoonful of mushed potatoes, onions and a small lump of bacon and swallowing it. His face turned a little puce as he gulped it hurriedly down, 'A tad cold and the bacon is rather fatty but nonetheless good enough to survive on,' he gasped as he hurried for the door and the outside toilet!

The rest of the day was a blur for the family; they tried to take stock of the situation ending with Jane gathering them together in the sitting room after Maureen returned from a visit to Terry in Ashington Hospital.

Jane told them, 'We need to keep going and be prepared tomorrow for some derogatory comments from some people but it is best to just ignore them and act as normal as far as we can,' she finished by saying, 'I'll take Tommy and we'll walk with Maureen to her shop before I take him on to Wansbeck School, then I'm going to Kirkup's Bakery to start my new job, if they still want me?' 'Ian you and Rafe will have to face your school friends on your own but I'm sure you will manage just as long as you ignore any snide comments that may be passed.'

The reporters began interviewing the other residents of the Row, keen to gather as much information as they could on the disabled War Hero held for murder as well as any information they could sniff out about his family.

Some refused to speak to them while others were only too happy to tell them how vile Nick was and how he had mistreated his lovely family but it was left to George Holland to sow the seeds of a great story – 'War hero my arse, he's a gutless little coward, I've hurd tell that Eddie Thompson should have got that medal not blidy Nick Shepherd.' That was enough to have several of them scuttling off in search of Edward who when they found him, refused to talk to them. However, that did not deter two of them who stayed in the Row, hovering vulture like a few yards from the Thompson's house; waiting for the opportunity to interview his parents.

Nick was having another bad day! He admitted to murdering PC John Tate and stabbing Terry Proudlock – a signed confession to his drunken spree. DCI Fairbanks told him with venom, 'That's Capital Murder Mr Shepherd; murder of a Police Officer in the execution of his duty and, in the course of resisting arrest and that me lad means Capital Punishment for you, I just hope that will be some sort of compensation for his widow and kids and all his pals who just want te get their hands on you.'

The Local and National newspapers all led with the murder;
'Ashington Man involved in Murder of Policeman!'
'Police Constable Murdered!'
'Father of Three Slain!'
'Murder!'

Despite the tabloids being full of the news of the murder of a policeman and everyone knowing of Nick's arrest, Monday went better than Jane could have hoped for. A constable accompanied her, Maureen and Tommy to Highmarket and Wansbeck School, keeping reporters at arm's length and Alice Kirkup welcomed her into the Bakery saying, 'I'm glad you've come Jane, I wasn't sure that ye would and there'll be nee questions from anyone here, but if ye want te talk all well and good, noo let's get you a white overall and show you the ropes.'

Ian and Rafe were treated like celebrities by the rest of the lads at school, all of them trying to get close, hoping to hear some gory details of Nick's misdemeanours but they steadfastly refused to give any. Geordie Robertson hung back – biding his time.

As Nick Shepherd's solicitor talked him into going for a plea of, 'not guilty of murder' but 'guilty of manslaughter,' convinced that Nick's war record would save him from hanging, Peter Mansfield from the 'Daily News' interviewed Harry Thompson, Edward's father.

'Noo Aah'll tell ye sumat else aboot that little waster, he niver deserved that Military Medal, he hid behind his deed pals until the shooting was ower, it was wor Edward that shud have got the medal not that murdering swine!'

Peter Mansfield stopped writing and asked, 'Who told you that Mr Thompson, your Son?'

'Aye but it's nee gud ye asking him, he winit tell ye owt, he's always said it's up to Nick blidy Shepherd to tell the truth, ye should speak to Brigadier Cartwright, he was the Officer there, it was him that recommended Shepherd for the medal.'

Peter intended to do just that; he also needed to call in a few favours and interview Shepherd, if at all possible!

Appearing briefly in Magistrates Court, Nick was told that he was being held in custody to be referred to Crown Court due to the charges against him being indictable. Stephen Caldecott, his solicitor, explained to him that this was normal procedure and that he would appear in Crown Court within a few days when the Judge would read out the charges against and ask him if he pleaded 'Guilty' or not 'Guilty.'

Caldecott went on to say, 'We'll plead 'Not Guilty' to the murder charge which will mean a trial then we will endeavour to have it reduced to manslaughter, which is our best hope, even if we are successful, it will mean a long prison term I'm afraid.'

Rubbing the Elastoplast covering the cut on his cheek, Nick looked contemptuously at the young Solicitor and sneered, 'And if we fail, Aah'll hang and wor boond te fail cos I killed a coppa, that's the end of it, Aah hevn't got a frigging hope man so it's bloody pointless isn't it?'

'There's always hope Mr Shepherd and your Barrister will plead diminished responsibility due to your intoxication, plus your war record is a great bonus.'

'Aah wouldn't put much store in that, it's boond to come oot that Aah should niver hev got that blidy medal man!'

Aghast, Caldecott asked, 'What are you saying Mr Shepherd, that you did not win the Military Medal?'

With a sardonic laugh, Nick replied, 'Aye that's what am saying, Aah blidy hid while aall the fighting went on, Edward blidy Thompson shud hev got the medal not me and he has niver said owt aboot it, whey more fool him.'

Shocked and horrified at what Nick had told him, Caldecott knew any trial would go very badly for Nick if it became common knowledge that he was a false hero and a liar. 'Whatever you do Mr Shepherd, do not talk about this to anyone, it would be most detrimental to your case.'

Nick looked away and took a long drag on the cigarette Caldecott had given him; 'Aye, whatever ye say, when de I meet me Lawyer then?'

'This afternoon, Mr David Johnston, he is coming to discuss your plea and how to take your case forward.'

'Whey Aah'll welcome him te the frigging sinking ship when comes then.'

Before he comes, a Miss Duncan has asked to see you and the staff here, want to know if that is OK.'

'Ginny,' said Nick, 'no Aah definitely divin't want te see her so divin't let the buggas let her in, what aboot me wife or mother, hev they asked to see me?

'No I'm afraid not Mr Shepherd, do you want me to speak te them?'

He sneered, 'Na, there's nee point, my wife hates me and me Mother's terrified of me!'

The following evening, nursing a badly bruised eye where Nick had hit her with the money satchel, and in the depths of despair, Ginny made her way to a non-descript house in one of the Rows and timidly knocked on the door. She had to wait a couple of minutes before the door opened, casting bright light into the backyard and silhouetting the huge shape of 'Fat Flora!'

A deep voice climbed up from within her huge bosom, gargling its way through her numerous chins, 'Come on in lass, divin't let the nosey neighbours see you standing there, or iviry bugga'll kna what yer here for and it'll be roond the Ra's in nee time.'

Two hours later Ginny was curled up in her own bed; in pain and very drunk, 'At least I won't be the mother of the baby of a murderer,' she said out aloud before burying her head in her pillow, sobbing from her pain and anguish.

Three days later as his family tried to rebuild their lives whilst coping with press harassment and the odd whispers from some folk in the Ra's; Nick was in Crown Court packed with reporters as he listened to the Judge read out the charges against him:

'Nicholas Shepherd you appear before me today on the following charges, Charge One, Grievous Bodily harm in that you stabbed Terrence Proudlock; Charge two, The murder of a police officer Police Constable John Tate, acting in the execution of his duty; Charge Three, Resisting Arrest and Charge Four, Threatening a police officer with an offensive weapon, all of the charges relating to the events of 30 March 1957, do you understand the charges?'

'Yes,' answered Nick.

The Judge looked into Nick's dead eyes and asked, 'On Charge One, How do you plead?'

Nick looked at his Lawyer briefly then answered, 'Guilty.'

'On Charge Two, the murder of PC John Tate, how do you plead?'

Nick again looked briefly at his Lawyer who raised his eyebrows and nodded slightly. Sneering at him, Nick turned back to the Judge and in a loud voice that echoed around the Court Room, answered, 'Guilty!'

The gasp from the public gallery and Nick's lawyer's incredulous, 'What?' were silenced by the Judge banging his gavel loudly before he continued, 'And on Charges Three and Four, how do you plead?'

'Guilty!'

Reporters elbowed each other out of the way as they scrambled out of the Court to file the news that a disabled War Hero had pleaded guilty to murder while back in the courtroom, the Judge ordered Nick to be taken down while he retired to consider sentencing. That is all but one reporter; Peter Mansfield , who the night before, had spoken to Brigadier Cartwright on the telephone.

In reply to Mansfield's questions on what had happened at Dunkirk and after some beating around the bush, the Brigadier finally said, 'Look here Old Man, this was the heat of battle, the action took place over a hundred yards from where I was and as either Shepherd or Thompson had thrown smoke, I could not make out who actually charged and threw the grenade that took out the machine gun. When we closed up, only Shepherd was alive, at least we thought he was the only survivor until we discovered later that Thompson was not dead. Shepherd took the credit for the action but then he was not aware that Thompson had survived so it is possible that he lied about his actions.'

Mansfield kept up the pressure, 'So what you are saying Brigadier is that, the Military Medal may have been awarded to the wrong man?'

'Yes, I suppose I am but only Shepherd and Edwards can verify or deny that!'

Whilst the other reporters were dictating their reports to their newspapers, Peter Mansfield drove round to the new council estate at Darnley Road in Ashington and tracked down Edward Thompson who he found working in one of the almost completed houses.

Wiring a cooker socket into the kitchen Edward scowled at Mansfield, 'Aah towld you, Aah didn't want to give an interview, noo bugger off before Aah throw ye oot!'

Mansfield was not about to give up and pleaded, 'Just a few moments of your time please Mr Thompson, did you know that Nick Shepherd has pleaded guilty to all charges against him?'

Edward put down his screwdriver and turned to look at the reporter, 'No I didn't, noo that is a blidy surprise as Aah cannit remember him ever deeing the right thing before!'

'I've also spoken to Brigadier Cartwright who told me that he could not be one hundred per cent certain that Shepherd threw the grenade that knocked out the machine gun nest, who threw it Mr Thompson?'

'Edward gave a wry smile and said, 'Well it certainly wasn't Nick Shepherd, he was hiding behind our dead mates.'

'So would I be correct in saying that *you* charged the farm and threw the grenade at the machine gun nest and *you* are the real hero and should have received the medal?'

Leaning back against the wall of the kitchen, Edward stared the at ceiling for a minute or two and then said, 'I'm no more of a hero than the brave men who were killed on that day and if you want to see some heroes, just gan on up to the pit and watch the men coming oot after a hard days graft, noo iviry one of them is a hero, an iviry day hero - this toon's full of them!'

Mansfield had his scoop, the following morning, while the rest of the newspapers headlines announced;

'Shepherd pleads Guilty!'
'War Hero Pleads Guilty!'
'Murderer is a War hero!'

The Daily news shouted;
'Liar and False Hero Pleads Guilty to Murder!'

210

Everyone in the Sixth Row and the rest of the Ra's discussed Nick's plea and the news that he had been awarded a medal that should have rightly been awarded to Edward Thompson!

No one was surprised, their feelings summed up by Aggie Galloway when later in the day she said to Jane, 'Eeee lass ye've had an aaful life since ye met that waster, we alwas knew he was a bad bugga but niver thowt he would dee something like this, yer weell shot of him Pet and alwas remember ye live in a street full of friends of ye and the bairns!'

There was much speculation as to whether or not Nick would receive the Death Penalty. The murder was a Capital Offence and he had used the knife to stab Terry earlier but he had been drunk! Nick had resigned himself to his fate, he had never felt so calm and detached, as though all this was happening to someone else and whilst he himself expected the Death Penalty, others tried to convince him that the Judge may be lenient, especially as there was a growing public outcry to stop Capital Punishment. He spent two nights lying alone in his cell contemplating his fate, waking on the third day, panic stricken at the realisation of what he had done by pleading 'Guilty' and what his punishment would be.

He demanded to see his Lawyer but it was all too late, the Judge had made his decision and Nick's plea to his Lawyer to withdraw his Guilty plea in an effort to stop events and go for a trial were of no consequence, he was hauled struggling, into the dock. Unable to focus on what was happening and staring madly at the Judge, he mouthed silent obscenities at him.

Explaining his deliberations, the Judge spoke for some time, listing the fact that Nick had used a knife twice and had been prepared to use a knife again, that the murder of a police officer whilst resisting arrest was a Capital Crime. He also said that he had taken into consideration

211

that Nick was probably intoxicated when he committed the cruel acts; all of which he had carefully considered before deciding on his award. Nick was unable to comprehend what was being said and what was happening, that is until the Judge placed a small square of black silk on his head!

'NO,' he yelled as the police escort stopped him from collapsing into the chair behind him.

In a sombre voice that rose above Nick's moans the Judge awarded three consecutive prison sentences for the lesser charges before saying, 'By your own admission you are guilty of the murder of Police Constable John Tate; for this crime Nicholas Shepherd, you will be taken to a lawful prison where you will be hanged by the neck until dead.'

With the sun shining brightly on the following Sunday, Jane determined that the boys should get on with their lives and encouraged them to do so. In an effort to comply with her wishes, just after lunch Ian and Rafe pushed down on the pedals of the tandem, and cycled down the Row with Tommy sitting on a cushion in the barrow fastened securely to the back. Not wanting to spend money on a reflector for the rear of the barrow, Ian had crudely painted vertical red and yellow stripes on the back as a warning to motorists, none the less, Jane had lectured them on safety and extracted promises of safe cycling from the two boys before they set off for Newbiggin by the Sea to enjoy the spring weather.

Riding his smart Raleigh Tourer, Howard Holland cycled alongside with Jake Grundy riding behind yelling 'Haway the Hack Dortys,' as he rode Mary Holland's bicycle that she had unknowingly lent to him for the day! Standing outside her house with her older sister, Peggy Reagan gave Ian a shy smile and little wave as they cycled past. Reg was waiting on his bike at the Fifth Row and joined them as they yelled and whooped their way onto the main road, past the Store Corner and through Ashington to bike the couple of miles to Newbiggin.

Back in the Sixth Row, Mike Joined Albert Grundy outside his shed where he was polishing his James Motorcycle, 'How come ye divin't ride yer motorbike Mr Grundy? He asked.

Rubbing the petrol tank with a tatty rag, Albert replied, 'Whey, Aah hevn't got a licence, Aah cannit afford to run it and Flo wudn't let me ride it anyway but Aah hev it running champion noo and Aah mean te sell it.'

As Mike walked around the bike to appraise it, Edward Thompson joined them, 'Selling Mike yer James then Albert?'

'If the lad wants te buy it he can.'

Mike said, 'Aah would love te but Aah doubt Aah can afford it, hoo much de ye want for it?'

Albert lifted his cap and rubbed his bald head, 'Whey hoo aboot fifteen pund lad?'

Edward said, 'That's a good price Mike, the bike is well worth that and more now.'

'Aye am sure it is,' said Mike, 'but Aah cannit afford that, not on an apprentice's wage.'

Albert smiled and said, 'Aah'll tell ye what lad, give me ten bob a week until it's paid for, hoo aboot that?'

'That would be great but Aah'll hev te ask me Mam; can Aah hev a ride on it?'

Stepping back, Albert said, 'If ye kna hoo te, gan on help yersell.'

Mike straddled the motorcycle and gripped the handle bars but did not start it up, his attention being drawn to two swarthy and very rough looking men dressed in black double breasted suits with fedoras on their heads instead of the normal flat caps. The two men walked past them toward the end of the street!

Albert said, 'Aah've niver seen them Buggas before, tha a right rough looking pair!

Edward turned to watch the men saying, 'I wonder where tha ganning, we'd better keep an eye on the shifty looking sods.'

As the three of them watched, the strangers continued walking all the way to the end of the Row, stopping outside Number 60

'Bloody Hell, Mike said, 'tha ganning into wor hoose!'

Jane and Aggie Galloway were making scones at the kitchen table when their efforts were stopped by a loud and determined knock on the back door.

Walking to the door, Jane said, 'I wonder who on earth that is, knocking like that? Opening the door, she was taken aback by the menacing look of the two spivs standing with forced smiles on their faces.

Joe McArdle put his foot onto the door step and said, 'Hello Missus, you'll be Nick Shepherd's wife, will you?'

Jane immediately felt intimidated by the two men but held her nerve, 'Who are you and what do you want here?'

The McArdles began their double act;

'Well it's like this now Missus Shepherd, Nick owes us three hundred and eighty quid,' said Pat.

Joe added, 'And we would very much like that money Missus.'

'And we were wondering how ye were going to pay it?' said a sneering Pat.

Jane tried to push the door shut but Joe stopped her holding the door firmly in his grip, 'Now Missus that's no way to behave to two fellas who ye owe money too!'

A few feet away, Aggie listened intently to the conversation then quickly sped through the sitting room and out the front door, into the garden and turned toward her own garden where Arthur was leaning on his spade talking potatoes to big George Holland on the other side of his hedge.

'LISTEN,' she shouted at the two men, 'there's two bad men at Jane's door demanding money, get yerself aroond there and chase the buggers off, noo go on get ganning.' Arthur and George looked at each other briefly then both headed into their own houses and hurried through and into the back lane, Arthur still clutching his spade. Walking through their yards, they met Mike, Edward and Albert who were walking briskly toward Jane's house.

Aggie followed her husband out of their back door and scurried down the Row to find more men!

The McArdles were slowly but forcibly pushing the door back as Jane tried desperately to stop them from entering her house, Pat snarling, 'Come on Missus let us in and we'll just talk about how you are going to pay us back now.'

Edward's booming voice stopped them, '*What's ganning on here?*'

The two spivs turned to see Edward stepping into the small back yard with the huge shape of Arthur Holland at his shoulder and two smaller men behind, one of them clutching a spade menacingly.

'There's no bother here boys,' said Joe, 'we are just telling Mrs Shepherd here how sorry we are to here that her husband has been locked away.'

Edward stepped in front of Joe and looked down into his sneering face and asked, 'Is that true Jane?'

Jane swung her door open and said firmly, 'No these two say that Nick owes them three hundred pounds and that they want the money from me!'

'Three hundred and *eighty* pounds Missus,' corrected Pat McArdle.

Without taking his eyes off Joe, Edward said, 'I don't know who you two are but if Nick Shepherd owes ye money then Aah suggest ye tek it

215

up with his solicitor or the police, not with Mrs Shepherd, have ye got that?'

Pat looked past the men crowding into the yard and saw another two arriving with a stocky little woman who was wearing a set and determined look on her face. Gripping his brother's arm he said, 'Come on Joe, it doesn't look as though we will be getting our money here today,' and tried to walk out of the yard but Edward and George Holland stopped them.

Big George Holland spoke next; placing his huge hand on Joe's shoulder he said in his deep powerful voice that had suddenly developed a very hard edge, ' Aah divin't kna who ye two blidy wasters are but Aah'll tell ye this, if either of ye two come anywhere near this street again, we'll hunt ye doon like the mangy dogs ye are and by God we'll fettle ye right good and proper, noo bugger off oot of wor street and niver come back again, got that?'

Wincing under George's powerful grip, Joe said, 'Aye, right we've got it now let go.'

George swung Joe toward the gate and pushed him through as Edward bundled Pat after him warning, 'Tek heed of what George has said because we look after wor own here and I'll be talking te the police about you two.'

'There's no need for that Mister, said Pat, 'we won't be coming back to your stinking street again,' and he hurried down the street with his brother with the Sixth Row men following behind.

Emboldened by the big strong men around him, Albert Grundy stepped quickly forward and booted Pat McArdle hard up the arse saying, 'Aye ye better not show yer faces roond here again,' but scuttled back behind George when Pat turned around with a savage glare in his eyes. The sight of the other men was enough to deter Pat from doing anything and the two brothers hurried out the Row muttering obscenities but both new that they would not be venturing down the Sixth Row again.

The Sixth Row men stood talking for some time before dispersing back to what they had been doing before the little excitement had interrupted their Sunday afternoon routines. Edward walked with Mike back to Number 60 where Aggie was making a cup of tea for Jane who, visibly shaking was sitting at the kitchen table staring out of the window.

Hurrying in Mike asked with some concern, 'Are ye alright Mam?

'Jane nodded, answering, 'Yes Michael, I'm alright now and I feel very blessed that we live next to so many good people.'

Edward asked, 'Do you know who they were Jane?'

'I have never seen them before but I imagine Nick owed them money from his betting.'

'Edward took the cup of tea that Aggie offered, 'I'll call in at The Police Station on the way home later and let them know what happened.'

Jane smiled at Edward and said, 'I'll phone Sergeant Norman tomorrow and tell him, he said I should let him know if I had any problems.'

The Hacky Dortys enjoyed the bike ride to Newbiggin, the spring sunshine lifting their spirits as they sang Rock and Roll songs and chattered their way along North Seaton Road and into Newbiggin. The seaside town's handsome main street was a welcome change after the drabness of the Colliery Rows and an almost euphoric holiday feeling swept over the lads as they pulled up in the square formed by Bertorelli's art deco Café Riviera on one side, the Coble Inn and sailing club opposite, with the promenade joining the two.

217

The tops of the 'Shuggy Boats' on the beach could be seen at the other side of the promenade and never having seen them before, Rafe asked, 'What are those huge swings?'

'SHUGGY BOATS' yelled Ian, Howard and Jake as they ran toward the gaily painted boat like swings, digging in their pockets for three pennies for a ride. With Tommy next to him, Ian climbed into one with Rafe sitting opposite as Howard, Reg and Jake climbed into another.

The lads soon had the boats swinging high, whooping and yelling with delight at the end of each upward swing that lifted them from their seats, until the attended shouted, 'Gan blidy canny man lads!'

The shuggy boats set the tone for the rest of the afternoon, although it was too cold to go into the sea, the beach and promenade was busy with people enjoying the spring Sunday afternoon.

The Hacky Dortys ran along the long wide beach of the picturesque bay to the rocks at 'Needles Eye' at the south end where they clambered about the promontory exploring rock pools for hermit crabs and starfish.

Rafe held up a black curled shell and asked, 'Is this a winkle?'

'A winkle,' Jake spluttered, 'Nur man it's not yor willy it's a willick!'

'A willick! Can you eat them? Rafe asked.

Ian grabbed his arm and said, 'Aye ye can, after ye've boiled them, tha lovely just like lang hot snots, but the best ones are at Church Point at the top end of the Bay, haway we'll gan an pick some te take home but first lets have an ice cream at Bertorelli's.

Climbing onto the prom, they headed back to the café, Jake wiping a dew drop from his nose and brushing sand from his damp trousers before he sat down to empty more sand from his sodden, battered leather shoes, asking Ian, 'When is yor dad getting hung, me Dad says it winit be lang as they divin't hing aboot when it comes to cop killers?'

Ian ignored the question and Rafe glared at Jake but it was Howard who hauled Jake to his feet and dragged him over to one of the shelters on the promenade where he snarled, 'Listen ye stupid skinny little git, we said we wudn't taalk aboot tha Dad noo keep your big gob shut ora Aah'll shut it for you!'

Taken aback by Howard's threat, Jake whispered, 'Am sorry man, Aah forgot, noo will ye tek yer hand off me arm cos yer nipping me skin and it bloody horts man!'

Howard pushed him away and warned, 'Aye whey divin't forget again or else!'

Irrepressible as ever as Jake ran ahead and shouted back, 'Forst one there's ice-cream is paid for by the last one there!'

Rafe was about to sprint after him but Ian said, 'Let him win, he never has any money so it's the only way he can get an ice-cream!'

Paying for his and Jake's ice-creams in Bertorelli's Howard growled, 'Isn't aboot time ye got a paper roond or sumat so ye can buy yer an ice-cream?'

Jake took a huge gulp of ice-cream and winced as the cold gave him a sharp pain in the temple, 'By that's frigging cowld man,' he said. 'I winit get a paper roond, cos me Mam'll just tek the money; anyway Aah nick empty pop bottles from the back of the clubs and sell them to the pop women or shops for tuppence each, so Aah have a job, divin't Aah!'

Half an hour after the McArdles visit as Mike was riding around the Rows on Albert Grundy's motorcycle, Jane was finishing off putting away the Sunday dinner dishes when there was another knock on the door but this knock was timid, barely audible. Jane walked to the door and opened it a few inches to peer through the gap until she recognised the visitor and swung the door wide open saying with great surprise 'Margaret!'

Neat, diminutive, grey haired Margaret Shepherd, Nick's mother smiled nervously at Jane and said quietly, 'Can I come in lass?'

'You are always welcome here, this is as much your house as mine,' said Jane as she stepped forward and taking her Mother-in Law's arm, led her into the house and through into the sitting room. 'Would you like a cup of tea Margaret? You'll need one if you've come on the bus.'

As Jane walked into the kitchen, Margaret sighed deeply as memories of her happy, young married life here with her husband Jim flooded back, that is until an image of her arrogant son Nick replaced them, reducing her to tears.

'Whatever is the matter?' Jane asked as she carried in the tea tray, setting it down on the coffee table.

Sitting down next to the sobbing Margaret, Jane put her arm around her shoulder to comfort her and sat silently for five minutes until she composed herself.

'It's a long time since I've been back here Jane, the memories got the better of me Pet, she said quietly.

It had been eleven years since Jim had died, eleven years since she had moved to Newbiggin, vowing never to return while her son was still here. During the first few years after her Mother-in-Law moved, Jane had taken the children to visit her in Newbiggin many times but Margaret had always seemed remote, almost off hand. She loved the children but was nervous, almost frightened when they visited, always asking, 'Is Nicholas with you?' Then, 'Is he coming?'

Nick never visited his mother and she had never returned to her home, that is not until today and Jane was curious as to why now but waited, hoping Margaret would explain. Margaret drank the tea Jane had handed her and asked how the children were and listened quietly as Jane told her of Tommy's accident and of Rafe.

Placing her hand on Jane's, she said, 'Aah heard about little Tommy and how wor Ian saved him Pet, Aah wanted so much to visit him in hospital but Aah couldn't, Aah was frightened that Nick might have been there!'

Nick only visited him once Margaret, Tommy would have loved to have seen you, he still remembers his Nana.'

This brought another tear to Margaret's eye but she composed herself and looking into Jane's she said, 'Noo's the time for me te tell ye why Aah left here and niver came back and why Aah was so scared when ye visited in case Nicholas was with ye.'

Jane shook her head and said, 'You don't have to explain anything, I'm just glad you're here.'

'Aye but Aah do hev to explain, you need to kna what I think happened to Jim and why am so scared of my own son, it's been eating me up for these past eleven years Pet.'

Jane asked, 'What do you mean, "Happened to Jim," he fell down the stairs when he was painting the ceiling at the top of the landing, we all know what happened?'

'Aye my poor Jim was fund at the bottom of them stairs with his heed bashed in but he didn't fall, not him, he was pushed or worse by Nick! His own son killed him and for what? a few bob's worth of insurance that he took most of, not that Aah wanted it but Aah kna he kept it and just gave me a few pund telling me that's all there was.'

Jane was horrified, she had never considered that Jim's death had been anything but an accident and thought that what insurance money there had been, had gone straight to Margaret. 'But Nick was at Jim's allotment that Saturday while we were at the swing park with the kids, Jim was on his own in the house, it couldn't have been Nick, could it?'

Margaret looked tiny and forlorn as she sat clutching the tea cup, 'That's what he towld everyone, that he was at the allotment but ye kna as well as me that he niver went there but on that day he just happened to be there to dig up some tornips, de ye believe that?'

'He was seen there by other people Margaret, so he must have been there.'

'Aye was seen there but it's only five minutes away, he had plenty of time to pop back here and....' 'And pop back, besides Aggie towld me that she thought she had seen him walking doon the back garden, she niver towld anyone else and Aah couldn't tell anyone, not aboot me own son, I knew he was a nasty bugga but I didn't think he could de that, not until it was too late and then I was terrified that he might harm me or ye and the bairns if Aah said out.'

Jane didn't know what to say, she was trying hard to rationalise what she had just heard - had Nick murdered his own father for a few pounds? A few weeks ago the idea that he had might have would have been difficult to believe but now, after recent events and Margaret's conviction that he had, it sounded very plausible!

'What are you going to do, are you going to tell the police what you think?'

Margaret shook her head, 'What good would it do to say owt now, he's already going to hang and just think of the upset it would cause the bairns!'

Jane agreed with Margaret, there was nothing to be gained by telling anyone of their suspicions; an inquiry would only delay the inevitable so the two women decided to keep it a secret between them.

Margaret then told Jane that she had been approached by a couple of newspapers, offering her money for her story on being the mother of Nick Shepherd and asked, 'Aah don't want to upset or embarrass you and the bairns, what de ye think Aah should do Jane?'

'Take the best offer, he has caused you enough pain in your life and from what you are saying, he stole Jim's insurance money so I think you should take what you can, besides people need to know what he was really like.' Jane did not tell her that she too had been offered money for her story but had declined, not wanting to upset the children any more than was necessary.

A few minutes later, Mike walked into the sitting room and smiled warmly when he saw his grandmother, 'Nana,' he said as he hugged her when she stood up, 'it's smashing te see ye.'

Margaret stepped back to admire her handsome grandson, he looked like a pleasant version of his father but with Jane's intense eyes; 'Aah bet you've got all the lasses roond here chasing ye Bonny Lad?'

Mike grinned and said, 'Am too busy playing football Nana and the lasses here aren't fast enough to catch me man but there is a lass in Morpeth!'

Margaret grabbed his arm and pulled him onto the settee saying, 'Come on then, tell me all aboot her.'

Margaret shed a few more tears when the boys burst into the house just after five o'clock and Tommy and Ian hugged her as a bewildered Rafe, looked on with a large bag of willicks in his arms. 'Who is this handsome young man then, is this Rafe wor Jane? Ye didn't tell me he was so handsome,' said Margaret, raising a blush to Rafe's cheeks.

Rafe stepped forward and held his hand out, 'Hello, I'm Rafe Jane's brother and you must be Ian's Grandmamma?'

Margret brushed his hand aside and pulled him down into a hug, kissing his cheek wetly, 'I am lad and am very pleased to meet ye, Aah only wish it had been under better circumstances.'

Margaret stayed for a few more minutes before she bade her farewells making promises to visit again shortly. Jane walked her to the bus stop and promised to visit her at Newbiggin when things quietened down and waved her off, both with tears in their eyes.

Later that night, In an effort to forget their problems, Mike, Maureen and Jane relaxed in the sitting room and listened to the 'Goon Show'. When it finished Mike told his Mother of Albert Grundy's offer to sell his motorbike for fifteen pound at ten bob a week and asked what she thought.

Jane asked, 'Is it worth fifteen pounds?'

'It's worth at least double that Mam, he's done a great job of doing it up, he's got it looking like new, Aah kna we're hard up but it will help me get aboot and Aah'll be able to pop over to Morpeth on it te see Jennifer.'

With a wistful smile, Jane rose from the sofa and walked to the sideboard at the back of the room where she opened a draw and looked at two envelopes pushed to the back, taking out a white envelope with an elastic band around it. As she took off the band she asked, 'How is it going with Jennifer, it must be difficult with what has happened?'

'It is difficult but she say's what my Dad has done doesn't alter hoo she feels aboot me but last night when her dad picked her up outside the Arcade, he didn't offer me a lift hyem and said he want's te see me the morn night at their house at seven o'clock.'

Jane sat down next to him and said, 'Well if you really do like Jennifer, then be careful when you talk to him, do not let him upset you or make you angry, whatever he has to say, stay calm and be polite do not give him any reason to think you are the least bit like your father because you are not, you are good enough for any man's daughter, now here's fifteen pounds to pay for the motorbike and no riding it until you have a licence and are insured, got that?'

Not expecting any money, Mike was taken by surprise, 'Thanks Mam but where did you get the money?'

Jane smiled, 'It's from the money the Policeman handed me on the night your father was arrested, so you could say the motorbike will be a present from him, and we'll use some of it for your wedding Maureen.'

Maureen sat up and said, 'Aah don't want anything from him Mam.'

Jane replied, 'Well in that case, as the money was given to me we will say that it is my money, now that's the end of it!'

Chapter 11
Showdown

The Shepherd's new daily routine kicked off with Ian and Rafe rushing out into a dull overcast morning at seven o'clock to deliver newspapers while Jane made tea and toast or poured cereal into bowls for the rest of the family. Mike left for work at seven thirty as Tommy chewed his way through a second slice of toast, making faces at Maureen sitting opposite eating her Weetabix before she too hurried out the door leaving Jane to walk to the Bakery in High Market and Tommy to meet up with Roger and Billy Grundy for the walk to Wansbeck School.

Ian, Rafe and Tommy had their lunches at school while Jane, Maureen and Mike had theirs at their work places. Tommy was normally the first home; just before Ian and Rafe who grabbed a biscuit before riding the tandem, less barrow, to Crisps to do their evening paper rounds. The two lads had yet to make a trip back to Coneygarth to restart their firewood sales but planned to do so on Saturday.

Jane was pleased that they were all busy as hopefully, it prevented them from dwelling on less pleasant matters! Even so the problems Nick had created were never far from her thoughts and it took all her inner strength and resilience to keep going. At eleven o'clock, she was reminded of the problems that he had created, when DS Jamie Norman parked his Ford Prefect outside Kirkup's Bakery and looked at his reflection in the rear view mirror, 'Not bad,' he thought as he smoothed down a blonde curl that immediately sprung back to its original unruly position.

Climbing out of the car looking like a young Michael Caine, he took off his glasses and slid them into his inside pocket before adjusting his tie unnecessarily and striding across the pavement to swing open the stiff door to the bakery just a little too hard, ringing the little brass bell loudly as the door bashed into the counter, clattering the glass display and knocking onto the floor a large cream cake and Swiss roll from the top where they had been on display!

The tiny shop was busy with several women who were either being served or waiting to be served by Jane and Alice Kirkup, both of them stopping what they were doing as they stared at the clumsy, dishevelled Sergeant who was blushing madly.

'Och, I'm so sorry, I didna mean to knock anything over, I'll pay for the cakes,' he stammered.

Alice Kirkup crossed her arms over her ample bosom and looking over the top of her glasses at him, said none too softly, 'Indeed you will young man, now what do you want?'

'I've come to see Mrs Shepherd, if that is alright?

Alice glared at Jamie, 'No it's not alright, and ye can see that we are busy, so if you want to see Mrs Shepherd ye'll have te come back later!'

Jamie was about to pull out his warrant card and say who he was but the look Alice gave him was enough to deter him, 'OK, I'll call round and see you this evening Mrs Shepherd, if that is alright with you?' Jane nodded and Jamie pad for the cakes and hurried out the door with the remnants in a bag, glad to be away from the intense scrutiny of Alice Kirkup.

Later, when the shop was quiet, Alice asked, 'Who was that clumsy Scotsman then Jane?'

'He's a police sergeant Alice, he had probably come to talk about a little bother I had yesterday.'

'Oh I see,' said Alice grinning, 'And here's me thinking he was a boyfriend, well he certainly fancies you.'

Jane actually blushed, 'Nonsense Alice, he's just doing his job, that's all.'

'Aye mebe but I tell you he fancies you, mind he could do with a damn good ironing couldn't he!'

Ian and Rafe had finished their evening paper rounds and were cycling back in to the Sixth Row when they saw Mike talking to Albert Grundy outside his shed, Albert having just wheeled his motorbike out.

Pulling up next to them Ian said, 'We'll give ye a race Mike, ye'll niver catch us on that!'

Mike smiled, 'Don't dare me lad,' then looking past Ian, he said, 'it looks as if someone is waiting to talk to you.' Peggy was standing by her gate, wearing a pink blouse over a pink skirt that bellowed out over half a dozen starched petty coats; she looked very pretty.

Rafe said, 'Go on, I'll take the bike home,' and changed to the front of the tandem when Ian dismounted and shyly walked over to Peggy.

'Hello,' he said.

Peggy did a twirl making the skirt and petticoats spin high, 'Do you like my new skirt, I'll be wearing it at your Maureen's wedding; will you have a dance with me?'

Ian frowned and replied, 'They divin't dance in Church Man.'

'Not in church silly, at the reception in the Toc H afterwards.'

Ian blurted, 'Aye OK,' and kissed her lightly on the cheek before hurrying away as butterflies engulfed him and he worried about dancing ; 'How the heck am supposed to larn who te dance?'

Mike pushed the Motor Bike up the Row, around the gable end and into their shed where he spent some time unnecessarily polishing it as Albert already had the paintwork and chrome gleaming. Hearing a car pull up, he walked around to the back lane again and saw the tall Detective Sergeant climbing out of his little car, 'Hello Sergeant, me Mam's expecting you, just knock and gan in,' he said.

227

Jamie knocked on the door and stepped into the tiny hallway, 'Hello, Mrs Shepherd, it's me Detective Sergeant Norman,'

'I can see that it's you Sergeant Norman, come through to the sitting room,' said Jane smiling at the awkward policeman, noticing for the first time that he was rather handsome, if perhaps just a bit dishevelled.

He asked her about the McArdle's visit and said that he would be interviewing them both and would ensure they got the message to stay away, 'loud and clear'. 'Now I have some news for you Mrs Shepherd,' he said nervously.'

'Yes what is that?'

'I've heard that your husband's execution has been confirmed and the date set,' he paused as Jane looked down at the floor, 'it's three weeks today and will be at eight o'clock...'

Jane cut him off, 'I don't wish to hear any more details, thank you Sergeant.'

Jamie nodded and said, 'OK, I understand Mrs Shepherd, can I suggest that you and your children go away for a few days over that period as there'll bound to be reporters sniffing round.'

'We'll see,' Jane said, 'now if there is nothing else, I have my children's dinner to serve.'

Jamie stood up and said, 'I'm sorry to have troubled you Mrs Shepherd, I'll get from under your feet right away.'

'It's no trouble Sergeant and please, call me Mrs Trevelyan or better still Jane, I no-longer want to be called by *that* name.'

'Understood – Jane and it's Jamie, my name that is,' he replied before making a hasty exit to conceal his embarrassment and delight.

Just before seven o'clock and wearing his blue suit with freshly pressed white shirt and blue striped tie, Mike walked up Thorp Avenue in Morpeth looking for the number Doctor Metcalf had given him. Finding it on the door of a large, handsome semi-detached house, he took a deep breath and walked up to the door to knock just as the Doctor swung it open.

'Come on in Michael,' he said without warmth.

Mike entered the large hallway and waited until Doctor Metcalf closed the door and led him into the comfortably furnished sitting room where Jennifer was sitting nervously waiting.

'Sit down Michael; do you want a cup of tea or anything?' Doctor Metcalf asked brusquely.

'No thanks.'

'OK, look, I'll not beat about the bush, Jennifer here says she wants to continue to see you but I, understandably I'll hope you agree, am not happy with my daughter going out with the son of a convicted murderer, dear God Lad, my dear wife would turn in her grave if she knew and besides that what prospects do you have!'

Jennifer pleaded, 'Daddy please!'

Mike cleared his throat and began his rehearsed speech, 'I understand Sir; your concerns are very valid but I can assure you I am not at all like my Father, I would like te believe that I am like my Mother who is a wonderful woman, well-educated and the nicest, warmest most generous person you could ever meet, I would like you to come and meet her before you make your mind up about me and, I may only be an apprentice electrician but I have goals in life and believe I am as good as any man!'

Jennifer beamed with delight at Mike's little speech as her father stood and walked to the window and stared out for a few seconds before turning and saying, 'All right, that was well said for what it's worth; I will give you the benefit of the doubt and I would like to come to meet you mother and have a chat as I am totally unable to change Jennifer's mind when it comes to you.'

Jane was angry when Mike related the conversation he had had with Jennifer's father, she had had enough to contend with without some uppity doctor looking down on her son. 'Who does he think he is? I'm glad you have invited him here tomorrow, I'll give him a piece of my mind!'

Mike smiled and said, 'Now Mother, remember what you told me, remain calm,

As Jonathan Metcalf's sleek Rover 90 turned into the Sixth Row, Billy and Roger Grundy were kicking a battered, semi-inflated football against the brick side of the air-raid shelter that their father used as his shed, Albert was inside tinkering with a newly acquired moped, thanks to the fifteen pounds from Mike for the James Cadet.

'My God look at this place,' Jonathan said to Jennifer who was sitting quietly beside him, 'there's a steam engine at the other side of those out buildings, what number do they live in?'

'Number 60 Daddy,'

'There are no numbers on the doors that I can see, I'll ask one of these children where it is,' he said as he pulled up alongside the two Grundy kids, winding down his window as he did so, 'Hello boys, can you tell me where number 60 is?'

Roger pushed his National Health spectacles back up his nose and tilted his head back to look at the Doctor through his specs that had slid straight down again as Billy sniffed up a green snot that had been on the verge of escaping from his nose, both boys staring at the Doctor and the posh car but neither answering his question.

'Well, where is number 60?'

Albert stepped out of his shed and placed a very greasy hand on the pristine paint work of the Rover door, 'Number 60 is the last hoose up yonder at the end.'

'Thanks very much,' said Jonathon as he let the clutch out and drove slowly up the Row, 'My God did you see those children, they look inbred!'

Jennifer was horrified at his comment, 'Daddy what an awful thing to say, please don't be rude with Mrs Shepherd.'

He had gone with every intention of being rude but his intention evaporated when Jane Shepherd opened the door and smiled a beautiful disarming smile and said in a voice that stole his heart, 'Hello, you must be Doctor Metcalf and Jennifer, I'm Jane Trevelyan, Mike's mother, do come in.'

He followed her through the kitchen and into the sitting room, barely noticing the meagre and worn but spotlessly clean furnishings but he did notice the wonderful aroma of home baking and ignored Mike as he greeted Jennifer.

As Jane invited them to sit on the sofa he asked, 'What are you baking that smells so wonderful?'

Standing at the table next to window pouring tea, Jane answered, 'Scabby Aggie, it's a fruit cake that my Mother-in- Law taught me to bake, would you like a slice, I have some here I made yesterday?'

'Yes please, I'd love a piece,' he answered before asking, 'forgive me Mrs erm, Trevelyan but your name?'

'It's my Maiden name; I no longer use my married name for obvious reasons.'

'Of course and again I hope you don't mind me asking but your accent, you are not from Northumberland are you?'

Jane handed tea and slices of cake to the Doctor and his daughter, 'No, I'm from Coventry, I was educated at Brighton but have lived here since 1940; it's a long story!'

Jane's beauty and charm had already worked its magic on the Doctor; forgetting why he had come, he said, 'One that I would love to hear sometime.'

Ignoring his comment, Jane said, 'Perhaps we had better get back to the reason for your visit tonight Doctor Metcalf, Michael tells me that you are not happy that he is taking Jennifer out and can I say Jennifer, you are even prettier than Michael told me you were.'

Doctor Metcalf cleared his throat and said, 'Please call me Jonathon and without being rude you must surely understand my concern, any father would be the same under the circumstances, Mrs Trevelyan.'

Jane smiled her most disarming smile, 'It's Jane, Jonathon and I understand how you would worry and care about your daughter but let me assure you that Michael is not like his father, he is a caring and honest young man who would never intentionally hurt or upset anyone and he is also someone you can always rely on to do what is right. I have endeavoured over the years to teach my children right from wrong and would like to believe that I have succeeded.'

Right at that moment, if Jane had told him that the moon was made of cheese, he would have believed her but he had listened carefully to what she had said, 'Jane I apologise to you and Michael, I had obviously not appreciated the type of young man that Michael is; Jennifer had told me but I'm afraid I was not listening, now if it is not too late I would like to give my blessing to their courting and would dearly love to eat this, em, 'Scabby Aggie'!'

After running the Grundy kid's gauntlet, Jonathan was deep in thought as he drove home until Jennifer spoke, 'Thanks Daddy, I'm glad you can see how wonderful Mike is.'

'What a beautiful woman,' her father said.

'Dad, I'm talking about Mike!'

'Oh yes of course, a great boy with a remarkable mother!'

Later that night, fearing they would hear of the time of their father's execution on the radio or read about it in a newspaper or worse still, be told by one of their friends, Jane sat all her children, less for Tommy who was in bed, down in the sitting room and told them that their father was to be executed on the fifth of May and she was that they were all going to stay in a holiday caravan at Seahouses over that week in order to escape any press attention.

'On no account tell anyone where you are going and while we are there we will use my Maiden Name – Trevelyan, no-one is to mention the name Shepherd, is that clear,' she asked.

They all nodded but Maureen said, 'But Mam, I want to stay here with Terry, now that he's out of hospital.'

Jane took Maureen's hand and said gently, 'No Maureen, I insist, you are coming and you cannot tell Terry or his family where we are staying, that would be unfair on them, nor can anyone at school know, there will be only one other person told of where we are going.'

Mike asked, 'Will that be Aggie?'

'God no Mike, bless her, I love her so much but she would not be able to keep a secret like that, someone would trick her and find out. Now do not mention this to Tommy, I will talk to him tomorrow, just him and me.'

So who will know?' Mike asked.

'Mr Thompson but he doesn't know yet!'

Ian leant forward and asked, 'What about our paper rounds and my delivery job Mam?

'You'll have to see if any of your friends will cover for you.'

Ian nodded and Rafe said, 'We will organise something Sis, Howard and Jake might cover for us.'

Remembering Jake's last attempt to cover for him, Ian moaned, 'Jake, aargghh!'

That was the end of the discussion, apart from Rafe saying to Ian, 'Well you're a Trevelyan know Ian, how strange is that!'

The following Sunday, Jane walked along the Row to where Edward Thompson was as usual, cleaning his car and asked him if he would join her for a cup of tea and a chat, he almost beat her back to Number 60! Sitting on the sofa with a cup of tea in his hand, Edward looked at Jane admiringly and asked astutely, 'So what's up Jane lass, there's got to be a reason for asking me in, not that am not chuffed to be here?'

Jane told him of their plan to escape to Seahouses for the week of the execution and asked Edward if he would be willing to drive them over there as she did not want folk to see them catching a bus, 'We are all going but Mike will be riding over on his little motorbike, so can five of us squeeze into your car?'

'At a squeeze you could but I have a better idea, can you drive?'

'Em, yes I can but it's been a while but I have kept my licence up to date.'

Edward grinned, 'There you go, you borrow the Jowett and I'll use my van for the week, it will mean you have the car to run around in while you are there, you'll be able to show the kids just how lovely Northumberland is.'

Jane beamed, 'That would be wonderful Edward, I haven't seen much of Northumberland either; how can I ever thank you.'

'By having a good time with the kids, you are doing the right thing by getting away and I won't tell a soul, I tell you what, I can travel over with you on Saturday to mek sure you are happy with the car and Aah'll catch the bus back.'

'No Edward, that is too much, you got other things I'm sure you'd rather be doing.'

He replied, 'Not as much as taking you to Seahouses Pet, consider it done, thanks for the tea and I'll come over on the Friday night to familiarise you with the Jowett and then see you all first thing on the Saturday morning,' and then left whistling as he walked back down to his parent's house.

Apart from a couple of reporters seeking stories who were turned away, the next two weeks passed quietly, the family coping with their busy routines, trying to make enough money to survive and succeeding – just. Jane and Maureen booked the Methodist Chapel and the Toc H for Saturday the seventeenth of May and chose a cream summer two piece for Maureen from Doggart's small Department Store.

The Proudlocks friends and neighbours were all going to cook or bake for the reception dinner which would be served as a buffet and Jane bought several bottles of sherry to be used to toast the Bride and Groom. She also used some of Nick's gambling money to book a room in a hotel in Scarborough for the week for the newlyweds.

Although Jane said she shouldn't, Alice Kirkup said she would make the wedding cake as a gift for the two 'bairns which had Jane thanking her for her kindness while trying unsuccessfully to hold back a tear.

At the end of school on the Wednesday afternoon of the week before the execution, Ian walked through the school gates and turned right to walk down Third Row and head over to the 'Rec' to watch Rafe playing Rugby for the school before they did their paper rounds. Geordie Robertson and two of his cronies were waiting on the rough ground at the rear of the Fourth Row, opposite where the School Hall butted up against the last house of the Third Row!

As Ian approached the bully shouted, 'Right Shepherd, ye hevn't got yer poncy blidy Uncle te protect ye noo, get ower here and let's sort things oot!'

Remembering the advice Rafe had told him his Father had given him, Ian ignored the shout and tried to walk past but the three lads crossed the road and jostled him back over and behind the outhouses of the Third Row, 'Yer not se hard withoot him are ye Shepherd, are ye a coward like yer frigging murdering Faather?'

235

Ian tried to push past but the three lads held him there, 'Am not fighting you Geordie, I've no reason too, noo let me past.'

Geordie stepped back and snarled, 'Aah'll give yer a fucking reason to fight,' and with the two other lads holding onto Ian, he threw a viscous punch that smacked into Ian's right cheek snapping his head to one side and throwing him off balance. Geordie followed his first punch with two more, splitting Ian's bottom lip, splattering blood across his face as more blood trickled from his nose.

As a few more lads from school began gathering, Ian struggled in vain to break the grip of the two lads and suffered another stinging punch to the face until Robertson stepped back and swung his right foot at Ian's crotch. Ian saw it coming and managed to raise his right leg taking the impact of the kick on his thigh.

The sight of Ian's blood spattered face was too much for one of the other lads, he, let go of Ian and said, 'That's enough Geordie, haway, let's gan, ye've beaten him!'

'Fuck off then yer soft twat,' Robertson snarled, 'Am not finished with this fucker yet!'

The second lad let go of Ian, 'Haway man, ye've done enough, look, he's knacked, come on, let's gan.'

Steadying himself, Ian wiped blood away from his nose and spat a mouthful onto the dirt of the alley and glared at Robertson who scoffed, 'Aye that's the coward knacked alreet, am finished with him!'

As he turned to walk away, Ian barked, 'Am not finished with you though Robertson yer swine,' and turning to the two other lads warned, 'You two better stay out of this now ora I'll come after you as well.'

More lads had arrived, several of them pushing Robertson's friends to one side as Ian advanced on the still cocky bully who spat, 'Come on then Shepherd, noo Aah'll really knack ye!' He swung his right at Ian who ducked under it and barged into the bigger lad knocking him backwards and off balance allowing Ian to swing three or four blows of

236

his own into the face of his opponent, raising cheers from the spectators.

Geordie took the blows and swung back with a heavy right that knocked Ian against the brick wall of the back of a coal house. As he pushed himself off, Ian took another two punches to the head followed by a knee intended for his groin that crunched into his right thigh again, dropping him to his knee. Sensing victory, the bully rained punches down onto Ian's head until Ian, using the wall to again push off, heaved a mighty uppercut into Geordies chin, snapping his neck back and propelling him backwards, raising more cheers from the group of onlookers that continued to grow in numbers.

Ian barged into the off balance Geordie, knocking him onto his back and dived onto him but Geordie was too strong and threw him to one side, scrambling on top trying to pin Ian's arms with his knees. Ian struggled to resist but the heavier lad managed to pin them and battered Ian's unprotected face with two more crunching punches until Ian, summoning all his strength, arched his back and chest throwing Geordie forward and to one side. The two lads scrambled to gain their feet, Geordie kicking Ian in the ribs as they did so.

With twenty or more voices screaming encouragement a battered and bloodied Ian, ignored the blood oozing from his nose and cuts on his lip and above his eye and advanced toward Geordie who, blowing hard, wiped blood from his own nose and said, 'Aah've beaten yer noo bugger off!'

Ian answered with a flurry of wild punches, most of which missed as Geordie back pedalled but one right landed solidly on Geordies left eye making him wince and turn away. Ian felt neither pain nor exhaustion and ignoring his bruised knuckles weighed in again landing several more stinging blows until Geordie turned his head away and bent over, shielding his head with his left arm. Ian stepped back thinking his opponent had given up but as he did so Geordie seized the opening and

237

kicked out striking Ian on the side of the right knee that buckled, collapsing him onto his hands and knees as the bully swung two more powerful kicks into Ian, one smacking into his stomach and one his hip.

Geordie stopped to balance himself and swung another powerful kick aimed at Ian's head but Ian rolled to his left and sprung to his feet lunging at the now off balance opponent and barging him onto his back. Geordie scrabbled at the ground to regain his feet but Ian knocked him back with a barrage of punches and a crunching knee to the nose that left Geordie cowering on the dirt on all fours. Ian stepped back and looked at the beaten Bully and ignoring the mob's shouts to 'Kick Him,' growled, 'Come on then Robertson, stand up and fight!'

Staying on his knees, Geordie straightened his back and tried to wipe blood from his battered face before looking at Ian through rapidly closing eyes, he shook his head and moaned, 'Nur am knacked!' The little crowd went wild, shouting and cheering as Ian steadied himself, too sore and exhausted to feel jubilant, he turned and began making his way back through the throng of lads all wanting to pat his back as Geordie Robertson staggered to his feet and slunk off alone.

Jake Grundy appeared out of the throng, 'Bugga me Ian, that's the best fight Aah've iver seen, ye were like Rocky blidy Marciano man!'

Ian put his arm around Jake for support and said, 'Jake, shut up man.'

Unperturbed by the rebuke, Jake continued, 'Aye ye beat the bastard but fucking hell man ye look in an awful blidy Mess, yer mam'll gan spare when she sees ye, ye'd better come to wor hoose and get yer face washed forst!'

Flo Grundy was shocked when she saw Ian, 'Sit yersell doon lad while Aah get some hot water to wash yer poor feyce noo.'

Ian was happy to oblige as Flo washed the blood from his face with surprising tenderness using the not so clean towel that had been hanging on the pantry door, not that Ian cared. 'Ye might need a stitch in that lip and the cut above yer eye, I think ye better gan te the Medical Centre lad.

Ian sighed, 'Aah cannit, Ah hev me papers te deliver.'

'Not like that ye hevn't Pet, wor Jake'll deliver them after he's walked doon te the Medical Centre with ye!'

A few minutes later Jake helped Ian into the Medical Centre next to the Pit Head Baths and knocked on the hatch that was slid open by the duty nurse, 'Aye what's the matter lad?'

'It's not me Miss, it's him,' he said pointing to Ian who was leaning against the wall.

'Oh I see,' she said, I think I've just patched up the big ugly brute who did that to your pal!'

Jake grinned, 'Aye me pal won the fight; he beat the big bugga up!'

The Nurse tutted and warned, 'Don't swear in here lad and your friend doesn't look much like a winner to me, now bring him through.'

'Aye whey he did anyways,' muttered Jake as he helped Ian through.

She put two stitches on the inside of his lip and one above his eye that she covered with a plaster, 'There you are, that's that and I suppose you must have won the fight because the other lad needed four stitches!'

'Aah towld ye, didn't Aah,' Jake Shouted from the waiting room door.

The Nurse then went over to her desk and asked, 'Your father does work at the colliery, doesn't he?'

Ian looked at Jake standing in the doorway and answered, 'Yes, Albert Grundy, he works in the stables.' Jake was about to speak but Ian's glare silenced him.

'And your name and age?' the Nurse asked,

'Jacob and am thirteen,' Ian lied.

Outside a grinning Jake asked, 'Why did ye tell hur yer wor me?'

'Whey think man, Aah didn't want te tell her who my Faather was did Aah?'

Jake looked puzzled for a moment then the penny dropped, 'Ur nur, Aah see, cos yer Dad doesn't work for the Colliery anymore.'

'Aye that as well,' said Ian, 'now am off te de me paper roond are ye coming with me?'

'Aye of course marra - for a bob!' answered the grinning Jake.

A concerned Rafe said, 'I wondered why you did not come to watch the Rugby,' when Ian walked into the room used to sort the newspapers at the rear of Crisps. Aided by an excited Jake, Ian told Rafe of the fight and the visit to the Medical Centre.

Rafe listened quietly until Ian finished than said, 'Well I hope that is the last bother we have with that gross swine but God knows what Sis is going to say when she sees you later?'

Jane had a lot to say, including wanting to inform the Police of the assault on Ian and would have done so if Mike had not been there, 'Look Mam, there are fights amongst lads every day and I know it was assault but if you go to the Police, Ian will lose support from all the other lads, it's just not done and anyway, judging by his knuckles he gave as good as he got if not better and think, do we really want any more Police involvement with our lives at the moment?'

Jane calmed down and examined Ian's wounds for the third time in as many minutes, 'Judging by the bruising, you are lucky he did not break your ribs, please God let that be an end to it, I don't want you turning into a thug or worse.'

Mike ruffled Ian's hair and said, 'Not him, he's a lover not a fighter from what I hear, eh Ian?'

Later, Howard agreed to do both of Rafe's paper rounds and Ian reluctantly walked along to the Grundys and knocked on the door, there was no answer so he knocked again but again there was no answer so he opened the door and shouted 'Jake are you in?'

The kitchen was occupied only by the stale smell of burnt onions but a muffled voice from the sitting room shouted 'Wa in here.' Ian walked through the kitchen and pushed open the door to the sitting room to look at the backs of all the Grundys; Albert, Flo, Jake, Billy and Roger, all sitting on various chairs and crackets giggling and laughing at two wooden pigs that were dancing and singing on the twelve inch television that they were gathered around! Ian watched the antics of the two puppet pigs that sang with weird high pitch voices for a moment and although they were funny, they were not nearly as funny as the expressions of delight on the Grundy Familie's faces as they chortled at the antics of the pigs. Flo in particular looked like a little child watching a Punch and Judy show for the first time, every few seconds gasping, 'Whey ye buggas a hell!'

Ian nudged Jake who had not taken his eyes of the screen, 'How, I'm ganning away next week, will ye dee my paper roonds and grocery deliveries?'

Jake nodded and without turning said, 'Aye, nee bother, dee ye like wor new telly?'

Before Ian could answer, Albert said, 'I've hired it from Rediffusion, Aah, used some of the money yor Mike gave me for me motorbike for the deposit, grand isn't it?'

Flo said, 'Will ye buggas shut up man, am trying to listen to them blidy pigs sing!'

Jake whispered, 'Where ye ganning?'

'Just away for a week, Aah cannit tell ye where, so ye'll dee my paper roond and grocery job and dee it properly this time?'

241

'Aye of course Aah will, noo haway and waatch Pinky and Perky man.'

'Nur thanks, I'm ganning for me dinner, I'll see you later,' Ian said and walked back out in to the street where Peggy was expertly bouncing three tennis balls off an air raid shelter.

The balls went flying when she saw Ian's face and she lost her concentration, 'Whatever's happened?' she demanded as she gently touched his swollen cheek.

'Ur nowt man, Aah just had a fight at school that's all.'

Peggy fired a barrage of questions until Ian told her of the problems he had had with Geordie Robertson and of the fight as she stood listening quietly, her lips tightening as her anger built until she vowed to boil Geordie Robertson's head in oil if she ever met him!

Chapter 12
Over and Done With

The sun was burning away the last remains of an overnight frost as Mike wheeled the James out of the shed and into the back lane. He had already strapped his rucksack containing his clothes and washing kit onto the back and rubbed his hands to warm them as he walked back into the house, stepping over the two suitcases standing at the foot of the stairs and into the kitchen where the rest of the family were sitting with their engines ticking over, waiting for Edward to arrive.

'It's just five to seven Mam, he said he'd be here by seven, just relax,' Mike said.

'I'm perfectly relaxed Michael,' Jane said although she clearly wasn't, keen to be away before neighbours were up and about, she leapt out of her chair when Maureen, pulled the net curtain back and said, 'He's here!'

By the time Edward had turned the car around, the family were standing on the pavement with suitcases in hand, ready to go! Climbing out of the car, he said, 'Morning everybody, fancy a trip to the seaside?'

In her rush and excitement to be off, Jane forgot herself and stepped forward and kissed Edward on the cheek, blushing instantly as she realised what she had done. 'Come on into the back of the car,' she ordered her older children, as she tried to hide her embarrassment.

The satisfied grin on Edward's face disappeared when he saw Ian, 'Blidy hell lad what happened to you?'

Ian touched his bruised eyes and replied, 'Aah had fight at school Mr Edwards.'

Edward frowned, 'It wasn't because of yer Dad was it?'

'Not really, it's been ganna happen for a long time.'

'Who was it that did this te ye then?'

Ian half smiled, 'Geordie Robertson but I won the fight like!'

'That lad's nowt but trouble, let me know if ye have any more bother with him.' Edward said as he opened the boot and piled in the suitcases as Maureen, Ian and Rafe climbed into the back of the car while their mother stared nervously at the driver's seat. Edward said to Tommy, 'Right young man, into the front,' and Tommy excitedly climbed onto the front bench seat as Jane slid in behind the steering wheel.

Edward climbed into the passenger side and asked, 'Can you remember where all the controls are from when I showed you last night?'

Jane gave him a cheeky smile, turned on the engine, engaged first, released the handbrake and pulled away slowly but smoothly with just a tiny judder as she changed up to second. They saw no one as she drove out of the Row with Mike following behind on his motorcycle.

It had been a long while since Jane had driven so she concentrated on driving smoothly and safely and did not go over thirty miles an hour as they drove past New Moor Marsh framed by the steaming collection of pit heaps half a mile beyond and on into the pretty village of Ellington where Tommy pointed to the square sandstone Plough Inn and said, 'Look, that's called the 'Plodge Inn', de you gan plodging here?'

Edward chuckled, 'Ye can if ye can find any weter here Tommy but that's pronounced "Plough" not "Plodge"'.

The mood in the car was sombre, all but Tommy remembering why they were escaping Ashington's drab, smoky Colliery Rows for a week as they drove past the hamlet of Widdrington and just beyond, the massive ugly hole in the ground where the mighty crane 'Big Geordie' scooped tons of earth and coal from the opencast mine. Through the quiet and unexciting Red Row and onto Amble where the 19th century coal mine and terraced miners cottages sat close by the older and grander sandstone buildings of the fishing port.

The road out of Amble descended a short hill onto a wide plain flanked on the right by the River Coquet with a mile ahead the imposing Warkworth Castle standing proudly above the picturesque village that nestled in a loop of the river.

'Gosh, look at that Castle,' said Rafe.

'Aye that's Warkworth Castle, it belonged to the Percy's, it was Harold Hotspur's place,' said Edward before providing a potted history of Warkworth, the Castle and the Dukes of Northumberland; impressing everyone with his detailed knowledge before finishing with, 'Mind, if ye think Warkworth is big, wait until ye see Bamburgh!'

The family slowly relaxed and began enjoying the drive along the stunning Northumberland Coast, past beautiful Alnmouth standing above the Aln estuary that glistened in the morning sun, through Lesbury, Longhoughton, Embelton and eventually quaint Beadnell and finally, alongside the sand dunes into the small seaside town of Seahouses with its bustling harbour packed with fishing boats.

As they reached the town, Jane turned right off the main road and along a side road for a hundred yards before entering the static caravan park where she stopped in front of a red brick built shop as Mike pulled up behind them.

Edward accompanied her into the shop as she walked up to the counter and said to the cheery middle aged women behind, 'Hello, I'm Mrs Trevelyan; we are booked in for a week.'

The woman consulted a large open book behind the counter and then took a key from a numbered board, handing it to Edward, 'Here ye are Mr Trevelyan, it's; number fowerty one, half way doon the third row.'

Edward took the key and said 'Thank you,' as he grinned sheepishly at Jane.

Outside he handed her the key and said, 'I thought it was best to say nowt to her.'

Jane nodded and hiding a smile, replied, 'Yes you were right Edward, it's probably best that she thinks you are my husband but she may think it strange when she doesn't see you anymore, I'll have to tell her you are working.'

'Aye, well I am aren't Aah!'

The caravan was 30 foot long and 11 foot wide and although not brand new it was in excellent order and spotlessly clean; Tommy was first inside and shouted, 'A television look,' then wandered through the sitting area, past a small dining area and kitchen that led to a small hall with three doors leading to a double bedded room, a smaller room with bunk beds and a small bathroom with wash basin, toilet and half size bath.

Ian was first into the bathroom that smelt strongly of pine disinfectant, 'Look at this,' he shouted, 'not only hev we a television, look in here tha's an inside netty and a bath, it's better than wor hoose!'

Tommy had climbed onto the top bunk in the tiny second bedroom and shouted, 'Can we live here?'

Jane checked through the kitchen area that smelled of a mix of burnt gas and disinfectant as Maureen locked herself in the bathroom. Jane then organised sleeping arrangements, 'Maureen and I will sleep in the large bedroom, Ian, you and Tommy on the bunk beds and Mike, you and Rafe on the sofas in the siting area.'

Edward who had been standing in the doorway joshed, 'And what about me, where am I sleeping?'

'Back in your own bed,' answered Jane smiling at him. Edward had a cup of tea with the family before wishing them a pleasant stay and after saying his goodbyes he walked off to catch the bus back to Alnwick for the connection to Ashington. Jane walked with him to the gate of the caravan park and thanked him for his help and the use of his car for the week.

'Think nothing of it Bonny Lass,' he said, 'ye kna I would de owt for ye and the kids, Aah hope ye hev a quiet and peaceful time,' and with an unexpected boldness, kissed her on the cheek and turned and hurried off.

The Caravan Park was on top of a small cliff at the south edge of the town, a hundred yards or so from the harbour and after lunch of tinned hot dogs between squashy bread rolls, the family strolled to the bank above the harbour. The harbour was packed with brightly painted fishing boats moored two or three abreast, all of them festooned with fishing gear with men clambering over them readying them for the next trip to sea as the not unpleasant smell of sea, seaweed and fish reached them on a gentle spring breeze.

The harbour consisted of at the north-side; three distinct mooring areas separated by huge stone jetties, the outer one with a high wall built to provide some respite from the cold north easterly winds. The south-side consisted of an outcrop of rocks that ran from the foot of the cliff next to the caravan park and out to sea for fifty yards to where a second lower breakwater stretched toward the northern one leaving the entrance to the harbour between the two Jetties. A small stone hut had been built on the highest part of the rocks at the south-side to provide an emergency shelter for anyone unfortunate enough to be caught by high tides or storms that often cut off the southern break water.

At the northern end of the harbour, the lifeboat station and a boat builders shed stood side by side with the skeletal ribs of a fishing boat under construction outside. Massive redundant brick built kilns that had been turned into boat sheds lined the land side of the harbour with the picturesque Bamburgh Castle Hotel sitting above with its magnificent views out to sea that encompassed the wild and rugged Farne Isles.

Mike pointed north over the harbour to the dark and imposing shape of a castle a few miles along the coast, 'That must be Bamburgh Castle.'

'It is,' said Jane, 'and the smaller shape out to sea a bit further on is Lindesfarne Castle on Holy Island; we'll visit them both this week.'

The boys raced off down the slope and excitedly explored the harbour and its surrounds. A little later they met up at the milk bar in the centre of the small town that was made up of a mix of shops and a newly opened smart Fish and Chip Bar.

Slurping a strawberry milk shake, Tommy asked, 'Can we have fish and chips for dinner Mam?'

Jane looked into her purse and said, 'We will tonight as a treat, but that will be the only time we eat out, I have only enough money for a gallon or two of petrol and a visit to Bamburgh Castle on Monday, we will take sandwiches and flasks for our lunches and have dinner in the caravan so please do not expect any treats other than exploring the area, okay everyone?'

Ian said, 'There's plenty to explore here, it's going to be great Mam.'

'A terrific place Sis, thanks so much,' added Rafe.

The fish and chips served with bread, butter and pots of tea were superb and ended a great afternoon as they walked back to the caravan just after six o'clock looking forward to watching television, regardless of what was on.

Everyone was in bed by ten o'clock and as they settled down Mike asked, 'Rafe I don't understand how ye can be so happy living with us in the Sixth Ra after the life you've had, hoo come?'

There was silence for a while before Rafe answered, 'Mike, my home life was never exactly happy, my Mother, when she was alive

248

rarely showed me any affection which I found very upsetting and my father was also very remote, he was always very busy at work and I hardly saw him. When I went off to Rugley I hated it initially and was very lonely but it did get better and at times I preferred to stay there rather than go home for weekend hols.'

'So how come living with us in a tiny hoose with a mad murderer for a father and an outside netty and nee bath is better?'

'I admit I miss the comforts of my old home but that is more than made up for by the warm welcome I received from Sis and you lot, I love being part of the family and love the excitement of living in Ashington and the freedom we have, as for your Father, what can I say, I think you are all going to be much happier without him.'

Mike turned over and pulled his blanket under his chin, 'Ye can say that again, good night Rafe Lad.'

'Goodnight Mike.'

The next morning having checked the tide table and with Mike sitting in the front alongside her and Tommy, Jane drove up the coast to Holy Island where with much excitement from everyone in the car, she drove across the causeway that was still damp from the outgoing tide and onto the beach of the south-side of the Island and along to the village dominated by the ruins of the once mighty Priory. The small but beautifully proportioned castle sitting on a huge rock on the outskirts of the village dominated the bay that had a collection of cobles, yachts and dinghies anchored in its safe shelter.

They had a wonderful couple of hours exploring the old village and Priory before eating their packed lunches as they sat on the edge of the tiny harbour that was made up of a stone jetty protecting a corner of the bay whose shore was lined with up-turned boats that had been tarred black and now used as boat sheds.

Back at the caravan, as Jane prepared dinner with Maureen and despite her efforts to keep everyone cheerful, the mood was sombre as Nick's last few hours ticked by.

Sensing the problem, Mike ventured, 'Right who fancies a game of three card brag after dinner?'

Jane was shocked, 'Mike, there'll be no gambling in this house!'

'Don't ye mean caravan Mam? Anyway it'll be just for matchsticks, Aah thought it would...'

Realising what her son was trying to do Jane interrupted, 'Yes that's a good idea Mike and the one with the most matches at the end will not have to do any washing up whilst we are here!'

The card game and television helped a little but only Tommy slept well that night!

At Strangeways Prison, Nick had hardly slept at all during the past week and was barely conscious of what was happening to him when on Sunday evening, he was giving his own freshly cleaned clothes to wear before being taken to a cell in a different part of the prison. The cell was the same drab battleship grey as his last but was larger with a small square table and three chairs occupying the centre, his bed in one corner with a toilet and washbasin opposite and a large wooden wardrobe against one wall.

He did not eat much when his food was brought in just after five o'clock, his stomach was a tight ball and it took a great deal of effort to even swallow the luke warm tea in the large enamel mug as he glared morosely at the two Warders who would stay with him until the end. He had talked almost non-stop during the afternoon but now tiredness and fear robbed him of the will to do anything other than lie down on his bed and stare at the ceiling as he slowly drowned in a sea of self-pity.

In the early hours of the morning, he had to be helped to his feet by the Warders when he needed to use the toilet and again a little later when they roused him to wash and shave. He refused breakfast with a shake of the head and instead sipped at a final mug of tea and again shook his head when asked if he wanted to speak to a priest. A little later he spoke for the first time in twelve hours, 'What time is it?'

His question was never answered; following a well-rehearsed routine, a tap on a door behind the wardrobe was the signal to the two warders; they stood up and slid the wardrobe to one side revealing a large wooden door that they threw open as Nick looked up. Two dour faced middle aged men strode into the cell as the Warders turned back and lifted Nick to his feet. The Hangman and his assistant pulled Nick's hands behind him and strapped them together with a stout leather belt, then turned and marched out through the door onto the wooden decking beyond where the Prison Governor, Doctor and Chaplain stood silently waiting.

The Warders led Nick out; quickly positioning his feet over an inverted T chalked on the decking as the Hangman stepped forward and placed a white bag over Nick's head. He then slipped the noose around Nick's neck and tightened it while his assistant strapped Nick's ankles together. The two Warders ensured they were standing on the two bridging planks either side of Nick and each grabbed a dangling rope attached to the gallows to support themselves.

This happened in seconds, giving Nick little time to think or react but as he heard the Hangman step back and slide a safety pin out from the base of the operating level, his knees buckled but he was held firm by the Warders.

A scream of terror started in his stomach and raced to his throat but was silenced before it could be heard as the Hangman threw the lever forward!

Deep in thought as she stared out of the condensation clouded window above the kitchen sink in the caravan, Jane gave a little shudder, looked at her watch and thought to herself, 'I hope you are at rest now Nick Shepherd,' then turned to her family who were sitting quietly at the small dining table. Sighing deeply she said, 'let's get ready for Bamburgh Castle.'

'Aye,' said Mike, 'that's over and done with then!' Nothing more needed to be said.

As magnificent as it is, Bamburgh Castle did not succeed in lifting the sadness of the day, even Tommy was unable to enjoy the chance to become an imaginary Knight and instead of spending a full day there, by twelve o'clock Jane had driven them onto the beach of the huge sweeping sandy bay that the mighty Fortress domianted.

They ate their sandwiches in silence before Jane said, 'OK, a walk, come on while the sun is out we'll have a walk along the beach.'

The bracing sea air helped lift their spirits so much that Mike said, 'Mam, I'm ganna walk back to Seahooses alang the beach, it's only a couple of miles, what about ye lads, de ye fancy walking back?' The four boys agreed and set off at a brisk walk as Jane and Maureen walked slowly back to the car chatting about wedding arrangements in an effort to forget the morning's sadness that was tinged with relief that Nick was now hopefully, out of their lives for good!

Chapter 13
What Next?

For the rest of the week Jane did her best to keep the family entertained, driving them around the coast and as far up as Berwick upon Tweed but by Thursday the boys were happy enough spending their time in and around the harbour, fishing off the jetties with lines and exploring the rock pools below the caravan park. Jane had removed the stitches from Ian's face and with the swelling gone; all that remained of his battle were some discolouring below his eyes.

A strong North Easterly wind picked up on Friday morning sending waves crashing spectacularly over the southern breakwater and rocks, the excitement of which was a magnet to Ian, Rafe and Tommy. They joined a couple of hardy men who were fishing very successfully for Pollock from the breakwater and tried in vain to catch some with their lines and sinkers. All of them were so absorbed in fishing and dodging waves that they failed to notice the sea crashing over the rocks behind them, cutting off their route back to the shore.

As more waves crashed over the breakwater, it became clear that they could not remain there safely! One of the two men shouted, 'Howay lads, we'll hev te get into the shelter.' That was easier said than done as waves were crashing on to the back of the tiny stone building but the holding onto each other, the five of them shuffled from the breakwater, over the rocks and into the shelter where soaked to the skin they stood shivering, glad to be out of the spray, 'Well that was jolly exciting,' said Rafe!'

It was over two hours before the tide had receded enough to make it safe enough for them to walk through now torrential rain, back across the rocks to the shore where they received a stern talking to by a Coast Guard Officer and a member of the life boat crew who had been called out in case they were needed. Suitably chastised the boys made their way back to the caravan park as the Coast Guard Officer continued to remonstrate with the two fishermen!

Standing dripping water on the doormat of the caravan, the three boys looked pathetic, 'Look what's washed up in the storm, three smelly kippers,' said Mike laughing.

Jane was angry, 'You think you two would have more sense than to be out in the rain, especially with Tommy having been so ill, where have you been?'

Rafe looked at Ian and answered for them, 'Just fishing Sis and we got caught in the rain.' Tommy was about to speak but Ian silenced him with a nudge and a wink.

Jane issued orders, 'Right, a hot bath for you Tommy and you two can go over to the wash rooms and have showers but hurry back, we are having an early dinner as Mike is going home tonight.'

Mike had telephoned Jennifer at home and arranged to meet her at Morpeth for a night at the cinema after first calling at home to check that everything was okay and to relight the fires.

It was just after 6 o'clock when he parked his motorbike outside the front of the house and Aggie Galloway came galloping along to intercept him before he could retreat inside; 'Eeee, hello Bonny Lad, where hev ye been, where's yer mam and the bairns, we were worried sick man, we thowt ye had aall gone for good, is yer mam back tonight, de ye need owt, Aah'll bring a pot of tea alang or should Aah put yer kettle on, Eee am glad te see ye back, is iviry body aall reet, tha's been lots of nosey reporters aroond here looking for ye's and that taall Scotchy Policeman, Monday must hev been aaful for ye's aall, eee, am sorry, Aah shudn't hev mention that, am sorry lad, noo what can Aah dee for ye?'

Glad to see Aggie, Mike stood smiling and when she finally gave him the opportunity to speak, he answered, 'Everybody is fine Aggie, me

Mam and the rest are coming back tomorrow morning, we've been up to Seahouses for the week to be out the way, I'm just going to light the fires and mek sure everything is all right before I ride ower te Morpeth te see me girlfriend; it would be good if you didn't mention Monday when me Mam gets back the morn and, Aah would love a cup of tea please.'

Aggie scuttled home to make a pot of tea as Mike opened the back door and stepped in picking up two official looking brown envelopes addressed to his mother that he placed on the kitchen table before he set about cleaning and lighting the fires.

The following day, Aggie had been busy when Jane pulled up outside Number 60 just after lunch time; the fires in the kitchen and sitting room were glowing fiercely, the tea pot was ready and waiting for boiling water, the kitchen table was set for lunch and a large Pan Haggerty sat on the open oven door filling the kitchen with the welcoming smell of cooked bacon and cheese. She rushed at Jane crushing her with a bear hug before turning her attention on poor Tommy who she plastered with large wet kisses that was a signal for Ian and Rafe to escape before they suffered the same fate. Rushing back out the door Ian said, 'We'll be back in a minute Mam, wa just ganning te check with Howard and Jake that tha was nee problems delivering papers.'

Mike carried the suitcases in from the car as Jane picked up the two letters on the kitchen table and placed them behind the clock on the mantelpiece, 'I'll read them after we had some of Aggie's lovely Pan Haggerty,' she said as she hugged Aggie again.

Ian and Rafe found Howard swinging on the Tarzan rope the lads had tied to the tallest of the trees in the scrub behind the outside toilets. As he swung in a large circle below the tree, Ian shouted, 'Hi Howard, any problems with the newspaper roonds?'

255

Jumping off the rope with a thud, Howard replied, 'The only problem was making sure that useless sod Jake was oot of bed in the mornings, three times Aah had gan up his stairs and inte that smelly room and drag him oot of bed, Aah divin't kna who smells the worst him or his bloody dog!'

'But did he deliver them alright?'

'Aye as far as a kna but he's slow man!'

Climbing back over the wall between the toilets and coal houses Ian said, 'Aah better gan and check that he's delivered the groceries withoot any bother,' and ran down to the Grundy's followed by Rafe and Howard.

Flo answered the door, 'Nur he's not back yit son, who's yer mam, is iviry body alreet?

Ian nodded, 'Aye, we are all okay thanks Mrs Grundy can ye tell Jake te come and see me when he gets hyem?

Ian and Rafe jogged home and sat down to enjoy Aggie's Pan Haggerty with the rest of the family, apart from Mike who had already left for football practice. They were busy clearing away when the back door swung open and Jake walked in, 'By that smells champion, hev ye got any left Mr's Shepherd?'

Ian turned and said with some exasperation, 'Jake, Aah telt ye before we left, wor name's Trevelyan noo man!'

'Ur aye ye did, sorry like but is tha any of that food left?'

Jane said, 'Sit down Jake and I'll scrape what's left on a plate for you.'

'Ta Mrs Shep – sorry Mrs Trevlan,' Jake said as he eagerly pulled up a chair and was joined by Ian and Rafe who sat either side of him keen to know if he had delivered the groceries without problem. As Ian began his inquisition, Jane took the envelopes from the mantelpiece and sat down in the sitting room to read them, Maureen had rushed out to hurry round to the Proudlocks to see Terry while Tommy dragged his toy soldiers out for a muster parade on the sitting room fireside rug.

Ian and Rafe watched in awe as Jake devoured the remains of the Pan Haggerty in seconds before lifting the plate to lick every last trace of the food. 'Any problems with me paper roond Jake?' Ian asked.

'Nur, why shud tha have been like,' he answered, having placed the plate back on the table he used a grubby finger to wipe up the last vestiges of grease, sucking them from his finger noisily.

Rafe asked 'You had no problem in rising in the morning?'

'Nur man, who telt ye Aah did, Aah bet it was that big bugga Howard, he was alwas ower urly man, I wud hev got up in time withoot him man!'

Ian shook his head, 'Aye whey thanks for that but what about the groceries any problems we them?'

'Nur man – whey not big problems – not really,' Jake said as he rose to leave.

'Ian pulled him back down into the chair, 'Had on a minute, what de ye mean, not really?'

'Nowt man, one of them snotty blidy wimin doon Wansbeck Road said tha was a cyek missing oot of her box.'

'Cyek!' Rafe said, imitating Jake's pronunciation, 'what on earth is a cyek?'

'A cake,' answered Ian before turning on Jake, 'and was tha one missing and did ye eat it?'

'Aah might hev done!'

'What de ye mean, Ah might hev done, did ye or didn't ye?'

'Whey man Aah was blidy starving, Aah just had the one – and a piece of cheese but she didn't kna Aah had that cos a wrapped the paper back all reet!'

Ian glared at him, 'Did the manager say owt?'

'Nur man, it's alreet – whey, he did say he wudn't trust me te de owt again and asked when ye wor back, and ye kna he took thrupence of me money and made me tek another cyek doon ta that snotty woman and telt me te apologise te hur!'

Ian asked, 'Did ye?'

'Did Aah waat?'

'Apologise,' said Rafe.

'Ur aye, whey sort of like.'

Ian leant toward him and demanded, 'Sort of like what?'

'Sort of like, Aah said, "Here's ya cyek Missus!"'

Relieved to be home and ready to start life anew, Jane sat smiling as she listened to the boy's banter, 'Maureen's wedding next' she thought as she slid her finger under the flap of the first envelope to open it. It was a short, pithy formal letter from the Governor of Strangeways Prison informing her that in accordance with the sentence handed down to him, Nick had been executed at precisely eight o'clock on Monday the fifth of May 1958 and that he was pronounced dead by the Prison Doctor at ten minutes past eight o'clock. A Death Certificate was attached to the letter.

Having neatly re-folded the letter and Death Certificate, she slid them carefully back into the brown envelope and sat staring into the fire for a second or two, 'Well that really is that Nick,' she thought.

She opened the second envelope and taking out the single sheet of paper, opening it up she saw typed across the top, 'National Coal Board.' She read the two paragraphs slowly then stared into the fire again as a tear rolled down her cheek and she whispered 'Oh my God, not now surely!'

Holding back waves of panic and despair, she re-read the letter;

Dear Mrs Shepherd,

Number 60 the Sixth Row was allocated to Mr N Shepherd (deceased) a former employee of Ashington Colliery.

In accordance with NCB regulations concerning occupancy of allocated housing, we hereby give you notice to vacate number 60, the Sixth Row at your earliest convenience but no later than the 6th of June 1958.

Hearing his mother sigh, Tommy looked up and saw tears running down her cheeks, 'What's the matter Mam?' he asked as he got up from the floor and sat next to her.

Jane composed herself and answered, 'Nothing Tommy, just another little set back but nothing for you to worry about, now get back to your soldiers, I'm popping next door to see Mrs Galloway.'

The three lads had already left when Jane walked through the kitchen and to the back door just as Edward Thompson knocked. 'Hello Jane,' he said when she opened the door, 'how was your week?'

She smiled at him and replied, 'It was lovely to be away for a week Edward and thanks for the use of your car but,' she was unable to speak as her emotions got the better of her.

'What's up lass,' he said placing his hand gently on her shoulder.

'Just when I thought we could move forward,' she said as she walked back into the kitchen, 'this was waiting for me.' She handed the letter to him and waited whilst he quickly read the two paragraphs.

'That's a bugga Jane but were you not expecting it?'

'To be honest, not really, what with everything that has happened, I never for a moment imagined we would be evicted, it has knocked me back, I'm not sure what we are going to do and it's Maureen's Wedding on Saturday! I think I may have thought that the house could be transferred to Mike as he works for the NCB and is now the man of the house but I don't know, so I was on my way next door to speak to Arthur, he is an NUM Rep isn't he?'

259

Edward handed back the letter replying, 'He is Jane, if anyone can do owt he can.'

The two of them walked next door where Aggie welcomed them in, 'Come on in, Aah'll put the kettle on, noo sit your sell's doon and tell me yer news,' she said excitedly.

Jane asked, 'Is Arthur in Aggie?'

'He's in the garden Pet but ye can tell me yer news forst can't ye?'

'I'm sorry Aggie I haven't got any news, just a problem I thought Arthur could help me with.'

Aggie looked crestfallen, 'Oh I see, I thowt ye had something te tell me aboot ye two, I'll just call Arthur, hang on,' she said as Jane looked at Edward with a puzzled expression but he looked equally confused at Aggie's comment and shrugged his shoulders.

Arthur kicked off his boots at the front door and walked into the sitting room, pulling his braces back up unnecessarily as a large leather belt was doing an admirable job of supporting his grubby gardening trousers. Hello Jane, nice te see ye back pet, the Gallowa says ye want te see me?'

Handing him the letter, Jane said, 'I received this today Arthur and I was wondering if there was anything that the Trade Union could do to help me?'

After reading the letter he sat down in a large armchair by the fireplace and asked Aggie, 'hev ye got the kettle on, Aah think we'll need a cup of tea.'

'Aye the kettle's on but what on Earth is the matter?' Aggie replied.

'It's Jane's eviction notice,' he said solemnly.

'Aggie almost stamped her feet with indignation, 'Bye tha blidy quick off the mark, aren't tha?'

Jane lent forward and asked Arthur, 'Is there anyway the house can be transferred to Mike, he works for the NCB?'

Arthur grimaced before replying, 'I'm sorry Bonny Lass, Aah don't think see, he's not owld enough and he's still and apprentice, Aah'll check for you on Monday but Aah divin't think it's very likely but Aah'll see what Aah can dee.'

Aggie handed cups of tea round and said, 'Listen Pet, ye've got a lot of friends in this Ra and we'll all look after ye and the bairns, so divin't worry ower much, ye've got the wedding on Saturday te sort oot forst.'

Jane sighed deeply, 'Yes Aggie and I feel blessed that I have you for a neighbour but it looks as if that won't be for very long does it?'

Edward placed his hand on her shoulder again and asked, 'Whatever you do we will all be here to help you, anything you need or want doing, you've just got to ask.'

Jane thanked him and said, 'Please don't tell anyone of this until after the wedding, I don't want to upset the children so I won't tell them until next Sunday, in the meantime, I had better start looking for a cheap flat and go to the council to see what they can do for me.'

Edward said, 'The new council hooses doon Darnley Road are smashing, you might be able te get one of them as you are being made homeless.'

Jane smiled, 'We'll see, another bridge to cross, I must try and stay positive for my family.'

Edward wanted to take her in his arms and say, 'Don't worry about a thing, you and the family can come and live with me,' but knew that was just an impossible dream.

Jane found the next six days hectic and very stressful; working in the bakery took up most of the day but Alice did allow her a couple of hours off to go down to the council offices with her eviction notice and register for a council house. The staff were understanding and very helpful, apart from one woman who said rather frostily, 'Considering what you're late husband did and what happened to him, I would have thought you would have wanted to leave the area?'

Jane replied, 'My life is here in Ashington, all my friends live here, my children's friends live here, I have no intention of moving anywhere else.' As helpful as the staff were they could only offer a house in South Villas at the other end of the town from the Ra's which would mean a change of school for the children and was too far for regular contact with her friends in the Sixth Row. She did not turn it down but began looking for somewhere to rent around Highmarket, not easy considering funds were so very tight.

She kept all of this from the children, planning to talk to them after the wedding but at the moment her priority was to ensure that Maureen had the best day possible, considering the circumstances. Her biggest worry though was money, with Maureen leaving that would be a few pounds less for the kitty, leaving them to survive on her wage, a couple of pounds from Mike's apprenticeship wage, the few pounds Ian and Rafe made from their various jobs and of course Rafe's £5 allowance which without, they certainly would be unable to manage!

Jane had initially thought that the wedding would be a quiet affair with only the two families in attendance but she had not taken into account the size of the Proudlock extended family. Terry's parents, Jim and Sarah both came from large families and it was likely that most of them were going to attend. In addition, Aggie Galloway had roped every woman in the Row to bake or cook for the buffet and they all naturally thought that was an invitation to attend along with all their families!

Twenty minutes before the ceremony on a beautiful spring day, every seat in the tiny Methodist red brick chapel was filled and in addition, well over a dozen more people crowded into the space behind the last

262

row of pews. Jane, after doing Maureen's hair, ensuring all the boys were dressed, checking with Aggie that the trestle tables had been arranged in the Toc H hall along with plates and glasses and that the wedding cake was in place; said to her very nervous daughter, 'You look beautiful sweetheart, now relax and enjoy the day.' She then chased out the scrubbed and polished boys along with Jennifer into Edward's car in which they travelled around to the Chapel.

Standing nervously by Doctor Metcalf's Rover, Mike who had just checked his watch for the umpteenth time, breathed a sigh of relief when Maureen finally stepped shyly out of the house and climbed into the back seat, being careful not to crease the fitted skirt and jacket of her cream suit. As he drove off, Jonathan Metcalf said over his shoulder, 'You look stunning Maureen, and the sun is shining for you.'

The Sixth Row was empty but as they drove up and into the Fifth Row a handful of housewives had gathered to wave at the bride as the big car purred past, their waves answered by a shy gloved hand from the rear window. 'Eeh doesn't she look lovely?' said one of the women.

'Aye but she's ownly a bairn man,' said another.

'Aye tha's nee white wedding dress there is tha, silly little bugga.'

Oohs and aahs, accompanied Maureen as Mike proudly walked her up the Isle to Terry who turned and smiled at her as she looked nervously through the tiny net hanging from her neat hat.

The ceremony was soon over and the Happy Couple posed for a photo in the small chapel porch before leading everyone the few yards into the Toc H Hall that had been spruced up with bunting left over from the Coronation Party a few years earlier. The wall opposite the door was lined with white cloth covered trestle tables that groaned under the weight of the food on offer; plate pies of corned beef, lamb, bacon, cheese and just about any other ingredient that would fit under a crust, lined up with heaps of scones and cupcakes, rows of sandwich and sponge cakes, piles of sausage rolls and pork pies, and one table

263

was heaped with piles of all types of sandwiches. A separate table was lined with glasses and cups and saucers with two large urns, one containing tea and the other orange squash.

On its own at the top end of the hall, Alice Kirkup's wedding cake took pride of place standing three tiers high on a small square table covered in a damask cloth with pink ribbons on each corner.

As the hall filled with the congregation many of whom were lighting cigarettes, Aggie scuttled up and down the buffet tables lifting of sheets of grease proof paper that had been used to protect the food during the wedding ceremony while George Holland and Edward began opening bottles of sherry and filling several lines of glasses as fast as they could. Albert Grundy joined them but after drinking two glasses, was sent packing by an irate George.

George's daughter Mary was already in the hall manning the record player that was connected to an antiquated loud speaker system and as Terry and Maureen walked in, she dropped the needle onto the first 78 record of a stack of five; Tab Hunter began to croon 'Young Love':

'They say for every boy and girl
There's just one love in this whole world
And I know I've found mine.

The heavenly touch of your embrace
Tells me no one could take your place
Ever in my heart

Young love, first love
Filled with true devotion
Young love, our love
We share with deep emotion.'

Mary knew that the song was Maureen's favorite and hearing it brought a huge smile to her face but the meaning of the song was lost on most of the gathering as they hurried to grab plates to fill from the buffet and shuffle off to various corners to enjoy their booty.

Edward and George guarded the sherry until everyone had had their first fill of food and nodded to a tall and very nervous Martin, Terry's Best Man, the nod being the signal for him to bring the newly Married Couple and parents over to collect their glasses before the rest of the adults collected theirs'.

Jake Grundy, resplendent in a pair of his older brother's trousers that came up to just below his chest and gathered around his ankles at the opposie end, a shirt with cuffs that kept swallowing his hands and collar that barely touched his neck from which a brand new tie hung down almost to his knees. With his hair plastered flat with Vaseline, he thought he was the height of sartorial elegance and sophistication as he waited in the queue for a glass of sherry.

He was disappointed when Edward turned him around and gently pushed him away saying, 'I'm sorry Beau Brummel, yer just a bit ower young for sherry.' He retreated to a corner where Ian and Rafe, smartly dressed in double-breasted suits from Rafe's trunk, stood awkwardly beside an ever-growing group of girls. Noticing one of the girls smiling at him as he swaggered by, Jake hitched up his trousers even higher and grinned inanely back, a grin that brought blushes to the girl's cheeks.

'Did ye see that, she fancies me?' he said to Ian and Rafe.

Rafe nodded and answered, 'Yes Jake, I do believe she was impressed by your roguish attire!'

'Me whaat?'

'The smart way you're dressed,' said Ian.

'Aye Aah thowt that's what he meant and she must be, eh?'

265

Martin banging loudly on a table was the signal for Mary to lift the needle from the record player and for him to step forward to wait for the chatter to stop, 'Ladies and Gentlemen,' he almost shouted as his nerves got the better of him. Lowering his voice, he began again, 'Ladies and Gentlemen, please raise your glasses and toast the Happy Couple – Terry and Maureen.'

'Terry and Maureen' was repeated round the room as the Couple beamed at each other. Martin raised his voice again, 'Ladies and Gentlemen if you would like te tek yor partners we'll be kicking off the dancing in a minute with the Bradford Barn dance.'

For the third time in as many minutes Albert Grundy surreptitiously poured whisky from the half bottle he had hidden in his inside jacket pocket into the tumbler of lemonade that now contained two thirds whisky! Lifting the tumbler to his lips he was just about to take a gulp when Flo came up behind him, 'Niver mind hiding in the blidy corner, come on Hinny, wa dancing,' and grabbing his arm pulled him toward the dance floor. He just had enough time to place the tumbler on the edge of a table before Flo dragged him to join the pairs of people lining up behind the Bride and Groom.

Peggy and Ian joined the dancers as Rafe turned to the girl nearest him and holding out his arm asked, 'Shall we?'

That left Jake and the dark haired girl who had smiled at him; he looked at her and she gave him a nervous expectant smile but he walked over and said, 'Aah canna dance so it's nee good looking at me,' and then stood in embarrassed silence as the music started and the pairs began to dance around the room changing partners every few twirls. Feeling very awkward Jake muttered, 'Am ganna get a drink, de ye want one?' The girl nodded and Jake walked off in search of drinks, finding the tumbler of amber liquid his father had left on the table.

He picked up the drink and took a large gulp. Almost choking he spluttered a small amount across the floor but managed to swallow most of the fiery liquid. 'Bah that's blidy strong ginger beer,' he thought to himself as he grabbed another glass and filled it with orange juice before walking back around the parading dancers to where he had left the girl but she had gone. 'Bugga it,' he said aloud and took another long drink of 'Ginger Beer' enjoying the way it burned his throat before it travelled down to explode in his stomach.

As the dance finished, Jake drank the last of the whisky/lemonade and belched loudly as the dark haired girl returned, 'I've just been to the, ye know what, did you get me a drink?'

'Aye, here it is,' he replied, grabbing the drink from the floor where he had placed it, almost falling over as he stood up. Another dance involving marching up and down the hall began as Albert managed to leave Flo and sneak off to grab his drink. Standing next to the table where he had left it, he looked angrily around the hall trying to see who had pinched it. He saw no sign of his tumbler but did notice Jake grinning stupidly as he said something to a pretty dark haired girl in the corner who was giggling at whatever Jake was saying.

Jake was trying to tell the girl that he thought she was very nice but he was having difficulty forming the words properly, so eventually gave up and just stood there grinning as Mary Howard placed another record on the turntable and said confidently, 'Please take your partners for the waltz.'

Edward had been waiting for this - his opportunity to dance with Jane who was talking to Mike and Jennifer by the wedding cake. 'It's now or never lad,' he said to himself as he marched toward them but before he reached her, Jonathan Metcalf stepped forward, stopping Edward in his tracks. As the Jonathan led Jane past him and onto the dance floor, she gave Edward a little smile and he watch enviously as the couple waltzed gracefully round the hall.

Ian and Rafe had rejoined Jake who was still grinning like a mad man.

Ian asked, 'Did ye not get up te Dance Jake?'

Jake shook his head violently, 'Aah canna blidy dance, am ganna hev a sit doon,' and wobbled off to sit alone in the corner of the hall while Ian and Peggy joined the dancers on the floor.

Rafe turned and asked the girls if anyone could dance the waltz to which the tall and pretty, Fourteen year old Audrey Smith from Number 51 put her hand in front of her mouth to hide her brace and stepping forward, grabbed his hand saying, 'I do Rafe,' and led him onto the dance floor where they waltzed as though they had been dancing together for years and were applauded by some of the adults when the music finished.

Edward had waited patiently in vain for Jonathan to lead Jane of the dance floor and was upset when any further chance of a waltz vanished as Ian spoke to Mary Holland, 'Haway Mary put some of your Rock and Roll records on for us young'uns.'

Mary smiled and replaced the stack on the spindle for another five 78s she had been waiting to play. Elvis's voice burst out of the loud speaker singing, 'They said you were high class, but that's just a lie,' - the beginning of last year's hit, 'Hound Dog.' All the adults quickly left the dance floor as the younger members began to move forward, and although there were a lot of heads nodding to the Rock and Roll beat, none of them were brave enough to be first to jive.

The music reached Jake Grundy who was slumped in a chair in the corner of the room at the rear of the Hall! As the music slowly perculated through his alcohol befuddled brain, his right foot began to twitch, slowly at first until it picked up the beat and then it began to tap in rhythm, the movement of the foot increasing until it was stomping; this led to his whole leg bouncing up and down until with a whoop, he leapt to his feet his legs gyrating wildly just as Elvis had done on the News Reel at the Regal.

His legs appeared to have taken control of his body; twisting and stomping they danced into the middle of the dance floor as he waved his arms above his head in abandonment - 'Elvis Jake Presley' took the Hall by storm! His dancing had frozen everyone to where they stood as he gyrated in a better than good impersonation of the American Rock and Roll idol. His upper lip began to curl upward until with a nod of his head he growled 'Ar huh ar,' as he tried to release his inner Elvis! This had the adults chortling and laughing at his antics while all the young ones gathered round him clapping in rhythm and cheering as Jake danced his heart out.

While he danced almost oblivious to everyone around him, a tall and attractive middle-aged blonde woman whose beauty was just beginning to fade, rather like the elegant but well-worn clothes she wore, stepped into the hall. Holding a long cigarette between her leather gloved fingers, she put it to her bright red lips and inhaled long and slowly before blowing smoke upward as she cast her eyes around the room.

The record ending, brought Jake's gyrating to a stop leaving him swaying in the centre of the cheering and clapping teenagers until he gulped deeply, clasped his hand to his mouth and bolted for the door, bumping into the horrified blonde who swatted at him as he fell past her, collapsing onto his knees and throwing up at the entrance way, narrowly missing several men including his father, who were drinking bottles of beer brought over from the Fell-em Doon.

Albert stepped forward and lifted Jake to his feet and smelt whisky on his breath as he held him steady, snapping angrily, 'You drank me blidy whisky ye little sod ye!'

Albert had not seen Flo scurrying up to see to her son but she, heard Albert and digging him in the ribs, demanded, 'What whisky, hev ye brought whisky ye blidy waster ye?'

269

Albert let go of Jake who collapsed back on his knees muttering, 'Aah've just had ginger beer man,' and wretched again.

'Aah hevn't got any blidy whisky woman,' said Albert confidently, having disposed of the empty bottle a minute or two before.

'Aah divin't believe ye, ye useless waster ye, ye'd better tek wor Jake hyem and mek sure he's put te bed.' Albert was about to argue but looking at Flo's angry face, he thought better of it and lifting Jake back to his feet, he dragged him back through the cuts to the Sixth Row.

Inside Terry and Maureen were posing by the cake with knife in hand as one of Terry's uncles took several photos of them. While pieces of cake were served to those that wanted it, the blonde woman spoke to a man by the door who, in response to her questions, pointed to Rafe who was jiving with Audrey. After a few more words the man walked onto the dance floor and tapped Rafe on the shoulder saying, 'How Rafe lad, tha's a woman ower here wants a word with ye.'

Rafe turned and looked at the blonde and asked the man, 'Who is she?'

'Aah divin't kna son, she says she wants te speak te ye.'

Taking Audrey by the hand Jake walked across to the woman, noting as he did so how well dressed she was and how high her stiletto heels were. 'Hello,' he said smiling, 'Do you want to speak to me?'

In her high heels, the blonde was a couple of inches taller than Rafe and looking down at him she gave him a sickly false smile and asked, 'Are you Ralph Rorke Trevelyan?'

Rafe gave her a quizzical look and answered politely, 'Yes I am but who are you, may I ask?'

'I'm your mother Ralph, I'm Liz; I mean Elizabeth Wilson but was Rorke!'

Rafe was bewildered; who on earth was this woman and why was she saying she was his mother, he said slowly, 'My mother was Rosalind

Trevelyan, she died some years ago, why on earth would you say you were my mother?'

Taking another long drag from her cigarette, she answered matter of factly, 'Because I *am* your mother sweetie and I have come to take you back to Australia!'

Rafe was confused and just a little angry, 'Why would you say these things, who on Earth are you?'

'I've told you sweetie, I'm your mother and I've come to take you home.'

Rafe turned to look for Jane and seeing her talking to Edward and Doctor Metcalf, he walked briskly over to her, 'Sis, there's a woman here saying she is my mother and that she is taking me home,' he said with some panic, 'do you know who she is?'

Jane grabbed his arm and asked, 'Where is she?'

'She's over there by the door but why is she here, why would she say is my mother?'

Looking across at the blonde, Jane replied, 'Rafe it is probably best if you stay here with Edward while I go to speak to her,' and walked across to the blonde.

Jonathan Metcalf looked at Edward and raising his eyebrows said, 'What an unusual family this is, but isn't Jane wonderful?'

Edward nodded and turning to Rafe asked, 'Are you okay lad?'

'Yes thanks Mister Thompson, I'm just a tad shocked and mightily confused.'

As Jane approached the blonde she recognized the small diamond encrusted broach of a butterfly on her jacket lapel, 'Are you Elizabeth Rorke?' she asked.

Liz Rorke looked the younger prettier woman up and down and said, 'Yes, well I'm Wilson now but my Maiden name is Rorke and you must be Jane, do you know me?'

'I know of you; my father's solicitor told me all about you; I see you are wearing one of my mother's brooches.'

Liz touched the brooch and replied, 'Was it your mother's? Your dear father gave it to me.'

Jane paused and asked quietly, 'What – for services rendered?'

'Now now sweetie,' Liz said, 'let's not be rude, we wouldn't want a scene here would we?'

Controlling her mounting anger, Jane asked, 'Why are you here, why on earth have you told Rafe who you are?'

'Rafe is it? Isn't that obvious, I'm his mother, he should be with me now that his poor father is dead!'

Jane looked Liz up and down, noting the premature lines around her eyes and mouth beneath the heavy makeup that also hid the damage that year's of chain smoking had done to her skin.

'As you can see there is a wedding going on, this is neither the time nor place to discuss this, I suggest you come to my home tomorrow morning and we will sit down and discuss it then.'

Liz sneered at Jane, 'Why can't we discuss it now, are you afraid I am going to take away your little money pot.'

Jane was furious but controlled herself, 'I have told you that we will discuss it tomorrow morning now please leave or believe me I will have some of these men throw you out, we will speak tomorrow.'

Liz glared at Jane and demanded, 'And where am I supposed to spend the night in this God forsaken hole, I went around to your hovel before I came here, so please don't ask me to stay with you.'

'I have no intention of offering you a bed, where you stay is of no concern to me, I suggest you climb in that taxi you have waiting and go to Morpeth for the night.'

Lightingt another cigarette, Liz said, 'OK sweetie, I'll see you around lunch time tomorrow, you might have Ralph or Rafe or whatever he calls himself, pack his belongings so he is ready to leave with me, toodle pip,' and turned and strode out to the waiting taxi.

Still clutching the hand of a worried Audrey, Rafe walked quickly over to Jane and asked, 'Who is she Sis?'

Jane took his other hand in both of hers and said, 'It's a long story Rafe, I will tell you after Terry and Maureen leave in a few minutes I promise but please, please just wait for a few minutes.'

The three of them walked back over to Join Maureen and Terry and his parents just as the nervous best man announced that the Bride and Groom would be leaving in five minutes to catch the train to take them on their Honeymoon to Scarborough.

After hugs and kisses, Terry and Maureen climbed into Edward's car and amid cheers and clapping, Edward drove off for the railway station, slowing down at the corner to allow Maureen to throw a large handful of coins out of the car window to the group of waiting children who scrabbled to collect them.

Back inside the Hall, Aggie, Alice Thompson and Mary Holland began clearing away the remnants of the buffet, ensuring that any pie, cake or sandwich that was still intact was placed carefully on a separate table for distribution later, the best of them earmarked for their own consumption. Young Mary Holland continued to play records for a group of a dozen or more cavorting ten to sixteen year olds who demonstrated several different versions of 'Bop'.

Jane waited until the wedding car was out of sight before walking back to Rafe who was standing by the Chapel wall, 'Well Sis, who was that dreadful woman?' he asked.

'She *is* your mother Rafe, at least she gave birth to you but it was my mother who brought you up as her own even if she did not always show you very much affection.'

Rafe's face clouded with confusion, 'I don't understand; how could this woman give birth to me when Father was married to Mother?'

273

'Our mother was unable to have any children after me so Father paid this woman to have his baby – you; she also signed a letter that father's solicitor has, basically saying that she gave up all claims or rights over you, I thought she was in Australia!'

'How long have you known about her,'

'Only as long as I have known about you, the Solicitor thought it better that you were not told about the arrangement, he never thought that she would turn up like this.'

'So why is she here, now? Why is she saying she is going to take me with her, can she do that?'

'Jane took Rafe's hand again, 'I can only think that she has come looking for more money and she cannot force you to leave with her Rafe, she may be your birth mother but if you don't want to go with her she could not take this to court as I'm sure what she did must have been illegal. Even if it was legal, I doubt if she could win a custody case because of, well basically selling you to father. It is up to you Rafe; you know you will always be welcome with us.'

He nodded and said thanks' Sis, I cannot for a moment imagine living with that woman, no matter what she says.'

Jane took his arm, 'Come on, we will talk about it some more when we get home but I have to talk to Terry's parents and I see Audrey is waiting for you.'

With the dancing finished, the Proudlocks took the remains of the wedding cake and a selection of sandwiches when they left just before five o'clock as Jane and her helpers returned the Hall to normal. The boys had left earlier carrying left over plate pies and sausage rolls that Aggie had handed them saying, 'Haway lads, carry this lot hyem for yer dinners before the vultures get them.' 'The vultures' were a group of about six women who had been hovering near the left overs, keen to swoop on any unattended food; they did not leave empty handed!

Liz Wilson had lit another cigarette when she climbed into the back of the taxi, ordering, 'Take me to the best hotel in Morpeth.' It had been a frustrating and annoying few days since she arrived back in England and her mood had not been lightened by what she had seen in Ashington and the Sixth Row, 'There's no damn money here,' she thought to herself, 'it is beginning to look as if this whole trip has been an expensive waste of time!'

Life had been good back in 45 when she first moved to her new home overlooking the beach and ocean at Bondi, she had joined the Golf and prestigious Life savers Clubs and enjoyed the high life, marrying a dashing Australian in 1948. However, the marriage was a disaster; her new husband, Trevor Wilson, turned out to be a bigger 'Gold Digger' than her and was far from being faithful loving. Finding him in bed with another woman, she divorced him in 1952 but he had already spent a substantial amount of her cash, forcing her to search unsuccessfully for a wealthy widower to finance her lavish lifestyle.

She had even written in an almost threatening way to Robert Trevelyan asking for more money but it had not worked; he returned her letter in kind and warned her never to contact him again. As her money dwindled she was eventually forced to sell her beautiful Bondi home and buy a small flat in the Kings Cross area of Sydney. The money she had left provided her with a modest life that was far from the excesses of her first few years in Australia and with her looks slowly fading, she entered into several relationships that all ended badly as her motives became obvious to her targets.

Reading of Robert Trevelyan's death she had travelled to England to lay claim to any inheritance that may have been left to her son but was bitterly disappointed when Mr. Penrose the Solicitor told her the extent of Robert's debts, his bankruptcy and his suicide. Her hopes did rise when he admitted that Robert had left a small amount of money in a

Trust Fund of which he was the executor and out of which he paid a modest amount to Mrs. Shepherd for Rafe's upkeep. Despite her badgering, he of course had not told her how much money was in the Trust Fund or how much Jane received.

Leaving his office in a foul mood, she determined to track Jane down and find out how much money she was receiving from Penrose, 'I may yet be able to salvage something from this damn trip,' she had thought.

It was on the train journey north that she read an article in the Daily News about Nick Shepherd the 'False Hero' hung for murder – 'My God, Rafe was living with a murderer, I can use that to my benefit I am sure,' she thought.

Back at Number 60, Jane and the boys sat at the kitchen table eating a supper of bacon and egg plate pie as they discussed Rafe's mother and why she was there. Jane thought it was only fair that all the boys including Tommy, were aware of what had happened and who she was and Rafe was more than happy that they knew about his parentage.

Mike said, 'She sounds like a right charmer, should we not tell the Police about her?'

Shaking her head, Jane said, 'I'd rather not, and I think we've had enough of Police for the time being but if she does force matters then I will call Sergeant Norman for advice but not yet.'

Leaning forward, Rafe said, 'I know one thing for certain, I do not want to have anything to do with a woman who sold me as a commodity, the whole idea is frightful!'

'Frightful Rafe,' said Ian, mimicking Rafe's voice, 'one can always bide here like.'

Rafe grinned at Ian and said, 'Whey yor me family noo man!'

The banter between the boys continued for a few minutes until Jane said, 'We will deal with Mrs. Wilson tomorrow and after she has gone I want you all here at lunch time as I have something else to discuss with you all, don't ask me what it is now, we will deal with it tomorrow, just make sure you are all here.'

Liz Wilson spent the night drinking in the saloon of the old black and white, timber framed coaching inn in the Centre of Morpeth and had risen with a dreadful hangover and a continuation of yesterday's foul mood. Picking at breakfast, she complained loudly that there was no 'Bludy fresh fruit' demanding, 'Coffee not bludy stewed tea'!

Jane and Rafe watched through the kitchen window as Liz climbed out of a taxi just after eleven o'clock. They watched as she paid the driver, lit another cigarette and stared down the Row, shaking her head before stepping into the yard and knocking on the door.

Jane made her wait, 'Go into the sitting room Rafe and I will fetch her through,' she said before slowly walking to the door that Liz knocked on again. Opening the door she looked at Liz and said 'Please come in, we are in the sitting room.'

Liz followed her through the kitchen, tutting at the meagre furnishings as Jane stepped into the sitting room where Rafe was standing by the fire.

'She smiled her sickly smile at her son, blew a cloud of cigarette smoke at the ceiling and said, 'Hello Sweetie, are you packed and ready to leave this dump before someone murders you?'

Rafe controlled his anger and was about to reply but before he could, Jane said in a matter of fact voice, 'Please sit down, can I offer you a cup of tea?'

Liz looked at Jane with contempt and said, 'No thanks, I've come for Raiph, the sooner I get out of this dump the better.'

Rafe stepped up to her and said, 'This is my home and you are not welcome here, so I suggest you leave as I certainly have no intentions of going anywhere with you.'

Liz flicked her hair back as though she flicking away Rafe's words, 'Now Sweetie do be careful what you say, you wouldn't want me to leave you in this - this squalor, I'm taking you to Australia, now isn't that exciting, better than living with no hopers and murders Sweetie.'

Rafe shook his head, 'Look Mrs Wilson, you are probably the last person in the world I would want to live with, you sold me when I was a baby, I think you are absolutely vile!'

Liz's demeanour changed, she turned on Jane, 'Look, I am entitled to this wretch's maintenance and any other money he has, so get your hooks out of him, he and his money are coming with me.'

Jane smiled at Liz and said, 'Thank you for confirming why you are here, you are not in the least bit interested in Rafe's welfare, only what money you think he might have, now let me tell you that I receive barely enough to feed and clothe him, look around you, you stupid woman, we are not living in the lap of luxury nor are we living in squalor as you put it. Rafe will receive some money when he is twenty one but there is no way that you, I or anyone else will get their grubby hands on it; now get out of my house before I call the police.'

Liz flicked her cigarette stub into the fire and snarled at Rafe, 'Just as I thought, you are not worth the bother Sweetie, well I hope you are comfortable in this dump with your big bludy sister,' and turning to Jane, demanded, 'Phone for a taxi for me so I can get out of this godforsaken town.'

Jane shook her head and replied, 'You are an unbelievably stupid women, get out now, I have no telephone and even if I did, I would not use it to call a taxi for you.'

Liz was unperturbed, 'Keep your shirt on Sweetie; now where is the nearest telephone box?'

Rafe grabbed his mother's arm and marched her out through the kitchen and into the street where pointing down the Row, he said, 'Go to the bottom of the Street, turn right and follow the cuts to the main road, the telephone box is there, now go.'

Liz took out another cigarette and lit it before saying, 'Toodle pip Sweetie,' and walked off down the Row past where the local boys who were playing football stopped to glare at her as she passed them. Nearest the pavement, Billy Grundy tilted back his head to look at her through his grubby glasses and said, 'She looks like a witch!'

Glaring at him, Liz flicked ash from her cigarette onto his head and continued on and out of the Row.

Jane had not been looking forward to telling the boys the news of the eviction and had waited until they had finished Sunday Dinner and washed up before gathering them once more around the kitchen table for a discussion.

Sitting down opposite his Mother, Mike joked, 'What is it this time Mam, are we being hoyed oot?'

Jane looked at without smiling and replied, 'Yes Mike, I'm afraid we are!'

'Never!' Mike said incredulously as the other three boys looked shocked.

'We have been given an eviction notice by the National Coal Board and so must find somewhere else to live, I have spoken to the Council and they have said that they might be able to allocate us a house in South Villas within a few weeks.'

Mike was shocked, 'What, Chinky Toon, that's doon the bottom end of the Horst!'

Ian asked, 'Does that mean we hev te change schools Mam?'

'If we move there it would but I am looking for somewhere to rent around by the Store Corner and High Market but there's not much choice and quite frankly it is going to be difficult enough to pay Council rent let alone rent for a private house, remember we have been living here rent free and had free coal!'

They then discussed how they could make their money stretch almost bringing Jane to tears when Mike said, 'Hanks dad said he'd buy my motorbike for twenty five pund, so I'll sell it to him next weekend and Aah can always jack my apprenticeship in and get a job underground, it would be more than double me wages if Aah did!'

You'll do no such thing Mike, you will finish your apprenticeship no matter what but I think it is best if you do sell your motorcycle.'

They talked for a further hour, discussing possible ways of making more money but failed to come up with anything rational until Mike said with a huge grin, 'You could marry Jennifer's Dad, he's got plenty of money and fancies you!'

Jane blushed, 'That's enough nonsense Mike, we will just have to be very careful and I'm sure we will get by,' she said without conviction.

When Edward called to see how Jane was before he drove home, she invited him in for a cup of tea which the two of them drank in the sitting room, Edward asking, 'Have you decided on whether or not you are going to take the offer of a council house?'

Jane shook her head and replied, 'Not yet, the boys and I all want to stay up here for school and work, but financially, I don't think I have much option.'

Edward looked at Jane as she sipped her tea and for the first time let his heart speak, 'Jane, it goes without saying that you are beautiful but you are also the most remarkable woman I have ever met, no matter what traumas and problems are thrown at you, you always remain dignified – positive and dignified. The newspapers are now calling me 'the belated hero' but you are a blidy hero lass, especially the way you have coped these last few months, the lads are lucky to have you for their mother.'

His words were too much for Jane, tears filled her eyes and standing, she touched his shoulder saying, 'Excuse me Edward,' and hurried out and up to her room where her pent up emotions got the better of her as she collapsed crying into her pillow. Walking back down to his car, Edward cursed himself for having upset her and what he now thought, was his clumsy attempt of telling her how much he thought of her.

Ian and Rafe were chopping their latest double haul of pit props in the shed, discussing what other areas of Ashington they could try selling them, they even considered Jake's scheme of stealing empty pop bottles to sell in shops but discounted that as too risky.

Rafe changed the subject, 'The Headmaster sent for me last week and told me that based upon my Rugley School reports and how I have done at Bothal, that Morpeth Grammar School has said I can start there after half term which is next week for them.'

'What are you going to do?'

'I told him that I would discuss it with Jane but how can I? Especially after what has happened and not forgetting that you refused to sit your thirteen plus.'

'Aye it's a bugga Rafe, Aah bet you wish you could have stayed at Rugley eh?'

Rafe nodded, 'Sometimes but then I wouldn't be here with you unruly lot would I and I'd rather be here.'

'What about that woman this morning, yer mother?

'God wasn't she awful, hopefully I will never see her again, imagine selling your baby, unbelievable ay?'

'Blidy mad man, what a monster, ha ha, we're both sons of monsters!'

281

Despite looking at two terrace house; by Wednesday Jane had all but given up looking for somewhere affordable in the immediate area and was preparing herself to tell the boys that they were going to have to move to the other side of town and had even checked on bus fares for work. She hoped that Ian and Rafe might be able to complete their schooling at Bothal by cycling there on their tandem and had asked to speak to the Headmaster that afternoon – early shop closing day.

Chapter 14
More Unexpected News!

Leaving Kirkup's just after two thirty, Jane walked up Highmarket toward Bothal School and her appointment with the Headmaster. She was deep in thought as she reached the Fell-em Doon and almost bumped into Ginny who had just finished cleaning the bar after the lunchtime session and was heading for her flat. The two women recognized each other but neither said a word as they walked on, the part of their lives that had connected them was gone for good and there was nothing either one had to say to the other.

The middle-aged, balding and bespectacled Headmaster stood up when Jane was shown into his Office, 'Do sit down Mrs., erm Trevelyan?'

Jane smiled, 'Yes that's right Mr. Barton; I no longer use my married name for obvious reasons.'

The Headmaster nodded and sat down saying, 'Yes and rather appropriate as we are talking about Master Rafe Trevelyan today!'

Jane furrowed her eyebrows, 'No, I'm here to discuss my both my son Ian's and Rafe's future here at Bothal.'

'Oh I see, I thought you were here just to discuss Rafe's move to Morpeth Grammar but that does not involve Ian surely?'

Jane sighed deeply, 'I was unaware that Rafe was moving to Morpeth Grammar, I'm here because we may have to move to the Hirst and I was going to ask if the boys could stay on here, if and it is a big if, and when we move.'

The Headmaster rubbed his nose and answered, 'I don't see why not but what about Rafe, will he be allowed to move to Grammar School or will you prevent it as Ian was prevented from sitting his thirteen plus exam?'

Shocked at this evaluation, Jane took a small handkerchief from her handbag and wiped a tear from her eye, 'That's two bits of information I was not aware of, of course Rafe can go to Morpeth Grammar, now are we too late for Ian to sit the thirteen plus exam?'

'I'm afraid he has obviously missed last year's Autumn exam but he could be eligible for the exam next month that, if he was successful, he could be in Grammar School for the beginning of the School year, as you well know, he is one of our better students and we did have high hopes for him.'

Jane nodded, 'In that case, please ensure that he is given every opportunity to do so, he will be given my full support.'

Walking through the school gates, Jane's mind was in turmoil, she was distraught that Ian had felt it necessary to give up the chance of attending Grammar School, probably due to Nick and the way he controlled the family. She silently vowed to do everything she could to ensure that both he and Rafe left Bothal for Grammar School and wondered if Mike had done as Ian had?

Opening the back door, she hung up her coat and picked up a brown envelope that was lying on the floor and dropped it on the kitchen table as she wearily filled the kettle for a much needed cup of tea. Waiting for the tea to mash, she wondered what other bad news the letter contained and picked it up to exam the post mark. Reading 'Coventry' she wondered if it might be from Mr. Penrose, perhaps warning her of Elizabeth Wilson nee Rorke.

Sighing deeply again, she ripped open the envelope and quickly read the short letter; then clasping her hand to her mouth she sat down and read it again and still not fully understanding its contents she read it again!

All thoughts of tea left here head as she paced back and forth reading the letter again and again before she snatched her coat and handbag and walked briskly to the telephone box outside Bothal School. Trembling she dialed the number she had written in her diary that she kept in her hand bag, pressing Button 'A' when the voice at the other end said, 'Roddick and Penrose, can I help you?'

'Yes,' Jane said nervously, 'can I speak to Mr Penrose please, this is Mrs Shepherd?'

Penrose said, 'Hello Mrs. Shepherd, how are you, you appear to have had a very traumatic time since we last spoke, now what can I do for you?'

Jane composed herself, 'I am as well as can be expected Mr Penrose but I was wondering if you can shed some light on a letter I have just received?'

'Certainly if I am able to, who is the letter from and what is it about?'

'Trembling slightly, Jane replied, 'It is from the Midshire's Bank,'

'Yes Mrs Shepherd?'

'They have asked me what I want to do with the twenty five thousand pounds in my account.'

'And have you not yet decided?'

'Mr Penrose, I know nothing of any such bank account but you clearly do?'

There was a pause before Penrose said, 'The twenty five thousand pounds your father put in an account for you a year ago, almost to the day.'

'My Father, but he was bankrupt Mr Penrose, why did you not tell me about this before?

'But your father explained in the letter he left for you – you have read it haven't you?'

Jane paused, 'No Mr Penrose I'm afraid I have not been able to bring myself to do so.'

'Aah well that explains why young Rafe left Rugley, have you still got the letter?'

Jane could hardly speak, 'Yes,' she whispered.

'In that case I suggest you go and read it, I think you will find it rather sad but perhaps a little uplifting as well, please let me know if there is anything else I can do for you.'

Jane thanked him and walked slowly home, her head spinning; twenty five thousand pounds was a fortune, could this really be true, her thoughts were interrupted by Aggie as she walked past her house.

'Hello Jane, how are ye teday? Any news aboot hooses yet? Hoo are ye and the bairns? Didn't the two bairns look smashing and so happy when they went off on tha Honeymoon? Eeh God bless them, they'll need it, noo de ye want me te come and mek ye a cuppa cos ye look done in lass?'

Jane nodded and Aggie followed her into Number 60 and into the sitting room, Aggie saying, 'That's right pet you sit yersell doon and Aah'll gan and put the kettle on.

Jane took the letter from the draw before sitting on the sofa and with trembling hands slid a finger under the flap to rip it open carefully taking out the single sheet of paper, she began to read:

My Dear Jane,

How does one beg for forgiveness when they have been so stupidly cruel? I have written this letter a thousand times in my head but only now can I write it when everything I thought was good in life, crumbles around me. It is only now when it is too late, that I realize how wrong and how cruel I have been.

You will know by now that I have lost everything my father and I had built up over the years and that I have taken, rightly or wrongly, what I believe is the only course of action open to me. I hope you will forgive me for taking what may be thought as the coward's way out but my pride will not allow me to do otherwise.

I also hope that Mr Penrose has told you of my son, your half-brother Rafe, and whilst I do not for a minute expect you to understand or forgive me for what I did to your dear mother, I sincerely hope you will be able to accept him as your brother, he is a fine young man with an integrity I never possessed.

Jane my Dear, I know you will never forgive me for cutting you off from your Mother and the friends you once had here, I am led to believe that your life has been very difficult since you married that man and fervently hope it is not too late for me to make some amends. Last year when I realized I would not be able to save the Firm, I sold off some overseas assets and deposited the money along with what available cash I had, into an account with the Midshire's Bank. This account is in your name and is for you and you alone to use, the account number is at the bottom of the page. Perhaps you may wish to use some small amount to allow Rafe to continue on at Rugley?

I will trouble you no more my Dear, I wish you happiness and hope that the money may help,

Forgive me

Father.

10th of January 1958

Jane read the letter twice, the second time with tears streaming down her face, 'Eeeh what's the matter Pet?' said Aggie when she carried in two cups of tea, 'not more blidy bad news, ye've had enough te last any bugga a life time!'

Jane stood up, took the cups from Aggie, placing them on the mantle piece and turned to hug Aggie saying, 'No Aggie, not bad news, good news tinged with sadness but it is very good news!'

'Eeeh aboot blidy time pet, am thrilled for ye,' Aggie said as Jane let go and handed her one of the cups of tea.

She was almost bouncing with excitement as she waited for the boys to come home, Tommy was the first in and giggled as Jane snatched him up in her arms hugging tightly as she said, 'Everything is going to be good Thomas, everything is going to be fine.'

She put him down and grabbed his hands and was dancing around in a little circle when Rafe walked in! She ran over to him and surprised him with a hug and kiss on the cheek saying again, 'Everything is going to be fine, where's Ian?'

Jane's mood was infectious, grinning without knowing why, Rafe said, 'He's down the Row talking to Peggy.'

Jane interrupted, 'Go and get him quickly,'

Still grinning, Rafe ran down the back lane to where Ian and Peggy were talking, 'Ian come quickly, Sis wants you home now,' he said and ran back followed by Ian who had been infected by Rafe's smile!

Jane grabbed Ian and hugged him saying, 'You beautiful thoughtful boy, I love you so much,'

Ian's smile grew larger, his mother's happiness infecting all three of the boys, 'What's happened Mam, what's the matter?'

Jane stood back beaming at the three confused but grinning boys, 'We have great news boys but I can't tell you until Mike is here, you must all be together when I tell you.'

'That's great whatever it is Mam but Rafe and me hev wor papers to deliver noo.'

Jane frowned and the boys heard her swear for the very first time, 'Oh Bugga, go on then, be as quick as you can and hurry back, I will burst if I don't tell you the news shortly!'

An hour later Ian and Rafe raced the tandem up the back lane and leaping off, sped into the kitchen to find Mike and Tommy sitting at the table as Jane stood fidgeting by the fire, 'Come on, sit down quickly,' she said as she pulled back a chair for herself.

Mike said, 'Am glad yer back, Aah thowt she was ganna explode!'

Composing herself, Jane took a deep breath and said, 'My lovely boys, I received two letters today, I am going to read the first one out to you and you'll see why I am so excited, this letter is from the Midshire's Bank in Coventry.' She coughed as though she was clearing her throat and smiled at each of them in turn before reading out loud, 'Dear Mrs Shepherd, It is now twelve months since your bank account, number etc. was opened, can you please advise us if you wish the twenty five thousand pounds sterling plus an accrued interest of one thousand four hundred pounds sterling, remain in this account without further action,'

There was a stunned silence before Mike asked slowly, 'How much?'

Emphasizing each word, Jane replied, 'All together, twenty six thousand four hundred pounds!'

'That's a fortune,' Ian declared as Tommy looked bewildered, unable to comprehend what the letter meant.

Ian asked, 'But Mam where is the money from?'

Jane touched his hand gently, 'Now for the second letter which explains the money,' opening her father's letter she began, 'My Dear Jane.' but unable to read any further, she handed the letter to Mike and said, 'You read it Mike Dear.'

Mike read the letter slowly as Jane put her left arm around Tommy, holding her handkerchief in her right hand, she dabbed a wayward tear or two, sighing deeply when Mike finished and laid the letter on the table.

Jane smiled at the boys in silence until Tommy asked, 'Does that mean we're rich Mam?'

Jane hugged him and answered, 'Not rich but we are going to be just fine, money wise.'

Rafe was next to speak, 'Sis, I don't want to go to Rugley but I have been offered a move to Morpeth Grammar School which I would like to take.'

Jane nodded and said, 'Whatever you want Rafe, and turning to Ian, she gave a him a mock frown and she said, 'and you young man will be giving another opportunity to sit your thirteen plus next month so you had better start revising!'

Ian was shocked, 'How did ye know aboot that Mam?'

I spoke to Mr. Barton this afternoon; Rafe, you will be transferring to Morpeth after their half term break and Ian, if you pass your thirteen plus, you will be going after the summer holidays!'

Rafe put his arm around Ian's shoulder and said, 'Haway the Hacky Dortys!'

Jane turned to her eldest, 'Mike, tell me truthfully, did you have an opportunity to sit a thirteen plus exam?'

Mike grinned, 'Not me Mam, sorry.'

Jane patted his hand and said, 'You will still do well in life Mike, never fear.'

'Am not feared Mam, am happy deeing waat am deeing, what happens now, Aah mean, about moving?'

Jane sat forward, 'Well my mind has been racing away and if you all agree we will buy a house close by so that we remain close to the people that have been so good to us, I also want to buy Maureen and Terry a little house and help them set up; so with a few other things to buy we should have twenty thousand pounds or thereabout left to ensure you will all be looked after.'

Mike beamed and asked, 'Have you seen a house then?'

Jane nodded, 'I know it is silly to be rushing like this but yes, there is a house in High Market that I think may suit us, I obviously have not had time to make any enquiries yet.'

Mike asked, 'Do you mean the one that's for sale opposite the 'Gaffer's' hooses in Forst Ra, 'Hotspur Hoose' Aah think it's called?'

'That's the one, the detached Edwardian one with the double bay windows.'

'Wow, Aah kna that house,' said Ian, 'it's massive!'

Jane smiled, 'Well not massive sweetheart but I think it has four bedrooms and a bathroom.'

Tommy asked, What aboot a netty Mam?'

'There will be one in the bathroom as well as an outside one I think Pet,' she said as she rubbed his hair, 'now I must go round to the phone and call Maureen and Terry and tell them the good news.'

Ten days later, on a Saturday afternoon, Jane, Mike, Ian, Rafe and Tommy explored Hotspur House for the second time, this time Jane allocated bedrooms to the boys, Mike would have his own, Ian and Rafe would share a large rear bedroom and Tommy would move into the fourth and smallest bedroom. Ian said excitedly, 'The furniture is smashing Mam; the settee is as big as wor sitting room!'

Jane grinned, 'The furniture won't be staying, I'll be buying a few items from Laburnum's and Shepherd's as well as some more for Maureen and Terry's new house in Wansbeck Road.

Eight weeks later, Terry and Maureen had set up home in a terraced house opposite People's Park while Jane, the boys and Edward loaded what possessions they were taking to High Market into the back of Edward's Van. Aggie who could not stop telling people of the holiday her and Arthur were going to have in Scotland thanks to Jane, was already at Hotspur house unpacking crockery and cutlery that had been delivered that morning. Mike was also there putting together two new beds that had just been delivered.

Jane was carefully loading books into the back of her one year old Morris Minor Countryman estate as Tommy sat in the front pretending to drive when Flo Grundy tapped her on her shoulder, 'Thanks for all the things ye've given us Pet, especially the net cortains, wor's wor finished blidy years ago.'

Jane stood up and hugged her, saying, 'I'm pleased you can put them too good use Flo and there's still plenty of life left in that sofa.'

'Aye tha is and that lazy bugga of a husband of mine is already on it with his feet up and a fag in his hand, mind if he faalls asleep and burns it, Aah'll swing for the sod, no ye tek care Pet.'

Edward loaded a last box of pictures into his van and joined Jane at the back of the Morris, 'That's it Jane, you just have to lock the door now.'

Jane smiled and turned to Rafe and Ian who were straddling their new Raleigh Tourers, 'Go on boys, I'll see you round there and hurry, Aggie has stottie, pease pudding and ham for your lunch.'

The boys set of down the Lane noticing that just about everyone was at their back gates to wave them off, 'Ye'd think we wor ganning te Timbuctoo not Highmarket, Ian said laughing.'

Jake stood by his gate looking glum as he wondered if this would be the last he would see of his pals as they cycled by on their way to their posh new house but looked up when they braked to a halt a few yards further on. Ian shouted back, 'Haway man, Aggie's got grub on and Howard's already there, tha'll be nowt left if ye divin't hurry up!'

Jake reached behind the yard fence and dragged *his* new Raleigh out and jumping on pedaled after them as Rafe shouted, 'Haway the Hacky Dortys' and then all three yelled it as loud as they could, their voices echoing down along the Row and across the open ground in front of the Fifth Row.

Locking the door of Number 60 for the last time and locking the past behind her, Jane turned to Edward who was waiting by the gate and said with feeling, 'Edward thanks for always being here for me and the children.'

He looked down into her deep blue eyes and said, 'I will always be here for you Jane lass,' as she reached up and kissed him on the cheek before she climbed into the Morris and followed him out of the Sixth Row and on to her new home.

The End

To find out what became of Jane and her children, Edward and the folk from the Sixth Road, read the sequel 'Instinctive Heroes,' also available from Amazon.

Acknowledgement

My deepest thanks go to my dear Beth, whose advice and encouragement made this book possible.

My thanks also go to that select band of people who frequent the cyber 'Haway Inn' and 'Ashington Remembered' whose reminiscences were a great inspiration

Geordie/Pitmatic Words used in this book

Aah	I
Aaful	awful
Aalreet	alright
Aah've	I have
Alen	alone
An	own
Aroond	around
Bairn	Baby or small child
Bait	food carried to work
Boond	bound
Cannit	cannot
Cowld	cold
Cyek	cake
Daad	strike
Dee	do
Div	do
Divvint	do not
Doot	doubt
Droon	drown
Fyece	face
Forst	first
Fund	found
Gan	go
Gannin	going
Gis	give me
Grund	ground
Gully	large knife
Hoy	throw
Hurd	heard

He'ssell	himself
Hev	have
Hevn't	have not
Hoo	how
Haway	come on
Hord	heard
Iviry	every
Ivvor	ever
Kna	know
Lavvies	lavatory
Lowp	leap
Mair	more
Marra	friend or workmate
Mek	make
Mesell	myself
Nee	no
Nen	none
Nettie	lavatory
Nivvor	never
Nur	no
Nowt	nothing
Ower	over
Owld	old
Owt	anything
Plodgin	paddling
Reet	right
Roond	round
Sackless	dozy
Shows	the fair
Shull	shovel
Sowldgers	soldiers

Sumat	something
Taak	talk
Tecking	taking
Tha	they're
Tetties	potatoes
Thowt	thought
Towld	told
Tyeble	table
Whey	well
Willicks	winkles
Winnit	will not
Wiv	with
Wor	our
Worsells	ourselves
Yarking	beating
Ye	you
Yor	your
Yorsell	yourself

CPSIA information can be obtained at www.ICGtesting.com
Printed in the USA
LVOW04s1337210415

435339LV00044B/3178/P

9 781506 174792

i